"ARE YOU SUGGESTING . . . FOUL PLAY?"

Doc avoided Judith's gaze. "We'll know more tomorrow. September isn't a very lucky month around here. Over the years, most of the bad things that have happened seem to have occurred during September. People get superstitious. 'Remember September.' It's a catch phrase around here, and a somber one at that."

Suddenly looking weary, he finished his brandy and stood up. "I'd better head home now. It might be a good idea for you to lock up real tight. Just in case, you know."

Judith watched Doc go down the treacherous back stairs. A moment later he had disappeared out of the circle of floodlights. It had grown almost chilly and Judith hugged herself. She was shivering, though not just from the cold. Autumn was in the air. And so was death. *Remember September*, Doc had said.

Judith already wished she could forget.

———

"MARY DAHEIM IS ONE OF THE BRIGHTEST STARS IN OUR CITY'S LITERARY CONSTELLATION."
Seattle Times

Bed-and-Breakfast Mysteries by
Mary Daheim
from Avon Books

SCOTS ON THE ROCKS
SAKS & VIOLINS
DEAD MAN DOCKING
THIS OLD SOUSE
HOCUS CROAKUS
SILVER SCREAM
SUTURE SELF
A STREETCAR NAMED EXPIRE
CREEPS SUZETTE
HOLY TERRORS
JUST DESSERTS
LEGS BENEDICT
SNOW PLACE TO DIE
WED AND BURIED
SEPTEMBER MOURN
NUTTY AS A FRUITCAKE
AUNTIE MAYHEM
MURDER, MY SUITE
MAJOR VICES
A FIT OF TEMPERA
BANTAM OF THE OPERA
DUNE TO DEATH
FOWL PREY

MARY DAHEIM

September Mourn

A BED-AND-BREAKFAST MYSTERY

AVON BOOKS
An Imprint of HarperCollins*Publishers*

This is a work of fiction. Names, characters, places, and incidents are products of the author's imagination or are used fictitiously and are not to be construed as real. Any resemblance to actual events, locales, organizations, or persons, living or dead, is entirely coincidental.

AVON BOOKS
An Imprint of HarperCollins*Publishers*
10 East 53rd Street
New York, New York 10022-5299

First Avon Books paperback printing: August 1997

Avon Trademark Reg. U.S. Pat. Off. and in Other Countries, Marca Registrada, Hecho en U.S.A.
HarperCollins® is a trademark of HarperCollins Publishers.

Printed in the U.S.A.

20   19   18   17   16   15   14   13   12   11

September
Mourn

Hidden
Cove

Chavez
Cove

Dock

Chavez
Island

Salmon
Gap

1. Barber House
2. Turnaround
3. Garage
4. Shed
5. Woodshed
6. Doe (Cabin)
7. Buck (Cabin)
8. Fawn (Cabin)
9. Rafe St. Jacques
10. Helicopter Pad
11. Wicker Basket
12. Carr House
13. Stoneyhenge
14. Guest House
15. Boathouse
16. Temple

ONE

JUDITH MCMONIGLE FLYNN applied the brakes, got no reaction, and felt her blue compact crash into the retaining wall at Falstaff's Market. Jarred, but unhurt, Judith swore under her breath. She knew the brakes weren't working properly, but she'd put off having them checked. Summer was the busiest season at Hillside Manor, Judith's bed-and-breakfast establishment. Now it was the Tuesday after Labor Day; she should have gone to the mechanic before she went grocery shopping.

"Are you okay?" shouted a courtesy clerk who was wheeling a cart back toward the store. The disapproving expression on his youthful face indicated he thought Judith was drunk or stupid, or both.

Though still shaken, Judith nodded. "I think so, but some of my parts are lying in your parking lot. I heard them fall off."

"What?" The courtesy clerk, whose name tag identified him as Skip, seemed to be assessing Judith for missing appendages.

Seemingly convinced that Judith wasn't drunk and maybe not stupid, Skip investigated the car's front end. Judith got out and joined him.

"Your bumper took most of it," said Skip, fingering a chin that sprouted a fuzzy hint of beard. "But you

1

wiped out a headlight, and your grill's mashed in.''

''Rats,'' Judith muttered, trying to ignore the handful of customers who were watching from a discreet distance. Joe had offered to take the compact into the mechanic, but Judith hadn't wanted to bother her husband. Joe Flynn's schedule as a homicide detective was unpredictable, since murderers didn't punch a time clock.

The BP station on Heraldsgate Hill was located opposite Falstaff's Market. Judith jaywalked across Heraldsgate Avenue to make arrangements for repairing the brakes. Terry, the young but knowledgeable mechanic, told her she'd better do the bodywork first. Had she called her insurance company? The car should be towed in for an estimate. After the insurance people and the body shop had done their jobs, Terry could tackle the brakes.

Disconsolately, Judith trudged back across the busy street. She didn't think the front-end damage was sufficient to warrant all the inconvenience. Now she was stuck without a car. Joe needed his old but reliable MG to drive to work. Her insurance didn't provide for a rental car. Judith would have to hoof it all over Heraldsgate Hill or borrow a car from her neighbors, Carl and Arlene Rankers. Either way, it would be a bother.

So caught up in her dilemma was Judith that she didn't see the oncoming car until it screeched to a stop within a foot of her. The horn blasted as Judith reeled toward a Metro bus that had pulled into the stop by the service station.

''Coz!'' cried a voice that came from the direction of the car. ''Get out of the street before you get killed!'' Cousin Renie poked her head out of the Chevrolet sedan.

Judith was caught between the big car and the even bigger bus. With a sheepish expression, she scooted around the front of the Chev and jumped in beside Renie. ''My fault,'' Judith muttered, arranging her statuesque form in the passenger seat. ''I didn't look.''

''You sure didn't,'' Renie responded, then again leaned out the window to yell at the impatient drivers who had stopped behind her. "Oh, shut up! None of you are going anywhere except to the liquor store!" Renie goosed the accelerator but had to come to another quick stop, this time at the traffic light by Holiday's Pharmacy and Moonbeam's coffee shop. "So what's wrong? I'm going home, by the way. Are you coming with me?"

"I might as well," Judith sighed, smoothing her disheveled silver-streaked hair. As the cousins continued down Heraldsgate Avenue, she explained what had happened to her Nissan.

"Shoot," Renie said, braking to a full stop at the four-way arterial by S&M Meats. "Why don't I just take you home now?"

Judith gave Renie a slightly embarrassed look. "I still haven't done my grocery shopping. Would you mind . . . ?"

There wasn't much that the cousins minded doing for each other. As only children, they had grown up together, and were as close as sisters. Incapable of keeping secrets from each other, Judith and Renie could almost read each other's minds. Usually—but not always—that was a good thing.

"Oh, why not?" Renie replied, turning to head back up the hill. "I could pick up something for dinner. I'm running out of menu ideas with the kids still home for the summer. Next week, all three of them will be off to college, and Bill and I can eat real food, like meat and fish and vegetables. Where do these kids get such weird ideas about nutrition, like a yen for vegetarian chili?"

"Beats me." Judith shrugged. "Since Mike went to work for the park service in Idaho, I figure he's eating berries and nuts and tree bark. If he and Kristin really do get married, I wonder if she can cook. He can't."

"None of our children are ever getting married," Renie declared, untangling her maze of chestnut curls. "They're going to stay in school until they have so many initials after their names, it'll look like a foreign language. Why does Tom need a doctorate in German? He won't even eat sauerkraut. What will Anne do with an Ed.D? She doesn't want to teach or be an administrator. And Tony hasn't announced a major! Jeez, I thought that once they got into their twenties, they'd move out and hold down jobs and get married and have children of their own so that they, too, could be driven crazy! If I didn't take my estrogen, I'd be in the loony bin by now!''

Accustomed to Renie's rantings about her offspring, Judith dwelled instead on her own problems. ''You know, I always feel a letdown after the tourist season is over. Oh, I'm glad that things aren't so hectic, but between now and when the fall weather sets in and we can look forward to the holidays, there's about a two-week lull where I feel sort of disoriented.''

''It's not that I don't love my kids,'' Renie said, waiting to make a left-hand turn into the Falstaff parking lot, ''but wouldn't you think they'd want to get on with their lives? After four years of college, I was sick of the classroom. I couldn't wait to get out and try my hand at the graphic-design business. And earn some money, too.''

''Maybe it's the weather,'' Judith remarked. ''It stays too warm in September around here. I suppose after Labor Day, I automatically expect rain and cooler temperatures.''

''It's because they're spoiled,'' Renie asserted, finally entering the grocery-store lot. ''They have everything—we gave it to them, and now we're paying the price for taking away the need to acquire on their on. At least that's what Bill says. In our generation, we were still trying to better ourselves and move up another notch from where our parents stood on the economic ladder. But nowadays, according to Bill, we've reached a plateau where the next generation feels . . .''

''Pathetic,'' Judith interrupted, pointing to her blue compact, which was coincidentally parked next to the Chev. ''Look, my poor car seems lonely and forsaken. Maybe I'll call the insurance company from the store.''

''Save your quarter,'' urged Renie, who was used to being interrupted by Judith, especially when Bill's opinions were being parroted. ''Have you got a long list?''

"Long enough." Judith sighed, getting out of the car. "It'll take me about twenty minutes."

It took closer to thirty, since Judith ran into three fellow parishioners from Our Lady, Star of the Sea, the local head librarian, and Corinne Dooley, one of her neighbors. Renie whiled away the extra time by racing off to Begelman's Bakery and Heraldsgate Books. It was exactly 2:00 P.M. when the cousins pulled up in Hillside Manor's driveway.

"Hey, noodleheads!" yelled Judith's mother from the doorway of the toolshed that had been converted into an apartment. "You got any almond clusters in those grocery sacks?"

"No, Mother," Judith called across the expanse of yard. "The doctor says you're not supposed to eat so many sweets. Would you like a nice broccoli casserole for supper tonight?"

"*Broccoli!*" screeched Gertrude Grover. "How about bacteria and a couple of viruses? How about vaccinations for the pox? How about turnips and spinach and rutabagas?"

"I've got Brussels sprouts, Aunt Gertrude," Renie shouted.

Gertrude, who was wearing an ocelot-print housecoat and a baggy purple sweater, moved her walker closer to the cousins. She was followed by Sweetums, Judith's malevolent cat. "What's wrong with you young people these days?" she growled. "Have you forgotten how to eat? Whatever happened to steak and string beans and mashed potatoes? And almond clusters?"

Renie was bestowing a benign smile on her aunt. "You know, that's a funny thing—Judith and I were just talking about that very subject. Only we feel that *our* kids don't know what's good for them. Generation gap, huh, Aunt Gertrude?"

"Generation gap, my butt!" Gertrude snapped, banging her walker on the cement path and narrowly missing Sweetums, who fled into the nearest flower bed. "What's wrong with red meat and eggs and plenty of butter? How do you think I got to be this old? Protein—that's the ticket. Plenty of pro-*tein*." Gertrude put the emphasis on the second syllable.

"I have to unload," Judith said in a faintly feeble voice. "This stuff's heavy."

"Heavy," muttered Gertrude. "What's heavy about broccoli?" Clumsily, she turned the walker and stumped back to the converted toolshed.

Sweetums reappeared, holding something in his mouth. Nudging the screen door open with her elbow, Judith turned to see the cat deposit the object on the small patio and then bounce it in the air with his paws.

"Damn!" Judith breathed. "He's got a bird! I hope it's a starling. They're a nuisance. They scare the songbirds away."

It was indeed a starling which Sweetums was now conveying to the back porch. Just as Judith managed to get through the doorway, the cat angled between her feet and dropped the bird on her left shoe. He then settled his furry orange-and-white-and-gray body directly in front of Judith. His gold eyes gazed up at her, as if seeking approbation.

Struggling to hold on to the grocery bags, Judith kicked the dead bird out of the way. "Dammit, Sweetums, why can't you leave your victims outside?"

Sweetums took umbrage. With a flip of his plumelike tail, he marched into the dining room. Hurriedly, Judith set the grocery bags on the counter, then chased after Sweetums. She reached the dining room just as he was sinking his claws into her new lace curtains.

Judith grabbed the cat; the cat scratched Judith. Judith let out a little yelp. The cat jumped out of her grasp, arched his back, and hissed. Having vented his spleen, Sweetums tore off into the kitchen, jumped up on the counter, and dived into the bag that contained his weekly ration of cat tuna. He didn't budge until Judith had opened one of the cans and emptied it in his dish by the back door. Sweetums ignored his prey, which was still lying in the rear hall by the pantry. Satisfied with the havoc he'd wreaked and the reward he'd received, the cat strolled to his feeding area and contentedly began to eat.

Judith picked up the dead starling in a paper towel and threw it in the garbage. "I'll bet Mother forgot to feed him. Again," she sighed, washing her hands at the sink.

"You're making excuses for the hideous little beast," Renie said. "You should get a bunny like ours. Clarence isn't any trouble, even if Bill does call him Triple D."

"Triple D?" inquired Judith as she wiped her hands on a towel.

"For delicate, dirty, and dumb. I'll admit Clarence has had some health problems. He goes in for an eye exam tomorrow."

Judith didn't want to hear about Clarence. "I'd cook him in a big pot," she muttered. "I'd do the same with Swee-tums, but he's too fat to fit in anything but an industrial-sized roaster."

Renie opened a can of pop while Judith unloaded the groceries. "Do you want me to call the insurance company for you?" Renie asked.

"I'd better check my phone messages first," Judith replied, putting fresh halibut and bacon and a small rack of lamb into the refrigerator. "I've only got two rooms full tonight, so I can't afford to ignore any late requests."

After loading milk, butter, and eggs into the fridge, Judith crossed the long, high-ceilinged kitchen to her answering machine, which sat near the computer she'd received as a Christmas present from Joe. The red light showed that there were three calls. The first was from a couple in Montana who wanted a reservation for two nights in November. The second was a woman asking if it was true that Judith didn't allow pets. It seemed she had a hedgehog that went with her everywhere. The third and last message was a voice that mildly startled Judith. She turned up the volume so that Renie could hear, too.

"Judith, this is Jeanne Barber, Jeanne *Clayton* Barber. The last time I saw you was at the state B&B association meeting in February." The voice continued, breathless and

shrill. "Before that, we met at our thirtieth high-school reunion a few years back. I won't say *how many* years back,
ha-ha! You remember that I told you I own a B&B on
Chavez Island? Well, I sent you a letter about that the other
day. Maybe you haven't gotten it yet. The mail doesn't
always go off the island every day. So please call me, and
I'll explain. I'm terribly anxious to talk to you. It's . . . a
matter of life and death. Bye-bye, hear from you soon."
The voice dropped an octave and ended on a hush.

Renie was fumbling through the sheep-shaped cookie jar
on the kitchen table, finding nothing more than crumbs.
"Jeannie Clayton, huh? I remember her—she was two
years younger than I was and light-years dopier. I didn't
know she owned a B&B. Did she ever get her teeth fixed?"

"No. Yes." Judith felt distracted as she tried to pull up
a mental portrait of Jeanne Clayton Barber. Tall, though
not as tall as Judith. Slim, slimmer than Judith. Pretty in
an unremarkable, sort of faded way, not at all like Judith,
who hoped that her strong features had better withstood the
test of time. "Her teeth are fine. At least they all go in the
same direction now. Maybe I'd better check the mail. It
hadn't come when I left for the store."

Judith had her hand on the swinging door that led into
the dining room when her mother banged at the back door.
"Hey!" Gertrude yelled, using the walker to push open the
screen. "You get any of those almond clusters?"

Judith glanced at Renie. "Oh, dear!" The words came
out in a whisper.

Turning toward Gertrude, Judith forced a smile. "No,
Mother. I think you asked me that when I came home."

"Oh." Gertrude leaned on her walker. Her small, wrinkled face puckered. "Broccoli casserole," she said, in an
apparent non sequitur.

But Judith knew better. She understood that her mother
was racking her brain to remember something not only recent, but of importance. At least to Gertrude.

"With chicken breasts and rice," Judith replied, and finally looked fondly at her mother. "Maybe I'll make bis-

cuits unless it's too warm to turn on the oven.''

''Warm?'' Gertrude shivered inside the baggy cardigan. ''It's darned cold, if you ask me.''

Judith wasn't sure if her mother was kidding or not. A year, even six months ago, Gertrude definitely would have been trying to provoke her daughter. But now Judith didn't know if her mother was serious. Gertrude's natural perversity, often feigned, had become all too real.

''I've got to get the mail,'' Judith said, changing the subject. ''Why don't you sit down with Renie, Mother, and I'll pour us some lemonade?''

''Nope,'' Gertrude replied, swinging the walker around. ''I'm going back to that cardboard crate you call my apartment. It's almost warm in there, but that's because I set fire to my undies. I'd better go put 'em out before the rest of the place goes up in smoke. So long, suckers.''

With a nervous sigh, Judith turned a quirky expression on Renie. ''You see? That last part sounded like Mother—perfectly normal, ornery and mean.''

Renie gazed up at the high ceiling, then got out of the kitchen chair and followed Judith to the front porch. ''Normal for her, yes. Well, she's old. So's my mother. She remembers too much. You can't win, coz. We don't change as we get older—we just become more of what we always were—only worse.''

''I suppose,'' Judith murmured, sifting through the bills, circulars, and pre-Christmas catalogues that had arrived in the mail. ''But it's still depressing. Middle age is well named—we're right in the middle of everything—kids, mothers, and husbands, who need us most of all and yet don't always ask for . . .'' Judith paused, waving an ecru-colored envelope at Renie. ''Ah! Here's the letter from Jeanne Clayton Barber. She's right—it took five days to get here from—what?—less than a hundred miles away? Of course there was the Labor Day weekend in between.''

The cousins retreated into the living room, where they sat down on matching sofas by the empty fireplace. The French doors at the far end of the room stood open, with the soft sound of the breeze ruffling the lilac and fruit trees outside. Near the baby grand piano stood a card table with the current jigsaw-puzzle-in-progress. In the corner by the bookshelves, Judith's prized grandfather clock ticked away the hours. The living room was a comfortable place, intended not only for the permanent residents of Hillside Manor, but the guests as well.

Resignedly, Judith opened the envelope. " 'Dear Judith,' " she read out loud. " 'Last year you and I had the most wonderful chat during a break at the state . . . ' " Judith frowned at the elaborate handwriting which flowed beneath a Chavez Cove Bed-and-Breakfast logo depicting a crescent moon over a small bay. "This is just a rehash of her phone message. 'High school together,' blah-blah . . . 'married Duane Barber three years after graduation,' blah-blah . . . 'took over Chavez Cove cabins twelve years ago,' blah-blah . . ." The frown deepened. "Oh, what a shame! I'll read this part. 'Duane died unexpectedly of an aneurism this summer. It couldn't have happened at a worse time, the very height of the tourist season. I practically lost my mind trying to cope with the guests *and* the funeral arrangements *and* all the loose ends that have to be tied up after losing a loved one. But of course you understand, Judith. As I recall, you lost your first husband some years ago. Though, if I'm remembering correctly, you didn't have the B&B to worry about at the time."

Judith looked up from the letter's second page. "I sure didn't. Jeanne had it easy. I'd like to know what she'd have done in my shoes, working at the library during the day and tending bar at the Meat & Mingle in the evenings. Plus, debts up to my eyeballs, we were about to be evicted, and Dan's booze bill was the size of a third world country's gross national product."

"Gross is right," said Renie who had slipped off her sandals and settled her feet on the coffee table. "At over four hundred pounds, Dan was definitely gross. But I quibble with 'loved one.' Dan wasn't a loved one—he was the size of several people. Our Tom used to call him 'Uncle Group.' ''

''Behind his back,'' Judith put in.

''Of which there was a vast expanse,'' Renie noted. ''But we digress.''

It was easy to do, even after eight years and a second, much happier marriage. Dan McMonigle had been an intelligent, well-mannered, generous man on the surface. But under the massive shield of flesh there lurked a hostile heart. Dan could only like people who were his inferiors. When Judith met Dan, she had felt inadequate. The man she loved, the man who had promised to marry her, the man with whom she had envisioned a charmed life, had dumped her for another woman. When Dan waddled into the breach, Judith had felt inferior to all manner of lowly things, including earthworms and poison ivy and agents from the IRS.

Judith resumed reading. '' 'Duane passed away July 29. Now, a month later, I'm finally getting to the end of the insurance forms, the banking matters, the sending of little remembrances to his relatives. As you know, September is usually a quiet month in our business, at least after Labor Day. My daughter, Marcia, has been urging me to get away (she insists I go to one of those ritzy spas in Southern California—but it sounds so self-indulgent, doesn't it?). On the other hand, I definitely need a break in my routine. So many memories, so much emotion, such an overwhelming sense of sadness! I see Duane everywhere, which makes it doubly hard to let go.

'' 'Now I come to the difficult part of this letter. I'm not one to ask favors. But everyone in the state B&B association says you're absolutely tops! Plus, we do go way back, don't we, Judith? Do you remember Mrs. Beecroft in eighth grade, and how she'd soak her dentures in a glass of water on her desk, and one day Jerome MacAfee put ink in the water, and Mrs. Beecroft didn't notice, and when she put her teeth in, her mouth turned blue! Such a riot! Jerome, I hear, is now a circuit-court judge.

" 'So what I'd like to propose is a trade. (There! I've said it! That wasn't so hard after all!) If you could come up to Chavez Island and take over the B&B while I go to the spa or wherever, I'll spell you at Hillside Manor after the first of the year. If that doesn't suit you, then I'd be willing to pay for you to come up to my place. (Yes, I know that B&B-sitters can be hired through the association, but I want a real pro—believe me, my offer would be generous.) I know this is asking a lot, but my nerves are shattered, and I feel so claustrophobic. I never felt that way while Duane was alive, but it's different now. Chavez Island is very small, and only a handful of residents live here. Not that they haven't been ever so kind. Most of them at any rate—don't believe everything you hear in a tiny place like this! I can't imagine a safer situation anywhere, and the month of September doesn't bother me the way it disturbs some of the other folks. Life's passages can be awfully hard on people.

" 'Of course you must feel free to say No. I'll understand. But if you come next week, I can promise lovely weather—we get a true Indian summer in the islands. Do call or write. My phone number is . . .' "

Judith tipped her head to one side. "I didn't need this. Not today."

"Then say no," Renie replied in a reasonable voice. "She gave you an out."

Chin on fists, Judith considered. "She wouldn't have asked me if she weren't desperate. She wouldn't have written *and* called if she weren't frantic. She wouldn't have bared her soul if she didn't need a friend."

There were times when Judith's generous spirit was too much for Renie. "Sap, sap, sap! You'll do it, won't you? I'm going home. You don't have any cookies."

"I'll talk to Joe and call her tonight, one way or the other." Judith slowly got to her feet while Renie put on her sandals. "The first thing I've got to do is call the insurance company."

Renie headed for the French doors. "If you decide to

B&B-sit, don't take it out in trade. Ask for money up front. As a freelance designer, I always try to get a retainer fee. Otherwise, clients weasel.''

''Right.'' Judith sounded uncertain. ''I don't suppose you'd . . . ?'' The unspoken question floated past Renie into the backyard.

But Renie didn't need to hear the unspoken words. ''No! Not in a zillion years! After the kids leave this weekend and Bill goes back on campus to get ready for the fall quarter, I'm going to become a will-o'-the-wisp. I may go shopping, I may go to lunch with a friend, I might even stay home and wallow around with a bowl of popcorn and a half-rack of Pepsi and all my favorite CDs. But no way am I going with you to Chavez Island, coz. September is a lull for me, too, while everybody in the corporate world returns from vacation and the bigwigs aren't ready to farm out the fall projects. Believe me, after a whole summer with everybody home, I need some time to myself. See you.''

The blue Chev reversed out of the drive. Judith wandered over to the toolshed and found her mother lurking in the doorway. ''Would you have a fit if I left town for a week?'' She already knew the answer.

''First off, I'd croak,'' Gertrude said in a deceptively mild tone. ''Then you'd have to get me buried and have Father Hoyle pray over my mortal remains. Next, you'd put on your caterer's hat and invite the mourners in for a big buffet. Salads, sandwiches, cakes, pies, rolls, maybe some olives and pickles. Candy, too. Say, how about those almond clusters you didn't get? I might enjoy them from my fluffy white cloud.'' With a flip of her baggy cardigan, Gertrude stomped inside the toolshed.

''Naturally,'' Judith said to Joe as he opened a can of beer, ''Mother is against me going. That should settle it, shouldn't it? I mean, she's so old and I worry that her memory is slipping. I'd be afraid to leave her alone.''

Joe settled back in his captain's chair and took a big sip of beer. ''You've left her before. I'm here, and so are the

Rankerses. Carl and Arlene always take good care of your mother. As for her memory, I haven't noticed it being any worse than it ever was.''

"That's because you almost never talk to her," Judith said, not without a trace of asperity. The bitterness between Gertrude and Joe was long-standing, a wound that had never healed after his alcohol-induced elopement with his first wife.

"She doesn't want to talk to me," Joe replied in a calm voice. "In fact, she'd rather talk to Herself. I mean to Vivian. Hey," Joe went on, his round, slightly florid face brightening, "Vivian could help out, too. She seems to like the old bat.''

"Don't call my mother an old bat," Judith snapped, though she realized that her anger actually stemmed from the reference to Joe's first wife, who had moved into the neighborhood six months earlier.

Joe picked up the evening newspaper and flipped to the sports page. "Okay, it was just a thought."

Repenting her sharp words, Judith sat down across the table from Joe. "It's not just Mother that worries me—it's you. Would you manage without me?"

Joe's green eyes regarded Judith over the top of the sports section. "Sure. I can cook, remember?"

Judith did. Joe was an excellent cook, who often prepared the evening meals, at least on weekends. "I'd be gone a week," Judith persisted, wishing Joe would say he couldn't live without her. "Arlene and Carl would have to take over the B&B."

"They've done it before. What's the problem, especially now that Carl's retired?" This time, Joe didn't look up from the newspaper.

The Rankerses were admirable stand-ins. Arlene and Judith shared Hillside Manor's catering arm. Not only were Carl and Arlene good friends and wonderful neighbors, but they had a knack for dealing with people, particularly Judith's mother.

"I hate to bother them," Judith murmured. The least Joe

could do was put up a token argument for keeping her at his side. "I'm going to have to borrow their car until I get mine back. The insurance company said it might take until Friday to assess the damages. They didn't get it towed away until just before five."

"If you aren't here, you won't need a car," Joe pointed out, turning the page.

"So how will I get to Chavez Island?" The triumphant note in Judith's voice indicated that she'd scored a point in her favor.

"I could drive you up to the ferry in the MG. If the island is as small as you say it is, why would you need a car? Anyway, wouldn't your old high-school chum leave her car?"

Judith sighed. "I suppose." Fidgeting in the chair, she frowned at the newspaper, which hid her husband's face. "Won't you miss me?"

"Of course." Joe appeared to be finishing an article. At last, he put the sports section aside. Gold flecks danced in his green eyes. *Magic eyes*, Judith called them, full of mischief even in middle age. Thirty years earlier, she had fallen hopelessly in love with the red hair, the trim physique, the engaging grin, the magic eyes. Though the red hair had thinned and was turning gray, and a hint of a paunch flawed the physique, the grin and the eyes were still intact. So was the mischief. And that was what worried Judith most.

"A lot?" Judith's voice was uncharacteristically meek.

"A whole lot." Joe's gaze was steady as he reached across the table to caress her cheek. "But the truth is, I've got a training session coming up. I'll be working overtime, and when I get home, I'll be cranky as hell. I always am during training sessions. So if you're going to be gone, next week is a good time for it."

Judith fell silent. Joe was right, of course. There had been other training sessions, and they always triggered an irascible mood. Still, there was the car repair to consider and her mother and the B&B and . . . Herself, two doors down in the house vacated the previous winter by the Goodriches.

In a startling move, Vivian Flynn had pulled up stakes in Florida and returned to the Pacific Northwest. She had come for Christmas and stayed forever. Or so it appeared. Vivian—or Herself, as she was known—hadn't yet caused any serious problems. She was too enamored of the bottle, and thus inclined to keep to her snug little house. On her rare forays outdoors, she called on Gertrude rather than Judith—or Joe. All the same, Judith wasn't keen on the idea of leaving her husband alone with the woman to whom he had been married for over twenty years. Though considerably older than Joe and eroded by alcohol, Herself retained a certain allure.

"I guess I'll do it," Judith said glumly. She rose from the table and went to the cupboards, where she got out the makings of her guests' hors d'oeuvres tray. "I'm going to ask for the money, though. We never go anywhere in January."

"We could," Joe said as he sifted through the front section of the newspaper. "How about catching some sun in Mazatlán or Hawaii or Alabama?"

Judith opened a tin of smoked oysters. "Could you take time off?"

"Maybe." Joe polished off his beer.

"Can we afford it?"

"No. But that shouldn't stop us. Sometimes you forget that we're a two-income family."

That was easy to do. After eighteen years of providing two meager incomes all by herself, Judith couldn't quite adapt to the concept of separate paychecks. On the other hand, Joe didn't always take into account how much of Judith's earnings were plowed right back into the B&B. During the first year of operation, she had figured that her biggest benefit from the enterprise was having a free roof over her head. Judith smiled weakly. "We'll see about a winter break." She reached for a box of crackers. The kitchen was growing warm from the oven and the late-afternoon sun. Spending a week alone with Joe definitely had its appeal. Jeanne Clayton Barber might make a generous offer, enough to pay for a January trip. Running Chavez Cove B&B could be a pleasant change of pace. Summers were draining. Autumn would be setting in, with the advent of the holidays and then winter and . . .

Judith made up her mind. If Jeanne needed a friend, her name would be Judith Flynn. Chavez Island sounded lovely in the fall. It was isolated, it was picturesque, it was *safe*. Hadn't Jeanne Clayton Barber said so?

TWO

RENIE WAS INCOHERENT. When she phoned Judith around eight, words tumbled out in a squawking jumble. Judith told her cousin to calm down.

"It was that stupid vegetarian chili," Renie declared, still speaking rapidly, if now rationally. "I spilled some on the stove, so I wiped it up with a paper towel, and then the phone rang. My mother, of course, making sure I got home from her apartment safely." There was a pause during which Judith could almost hear Renie's teeth gnash. She could definitely hear Bill and the Jones offspring bellowing in the background.

"Mom went on and on, as usual, and I forgot about the paper towel. Just as she was asking if I'd been approached by any white slavers on my way home, I smelled smoke. Then I *saw* smoke, but not much else. I finally got my mother to hang up so I could call 911." Renie ran out of breath.

"How'd you manage that?" Judith inquired, marveling at Renie's success in getting Aunt Deb to part from the telephone.

"Good question," Renie replied. "I've used the-kitchen's-on-fire routine so often that I had to think of something else. I told her there was a man with a knife at my door."

"It sounds like it worked," Judith remarked. "Are you okay? What about damage?"

Renie let out a groan. "Nobody but me was downstairs, so we're all okay, except I had a coughing fit from the smoke. But the kitchen's a mess—and Bill just got through refinishing the cabinets on his summer break! Which, the firemen told us, was a good thing, because if they'd been layered in grease, the whole house might have gone up."

Judith couldn't resist a small laugh. "What a coincidence—we both get to call our insurance companies the same day!"

"Funny, funny, coz," Renie said in a voice indicating that her sense of humor had also gone up in smoke. "Our people from LUMPCO won't be able to come out until Thursday. We've got to spend the night in a motel."

Judith thought of the three spare bedrooms on the second floor. "That's ridiculous. Come over here. You and Bill can stay in the front guest room, the big one. I can put Tom and Tony in the room at the end of the hall, and Anne can take the little room off the stairs."

Though Renie demurred, Judith finally talked her cousin into bringing the Jones family under the sheltering eaves of Hillside Manor. An hour and a half later, Bill, Renie, and the three grown children pulled into the drive. Bill, who was an early riser, immediately proclaimed that he was going to bed. Tom and Tony declared that, having missed dinner, they intended to raid the refrigerator. Anne dumped off her suitcase in the smallest of the guest rooms and announced that she had a late date with Arturo.

"Who's Arturo?" Judith asked, as Anne disappeared into the small bathroom off the entrance hall.

"An Italian foreign student," Renie answered in an uncharacteristically dazed voice. "This is a bad idea."

Judith lifted her dark, even eyebrows at her cousin. "What is? Arturo?"

"Huh?" Renie was gazing distractedly around the dining room, where the oval oak table was covered with an Irish linen cloth and already set for breakfast. "Oh, Arturo!

Maybe, I've only met him once. No," she continued, now resting her brown eyes on Judith. "This whole idea of staying here. It may be days before we can go back home. What are your bookings for the rest of the week?"

Judith winced. "I've got four rooms filled tomorrow night, three on Thursday, and then we're full over the weekend. But still, if I've saved you the insurance allowance for one night at a motel, you ought to come out okay."

Renie sank into the chair at the head of the table, which was the only one of the set with arms. Grandpa Grover had used the chair as his place of honor. The previous spring, Judith had finally replaced Grandma Grover's original needlepoint covers.

"I suppose," Renie said in a small voice. "I think they allow no more than fifty bucks a night. Where can we stay in this town for so little and still get room service? You know what our children are like."

Judith had never quite approved of the Jones family's insistence on never staying at a hotel or motel that didn't rate at least three stars in the AAA guidebook. The result was that Tom, Anne, and Tony—not to mention Bill and Renie—expected every possible amenity, including a complete menu at three A.M. Judith hoped that the Joneses didn't expect such elegant treatment at Hillside Manor.

The front door slammed, indicating that Anne had left with Arturo. Renie looked mildly interested. "I think he's studying American art," she murmured. "Or does Anne call him Art?"

"Call it a day," urged Joe, who apparently had just descended the back stairs from the family living quarters on the third floor and entered the dining room through the kitchen. "It's almost ten, and both of you have had a long, destructive day."

"It's too early," Judith protested. Despite the need to rise at six and make breakfast for her guests, she usually didn't retire until around eleven.

"Are you kidding?" Renie asked. In contrast to her husband, she was a veritable night owl, seldom heading for bed until after midnight. "I have to wait up to let Anne in. She has no key."

Under the undeniably hideous paisley bathrobe Gertrude had given her son-in-law a couple of Christmases past, Joe shrugged. "Whatever. I'm going to watch TV. Something restful, like a violent cop show. Meanwhile," he added for Renie as he turned to the swinging door, "tell your sons that the freezer control knobs aren't edible."

"Sorry." Renie gave Judith a sick little smile. "You know how my kids love to eat, even if they do enjoy weird food groups."

Judith also knew how Renie loved to eat. "Did you get any dinner, coz?"

"No." Somehow, Renie managed to look as if she hadn't consumed even the tiniest morsel in days. Her cheeks sank in, her eyes grew hollow, her very skin seemed to turn ashen. "I could use a little meat. And potatoes and maybe a small but earnest vegetable."

Judith laughed. "As soon as your boys vacate the kitchen, I'll whip up some chicken breasts and rice and what's left of the fresh broccoli." She paused, hearing the retreat of footsteps from the kitchen. "I think they're going upstairs now. Shall I turn on the stove?"

Renie smiled feebly. Five minutes later, the cousins were in the kitchen, listening to the sizzle of skinless chicken breast, the burble of boiling broccoli, and the hiss of steaming rice.

"What," Renie asked from her place at the kitchen table, "did Jeanne say when you called?"

"Jeanne?" Judith blinked. "Oh—you mean Jeanne Clayton Barber."

"Right." Renie rolled her eyes at the high ceiling.

"I haven't called yet," Judith hedged, turning down the rice. "I don't think Joe wants me to go."

"I don't blame him," Renie allowed. "It'll wear you down, just when you should be taking a breather. It's always harder to shoulder somebody's else responsibilities than your own."

"It's not that . . . exactly." Judith busied herself with the chicken breast.

Renie didn't coax. Instead, she spread a paper napkin on her lap and gazed expectantly at the stove. "Cluck, cluck," said Renie.

"Actually," Judith admitted, "Joe doesn't care. That's what bothers me." She gave Renie an anxious look.

"Huh?" Renie's expression was blank.

"Herself." Judith savagely speared the chicken breast to lift it from the pan.

"Oh, Jeez!" Renie clapped a hand to her head. "You aren't worrying about Joe and Herself, are you? Come on, coz!"

Dishing up rice and broccoli, Judith sighed. "I know, it's stupid. I don't think Joe's seen Herself more than six times since she moved into the neighborhood last January. But they *were* married for almost twenty-five years, and they had a daughter together. Sometimes I feel as if I were an interloper in Joe's life."

Renie was evincing disgust even as she lavishly buttered her rice. "That's silly. Herself was the interloper, coming between the two of you, and almost ruining your lives."

Renie was right, of course. As Judith ran water into the kettle that had held the rice, she made up her mind. "I'll call Jeanne now and tell her I'm coming."

"Fine," Renie said with her mouth full. "Tell her I'm coming with you."

Renie's rationale was simple: She couldn't live at home until the repair work on the kitchen was done, the kids would be off to college in three more days, and Bill would be tied up at the university during the week. It might be possible for him to get a motel room for under fifty dollars.

"He doesn't use much room service," Renie explained.

Judith dialed Jeanne Barber's number on Chavez Island. The ringing in Judith's ear had a strange, hollow sound. "I feel like I'm calling Land's End," Judith murmured.

Jeanne was effusive, elated, grateful. "I was so afraid you'd say no! When can you get here?"

"Monday morning?" Judith offered. "I'll have a full house over the weekend, so I'd rather wait. I also need to ask my neighbors to fill in."

"What a good friend you are!" Jeanne enthused in her strident voice. "Even after all these years! Now here's how you get to Chavez Island . . ."

Somehow, Judith had assumed that she need only drive some seventy-five miles north to the terminal where the ferryboats sailed off to the Santa Lucia Islands chain, and arrive an hour or so later at her destination. But Chavez Island was too small for a scheduled ferry stop, Jeanne told Judith.

"You'll have to leave your car on the mainland," Jeanne said a trifle apologetically. "You won't need it once you get here—the island is only a little over one square mile. Walk off the ferry at Laurel Harbor on Perez, the big island, and then Rafe will bring you to Chavez Cove in his cruiser."

"Rafe?" Judith frowned into the phone.

"Rafe St. Jacques," Jeanne answered promptly, then giggled. "He plays many parts. One of them is to provide transportation between Chavez and the other islands. There's a nine-thirty ferry that'll put you into Laurel Harbor at ten-forty-five. It's an outgoing tide, but Rafe should get you to the B & B by eleven-fifteen."

"Okay," Judith said dubiously. She shot Renie a quick glance, but her cousin was absorbed in her food. It wouldn't do to mention the early departure time just yet. Renie wasn't a morning person. "See you Monday," Judith said to Jeanne, then listened to the other woman rattle off more thank-yous before hanging up.

"Well," Judith remarked, sitting down across from Renie, "that's settled."

Renie nodded. "It should be kind of nice. The islands are beautiful, especially this time of year."

"Coz," Judith began, gazing earnestly at Renie, "I re-

ally appreciate having you come along. Besides the pleasure of your company, it'll cut down on my responsibilities
and lighten the workload . . .''

Gobbling up the last morsel of chicken, Renie pushed
her chair away from the table and stretched. ''Who,'' she
yawned, ''said I was going to work?''

Judith merely smiled. It didn't matter whether Renie
helped or loafed. The cousins would be together on an out-
ing to Chavez Island. For a week, they could put their troubles behind them. Jeanne Barber's invitation began to take
on the aura of an adventure rather than an obligation.

Judith kept smiling.

By Monday morning, Judith's car had been declared a
disaster. The cost of fixing the blue compact was so close
to the low blue book value that the insurance company had
advised her to take the money and buy a new used car.
Judith wasn't pleased at the prospect, but Joe pointed out
that they didn't have much choice. His MG couldn't keep
going forever, and it was inevitable that sooner or later, one
of them would have to get another car. Sooner apparently
was now.

Since the Joneses were a one-car family, and Renie
couldn't leave Bill without the Chev, Joe suggested that
Judith figure out what kind of a car she'd like to try out
and rent one to take as far as the ferry dock. Upon their
return to the mainland, she could test-drive a different
model on the way home.

Thus it was that Monday morning Judith had gotten up
at her usual early hour to make breakfast for her guests,
but had left almost immediately upon serving them so that
Joe could take her to the nearest car-rental agency. Half an
hour later she was back at Hillside Manor with a dark blue
Subaru Legacy.

''What do you think?'' she asked of Renie, who had just
been dropped off by Bill on his way to the university campus.

"S'acar," Renie shrugged in her usual morning fog. "S'blue."

Gently but firmly, Judith steered Renie toward the back door. "Go have a cup of coffee. I've got to make sure Mother is okay before we leave."

"S'amother," Renie mumbled, staggering in the general direction of the porch.

Gertrude was up but not yet dressed. She sat in her favorite chair, swathed in a bright orange bathrobe. "I hate this bacon," she declared, pointing a gnarled finger at her plate. "It tastes like mole."

"It's low sodium," Judith said. "The doctor says it's good for you."

"How old's the doctor?" Gertrude demanded.

Judith considered. "Forty, forty-five. Why?"

Gertrude snorted. "Half my age. What can *he* know? I've been eating *real* bacon and *real* ham and *real* little pigs for twice that long. What do you bet that when the doctor's my age, he'll have been dead for twenty years?"

The point was unarguable, nor did Judith want to wrangle with her mother just before leaving town. "I've left a shopping list for Arlene. I'll make sure she gets you regular bacon. Is there anything else you need before Renie and I leave?"

Gertrude hunched down inside her orange bathrobe. "Hunh! You bet, kiddo!" Her eyes narrowed as she gazed up at her daughter. "A few internal organs that aren't on the skids, some arms and legs that don't creak, eyes that can see farther than my fingers, and ears that'll hear something quieter than an atom bomb. Well?"

The requests were as familiar as they were impossible to fill. Judith gave Gertrude a wry smile. "In other words, you're okay—all things considered."

"What things?" Gertrude stared at her hands.

Before Judith could think of a suitable reply, there was a knock at the door to the toolshed. "Mrs. G!" called the husky voice. "Mrs. G-G! Are you decent?"

"Herself," Judith muttered, covering the short distance to the door.

"Decent?" Gertrude echoed. "As in 'decent' *what*?"

Vivian Flynn looked as if she'd stepped out of the *Arabian Nights*. Or, Judith thought less charitably, a bad harem movie. Billowing purple pants were topped with an equally billowing magenta blouse and a gold-brocade vest. A dozen small coins dangled from each ear, and her feet were encased with embroidered slippers that turned up at the toes. It didn't seem possible to Judith that Herself could have completed the elaborate toilette at such an early hour; it was more likely that she had never gone to bed.

"How's my favorite neighbor?" Herself gushed, all but ignoring Judith as she made her way to Gertrude's chair.

"Finer than frog hair," Gertrude replied, stiffly accepting a big wet smack on the cheek. For reasons that eluded Judith, her mother had taken a liking to the first Mrs. Flynn. Perhaps it was sheer perversity on Gertrude's part, or maybe she genuinely enjoyed Herself's brassy manner. "How come you're all duded up like a circus freak?" Gertrude demanded.

Herself's laugh was loud and jangling. "Oh, Mrs. G-G, aren't you the one! This is my lounging costume. I wear it when I just want to loll around and do nothing except watch TV or read." Capturing some of the flowing purple fabric in one hand, Herself sat down on the arm of Gertrude's chair. "I hear your daughter is abandoning you." She darted Judith a sly look. "I just wanted you to know that if you need anything, I'm available."

"That's swell of you," Gertrude responded with a small smile. "It isn't easy for an old lady when her daughter goes off gallivanting to Shabby Island or whatever it's called."

"Now Mother," Judith began before the significance of Herself's words dawned on her. "Hey," she said, turning to the other woman, "how did you know I was leaving town?"

Herself's heavily penciled eyebrows arched in exaggerated innocence. "How? Why, I heard it through the grapevine, that's how. Isn't that what happens in a cozy neighborhood like this?''

It could be true. Hillside Manor was located at the end of a cul-de-sac, surrounded by longtime residents—except, of course, for Herself. Arlene Rankers was particularly generous in dispensing neighborhood news. Indeed, Judith often referred to her friend's limitless source of gossip as ABS—Arlene's Broadcasting System.

On the other hand, maybe it was better not to know. "I've got to get going," Judith said, summoning up a feeble smile. "I'll call you, Mother."

"You'll call me something," Gertrude muttered, but did her best to put her arthritic arms around her daughter. "You be careful and don't stick any nickels up your nose."

Herself flipped her platinum blond mane and laughed again. "Oh, Mrs. G-G! You're such a kick! While your daughter's off making pancakes for grumpy guests, let's party!"

"I'll bring the Tums," Gertrude said.

Herself laughed again, even louder. "Tums! Did you know that's *smut* spelled backwards?" She laughed some more. Judith left.

Two hours later, Judith and Renie boarded the superferry, which would take them to Laurel Harbor on Perez Island. The second Monday of September was golden, with the sun sparkling on the rippling waters, a few wispy white clouds drifting across the deep blue sky, and the wooded coastline rising up on the mainland to meet the mountains. As the ferry glided out of its slip and picked up speed in the open water, the cousins sat on the deck, feeling the brisk breeze ruffle their hair, sniffing the salt air, listening to the gulls and the waves and the thrum of the vessel's big engines.

"I haven't been to the Santa Lucias for years," Renie commented as a tourist family clicked pictures from the rail. "Bill and I came up with some other SOTS when one of our ex-pastors had the church on the main island, but that was at least ten years ago."

"We had a librarians' retreat at the big resort in 1971," Judith said, shielding her eyes from the sun. "Believe it or not, that's the only time I was ever on any of the islands. Isn't it weird how you can have such a tourist magnet in your own backyard and yet never visit it? Talk about taking things for granted!"

Renie nodded. "And putting things off. Bill and I are always saying how we should spend a few days in the islands—'they're so beautiful, they're so peaceful, they're so off the beaten track.' Except they aren't, at least not in the summer, when everybody from everywhere storms the whole archipelago. This year, I heard that it wasn't at all uncommon to have to wait overnight in your car to get on the ferry."

"It's like living a mile away from Niagara Falls and never going to visit." Judith smiled as three small children chased each other around in circles near the lifeboats. "We get spoiled in the Pacific Northwest. We may complain about all the growth, but even in the city, we're still pretty close to nature. If the weather's clear, you can hardly go anywhere without seeing two mountain ranges, a couple of lakes, and the Sound."

In silence, the cousins ruminated on their blessings. A few minutes later, they had visited the coffee shop, where they purchased doughnuts and hot chocolate. Since the ferry was now out in the open strait, where the winds blew harder and the currents ran stronger, they opted to have their snack inside. There were no empty tables; the ferry was filled to capacity, despite the lateness of the season. Upon boarding, they had noticed the dozens of bicycles, canoes, and kayaks which were being hauled onto the lower deck. Apparently their owners had all worked up an appetite. After standing in the cafeteria-style line for almost ten minutes, Judith and Renie finally found two empty spaces. They sat down next to a young, attractive self-absorbed couple, and across from a heavyset middle-aged man in a business suit who was partially hidden behind the morning paper.

"The Barber house is supposed to be pretty snazzy," Judith said as the ferry dipped from side to side in the heavy current. "Jeanne and Duane built it about ten years ago on the site of the original homestead."

"How many cabins?" Renie inquired. "Three?"

Judith nodded. "During the summer, Jeanne charges two hundred a night. Between Labor Day and Memorial Day, the rate drops to a hundred and fifty."

The young couple had wandered off, but the man across the table suddenly slapped his newspaper down on the Formica and let out a small yelp. "Are you talking about Chavez Cove?" he demanded.

Startled, Judith pushed back on the bench. "Why—yes. Do you know it?"

The man, whose graying hair was cropped close to a big skull with jutting ears and a large, irregular nose, narrowed his pale blue eyes. "You bet. I'm heading there now. But I'm paying two hundred, and it's after Labor Day. I'd better talk to the manager. She's going to hear what H. Burrell Hodge does to people who try to cheat him. And I promise, she won't like it one bit!"

Assuming that H. Burrell Hodge was in fact the man sitting on the other side of the table, and also assuming that she was about to become the manager of Chavez Cove, Judith conjured up a sheepish smile.

"I'm sure it's a misunderstanding, Mr. . . . Hodge."

"I'm sure it better be!" Hodge huffed as his face turned red with indignation. "Do you know this woman who runs the place?"

"In a way," Judith admitted. "My cousin and I are going there to . . ."

"Because if you do," Hodge said, getting to his feet, "you'd better warn her not to play games. H. Burrell Hodge doesn't like games." He picked up the newspaper and crumpled it loudly in his beefy hands. His chest puffed up and his jowls jiggled. "H. Burrell Hodge knew somebody would try to throw a spanner in the works. H. Burrell

Hodge is getting *angry*." The big man stomped off, impervious to the ferry's starboard list.

"H. Burrell Hodge is getting *loud*," Renie commented. "Are we going to have to listen to him for a whole week?"

Judith wore a worried expression. "I don't know. I'll see Jeanne's guestbook when we arrive. She said there shouldn't be any problems. But doesn't that suit look like a problem to you?"

"Huh?" Renie's round face puckered in puzzlement.

"Men in three-piece suits don't stay by themselves at bed-and-breakfasts, especially not in a rural area like Chavez Island. Think about it, coz."

"Coz is thinking," Renie replied, then tipped her head to one side. "You're right, they don't. They check into hotels with a corporate rate. Maybe he's been traveling from some other part of the country and hasn't had time to change."

Judith gave a shake of her head. "H. Burrell Hodge needs to change his attitude. I hope the rest of the guests aren't so difficult."

Renie withheld comment.

There was nothing difficult about Rafe St. Jacques, at least not in the sense that Judith had attached to H. Burrell Hodge. Rafe was more aptly described as tall, dark, handsome, and—if Judith could recall from the romance novels she occasionally read—conveyed a touch of mockery. Or irony, or self-deprecating humor, or cynicism. He was probably in his late thirties, though his age could have gone ten years either way. Muscles rippled under his white linen shirt, his black hair fell carelessly across a tanned forehead, and his azure eyes matched the richness of the sea.

Rafe had just helped Judith and Renie into the thirty-foot inboard cruiser when H. Burrell Hodge came huffing down the pier. "Is this the boat to Chavez Island?" he shouted, holding on to his dark gray hat with the hand that wasn't clutching a large suitcase.

"We're waiting for you," Rafe replied. Though courteous, his manner indicated he was very much in control of the situation, the passengers, the cruiser—and himself. "Come aboard. You must be Mr. Hodge."

"So I am, H. Burrell Hodge to be exact." The identification was again accompanied by the expanding of chest and the jiggling of jowls. Spying the cousins, Hodge frowned under his hat brim. "You're right—you're going to Chavez, too."

"I'll be darned," murmured Renie. "So we are." She shot Judith a caustic glance, indicating her disapproval of H. Burrell Hodge.

Rafe was consulting a small leather notebook. "That's it," he said, more to himself than to his passengers. "Three passengers this trip." He flipped the notebook shut and strode off to take the helm.

H. Burrell Hodge had planted himself on the cushioned seat opposite the cousins. He perched his fingers on his knees and sighed deeply. "Pretty area," he remarked. "Too bad I can't enjoy it."

Judging from Renie's sour expression, Judith figured there would be no conversational help from her cousin. Judith didn't blame Renie, but reminded herself that H. Burrell Hodge was an arriving guest, and she was his incoming hostess.

"I beg your pardon?" Judith said politely. "Do you mean this is a working holiday?"

The pale blue eyes regarded Judith as if she were a nincompoop. "Now what would you think, Mrs. . . . What was it? Barber?"

"No, no," Judith began, but was interrupted by a shout from Rafe St. Jacques.

"Killer whale! Port side!"

The cousins leaned forward; Hodge turned, though his attitude suggested indifference. At first, there was nothing to see. Then the killer whale dived out of the water, a graceful flash of black and white. Judith gasped, and Renie grinned. H. Burrell Hodge's hat flew off. With a curse, he snatched the hat from where it had landed next to Judith's feet.

"Whales! What next, crocodiles? This better be a comfortable setup. H. Burrell Hodge hates to be put out."

Judith and Renie exchanged covert glances. A silence fell over the little party as the cruiser cut through the water. Before the Ice Age, the Santa Lucias had been a mountain range, but the great glaciers had crept down to erode the peaks and create valleys which eventually had let in the sea. Large deposits of gravel had been left in the glaciers' wake along with a kindlier till that allowed forests, shrubs, and meadowlands to flourish. In the distance, the cousins could see the other islands, some large and inhabited, others the size of a big rock. But all were covered in greenery, from tall evergreens to soft moss. Trying to ignore H. Burrell Hodge, Judith sat back to enjoy the scenery.

Almost five minutes passed before Rafe St. Jacques cut the engine and began to steer the boat through the rocky shoals that led to Chavez Island. He maneuvered skillfully, at one point coming almost within touching distance of the granite boulders which formed the island's banks. Masses of kelp floated on the tide, indicating the presence of dangerous reefs. The harbor was no more than a small inlet, with a dock that could moor a maximum of three pleasurecraft at one time. Judith saw the wooden steps that led up the steep hill from the water, and beyond, in the shelter of a half dozen cedar trees, she could make out huge glass windows and a stone chimney.

"Is that the house?" Judith asked Rafe, who was adroitly tying the cruiser to the dock.

"That's it," he replied, keeping his eyes on his work. "Watch your step, *Fannie* bobs quite a bit."

Judith frowned. "*Fannie*?"

"The cruiser," Rafe replied, finishing his task and reaching out to give Judith a hand. She couldn't help but admire the muscles in his forearms as he helped her onto the dock.

"Oh." Judith smiled, but Rafe had already turned his back to assist Renie.

Renie, however, disdained Rafe's help. "I'm fine. My father was a seagoing man. I know my way around ships and such just fine. The only problem is, I can't swim." With a less than graceful lunge, Renie landed next to Judith on the dock.

They were halfway up the long wooden stairs when Judith heard someone call her name. Craning her neck, she saw a woman standing on the top step. "Jeanne?" Judith shouted back. "Hi!"

Jeanne Clayton Barber greeted Judith effusively. "This is so wonderful! I can't believe I'm actually getting away for a while!" She kissed Judith soundly on both cheeks, then made as if to enfold Renie in a bear hug. "You must be the cousin! Reneé, is it?"

"Renie, as in weenie," Renie answered, wincing as Jeanne embraced her. "It's short for Serena, not for Reneé. Ooof!" Catching her breath, Renie stumbled away from Jeanne.

Rafe, who was carrying the visitors' luggage, announced he would put the suitcases on the deck. Jeanne, still beaming at the cousins, nodded. Her face fell when she saw H. Burrell Hodge.

"Oh! Mr. Hodge? I didn't realize you were taking an early ferry!" Jeanne put out a reluctant hand. "How very nice!" Her tone belied the words. Jeanne's small mouth pursed, her gray eyes displayed alarm, and her angular frame seemed to tense.

The newcomer's stance was belligerent as he confronted his official hostess. "What's this about charging me the summer rate? Labor Day was one week ago. I demand a refund of the seasonal charge!"

Jeanne's flustered charm evaporated. "You must have misunderstood. This is still officially summer. The rate doesn't change until next week."

Seeing that H. Burrell Hodge looked as if he were on the verge of an explosion, Judith intervened with a forced smile. "I made the same error, Mr. Hodge. I thought Labor Day was the cutoff, too. But I—we—were wrong."

"Chicanery!" Hodge declared. "I was deliberately duped! H. Burrell Hodge doesn't forget ill treatment!" Despite his claim, he appeared to be quitting the field, at least temporarily. Hodge brushed past his hostess. "Which cabin have I got? I'm half-starved. What time is lunch served?" The question sailed over his shoulder as he stalked up the narrow footpath.

Jeanne avoided Judith's curious gaze. "Oh, my!" she laughed. "Mr. Hodge seems rather particular, doesn't he? Well, Judith, I'm sure you're used to people like that. Good luck; I hope you enjoy your stay."

"Whoa!" Judith cried, grabbing Jeanne's arm. "You're not leaving right away, are you?"

Jeanne's smile was forced. "Well, actually, I am. I've got to catch the next ferry out of Laurel Harbor if I'm to make my flight to Palm Desert. Rafe is getting my things now. I hope." Her thin face looked strained.

Judith's usual good nature was beginning to erode. "But Jeanne, we haven't even seen the house yet. There must be a lot of things you need to show us. What about supplies? Who are the other guests? And what the heck are we supposed to do with H. Burrell Hodge?"

Rafe St. Jacques came gliding down the footpath, carrying two suitcases and a garment bag as if they were tissue paper. "Ready, Mrs. B.?" he asked, his manner just short of being deferential.

Jeanne Barber gave Rafe a grateful smile. "I think I have everything. Yes, we'd better dash." She leaned toward Judith and gave her another smacking kiss. "You're an angel. I'll see you when I get back a week from Wednesday."

"Wednesday!" Judith cried. "I thought we were here only until Sunday! Wait, Jeanne!" Judith started after the other woman, but Rafe blocked her path.

"Sorry, ma'am." His smile seemed to convey a warning. "That ferry isn't going to sit there until we pull in."

Judith started down the stairs behind Rafe. "Jeanne! Please! Give me ten minutes! I feel at a complete loss! *Jeanne!*"

But Jeanne had reached the dock and didn't look back. Neither did Rafe St. Jacques. Disconsolately, Judith watched the two figures get into the cruiser. "Damn and double damn!" she exclaimed, her mouth settling into an angry line. "This is crazy. I can't stay until a week from Wednesday. How could Jeanne run out on us like this?"

"It looked pretty easy to me," Renie remarked. "For now, I'm with H. Burrell Hodge. When's lunch?"

Judith sighed. Renie could eat under any circumstances, no matter how dire. Hearing the inboard motor kick in from below, Judith resigned herself to being stuck on Chavez Island. There were certainly worse places to be marooned.

Maybe.

THREE

JUDITH STARTED UP the path. As the cousins drew closer, they were rewarded with a full view of the impressive dwelling built by Jeanne and Duane Barber. The house seemed to grow out of the rocks, though the ground was so uneven that most of the expansive three-level deck was on stilts. There appeared to be no easy access from the front to the rear, except by going through the house itself. At least a third of the facade was glass, huge, tall windows that looked out to the water through the ever-green trees. The exterior was finished in rough-hewn fir and spruce, which had acquired a mellow weathered look over the years. Judith picked up her luggage from the suitcases Rafe had left on the deck and pushed the screen door open.

"Nice," she admitted, though still feeling put upon. "Jeanne may not have good sense, but she's got good taste."

The kitchen was large, with a high, open-beam ceiling, bright blue tile on walls and counters, a Franklin stove next to the gas range, and a goose motif that seemed to run amok. Judith had a sudden qualm about Jeanne's good taste.

But the rest of the house was both stunning and comfortable. The stone fireplace in the living room also served the master bedroom. Near the back door was a small stone grotto with a waterfall that cascaded through native plants. The loft that overlooked the living room also shared the view through the floor-to-ceiling windows. There were two baths, one with a Jacuzzi, a sunroom off the kitchen, and a compact exercise area.

"Plush," Renie remarked, after she had taken her suitcase up to the loft. "What's in the fridge?"

The refrigerator was well stocked, as were the cupboards and counters. Jeanne had left three pages of notes. Her first caution dealt with the severe water shortage in the Santa Lucias. While Chavez hadn't been overbuilt like some of the larger islands, there was only one well and two catch basins. There was, however, no shortage of food: Each guest was entitled to a complimentary bottle of champagne, a fruit-and-cheese basket, and a hand-delivered breakfast of muffins, juice, coffee, tea, and more fruit.

"Visitors eat in their cabins," Judith noted. "Here are her muffin recipes." She tapped the three-by-five index cards that sat on the counter next to the refrigerator. "Plain, poppyseed, and blueberry. I suppose that's easier than putting on the full-course breakfasts I make at Hillside Manor. The cabins have kitchenettes and guests are asked to bring their own food, especially for dinner."

"What about *lunch*?" Renie persisted.

Judith glanced up at the round clock which depicted yet another goose. The wings indicated the hours and minutes. "Hold on," Judith said. "I haven't finished these instructions. Besides, it isn't noon yet. I want to have a look at those cabins before the other guests arrive. We also have to deliver Mr. Hodge's suitcase. Rafe left it on the deck." Judith removed a heavy key ring from a peg by the front door, then picked up H. Burrell Hodge's brown leather suitcase. Its weight surprised her.

"He must have a brick in here," Judith grumbled.

"It's probably his complaint log. Maybe it's a real log." Renie grabbed an apple from the fruit bowl and followed Judith. A single step led from the kitchen to the living room and rear hallway. Outside the back door was a long flight of covered wooden stairs. Alcoves jutted off the small porch, enclosing a barbecue on one side and a wicker love seat on the other. The narrow, steep steps were entwined with thick tangles of ivy which were decorated with tiny gold fairy lights that, according to Jeanne's note, were on a timer that turned on at dusk.

The cousins descended cautiously, hanging on to the wooden rail. At the bottom of the stairs, an open area apparently served as parking place and turnaround. On the right, nestled among the berry vines and vine maples, stood a garage and what looked like a storage shed. A rough dirt road led out of the open space, and on the left was a path that wound through the woods. Between the path and the staircase, hybrid rhododendrons had grown up to a height of at least seven feet. The big, glossy-leafed shrubs almost overshadowed the more modest plantings of azaleas, Oregon grape, foxglove, and Saint-John's-wort.

"Let's try the path," Judith suggested.

It was well-worn and came out into another, larger clearing carpeted in long grasses and lined with madrona trees. Three separate flagstone walks led to the trio of identical cabins that sat on the edge of a bluff overlooking the water. The buildings were small, with cedar shake roofs and stout stone chimneys. The exterior shingles had been stained a dark brown; the trim on the casement windows was a vivid red. A barbecue pit, a collection of sports equipment, and a covered woodpile sat next to a carefully cultivated rock garden. As the cousins went around to the front, they noted that each had a porch that ran the width of the cabin. Pristine white lawn chairs sat under the overhang, and flower boxes offered a cheerful welcome.

H. Burrell Hodge offered no welcome at all. He was sitting in one of the lawn chairs on the front porch of the middle cabin. "It's about time," he growled. "Be careful with my luggage. It's top-of-the-line. H. Burrell Hodge doesn't travel second-class. You'd better have my key. And lunch."

Hiding her impatience, Judith set the suitcase by the door. While Hodge watched her with a critical eye, she sorted through the keys on the heavy ring. Small pieces of tape were marked Front Door, Back Door, Garage, Storage, and Supplies. A duplicate set read Fawn, Doe, and Buck. Judith assumed that the last three names were those given to the cabins. Sure enough, above the door a slab of polished wood bore the name *Buck.*

Somewhat clumsily, Judith finally freed one of the two keys to the cabin called Buck. "Here, Mr. Hodge. I'm sorry about the delay, but we were expecting Mrs. Barber to . . ."

"I'm expecting Mrs. Barber, too. Where the hell is she?" Hodge demanded, heaving himself out of the lawn chair. "She's supposed to take me to meet the Danfields."

Judith gave Hodge a puzzled look. "The Danfields?"

Hodge had loosened his tie and now struggled to take off his suit jacket. "Bates Danfield and his wife practically own this island. If you don't know the Danfields, you don't know much. Now where's that Barber woman?"

Judith gritted her teeth. Explaining anything to H. Burrell Hodge seemed hopeless. The man wouldn't shut up long enough to listen. "See here, Mr. Hodge," Judith began, resurrecting the tone she had used on unruly library patrons by day and raucous barflies by night, "Mrs. Barber has gone away for the week. I'm Mrs. Flynn, and I'm taking over for her. I don't know anything about the Danfields or Chavez Island. As you're aware, I arrived here at the same time you did, less than an hour ago. Now explain what you'd like me to do, and I'll try to accommodate you."

Proud of finally having her say, Judith took a deep breath and waited for Hodge to respond. Instead, he picked up his suitcase, turned to the front door, inserted the key, and went inside. The door and the screen both slammed behind him.

"Oh, good grief!" Judith exclaimed. "The man's impossible! I hope the other guests aren't such jerks!"

"You've had worse," Renie pointed out, as Judith paused to inspect the sports equipment which sat in an orderly manner next to the woodpile. Badminton and horseshoe paraphernalia flanked a croquet set which was organized by color. It occurred to Judith that although Jeanne Barber might seem muddleheaded in some ways, she appeared to take her hostelry duties seriously.

"Well?" Renie demanded. "What about the guy in the loincloth who wouldn't use the stairs and went in and out of the second-story window on a rope? Or the woman who dressed up like Cleopatra and fell on her asp? Not to mention a couple of your more unfortunate visitors who checked out permanently."

Judith didn't want to be reminded of past pests, particularly those who had met their demise during or shortly after coming to Hillside Manor. Coping with all facets of human behavior was an occupational hazard. As far as Judith was concerned, travelers didn't leave their troubles behind them.

"Skip it," Judith said, tight-lipped.

"So who are the guests moving into the other cabins?" Renie asked in a relatively mild tone.

Judith thought back to the guestbook at which she'd only glanced. "A woman with an Irish name. A couple with a Hispanic name. Or Italian, maybe. I suppose Rafe is bringing them back from Laurel Harbor. Now what do I do about feeding H. Burrell Hodge?"

"What about feeding Renie? It looked to me as if there was plenty of food in that kitchen. Let's eat." Renie started for the flagstone walk.

They got as far as the parking area of the main house when an older man appeared at the head of the dirt road. He was short, wore wire-rimmed glasses, was inclined to stoutness, and had wisps of white hair peeking out from under a Greek fisherman's cap.

"Aha!" he called in a jovial voice. "You must be the caretakers. I'm Doc Wicker, proprietor of the Wicker Basket, provisioner for Chavez Island, postmaster, and first-aid attendant. How's it going?"

Doc Wicker's friendly manner was in such contrast to H. Burrell Hodge, that Judith broke into a big smile and vigorously shook the newcomer's hand. "We're off to a rocky start, I'm afraid," Judith confessed after introducing herself and Renie. "We didn't expect Jeanne Barber to take off so quickly."

Under the brim of his cap, Doc raised his fluffy eyebrows. "In a hurry, was she? Well, now." His fine gray eyes shifted away from Judith. Up close, Doc looked younger than Judith had first thought, closer to sixty than to seventy. "Left you stranded, eh?" he remarked after a pause. "Is there anything I can do to help?"

"We'll get along," Judith replied, "but one of our guests expected Mrs. Barber to introduce him to somebody named Danfield. Do you know who that is?"

Taking a Meerschaum pipe out of the pocket of his loosely knit cardigan sweater, Doc chuckled. "Mrs. Flynn, do you realize there aren't but seven people living year-round on this island? And that counts Jeanne Barber. There's Bates and Esther Danfield, Rafe St. Jacques, and the Carrs—Rowena and her daughter, Priscilla. But then you must know about Cilla."

Judith's confusion had returned. "Cilla? No, Jeanne didn't mention her by name."

Doc shook his head. "Looks like Jeanne left you in the lurch. Cilla Carr helps out at the cabins. Part maid, part carpenter, part just about anything you can name that needs doing. Cilla and her mother haven't been here long, but their coming was timely. I don't know what Jeanne would have done without Cilla after poor old Duane died. You give Cilla a call. Her number's Five."

"Five?" Judith was still confused.

Digging his pipe out with a small tool, Doc nodded. "The Barber house is 1, the Danfields are 2, I'm 3 and 4, depending on whether you ring me in the store or upstairs in my living quarters. Rafe's 6. Oh, we're connected to the outside world like regular phone customers, but here on Chavez we've got this setup kind of like a tie-line. The cabins don't have phones." Doc undid the strings of a small leather tobacco pouch. "You want to stroll over and check out the Wicker Basket?"

Despite Renie's show of reluctance, Judith agreed to go along with Doc. "Where do these other people live?" she inquired, as they headed down the dirt road.

"The Carrs are about a quarter of a mile from here on the southwest side of the island," Doc answered, now attempting to light his pipe even as he walked at a brisk pace. "They moved to Chavez last spring, bought their place from Tom and Peggy Lowman, who'd come here to get away from the city. *Too* far away, as it turned out, once their kids got to be school age. They found themselves a house on Perez Island, where there're schools and other youngsters. Isolation isn't for everybody."

"You must like it, though," Judith said, as the road curved to allow a glimpse of the strait between the trees.

"Mmmm." Doc sucked on his pipe, but didn't directly address the comment. "Rowena Carr likes it real well. She's practically a recluse. Couldn't be much different from her daughter. Cilla's wonderful, an outgoing girl, packed with fun and energy. The Danfields have a big fancy place on the south side. Rafe's not far from me, just on the other side of the helicopter pad, by Hidden Cove."

"There's a helicopter pad?" Judith evinced surprise.

"It's only for emergencies," Doc replied, then gestured with his pipe at a green roof that rose above a small stand of Douglas firs. "There's the Wicker Basket. You need anything?"

Doc's store was small, but surprisingly well stocked. The shelves were crammed with canned goods, beverages, pharmaceutical items, fishing tackle, hiking gear, housewares, and even a few articles of clothing.

"Rafe delivers fresh meat and produce and dairy products just about every day," Doc explained, moving behind the wooden counter with its glass case containing candy, gum, cough drops and cigarettes. "He brings the mail, too. Depending on how many guests are staying at the cabins, sometimes he makes four or five trips a day.''

"Has he been here long?" Judith inquired.

Doc shrugged. "Three, four years. He showed up one day from out of nowhere and the next thing we knew, he was living in the abandoned boathouse in Hidden Cove. Six months later, he had the place all fixed up and snug as can be. Duane Barber and I'd been doing all the fetching and carrying 'til then, but neither of us were as young as we used to be. We were both glad to turn the task over to Rafe. You sure there's nothing you need?''

"Not that I can think of," Judith replied. "Jeanne left us in pretty good shape.''

Apparently, Renie didn't agree. Unnoticed by Judith, she had been foraging in the food section of the Wicker Basket and now appeared at the counter laden with hot dogs, buns, potato chips, soda pop, cheddar cheese, sweet pickles, carrots, bananas, and three boxes of microwave popcorn.

"This'll do for now," she said, unloading her hoard on the counter. "How much?''

"Coz . . ." Judith began.

"I'll eat it here," Renie announced, as Doc began ringing up the items on his old-fashioned cash register.

"Coz!" This time Judith spoke sharply.

Over her shoulder, Renie gave Judith a sheepish look. "Okay, okay, so I'll wait until we get back to the house. But I'm not taking any chances. It's been a while since noon, and I'm about to pass out from hunger.''

"That'll be thirty-two dollars and twenty-three cents," Doc informed Renie.

"*What*?" Renie's jaw dropped. "This stuff would come in under twenty bucks at Falstaff's!''

Doc gave Renie a self-deprecating smile. "I don't know what Falstaff's is, but you're on Chavez Island. It costs a bundle to bring merchandise to an isolated place like this. I'm afraid prices are a bit steep. Take gasoline—it's at least 20 percent more on the islands than the mainland. That's because when deliveries are made, they have to come over on a special ferry run in the middle of the night, and after they unload, the boats are completely washed down to make sure there's no spillage. The environment, you see. We've suffered enough from careless sea captains around here. I don't sell gas because nobody drives much on Chavez.''

The rationale was lost on Renie. Grumbling, she counted out the required amount and handed it to Doc. Judith decided it was time to get her cousin out of the Wicker Basket.

''Thanks so much, Doc,'' she said, moving toward the door. ''It's a comfort to know that you're close by. You may see H. Burrell Hodge. He's the one who's looking for the Danfields.''

Doc's smile evaporated. Indeed, Judith thought that he suddenly looked stricken, but the storekeeper quickly recovered his aplomb. ''Hodge, eh? Right, I'll keep my eye out for him. Good luck.''

Songbirds vied with bluejays as the cousins made their way back along the dirt road. The afternoon sun filtered through the trees, creating filmy shafts of light and dancing off a lazy creek that meandered among huckleberry, salal, and Oregon grape. The small world of Chavez Island seemed infinitely peaceful, a square mile of rustic calm.

''That was odd,'' Judith remarked, breaking the tranquil mood. ''Didn't you notice Doc's reaction when I mentioned Hodge's name?''

''I noticed I got screwed on these groceries,'' Renie retorted. ''What else do I need to know?''

Judith started to expand on her observation, saw her cousin's pouting lower lip, and thought better of it. Renie would be more reasonable once she'd eaten. Or maybe Judith was being overly sensitive. As a fascinated student of human nature, she sometimes let her imagination get the better of her.

Upon reaching the house, Judith realized that she hadn't bothered to lock the door behind her. ''I suppose it's safe up here,'' she said, resuming her perusal of Jeanne's instructions. "With so few people in such a remote place, I can't imagine there's any crime."

"Are you kidding?" Renie was unloading her groceries. "Doc Wicker just robbed me blind. Want a hot dog?"

"Why not?" Judith had her head in the refrigerator, studying the items that Jeanne had provided. "There's plenty here—for us. How about prawns and fusilli? Lamb chops and baked potatoes? Rib steak and fries? Salmon with fettuccine?"

"Sounds good," Renie replied, dropping four hot dogs into a kettle. "All of it."

Judith shot Renie a wry look. "Let's concentrate on the prawns. They're fresh, and . . ."

A single knock on the back door interrupted Judith's inventory. Before she could reply, a cheerful voice called out:

"Yoo-hoo! Hey, hey! It's me, the truly excellent house-keeper-handywoman!"

A small blond dynamo in her mid-twenties charged into the kitchen pushing a bucket filled with mops, brooms, and other cleaning utensils. "Hi! I'm Cilla Carr. Where's the dirt?" Her big smile revealed deep dimples and sparkling green eyes. "You must be Flynn. One of you, anyway." Her elfin expression grew uncertain as she saw Renie eating sweet pickles straight from the jar.

Judith put out a hand. "I'm Judith Flynn, and the pig at the counter is my cousin, Serena Jones. Don't talk to her until she's full."

Cilla Carr's laugh was as genuine as it was musical. "I didn't know there were two of you! Does it really take twice as many hostesses to replace Jeanne Barber?"

Judith made a face. "Well . . . probably not. But Renie—Serena—is just along for the ride. Moral support, as it were."

Cilla shot Judith an enigmatic look which didn't jibe with her exuberant personality. "That depends, I guess. How well do you know Jeanne Barber?"

Judith blinked at Cilla. "We went to high school together. Actually, I haven't seen her much over the years except at . . . what do you mean?''

Cilla grabbed a mop, clutching it as if it were a dance partner. ''Oh, nothing!'' She began to sway in tune to a song only she could hear. ''Dum-de-dum . . . la-la-de-da . . . deedle-um-dee . . . I didn't mean anything, really. Jeanne's great. She's just . . . strange sometimes. Moody. Shall I start with the bathrooms?''

That was fine with Judith, though the house looked quite clean already. ''What about the cabins?'' she asked, following Cilla out of the kitchen.

''I did them first thing this morning,'' Cilla replied, opening the door to the red-tiled guest bathroom under the stairs. ''All the weekend guests left on Rafe's first trip to Laurel Harbor.'' Uttering Rafe St. Jacques's name seemed to provoke Cilla's dimples.

''The other newcomers should be here soon, I imagine. How many ferries are there to Laurel Harbor every day?'' asked Judith, who was studying a duck decoy that sat on one of the shelves that housed the TV, VCR, stereo, and an eclectic variety of videos, tapes, and compact discs.

''This time of year, there are four—the one you must have come on, the twelve-thirty, the three-fifty, and a seven-fifteen. The schedule changes with the seasons, and it isn't the same from year to year. It's confusing, even for people who live in the islands. Plus, the state ferry runs don't always make the same stops. You have to ask when you board to make sure you can get where you're going. There's an independent ferry, though, sort of a water taxi, that goes between several of the medium-sized islands. But it doesn't stop here because the Chavez Cove channel's too narrow and rocky.'' Cilla bustled around the bathroom, her neat little figure a whirlwind of activity with cleanser and rags.

''So if someone wanted to leave the island,'' Judith said, making calculations in her head, ''they'd have to get off Chavez no later than six-thirty, right?''

''Right,'' Cilla agreed, briskly polishing the oval mirror

above the vanity. "Of course the ferry doesn't actually leave until seven-forty. Depending upon the number of passengers, it takes about twenty minutes to load and unload." Emerging from the bathroom, Cilla beamed at Judith, displaying those devastating dimples. "Don't tell me you're thinking of getting out of here already?"

"Oh, no," Judith laughed, a bit weakly. "I was just looking ahead. By the way," she added, as Cilla started for the master bedroom, "the guest in the Buck cabin somehow got the idea we served regular meals here. Should I tell him to buy food at Doc Wicker's or make arrangements for Rafe to get a list from Mr. Hodge and pick it up on his next trip to Laurel Harbor?"

Cilla's hand tightened on the carpet sweeper. "Mr. Hodge? What Mr. Hodge?"

Renie was bringing a hot dog and bun to Judith. "H. Burrell Hodge," Renie said. "The H stands for Horse's Hind End."

Cilla's green eyes were wary. "Is he a fisherman?"

Judith hesitated. "I don't think so. He didn't mention it, and he's dressed in a three-piece suit."

"I don't like the sound of that," Cilla declared. "He must be a businessman. I don't trust businessmen. They're all sharks." Her elfin features were set, then she appeared to relax. "Have Mr. Hodge get what he needs from Doc Wicker. Just make sure he doesn't put it on the Chavez tab. You can't trust anybody in business." Cilla descended the four steps to the sunken master bedroom.

Judith and Renie went back into the kitchen. "That's it!" eyeing Jeanne's notes on the counter. "I haven't put the guests' baskets together. Let's do that, and when we take Hodge's over to his cabin we'll tell him about Doc's store."

Hurriedly finishing lunch, Judith found the big fruit baskets in a lower cupboard. Each was lined with a bright linen cloth. Checking Jeanne's list against the provisions, she filled the baskets with oranges, apples, bananas, pears, grapes, three kinds of cheese, crackers, packets of tea and coffee, smoked salmon, beefstick, and a bottle of champagne.

"H. Burrell Hodge won't starve, even if he doesn't make it to the store," Judith declared with a satisfied smile. "Maybe this will hold him until I bring the muffins and the rest for breakfast."

"Maybe." Renie sounded dubious, no doubt in consideration of her own ravenous appetite.

Cilla was now in the loft, humming a perky tune. Judith called to tell her they were heading out to the cabins.

"Good luck," Cilla said, leaning over the rail to look down into the living room. "If you see Rafe, tell him I need a new hammer. Standard issue, solid steel. I lost my old standby. Oh—and bleach, the biggest jug they've got at Laurel Harbor. I do the laundry, you know."

Judith didn't. "Jeanne's got it made," she said under her breath as the cousins went out the back door. "Except for making muffins and filling those fruit baskets, I can't see that she does much work. I envy her. Even with a cleaning woman, I run my tail off all day long."

"What did Duane do?" Renie asked as they trod carefully down the steep back steps.

Judith wrinkled her brow. "I don't really know. In fact, I'm not sure how long the Barbers have been on Chavez Island. Ten years at least, but the only time I really had a long chat with Jeanne was at that reunion four or five years ago. We were never close, even in high school."

"Do they have kids? I thought Jeanne mentioned a daughter." Renie followed Judith down the path that led to the cabins.

"A girl named Marcia, but she's grown. Married, maybe. I saw some photographs in the master bedroom. One was a wedding picture that looked fairly recent."

"Married. Out of the house. No more college tuition." Renie's tone had grown morose. "No wonder she can fly off to a ritzy California spa. Lucky Jeanne."

"Not so lucky being a widow," Judith pointed out.

"No?" Renie snickered. "I'm not talking about Bill, of course," she added hastily.

"It wasn't luck that killed Dan," Judith said, as they approached the cabin called Buck. "It was gluttony and drinking and self-loathing." She shook her head at the memory of her first husband's self-destructiveness.

Despite the warm afternoon, Hodge's door was closed. Judith knocked twice, but got no reply. She waited, then knocked again. Still no one answered. Judith got out the extra key and unlocked the door.

The cabin was compact, but comfortable. The living room was furnished in the same cheerful, airy decor as the main house. The stone fireplace was smaller, and the kitchenette was separated by a counter. The bath and the bedroom were off a narrow hall. Judith set Hodge's basket on the counter, then decided to write a note about securing his other meals. Renie, meanwhile, wandered into the bedroom.

"He hasn't unpacked, except for a briefcase," she reported, coming back into the living room. "What an impatient jerk—it looks like he used a crowbar to open the briefcase. I suppose he couldn't find the key."

"Oh?" Judith signed her name and stuck the note between a packet of Irish breakfast tea and a box of sesame crackers. "What do you mean?"

Renie was admiring Judith's handiwork with the fruit basket. "It's a very handsome leather case, the kind that a lot of the CEOs I work with carry around. It had a couple of fresh scratches in it, as if H. Burrell Hodge couldn't be bothered looking for the key."

Judith grew thoughtful, then headed for the bedroom. "You're right," she said, examining the briefcase which bore two one-inch gouges by each of the locks. "Let's hope it was Hodge who did it."

"Oh, come on," Renie urged. "Don't look for trouble. You've got enough to worry about."

Judith ignored the remark, but it was all she could do to resist the temptation of trying to open the briefcase. "He definitely came here to work," she observed, reluctantly leaving the bedroom. "Maybe his job requires seclusion. His registration lists an address in town, but no business information. But then I don't suppose Jeanne offers a corporate rate. I don't, either."

Outside, the bright sun was glistening off the water. Judith and Renie paused to admire the view. A dozen small boats, probably pleasurecraft, could be seen about a half mile away. Farther out was a large commercial vessel, possibly a tanker. Only a narrow ribbon of beach was visible from the bluff, but the slap of the waves against the sand could be heard as the tireless, rhythmic tide edged ever closer. The air was tinged with salt and evergreens and the wild roses that grew around the cabins. A faint breeze stirred the trees behind the cabins and ruffled the long grasses.

"The Santa Lucias may be farther north," Renie said, "but they have a milder weather pattern than we do in the city. It's because of the warming current that comes through the strait. Still, my dad always warned me never to travel by sea during the vernal and autumn equinoxes. The weather can be very unpredictable then, even dangerous, especially on the water."

"It doesn't seem dangerous now," Judith said. "It's lovely. Quiet. Peaceful. Soothing. I can almost forget my car's a wreck and my mother's going batty and my husband is probably being sexually assaulted by his ex-wife."

Renie said nothing. Judith understood that the silence didn't imply complaisance, but sympathy. The cousins were still taking in their agreeable surroundings when they heard voices behind them.

Rafe St. Jacques was leading three people down the path to the cabins. A woman, who was almost as tall as Rafe, was talking in overloud clipped tones. The young couple who trailed behind were holding hands and grinning as if they knew a delicious secret.

"Mrs. Flynn," Rafe called in his deep, mellifluous baritone, "I've brought Ms. Hennessy and the Estacadas."

"That's *Miss* Hennessy," said the tall woman with the

short gray hair, and then uttered a hearty laugh. "All this P.C. business! Not conducive to accuracy! *Miss* June Hennessy, Ed.D., high-school history teacher, and headmistress of Laurel Glen Academy. Howdjdo, *Mrs.* Flynn." Her shrewd gray eyes swerved in Renie's direction. "And you?"

"Just plain Jones," Renie replied. "My family was too poor to give me a title."

Miss June Hennessy blinked twice at Renie, but Judith quickly intervened, lest her cousin go off on one of her whimsical tangents. "You must be the Estacadas, from Stockton," Judith said warmly. "You're in Fawn."

"We're in love," the female half of the Estacadas said in a small, slightly dismayed voice. "We're on our honeymoon."

Judith winced at the misunderstanding, but kept smiling. "I mean, the name of your cabin is Fawn. Miss Hennessy is in Doe."

"The cabins look very nice," the bride said, her large brown eyes never leaving her husband's face. "Don't they, Rob?"

"Real nice," Rob replied, squeezing his wife's tiny waist. He was a dark-haired young man of average size, with pleasant if undistinguished features, and a stolid demeanor. "Is there any place we can rent a canoe?"

Judith didn't know, and felt chagrined at her ignorance. She suggested they ask Doc Wicker. Miss Hennessy, however, was better informed than her hostess.

"There's a canoe and a kayak," she said. "At least there was when I was here last year. He'll know." With a long, rangy arm, she pointed to Rafe, who had been delivering the guests' luggage to their cabins.

"What fun!" squealed the bride, clapping her dainty hands. "We can paddle all around the islands."

In his graceful, catlike manner, Rafe had returned to the little group. "Yes, you can—but you have to be very careful. Unless you've had ocean travel experience, I'd avoid the open water. No matter where you go, check the weather conditions first. You'll have to watch for tidal currents and tide rips. Not to mention changes in the wind. I've got some nautical charts which will help.''

''Wow!'' exclaimed the bride, her heart-shaped face registering dismay. ''Maybe we should just stick to hiking.''

Rob gave her another squeeze. ''Don't worry, Stacie. I did some canoeing when I was a camp counselor at Shasta Lake.''

Rafe's bronzed forehead furrowed. ''I'm afraid that's not the same thing,'' he said in his easy manner. ''Lakes don't have tides. But I'll do my best to give you a short course in navigating the sheltered waters.''

Stacie bounced on her sneaker-clad feet. ''Oh, that's too nice of you!'' She turned to Judith. ''Maybe you can tell us where we can go to picnic on the other side of the island.''

Again, Judith had to reveal her ignorance. ''Well . . . ah . . . I'm not really sure . . .''

This time, Rafe intervened, though his ironic mien altered almost imperceptibly. ''There are no public lands on Chavez Island. It's all private property. If you want to picnic here, you'll have to use the barbecue setup or the beach below the bluff. But there isn't much beach except at low tide. Tomorrow around noon would be a good time to be on what beach there is because we'll have a minus tide.''

Stacie Estacada leaned against her husband, as if seeking comfort for her disappointment. ''Oh, drat-drat-drat! Does that mean we can't hike?''

''As long as you stay on the trails and keep off the posted areas,'' Rafe replied, giving Stacie a sample of his engaging smile. ''The same goes for the road—there's only one, and it doesn't go all the way around the island. But there's plenty to see, including a bird sanctuary at Eagle Lake.''

Stacie's roller-coaster emotions were on the rise again. ''A bird sanctuary! How dear! Come on, Rob—let's unpack.'' Dragging her husband by the hand, she all but ran toward the cabin marked Fawn.

Miss Hennessy's shrewd eyes followed the couple as

they hurried down the flagstone walk. "Honeymooners," she murmured. "Very sweet. Let's hope they keep to themselves."

"Honeymooners usually do," Judith said, still smarting from her latest inadequacies as a hostess. "Would you like to have us show you around the cabin?"

Miss Hennessy lifted one unplucked eyebrow. "Show me *what*? I've been here before, remember? Laurel Glen Academy doesn't open until October first. I always spend a few days at Chavez Cove before school starts. In the spring, we hold our annual faculty retreats here as well."

"How nice," Judith said, and meant it. "What kind of a school is Laurel Glen?"

"Private high school." June Hennessy bristled with pride. "I taught in the public schools for years, standards kept slipping. Particularly discouraging to work with underprivileged students. So much extra attention needed, which wasn't always possible. I had a dream—a private school catering to their special needs, and at the same time, remove them from insidious city influences." Miss Hennessy's face had taken on a glow, and her eyes were very bright. "An aunt of mine died. She left me some property near Laurel Harbor, and a generous monetary sum. I built the school, and I'm able to subsidize tuition costs. Of course I can only accept sixty students each year. But if we can change the lives of those sixty, we've changed the world."

"That's very admirable," Judith said, appreciating the fervor in June Hennessy's tone. "It's a boarding school, I gather."

Miss Hennessy nodded vigorously. "Yes, indeed. An academy, actually. The students are allowed to go home only at Thanksgiving, Easter, and Christmas. And summer break, of course." Her expression changed dramatically. "I hate summers," she lamented. "The pupils become exposed to so many ugly situations, even within their own families. I'd love to extend the school to a year-round schedule. The students could use the extra classroom time.

By high school, they've got so much catching up to do. It's ridiculous for anyone to think we aren't making an enormous difference. Mrs. Barber has always been a staunch supporter. Where is she, might I ask?''

"She's gone," Judith admitted. "Mr. Barber passed away a few weeks ago. Mrs. Barber needed to . . ."

"Yes, I heard about Mr. Barber. We hear a great deal back and forth between the islands." Miss Hennessy now wore a sour expression, which made her plain face downright homely. She turned away from Judith and inclined her head at Rafe. "Thank you, Mr. St. Jacques. As ever, I appreciate your courtesy. Good day." With a long-legged step, June Hennessy headed toward Doe.

Between the warm afternoon sun and her own shortcomings, Judith felt a headache coming on. But she also offered her thanks to Rafe. "I'm afraid I'm kind of a washout as Jeanne Barber's stand-in," she said apologetically.

Rafe's engaging smile returned. "It's not an easy job, taking over for someone else." The smile twisted in irony. "I've got an idea that the part you're going to enjoy most is leaving. September seems to be a hard month around here. See you later, Mrs. Flynn, Mrs. Jones."

Rafe St. Jacques's catlike step took him out of earshot before the cousins could say a word.

FOUR

JUDITH FELT THAT the least she could do was explore the island. "If I know what this place looks like, I won't feel like such a dope," she told Renie, as the cousins headed down the dirt road. "Maybe Doc can give us a map."

But Doc wasn't in. A "Closed" sign was on the door, with a little cardboard clock that indicated he'd be back at three. There was, however, a map of Chavez Island nailed to a freestanding bulletin board by the side of the store. Judith chewed her lower lip and tried to figure out which way they should go next.

"If I understand it right, Rafe's place and the helicopter pad are that way," she said, gesturing to her right. "The hiking trails go off from somewhere in back of the cabins. Look," she said, pointing to the map. "The main trail branches off at Eagle Lake. One spur goes over to the north side of the island and the other to the east, by Salmon Gap where there's another cove and some beach. What do you think?"

"I think," Renie said, lifting one sandal-shod foot, "that we should avoid the trails for now and stick to the road."

"Why don't you wear real shoes?" Judith groused.

"Your Keds aren't exactly made for rugged terrain,"

Renie pointed out. "Besides, don't you want to meet the neighbors?"

"True," Judith agreed. "The map shows two houses, one marked Carr and the other, Danfield. Cilla and her mother's place looks as if it's just up around the bend."

In less than a hundred yards, the cousins came upon a modest two-story white clapboard house flanked by a profusion of gold, red, orange, and lavender dahlias. The house looked as if it had been freshly painted, and the gray-blue composition shingles on the roof also appeared new. The widow's walk was old, however, though its iron rails had been painted white to match the house.

"Shall we see if Cilla's home?" Judith didn't wait for an answer but unlatched the gate in the white picket fence and started up the walk. She stopped abruptly just before reaching the four steps which led to the small porch. "Blast! I forgot to give Rafe the message about what Cilla needs from Laurel Harbor. Gosh, coz, I feel as daffy as my mother!"

"You don't look that daffy," Renie said in mock sympathy. "Yet."

Judith turned and gave Renie a small shove. "Let's get out of here. I don't want to admit I goofed again."

The cousins were going through the gate when a thin voice floated somewhere behind them and over their heads. They turned and looked up. A figure stood at an open upstairs windows, partially concealed by the gauzy curtains that ruffled in the breeze.

"You're not wanted here," the voice said, sounding ethereal and menacing on the afternoon air. "Go away."

"We're doing it," Renie called back. "Bye." She scooted ahead of Judith and turned into the dirt road.

"Mrs. Carr?" Judith shouted, forcing a smile. "I'm Mrs. Flynn."

"That's not my fault." Mrs. Carr slammed the window shut. Part of the curtain got caught and fluttered above the sill. It seemed to be waving farewell to the cousins.

"Cilla's mother isn't a bit like her daughter," Judith said

in annoyance. ''Doc was right when he said Mrs. Carr was sort of a recluse. She's also very rude.''

The road wound among the western red cedars, Douglas firs, maples, and cottonwoods. An occasional madrona, with its red bark and glossy leaves, leaned toward the sea. Just at the point when Renie was beginning to complain that her feet hurt, the cousins glimpsed a black-tail deer. The animal stared at the intruders, then leaped into a thicket and out of sight. The cousins waited quietly, hoping that they might sight another animal. They knew from their experiences at the family cabin that deer often traveled together.

But the only wildlife in evidence was the sound of birds in the branches overhead.

''The animals don't like us either,'' Judith groused. ''Whatever I told Jeanne I'd charge her wasn't enough.''

''Did you get it up front?'' Renie asked.

''No,'' Judith admitted. ''There wasn't time. I mean, I didn't tell her I was coming until Tuesday night and then we didn't talk again until Thursday and at that point I knew she couldn't get a check to me before I got here and when I did, she left.''

Renie sighed. ''Sap. I told you to get the money first. She'll diddle you, just wait and see.''

Judith was trying to think of a way to defend herself when she caught sight of an imposing stone edifice behind a daunting stone wall. Square, three stories, solid granite, glowering on the crest of a sloping hill that overlooked the water, the Danfield house looked more like a fortress than a home. As the cousins drew nearer, they saw at least three outbuildings made of the same native granite. They also saw a large sign printed in looming black and red letters:

NO TRESPASSING. PRIVATE PROPERTY. KEEP OUT.
SURVEILLANCE SYSTEM IN OPERATION.

Judith scowled at Renie. ''Oh, shoot!''

Someone did. The shot sailed just over Judith's head.

Both cousins dropped to the ground, uttering terrified screams.

"Don't move unless you want to meet Jesus!" The gravel-voiced command came from behind them. "State your names and your intentions. Do it now, or the next shot won't miss."

Judith found her power of speech, which seemed to have been stifled by fright. "I'm Mrs. Flynn, from Chavez Cove. We're neighbors, not trespassers. This is my cousin, Mrs. Jones." She turned her head ever so slightly, trying to make sure that Renie was all right. In the pause that followed, Judith discovered that the fall had jarred her. She was bruised, and pebbles in the road were poking into various parts of her body. Renie's brown eyes were beginning to show anger instead of fear. Judith was afraid that her not always circumspect cousin might say something that would further incite whoever had fired the gun.

"We came to call on the Danfields," Judith said doggedly. "I guess we should have phoned first." She shifted her prone form ever so slightly, trying to relieve the pressure of the rocks.

"Get up." The abrasive voice conveyed impatience. "Slow, like."

The short, squat man with the sawed-off shotgun was at least seventy, as gnarled as a tree trunk, as hard as the granite stones that surrounded the house. His eyes never seemed to blink.

"I never heard of any Flynns or Joneses around these parts," he said, lowering the shotgun a trifle. "You got proof?"

"We didn't bring our purses," Judith replied, dusting off her slacks and T-shirt. "I'm taking Jeanne Barber's place while she's away. Call Doc Wicker. He knows who we are."

The eyes still didn't blink, but a glimmer of recognition passed across the weathered face. "I heard something about that. Already doffed her widow's weeds, I'll bet. She gone off to a fat farm?"

"Something like that," Judith said in a weary voice. "Are you Mr. Danfield?"

The worn old face broke into a fearsome grin. "*Mr. Danfield*? You're one dumb broad, lady. I'm Elrod Dobler. I watch out for this place. Anybody who shows up unannounced takes a big chance of leavin' feet-first." Dobler waggled the shotgun at the cousins.

"We wanted to introduce ourselves," Judith said in exasperation. "If the Danfields aren't hospitable, then we'll leave. But I've got a guest who has an appointment with them. I feel duty-bound to make sure he's received with courtesy."

At last Dobler lowered the shotgun. "You mean that Hodge fella? He's been here already. I shoulda peppered him with this." He waved the shotgun. Then he pulled the trigger and blasted a branch out of the nearest cedar. It fell at Judith's feet.

"I guess we'll be going now," Judith said, again more nervous than annoyed.

"Hell, no," Dobler said. "I'll tell the Danfields you're here. Don't call *me* unfriendly."

"That wasn't the word that came to mind," Renie murmured, trying to wipe off some of the dirt that clung to her tank top. "I was thinking . . . 'circumspect.' " She gave Dobler a toothy grin.

Dobler regarded Renie with suspicion, but approached the entrance to the Danfield house. For the first time, Judith noticed a small wire mesh grill set next to the wall and a system of buzzers, as well as a round indentation that could have concealed a surveillance camera. With movements that looked like wizardry, Dobler unlocked the wrought-iron gates.

"The missus'll let you in. I'll wager she's been watchin'." Dobler cackled and wandered off down the road, the shotgun at his side.

Like the Barber house, the Danfield mansion stood on a bluff that overlooked the water. Judith and Renie approached the double front doors, one of which opened be-

fore they reached the single step leading to the wide
verandah.

"How nice!" exclaimed a silver-haired woman in
matching beige slacks and cashmere sweater. She exuded
good breeding, charm, and a placid air. "I considered calling over to Chavez Cove, but I thought you might be busy.
Do come in and have some ice tea. Bates will join us in
just a moment. He's in the den. I'm Esther Danfield." She
put out a graceful hand.

"Hello," Judith responded, sensing that her smile was
off-center. "I'm Judith Flynn."

"I'm Serena Jones," Renie said, still picking debris from
her clothes. "Are you armed?"

Surprise was swiftly replaced by amusement. "Goodness, no!" Esther laughed. "You must forgive Mr. Dobler.
I hope he didn't frighten you with that silly shotgun. He's
very protective. You wouldn't believe the trespassers we
get on Chavez. There are so many parks and campsites on
the other islands that visitors assume we have them here,
too. But we don't. During the tourist season, we get over-
run. It's very distressing."

Grateful for Esther Danfield's hospitality, Judith exuded
sympathy. "Oh, I'll bet it's awful! People can be so
thoughtless and selfish. They don't respect others, let alone
private property and the environment."

Esther's thin mouth turned down. "It seems to me that
many people respect the environment more than they do
human beings." As Esther Danfield voiced her opinions,
she led her guests through the entry hall. Off to the right,
Judith caught glimpses of both the living and dining rooms.
The decor was a homogeneous mix of contemporary and
antique furnishing, artistically arranged to give the fleeting
impression of a showcase.

Esther turned the latch on an arched door that led outside.
"Let's sit in the garden. Fall's coming, and we won't have
many fine days like this to enjoy before the cold and damp
set in."

The Danfield "garden" was a far cry from Hillside

Manor's backyard. Judith cherished her prosaic flower beds, the aging fruit trees, the small patio, and the statue of St. Francis. But she felt a pang of envy as she gazed upon the enclosed area with its stone floor, vine-covered walls, sleek wrought-iron furniture, flower-filled urns, and a marble lion's head that gently spilled water into a small pool. Two separate planting sections, one for flowers and one for herbs, were separated by a walkway with stone benches at each end. Privacy was ensured not only by the stone wall, but the big horse chestnut trees which had been planted around the grounds. Beyond the garden area stood one of the smaller stone outbuildings. It looked like a guest-house, but it crossed Judith's mind that it might be Elrod Dobler's residence. The ornery old codger had to live somewhere, after all.

"This is beautiful!" Judith exclaimed. "How I'd love to do something like this in my backyard!"

"You could sink your mother in cement and have her hold a hose," Renie murmured. "Then you could turn the toolshed into a giant planter."

Esther's blue eyes widened. "I beg your pardon . . . ?"

"Ah . . ." Judith struggled to explain. "Serena said my mother's sink has a dent that makes her hold her nose. We use the toolshed for a giant panther. Sort of." A vision of Sweetums on the prowl crossed Judith's mind. The cat bore little resemblance to any of its feline fellows, let alone a graceful panther. Often, Sweetums seemed to belong to a species of his own.

Esther appeared more bewildered than enlightened, but remembered her duties as hostess and asked the cousins to sit at the glass-topped wrought-iron table. A big jar of ice tea sat directly in the sun. Next to an urn filled with ivy geraniums was a tray containing linen napkins and tall frosted glasses.

"I have no sugar out here," Esther apologized, glancing at the stone wall behind the urn. Another grill was set in the stonework, though Judith couldn't see any sign of a camera's spying eye. "Do you mind, or shall I have Bates fetch some?"

Neither Judith nor Renie cared much for ice tea, with or without sugar. Having assured their hostess they required nothing extra, Judith watched Esther fill three of the frosted glasses with self-assured, graceful movements. The women had just settled back in their chairs when a tall, lean man in his fifties strolled into the walled garden. He was dressed in a tan safari suit with an ivory scarf at his neck. A trim gray mustache and a full head of wavy gray hair enhanced his debonair manner.

"How delightful," Bates Danfield declared after his wife had made the introductions. "We have so few friends call on us after Labor Day."

"What Bates means," Esther said with the tiniest of frowns creasing her otherwise remarkably smooth skin, "is that during summer, so many of the people we know visit on their yachts. Even though the weather usually stays pleasant through September, it's not the happiest of months in some ways."

Judith was puzzled. "You mean the change in seasons?"

Esther leaned forward, with a sidelong glance at her husband. "In a sense," she said. "Most of our friends are duty-bound to return to work after the summer lull. Except, of course, for those who are fortunate enough to be retired."

"Are you retired?" Renie inquired between brave sips of ice tea.

Esther's frown degenerated into a scowl, but Bates threw back his head and laughed richly. "You might say I've always been retired." He crossed one leg over the other knee, revealing the perfect crease in his safari slacks. "For three generations, my family has been in investments. My main job—if you can call it that—is to oversee the finances. What that actually means is letting an army of accountants and attorneys and financial advisors tell me where to sign my name. If anything, I'm a professional puppet."

He laughed again, this time in a manner that was meant to be self-deprecating.

"You've certainly found a beautiful spot to live," Judith put in after a discreet glance at Esther who had recovered her placid air. "Did you build this house?"

Bates shook his head. "My father built it seventy years ago. Esther and I moved here after we married." He paused, leaning in his wife's direction. "That was thirty-two years ago. Sometimes it seems like only yesterday, doesn't it, darling?"

Esther smiled at her husband. "There's a timelessness to Stoneyhenge," she said, then turned to Judith and Renie. "That's what this house is called. Bates's father was fascinated by Stonehenge in England. He had some marvelous theories about it, including one that it represented the solar system."

Bates reached over to pat his wife's arm. His touch was gentle, but his dark eyes had hardened. "There are many theories about the original Stonehenge. Let's not bore our guests with them, darling. I believe they'd enjoy a refill of their ice tea."

But Judith and Renie had downed all the ice tea they could stand. "We should be heading back to Chavez Cove," Judith said, getting to her feet. "Oh—I almost forgot," she added, mentally berating herself for another potential omission. "One of my guests, a Mr. Hodge, was planning to meet you. I gather from what Mr. Dobler said that he's already come by."

"A Mr. Who?" Esther asked.

"Mr. Hodge," her husband responded quickly. "He did drop by an hour or so ago. Fine fellow, very congenial. We went for a walk in the woods." His dark gaze avoided his wife's questioning look.

"Hodge?" Esther echoed. "Do I know him?"

Bates Danfield had also gotten to his feet. "I think not," he answered easily. "Hodge is another of those advisors who feels it's his job to pull my strings." Again, the rich laugh, as he regarded the cousins. "I've never seen any reason to bother my wife with the dull details involved in finances. Women are so much better at keeping house instead of worrying about how to pay for the running of it, don't you think?''

Judith thought about Dan. "Well—maybe." During her first marriage, she had worried a great deal about keeping the house, period. Indeed, they had defaulted on one mortgage and been evicted twice. Life with Joe was not only far more secure, but he had no qualms about letting Judith manage their money. "At our house, I'm in charge of expenses. My husband doesn't like to be bothered with money matters."

Bates seemed surprised. "Really? I should hate to trouble Esther with such mundane matters. Finances usually aren't a woman's strong suit."

The comment rankled Renie. "My husband and I believe in complete equality. Neither of us can add or subtract. Since we have no money, it's not a problem. We take turns standing on street corners holding up a sign that says 'Will Intellectualize for Food.' ''

The Danfields exchanged puzzled glances. Judith thought it best to redirect the conversation. "With such a big house and extensive grounds, I'm sure that keeping everything up requires a lot of time and effort. Do you have any help?''

"Elrod takes care of the garden," Bates said, opening the side door for the women. "We used to have Peggy Lowman as our regular housekeeper, but lately we've had to rely on someone coming over from Laurel Harbor. It's been rather trying. But finding good help has been a constant problem over the years. We've had every Tom, Dick and Harry—literally."

"Harry!" Esther gave a little shudder. "Do you have to remind me? He was an utter disaster!"

Judith could have sworn that an expression of alarm crossed Bates Danfield's handsome features, but it was gone in an instant, replaced by a fond smile for his wife. "Now, Esther, that was all a long time ago. Tom Lowman was very hardworking, and Dick Wicker has been invaluable.''

"You mean Doc?" Judith asked.

Bates nodded. "Doc Wicker's first name is really Richard. He hasn't actually worked for us, but having him here has been a source of comfort. It's cut both ways, of course," he added enigmatically.

"You must come for dinner while you're here," Esther put in quickly, as they walked through the entry hall. "We're expecting our children up for a few days, but I'm not certain when they'll arrive."

"Oh," Judith said, warming as ever to a sense of family, "do they live close by?"

"They're both city dwellers," Esther replied, assuming a softer expression that might have been maternal pride. "Elliott—our son—is an antiques dealer. Our daughter, Eugenia, has her own catering business."

"You know young people," Bates remarked as he opened the front door. "They like the city. Oh, they're keen on outdoor activities and all that, but those bright lights lure them away from our kind of solitude." With a gallant smile, he ushered Judith and Renie outside. "Do enjoy your stay on Chavez. It was delightful meeting you. Good-bye."

The iron gates, which apparently were electronically controlled, closed behind the cousins. "Did Bates just uninvite us to dinner?" Renie asked as they started back down the road.

"I'm not sure," Judith answered in a puzzled tone even as she kept one wary eye out for Elrod Dobler and his sawed-off shotgun. "In fact, I'm not sure about anybody on this island. Have you noticed how guarded everybody seems?"

"Guarded?" Renie considered. "I'd say edgy. At least when certain subjects come up. Often that subject is H. Burrell Hodge."

"That's true," Judith agreed. "As you said, it's not our problem. All we have to do is see to the guests."

"And feed me," Renie pointed out. "I believe you mentioned prawns."

Judith checked her watch. To her surprise, it was after four. The afternoon had flown as they made their brief rounds of the island. "I should relay Cilla's message to Rafe St. Jacques. Maybe I can call him instead of walking down to Hidden Cove."

"Good idea," said Renie. "All this walking has made me hungry."

"So would sitting or sleeping," Judith remarked dryly.

Renie gave a little shrug. The cousins continued in silence, enjoying the golden hue of the trees that were starting to turn color, the faint haze that had begun to rise from the grassy glens, and the soft dance of amber light that shimmered on the water.

The Carr house was quiet when they passed by. But around the bend, they saw Cilla riding toward them on a bicycle. She braked to a sudden stop and waved a hand. Her blond hair was wet and the oversize T-shirt appeared damp. Sand clung to her bare legs and feet.

"Hi, there! I just went for a swim at Hidden Cove. You've got to try it. Rafe won't mind. At least, it never bothers him when I swim there." A becoming flush crept under Cilla's tan. "Anyway, he's off somewhere in the kayak right now."

"It's a little late for a swim," Judith said with a smile. "Tomorrow, maybe. By the way, I forgot to tell Rafe about . . ."

Cilla laughed. "No problem. I left him a note. I've learned never to make assumptions. You can't always count on things—or people." She made a sudden, embarrassed gesture with her small hands. "It's not that I expected you'd forget *completely*—but you're new to the job, and anyway, Jeanne Barber got really absentminded after her husband died. She could hardly remember who her guests were. See you tomorrow." With another wave, Cilla resumed pedaling down the road.

At the back door to Chavez House, Judith found a note written in precise, yet bold penmanship:

Toilet plugged. Need plunger. Or tools.

                                        Miss Hennessy

"Oh, swell," Judith grumbled. "Now I'm a plumber. Where are the tools?"

"Don't fuss about it," Renie urged. "Didn't Cilla say she was a handywoman? Call her."

Judith did, dialing the single digit of 5, as Doc Wicker had instructed. A harsh female voice answered on the second ring. "Don't bother us. Nobody's here." The line went dead.

"If that's Mrs. Carr, she's worse than my mother," Judith said in annoyance. While Gertrude detested talking on the phone, she could rarely resist getting in a few insults before hanging up. But the phone rang while Judith was trying to figure out what to do next. Cilla's cheerful voice was a welcome sound in Judith's ear.

"Don't mind Mama," she said. "She's not very sociable. What's up?"

"How did you know it was me?" Judith asked.

Cilla laughed. "Rafe's out in the kayak, Doc Wicker went bird-watching, and Mama wouldn't dare hang up on the Danfields. That leaves you, right?"

"So it does," Judith said, impressed by Cilla's logic. It was a faculty she not only admired, but also tried to exercise. "I got a note from Miss Hennessy about her plumbing. About the cabin's plumbing, I should say. Could you take a look?"

"Sure," Cilla answered. "I'm just about to take a quick shower, then I'll go over there."

Relieved, Judith sought out the liquor cabinet, which was in a breakfront cupboard next to the stove. Like the rest of the house, it was well stocked. She poured a measure of Scotch for herself and bourbon for Renie. The cousins took their drinks out onto the roomy deck and sat down in a pair of matching wooden chairs.

"Dinner won't take long to fix," she said, watching a pair of cedar waxwings peck at food in the bird feeder that sat on the rail a few feet away. "There's a baguette in the freezer. I'll thaw it to serve with the pasta and salad."

"Sounds good," Renie commented. "I'll make the salad." She gave her cousin an amused look. "I'm not really going to sit on my duff and do nothing. I'd get bored."

Judith, well aware of Renie's nervous energy, had known that all along. "We can watch a movie tonight," Judith said. "I noticed quite a few good videos in the bookcase, both classics and recent releases."

Renie shook her head. "Jeanne and Duane knew how to live. They spoiled themselves, don't you think? I mean, this place has everything. I'm going to dive into the Jacuzzi this evening and wallow around like a baby seal."

"Sounds good," Judith agreed. "But don't forget the water shortage."

Renie wrinkled her pug nose. "That's true. I'd like to do a wash, too. My clothes got dirty while we were under fire at the Danfields'. I don't want to bother Cilla with our personal laundry."

Judith agreed. "She does plenty as it is. You have to admire her energy."

"She's young," Renie noted. "And all that work gets her away from her nasty mother."

"I wonder what's with Mrs. Carr," Judith mused. "I picture her as a grieving widow who moved away from the memories of her husband."

"As usual, you're probably being too kind." Renie shook her head at her cousin's endless fascination with human nature. "It's not our problem, remember?"

Judith said nothing. The cedar waxwings flew off. A pair of young raccoons approached boldly, stood up on their hind legs, realized they weren't going to be served, and disappeared under the steps of the deck's lower level. The cousins laughed; they were well acquainted with raccoons. Though they lived in the heart of the city on Heraldsgate Hill, there still remained wooded gullies and creeks and expanses of underbrush where the masked marauders thrived. Judith and Renie knew that it was unwise to feed them. The raccoons were cute, but they could turn into savage little pests.

The waves slapped onto the beach below the bluff. The tide was coming in, covering the rocky reefs that mottled the little cove. In the distance, there were more pleasure-craft and at least three larger vessels, possibly heading north to Canada. Just as Judith was about to get up to freshen their drinks, a kayak glided around the corner of the bluff.

"Is that Rafe?" Judith asked.

Renie had better distance vision. "I think so. He must be heading for Hidden Cove. According to Doc's map, it's not far from Chavez Cove, just around the part of the island that juts out over there." She gestured to their right.

The kayak passed across the channel and disappeared. Judith went back into the house. As she got more ice from the freezer dispenser, a knock sounded at the back door. It was Cilla, looking upset.

"That Miss Hennessy put something down the toilet that backed it up," Cilla complained, beads of perspiration standing out on her forehead. "She denies it, of course, but that's why it's plugged. I used my snake to clear the line, but my wrench is missing. Have you got it?"

"I don't know," Judith said, again forced to admit ignorance. "Where would it be?"

"In my tool kit," Cilla answered, looking as if she were on the verge of tears. "Except it isn't. First the hammer, now the wrench. And where are my rubber gloves?" She held her small hands in front of her. They looked too dainty to wield heavy tools. "I'm not careless! But after . . ." Cilla gave herself a good shake. She seemed to regain some of her composure. "I can't imagine anybody swiping my stuff. Maybe I'm just muddled. I could have left some of it here. Have you seen it?"

Judith shook her head. "Do you want to look in the garage or the storage shed? I've got the keys."

"No. There aren't any tools in the garage, just Duane's Jeep. And the shed is stuffed with ducks."

Judith blinked. "Ducks?"

Cilla nodded. "That's what Duane did. He carved duck decoys. Haven't you noticed them around the house?"

"I saw one on the shelf by the TV," Judith replied.

"There are more. Check the sunroom, the loft, the exercise area. Duane carved those things day and night. But he couldn't sell them." Cilla's pretty face evinced disgust.

"Why not?"

"Because," Cilla answered, wiping the perspiration off her forehead, "he always made mistakes. Look at the one in the bookcase. It's got three eyes. Excuse me, I'd better get home to start dinner." Cilla headed for the back door, her compact little figure still exuding frustration.

Renie was exuding impatience. "More booze? Who needs it? How about some dinner? I thought you were putting on the water to boil the pasta."

Judith explained about Cilla's predicament. Renie listened with mild interest. "I can imagine the plumbing problems they've got in a place like this," she allowed. "There's not much water pressure, probably because there's not much water. Let's hope we have enough to cook the fusilli."

Ten minutes later, Judith had the kettle boiling on the gas range. The trestle table that faced the deck was set with Jeanne's bright blue-and-pink pottery plates. Renie had filled a wooden bowl with romaine lettuce, tomatoes, green onions, and radishes. The baguette was heating in the oven and the prawns were sautéeing in garlic when H. Burrell Hodge appeared at the back door.

"It's six-oh-five," he announced. "H. Burrell Hodge likes to eat on time. Is dinner ready?"

"Excuse me?" Judith said, taken aback. "I left you a note. Didn't you see it?"

"I did not." Hodge seemed to be simmering with indignation. "And if I had?"

"It advised you to buy your food at the Wicker Basket," Judith responded, unable to prevent Hodge from barging into the house. "I provide breakfast. Period."

"This is the dinner period," Hodge countered, glancing at his watch. "Six-oh-six, to be exact. Where do I sit?"

Renie had come in from the deck. "How about not here? This is a private residence, not a restaurant."

"H. Burrell Hodge doesn't agree," the pompous man declared, heading straight for the trestle table that stood on the other side of the blue-tiled work counter. "What are we having?" He saw the highball glasses and recoiled. "Not alcoholic beverages! That won't do! I've already thrown that bottle of champagne into the garbage. Do you know how many lives have been ruined by strong drink?"

"Do you know how many dispositions have been ruined by strong opinions?" an incensed Renie shot back.

Hodge bristled. "Lips that touch liquor will never touch mine."

Defiantly, Renie took a big swig of bourbon. "You can count on it, Burrell. I wouldn't touch you with a ten-foot pole."

"Let's all calm down," Judith urged, as she counted the simmering prawns. There were an even dozen. Divided by three, that made four apiece. Renie wouldn't be happy to share.

"We're having dinner for two," Renie asserted. "Beat it."

Though appalled by her cousin's attitude, Judith knew she had to side with Renie. "It's a rule," she insisted. "Mrs. Barber doesn't do dinner."

"Mrs. Barber isn't here," Hodge countered. "H. Burrell Hodge is." He wedged himself between the table and the matching bench. "Ah! Do I smell garlic? H. Burrell Hodge is fond of garlic!"

"Guess what?" Renie said, placing a knee on the bench next to Hodge. "I'm not fond of rude people who try to steal my dinner. You're not eating our pasta, but you might end up wearing it. Am I being clear?''

Hodge glared at Renie. ''You're very maddening,'' he averred, picking up the silverware that had been intended for Renie. ''H. Burrell Hodge doesn't give in to silly threats from mouthy women who drink too much. Where are my prawns?''

''That does it!'' Renie was enraged. She snatched up the heavy blue-and-pink plate and cracked it over Hodge's head. The plate broke. Hodge let out a howl of pain. Clutching his head with one hand, he made a fist with the other.

''Damn your hide! I'm reporting this to the authorities! You assaulted me! I'll sue!''

Judith was staring at Hodge in horror, but the unrepentant Renie had gone to the cupboard to get another plate. ''I'll use a skillet next time,'' she snapped. ''Did you think I was kidding about the prawns? R. Grover Jones doesn't kid about *food*!''

A bump was already rising on Hodge's skull. Judith was torn. Her naturally sympathetic nature compelled her to render help.

''Let me put some ice in a plastic bag,'' she offered. ''Please sit, Mr. Hodge. I really feel bad about this, but we tried to tell you how things are run at Chavez Cove. After all, I didn't make the rules.''

Hodge's gaze was malicious. ''Don't come near me. You'll pay for this,'' he snarled. ''Both of you. My lawyers will be in touch, and so will the police.'' Still holding his head, he mounted the single step to the rear hall and went out the back door.

Renie was dishing up prawns with a vengeance. Judith, however, had lost her appetite. She leaned against the counter divider, feeling a little sick. ''Coz,'' she said in a plaintive voice, ''I honestly think you might have handled that with a little more . . . finesse.''

Renie's mouth was set in a stubborn line. ''I broke my word,'' she admitted. ''But at least I didn't touch him with a ten-foot pole. He's lucky I'm small instead of . . .''

Before she could finish speaking her piece, there was another great howl and a terrible crash. The cousins stared at each other, then raced to the back door. Far down at the bottom of the steep steps lay H. Burrell Hodge, in a motionless heap.

"Oh my God!" Judith cried. "He must have fallen!" She started down the steps, somehow mindful of hanging onto the rail.

Renie, now pale and shaken, remained in the doorway. "Shall I call 911?" she shouted after Judith.

Judith didn't answer. She was intent only on reaching Hodge's prone form. Taking a deep breath and steeling herself, Judith hurried to his side and felt for a pulse.

There wasn't any. Judith closed her eyes and groaned. H. Burrell Hodge was dead.

FIVE

THE 911 OPERATOR sounded as if she were on another continent, rather than just an island away. The telephone line crackled and squawked as Judith tried to explain what had happened and where the tragedy had occurred. In calm, if partly indistinguishable tones, the operator informed Judith that help would arrive as soon as possible. Dusk was settling in, and it might be too late to send a helicopter because there were no landing lights at the pad. But emergency personnel could come to Chavez by boat.

"Please stay calm," the operator urged before ringing off.

"Calm!" Judith held her head. "I can't believe it! How could this happen to me?" She sank onto a tall stool next to the kitchen counter.

Renie was still too stunned to speak. She wandered from the kitchen to the sunroom to the deck and back into the kitchen again. At last, she recovered her voice.

"It's not your fault, it's mine," she said, slipping onto one of the other stools. "Contrary to what you may think, I didn't try to kill H. Burrell Hodge because I wanted more prawns. In fact, I've lost my appetite. Let's call Doc. We can't just leave Hodge lying down there at the bottom of the stairs."

It took Judith a few moments to remember Doc's single-digit phone number. But when she punched 3, there was no answer. Growing frantic, she remembered that he had a second number, for his residence above the store. Judith dialed 4 and heard Doc's voice after the third ring.

Trying to follow the operator's advice and keep calm, Judith limited her account to the barest of facts: "Mr. Hodge came by expecting dinner, and when we told him we didn't serve meals at the house, he left. Apparently, he fell down those steep back stairs and killed himself. We've called 911, but it doesn't sound as if they'll get here right away. What should we do?"

"Good Lord," Doc burst out, sounding as shaken as Judith felt. "The man's dead? Are you sure? Never mind—I'll be right over." Doc hung up.

Judith told Renie that Doc was on his way. Renie gave her cousin a bleak look. "Do you really think I killed him?" she asked in a hushed voice.

"No," Judith responded without hesitation. "He fell."

"But hitting him with that plate might have made him dizzy." She glanced guiltily into the trash can, where she'd put the pieces of broken pottery. "He could have been disoriented. I might as well have killed him. Coz, I feel awful!"

Judith said nothing. Renie could be right. She had logic on her side. Judith slid off the stool and headed for the back door.

"Come on. I hate to do it, but we'd better go down to meet Doc."

In the interim between trips out the back way, the fairy lights had come on. Their golden glow danced among the ivy like so many fireflies. The charming contrast with the grisly scene at the bottom of the stairs made Judith wince. Both cousins avoided looking at Hodge's body. They cut a wide swath as they walked toward the road to wait for Doc Wicker.

Doc was huffing from exertion when he arrived less than

five minutes later. To Judith's surprise, he carried what looked like a medical bag.

"Let's have a look," he said grimly. "Turn on those floodlights by the garage."

It took Judith a few seconds to find the switch, but when she did, the open area by the stairs and the garage and storage shed was as illuminated as if it had been high noon. Doc bent over Hodge, then suddenly stiffened.

"What's this man's name?" he asked in a shaky voice.

"H. Burrell Hodge," Judith said, startled by Doc's reaction.

For a motionless moment, Doc continued to stare at Hodge. "A dead body is always a shock," he finally murmured, then composed himself and checked for vital signs. When he found none, he studied the dead man's head. With careful fingers, he pressed various parts of the skull, then leaned even closer to examine the ears.

"There's some sign of hemorrhaging behind the eardrums," Doc said, standing up and dusting off his baggy trousers. "That indicates a fracture. How'd this happen?"

Renie started to speak, but Judith interrupted. "He must have hit his head when he fell down the stairs." She shot her cousin a warning glance.

Doc gazed at the long staircase, then eyed Judith and Renie with what appeared to be suspicion. "Those steps are made of wood. I don't see how they could do this kind of damage. Maybe the bump on the head, but not the back of the skull. It looks to me as if it's been severely damaged." He fingered his chin, obviously perplexed. "I could be wrong, of course. In any case, we shouldn't move him; but a blanket might be in order."

"I'll get one," Judith volunteered. "We're sure lucky you know a lot about first aid." She caught an odd light in Doc's eyes just before she turned to hurry up the stairs. His words troubled her. So did his manner. It wasn't merely that Judith felt guilty about lying to Doc. There was something else that disturbed her. Searching the linen closet for a blanket, she reined in her imagination. The tragedy of H.

Burrell Hodge had scrambled her brain as well as his.

Returning to the bottom of the stairs, Judith noticed that Renie had wandered off by the garage, ostensibly to study the wild rhododendrons that grew at the edge of the woods. Doc had lighted his pipe, and was leaning against the banister. He had regained his poise, but signs of tension remained on his usually genial face. Judith also felt tense. Delicately, she covered Hodge's body with the blanket. Nothing showed but his shoes.

"Do you know who his next of kin are?" Doc asked.

Judith shook her head. "All I have is an address in town. Shouldn't we leave notification to the authorities?"

"Probably," Doc replied. "If the authorities ever get here."

"It's a sheriff's jurisdiction, I suppose," Judith said. "Santa Lucia County?"

Doc nodded. "We're way overextended up here. Too much growth and not enough funding. Tourism is the only real industry. Just about everybody else is either retired, independently wealthy, or some kind of artisan. Writers and painters, too. Some of the land's suitable for farming, but agriculture forms a meager 2 percent of the economic base."

"What you're saying is that law enforcement is limited," Judith remarked.

"County law enforcement, yes." Doc fiddled with his pipe, which was proving recalcitrant. "There are plenty of park rangers and such, but they don't have anything to do with the likes of us on Chavez."

"Oh dear." Judith sighed, running a frazzled hand through her silver-streaked hair. "Surely someone will show up tonight?"

"Let's hope." Doc was watching Renie, who still seemed absorbed in the local flora. "What's with her?"

"She's upset," Judith answered. "So am I. I'll have to call Jeanne at the spa and tell her what happened."

Frowning, Doc turned back to Judith. "Why? She's already had one death here in the last few weeks. Let her relax and unwind. That's why she left. There's nothing she can do about this mess from Palm Desert."

Judith didn't agree. "Hodge's heirs may file suit. Jeanne will need to contact her insurance company. Her lawyer, too. Does she have one?"

"I think so. Someone on the mainland." Doc was again observing Renie. "If I were you, I'd take your cousin inside and give her some brandy. You look like you could use a little jolt yourself. Come to think of it, I wouldn't say no, either."

Judith approached Renie, who jumped when she sensed her cousin's nearness. "I'm thinking of hanging myself," she muttered. "Do you suppose there's a rope in the storage shed?"

Assuming that her cousin wasn't serious, Judith found Renie's attitude reassuring. It wasn't like members of the Grover clan to give in to tribulation. As their grandmother used to say, it was better to laugh than to cry, and in any circumstances, a Grover should remember to, as Grandma put it, "Keep your pecker up."

Judith, Renie, and Doc went up to the house. It didn't seem right to leave H. Burrell Hodge lying there alone, but on the other hand, a vigil wasn't necessary. Nor was Hodge going anywhere. Judith got out the brandy and poured stiff shots into three snifters.

"Did you know anything about Mr. Hodge?" Judith asked Doc after the trio had seated themselves in the living room.

"Not really." Doc sat in a rocking chair which permitted him a full view through the tall front windows. His eyes seemed fixed on the pink-hued glow of the setting sun. "I don't keep track of everybody who comes to Chavez. There're just too many of them."

Renie took only a sip of brandy before getting up from the sofa. She held the snifter in both hands. "Sorry, I'm going to throw myself into the Jacuzzi. Maybe that'll un-knot some of my muscles. Let me know when the sheriff or whoever gets here."

"Don't drown in there," Judith said, only half-kidding.

At the entrance to the sunken master bedroom, Renie gave Judith a wry little smile. "Don't worry. I'm fine. You shouldn't have lied for me," Renie whispered, moving away from the door. "When the sheriff comes, I'm telling him what happened."

"No, you're not," Judith insisted, also keeping her voice down. "Yes, you hit Hodge with that plate. But he deserved it, he egged you on. He was an impossible person. And we don't know if your conking him over the head had anything to do with his fall or . . ." Judith stopped and stared at Renie. "That's it!" she gasped. "You conked him *over* the head!"

"I know," Renie said impatiently. "I just told you, I'm willing to admit . . ."

"No, no," Judith said excitedly. "I mean you hit the *top* of his head, not the *back*. All you did was raise a bump."

"So it caused him to fall down the stairs and bash his skull." Renie shook her head. "It comes to the same thing."

"Doc doesn't seem to think so." Judith's black eyes bore down on Renie's skeptical face. "Go soak yourself and think about it, coz. I'm getting some funny feelings about how H. Burrell Hodge died."

Renie didn't look as if she thought there was anything funny about H. Burrell Hodge, dead or alive. Shrugging into her bathrobe, she headed for the Jacuzzi. Judith finished dressing and returned to the living room just in time to see running lights approaching the dock down below.

"That's probably the emergency crew," Doc said, getting to his feet. "They'll come in through the front way. Let's go out on the deck."

As darkness settled in over the island, and the wind blew off the water, Judith could feel the first hint of autumn. Watching the bobbing flashlights, she shivered and wished she'd put on a jacket.

"Goodness," she said, as the newcomers were temporarily lost from view on their ascent from the dock, "how will they get Mr. Hodge out of here?"

"The same way they're coming in," Doc replied. "They've probably brought a gurney."

Three husky young men appeared first, carrying various types of crime scene and medical equipment, including a collapsible stretcher. They were followed by a tall, strapping figure wearing what looked like a regulation sheriff's hat. The quartet paused on the path, looked up at the house, and, after a barked command from the person in the hat, hustled forward.

"The lawman seems to be a take-charge type," Judith said in approval. "I'm glad it didn't take him and the medics forever to get here."

Doc's usually genial aspect had deserted him. "That's no lawman," he said in a vexed tone. "That's a *lawperson.* Deputy Lulu McLean, to be exact. She's one tough customer."

"Oh." The single syllable sounded very small.

Lulu McLean was very large. She stood well over six feet and probably weighed in at two hundred and twenty pounds. There was no fat on her, however—just well-toned muscle adhering to big, strong bones. Judith's first impression was that McLean probably ate raw tiger meat for lunch. After she'd wrestled the tiger to the ground, of course.

A clipboard dangled carelessly from McLean's left hand. "All right," she said in a resonant contralto, "where's the body?"

Doc gestured to the rear of the house. "At the bottom of the back stairs."

McLean surveyed Judith and Doc. "Wicker? Good, I know you. Who's this?" She jabbed a thumb in Judith's direction.

Doc explained that Judith was filling in for the absent Jeanne Barber. McLean looked Judith up and down with a critical eye. "Barber's the recent widow, right? How many stiffs are we going to have to haul out of this place, Doc?"

McLean didn't expect an answer, and none was forth-coming. She strode across the deck and went into the house, the three young men dutifully following her. One wore the dark blue jacket and pants of a county medic, but the other two were dressed in a uniform similar to McLean's. Doc joined the emergency crew, but Judith held back. She'd seen enough of H. Burrell Hodge's corpse. Indeed, she was still picturing his wounds in her mind when Doc and the deputy returned to the living room.

"There'll be an autopsy over at Laurel Harbor," McLean announced, setting the clipboard on the coffee table and shoving her hands into the pockets of her dark green uni-form. "It looks like he died from a blow to the head. Two blows, maybe." She turned to Judith, pinioning her with probing hazel eyes. "Well? Tell me about it."

"I didn't see anything," Judith said with a helpless ges-ture. "I was in the kitchen."

"So how do you know what happened?" McLean was pacing the width of the living room in a deliberate fashion. "Well?"

"I heard Mr. Hodge cry out. And then a sort of . . . thud. Or crash." Judith swallowed hard at the memory. "When I went to the back door, I could see Mr. Hodge lying at the bottom of the stairs. He wasn't moving. By the time I reached him, he appeared to be dead."

"And?" McLean pressed on, retrieving the clipboard from the coffee table. She made a few quick notes, though her eyes never seemed to leave Judith's face.

A faint smell reached Judith's nose. She sniffed experi-mentally, but couldn't quite identify what it was. "Ah . . . well . . . I guess that's when I called 911. And then Doc Wicker."

"What time did the accident occur?" McLean's pen was poised above the clipboard.

Judith considered. Hodge had mentioned the time, at least twice. Six-oh-five and six-oh-six. But how many minutes had elapsed during the melee with Renie? "Six-ten, six-fifteen," Judith finally answered.

McLean turned to Doc. "When did you get here?"

"Six-twenty-three," Doc replied promptly.

Judith was impressed by his accuracy. But she was diverted by the strange smell which had grown stronger. Suddenly she realized it was the baguette in the oven. With a little cry, she excused herself and rushed into the kitchen.

The bread, which had been wrapped in foil, was ruined, but at least the oven hadn't caught fire. Judith checked the stove as well, but somehow she'd managed to turn off the burners, probably just before Hodge had fallen down the stairs. A glance at the table revealed six lonely prawns sitting on each of the blue-and-pink plates. They had grown cold, and somehow struck Judith as pitiful. But everything about Chavez House now seemed pitiful. Two deaths had occurred in its precincts. Unfortunately, one of them had happened while Judith was in residence. She chucked the baguette in the trash, where it fell on top of the broken plate. Judith suddenly wished she had never come to Chavez Island.

Back in the living room, Doc was filling out a form. "Are we giving statements?" Judith asked.

McLean shook her head. She had removed her regulation hat, displaying an amazing mass of short red curls. "Not yet. Doc's filling out the death certificate."

Judith regarded Doc curiously. "But . . . don't you have to be . . ." Feeling foolish, she let the question trail away.

Doc, however, gave Judith a sheepish look. "That's right. You have to be a doctor. That's what I am, Mrs. Flynn." He chuckled, an almost bitter sound. "Why do you think they call me 'Doc'?"

Embarrassed, Judith tried to smile. "I'm sorry, I guess I thought it was a nickname, like 'Cap' or 'Professor' or something. I should have known when I saw your medical bag. Oh, dear—I feel so silly!"

"No need," Doc said, putting his fountain pen back into his pocket. "It's not something to brag about." Solemnly, he handed the form to McLean. "What else do you need from us?"

The deputy was looking out the front window. "My assistants and the medic are taking the body down to the launch. We might as well do those statements now."

Before McLean could hand them to Judith and Doc, a shuffling sound was heard, followed by a thud and a squeal. All eyes turned to the steps that led into the master bedroom. Renie was sprawled across the threshold, a cockeyed grin on her startled face.

"I fa' down," she said, rolling around on the carpet and trying to gather her bathrobe around her. "I mus' 'a tripped."

"Oh, good God!" Judith breathed.

"Who is *this?*" McLean demanded.

In her distraction over the interview with the deputy, Judith had forgotten about Renie's submersion in the Jacuzzi. Apparently, she had taken the brandy snifter with her. Indeed, Judith couldn't see the brandy bottle anywhere. She had left it on the stone hearth by the door to the bedroom. Renie must have snatched it away before getting into the tub.

"This," Judith said between clenched teeth as she hurried to help Renie to her feet, "is my cousin, Mrs. Jones. She's suffering from shock."

"I'm not suf'rin," Renie asserted, wallowing around on the carpet. "I feel swell."

Judith had never seen Renie drunk. Borderline tipsy, maybe, in their partying days, but definitely not drunk. She guessed that the combination of the Jacuzzi, the brandy, and the very real shock of Hodge's death had taken its toll on Renie. Also, she recalled fleetingly, Renie hadn't had a chance to eat.

"I'm putting you to bed," Judith said in a stern voice. As the taller and heavier of the cousins, she was able to drag Renie back down the steps and across the room. It wasn't easy, though; Renie's arms and legs went every which way, like a floppy doll. "Keep your mouth shut," Judith hissed. "And stay put."

"But I gotta tell 'bout the plate," Renie protested. "Truth'll out."

"*You're* out," Judith declared, somehow getting Renie onto the queen-size bed. "I told you, don't say another word."

"Mm-mm-mm." Renie nestled her head into one of the several ruffled pillows. " 'Night, Bill. Renie loves Bill. Does Bill love . . ." Renie faded off into slumberland.

In the living room, Doc wore a bemused expression, while McLean looked downright incensed. "Who is that peculiar person and why didn't either of you tell me there was somebody else in this house?" the deputy demanded in an angry voice.

"She's my cousin, and she's not well," Judith said. While not averse to telling an occasional fib for a good cause, Judith rationalized that this time, her words contained more than a grain of truth. "This episode with Mr. Hodge upset her so much that I had to put her to bed." Judith still had truth on her side, though it was drifting slightly behind her. "She's a very sensitive person." Truth disappeared somewhere in the vicinity of the empty brandy bottle.

McLean turned to Doc. "Check this woman out. See if she's really sick. Unless she's at death's door, I want to interrogate her. Now."

Doc picked up his medical bag and went into the master bedroom. "What's your cousin's name?" McLean barked, picking up the clipboard once more.

"Serena Jones. Mrs. William," Judith answered, trying to keep from peeking in on Doc and Renie. "She's a graphic designer. I asked her to come along to help me."

McLean looked skeptical. "Help you do what? Design graphics?"

"No. Just for moral support, really. It's not easy to take over somebody else's bed and breakfast establishment. I have my own B & B on Heraldsgate Hill, you see. That's why Jeanne Barber asked me to fill in for her."

McLean's hazel eyes narrowed at Judith. "Did you know

the victim before he came to Chavez Cove?''

"No. We happened to meet him on the ferry this morning," Judith answered, feeling on somewhat firmer ground.
"I hadn't even seen the guest list at that point, so I knew
nothing about him."

"You sure?" McLean looked dubious. "He was a city
type—like you. What do you know about Adhab?''

Judith's eyes widened. "Is that some kind of Middle
Eastern type?"

"Is that some kind of smart-assed answer?" McLean retorted, but didn't press the issue. As Doc returned to the
living room, she regarded him with an expectant air:
"Well? What's with Mrs. Jones?''

Doc smiled thinly. "You won't get much out of her tonight, I'm afraid. I . . . ah . . . gave her a sedative. She needs
all the rest she can get. I'm sure she'll be much better in
the morning." He darted a conspiratorial look at Judith.

The skeptical expression remained on McLean's face, but
she turned her attention to the matter at hand. "Okay, we're
heading out with the body. I think we've seen enough. Except for taking photographs, there wasn't much data to
gather. The autopsy report should be ready by tomorrow
afternoon. I'll let you know if you're right, Doc.''

Judith's eyes strayed to Doc Wicker. Apparently, some-
thing had passed between the doctor and the deputy while
Judith was out of the room. She held her tongue until Lulu
McLean had left the house and was headed for the dock.

"You have a theory?" Judith inquired in a mild voice.

Doc got out his pipe. "You mind?" Judith shook her
head. Joe was fond of an occasional cigar. "It's not exactly
a theory, it's a puzzle. If you ask me, Hodge's head indicated two separate blows, and he didn't suffer them in the
same way or with the same object." The shrewd gray eyes
searched Judith's face. "Do you have any ideas about
that?"

Judith sighed and sank down on the sofa. Renie was
right: The truth would have to come out. Doc seemed sympathetic, the kind of person in whom Judith could confide.

"My cousin cracked him over the head with a dinner plate. Hodge was being impossibly rude. But all she did was raise a lump. That's what you saw on the top of his head."

"I wondered." Doc seated himself in the rocker. "I figured something was up with you two. You should have told Lulu McLean. The autopsy will prove my findings, and McLean will be furious."

"I couldn't squeal on Renie," Judith said. "And thank you for your own part in the cover-up."

Doc waved a hand. "It was nothing. Your cousin didn't need a sedative, of course. She was out like a light. But there was no way McLean was going to be able to talk to her. And given your reticence about what happened, I figured I'd better have a word with you before our deputy put the thumbscrews on Mrs. Jones."

"It's very awkward," Judith admitted. "Renie was willing to talk. Except that she couldn't. At least not without letting McLean think she was some kind of sot. Honestly, Doc, my cousin doesn't usually drink like that. It must have been the Jacuzzi."

"Hmm." Doc's attitude was ambiguous. "So what are you thinking, Mrs. Flynn?"

"Please call me Judith." She paused for a moment, collecting her impressions. "He *could* have fallen."

"He could." Doc nodded, his pipe finally taking hold. "But he couldn't have suffered that kind of a blow to the back of his skull by hitting it on those wooden steps."

Judith felt herself turn pale. "Are you suggesting . . . foul play?" She could hardly utter the question.

Doc didn't answer immediately. He was again gazing out through the tall windows, though his eyes didn't seem to be taking in the view. "That's a terrible thing," he finally said. "No, I don't want to believe it. A freak accident, maybe. Though I don't understand it. Of course," he added with an ironic expression, "in matters such as this, I'm out of practice. Literally."

"I see," Judith said, though she didn't. "You're retired?"

"You might say that." Doc still avoided Judith's gaze. "We'll know more tomorrow. September isn't a very lucky month around here."

The phrase rang some bells in Judith's brain. "I've heard other people say the same thing. Rafe. Bates Danfield. Jeanne, too, though I thought she was only referring to the end of the tourist season. What's wrong with September?"

Doc frowned into his brandy snifter. "Coincidences, really. Over the years, most of the bad things that have happened seem to have occurred during September. People get superstitious."

"Duane Barber didn't die in September," Judith pointed out.

"No. But others did. 'Remember September.' It's a catchphrase around here, and a somber one at that." Suddenly looking weary, he finished his brandy and stood up. "I'd better head home now. It might be a good idea for you to lock up real tight. Just in case, you know."

Judith shuddered. "I'd hate to think there's a . . . criminal on this island."

"So would I." Doc went over to the fireplace and emptied his pipe into the grate. Collecting his medical bag, he put a kindly hand on Judith's shoulder. "Think positive. It was just a terrible accident. They happen. An uncontrolled fall, I believe it's called. Forget all the things I said about September. Most years have been just fine."

"Except this one," Judith noted.

Doc tipped his head to one side. "Yes. Except this one. Sorry you were here for it. Good night, Mrs . . . Judith." Doc smiled, a ghost of his usual genial expression.

Judith watched Doc go down the treacherous back stairs. A moment later he had disappeared out of the circle of floodlights. It might be wise to leave them on, she decided, closing the door and securing the double locks. Going to the front of the house, she stepped out on the deck for a breath of fresh air. It was not yet eight o'clock, but full darkness had descended over Chavez Island. Far out on the water, she could see the lights of a single ship, passing under the stars. It had grown almost chilly, and Judith hugged herself. She was shivering, though not just from the cold. Autumn was in the air. And so was death. "Remember September," Doc had said.

Judith already wished she could forget.

SIX

DESPITE DOC'S ENCOURAGING words, Judith knew he didn't think H. Burrell Hodge's death had been accidental. Judith didn't think so, either. Someone besides Renie had bashed in Hodge's head. But why? Being obnoxious usually wasn't a motive for murder. Who, Judith wondered as she went back inside, had wanted Hodge dead? The number of suspects seemed limited to the inhabitants and guests of Chavez Island. Judith already knew them, though she had yet to see the reclusive Rowena Carr up close.

She checked and rechecked the locks to the front door, then made a tour of the windows. When she reached the master bedroom, she shook her head at her cousin's inert form. Renie was sleeping on her stomach, snoring softly. Judith considered moving her own things to the loft, but decided to stay put. There was plenty of room in the queen-size bed, and Judith felt there was safety in numbers, even if one of them couldn't be roused by a nuclear bomb. As much as she hated to admit it, even to herself, Judith was uneasy. In fact, she was downright scared.

As Judith knew from experience, keeping busy was a proven antidote to fear and anxiety. Returning to the kitchen, she was putting the cold prawns in a plastic container when a knock at the back door startled her.

Warily, she peered through the spy-hole. Rafe St. Jacques was standing under the fairy lights.

Judith wasn't inclined to open the door. She hesitated before asking what he wanted, but called to him after he knocked a second time.

"I heard there was an accident," Rafe replied in his mellow baritone. "Are you all right?"

It seemed unkind to turn Rafe away. He was being solicitous, neighborly. According to Jeanne's notes, he often acted as Chavez Island security. Judith wondered why she hadn't called him in the first place, instead of summoning Doc Wicker. Maybe her mind really was going to pot, right along with her mother's.

Fumbling with the locks, Judith finally got the door open. Rafe's chiseled features revealed genuine concern. "I picked up the emergency call on my shortwave radio," he said, stepping into the living room. "Actually, I only heard it a few minutes ago, when Lulu McLean called into Laurel Harbor on the return trip. What happened?"

Judith debated whether or not to tell Rafe the whole story. Like Doc, he seemed sympathetic. But if H. Burrell Hodge had been murdered, Judith already had acknowledged that the number of suspects was small. Rafe was one of them. On the other hand, news would travel fast in a tiny community like Chavez Island.

"Mr. Hodge died from an apparent fall down the front steps here," she said, deciding on discretion. "There'll be an autopsy."

"Given what I heard over the radio, I should hope so." Rafe seemed troubled, his usual ironic manner shaken. "Have you informed the other guests?"

"Um . . . not yet." Judith grimaced. "Do you think I should? Or would it be better to wait until morning?"

Rafe strolled over to the stone fireplace. "I think you have an obligation," he said gravely. "If you like, I'll go with you."

Judith gave him a grateful smile, then checked herself. Heading out into the darkened woods with Rafe St. Jacques could be dangerous. "Maybe we should have Doc come, too. He signed the death certificate."

Rafe lifted one dark eyebrow, but his voice was smooth: "That's fine. Ring him up and ask him to meet us at the head of the trail." He glanced around the living room and into the kitchen. "Where's your sister?"

"She's my cousin. She's sleeping. Do you think it's okay to leave her alone?"

Briefly, Rafe looked uncertain. Then authority returned to his voice. "We won't be gone long. You and Cilla have the only keys, right?"

"I guess so," Judith replied. "Let me get my jacket."

In the bedroom, Renie was still sound asleep. Judith returned to the living room to discover that Rafe had gone into the kitchen. He was hanging up the phone.

"I called Doc," he said, starting for the front door. "He's not feeling well. We'll have to go without him."

Judith hesitated, wondering if she could believe Rafe. Or Doc. Then she gathered her nerve and went out the door. "Tell me about Doc," she said, turning both keys to secure the locks. "Why did he give up his practice?"

"Did he tell you that?" Rafe's tone was wary.

"More or less. What happened?" She stepped aside, indicating that Rafe should go first. Judith didn't want him behind her on the steep stairs.

"It was before my time," Rafe answered, taking a flashlight out from under his moleskin hunting jacket. He kept ahead of Judith, shining the light along the path.

"What was before your time?" she persisted.

"Whatever made him quit his medical practice." Rafe didn't elaborate, and Judith kept quiet for a few moments, keeping one eye on the trail, and the other on her companion's catlike stride.

"Something in particular made him quit?" She hoped the question was casual.

"So I've heard." They had come into the open area, where the flagstone paths branched off. Rafe stopped and gazed down at Judith, his azure eyes mysterious in the evening shadows. "Sometimes people are forced to stop doing what they love," Rafe said with feeling as Judith tried to keep her gaze steady. "It's not always their fault. Not really. But they blame themselves anyway. And they never forget." He turned away and headed for Fawn, the Estacadas' cabin. She sensed that Rafe wasn't talking only about Doc; the melancholy in his voice also might have been for himself.

The honeymooning Estacadas weren't pleased by the intrusion. Judith felt embarrassed, but Rafe took over. He informed the couple that Mr. Hodge had suffered a fatal accident. While there was probably no cause for alarm, any sign of a stranger should be reported immediately to him or to Mrs. Flynn.

"You mean there's a madman loose?" Stacie Estacada cried, clutching her black peignoir close to her slim body. "I thought you said it was an accident!"

"We haven't yet had official word," Rafe said quietly. "It never hurts to be careful."

"What kind of a place *is* this?" Stacie demanded, moving into the protective circle of her husband's arms. "We came here for a romantic getaway!"

"Now Stacie," Rob said in a soothing tone, "sometimes things just happen. Nobody can control events."

"How true," Rafe said grimly. "That's a lesson in life we all have to learn. Good night."

The Estacadas now looked more frightened than annoyed. But Rafe moved purposefully off the porch, with Judith trailing behind him. When they reached Doe, June Hennessy was already outside.

"What's going on?" she queried. "I heard voices."

Again, Rafe explained what had happened. Miss Hennessy's reaction was quite different from the Estacadas'.

"Just as I suspected," the headmistress averred. "That dreadful man was a troublemaker. If he had an accident, he probably brought it on himself. Now you understand why I feel so strongly about outside influences on my students. The world is full of scoundrels."

It seemed to Judith that June Hennessy's response was evidence of her vast experience with social ills and human nature. Judith grudgingly admired the other woman's raw candor, if not her cynicism.

After Miss Hennessy had stalked back into her cabin, Judith gazed in the direction of Buck. "Deputy McLean is supposed to notify Mr. Hodge's next of kin, but I don't think she found much information in his wallet. Should we check his belongings? I feel responsible."

Rafe concurred. Judith used her extra key, but paused on the threshold. Even before she flipped on the lights, she felt a sense of desolation. H. Burrell Hodge hadn't spent much time in the cabin, but he'd left his mark. With her nerves on edge, she was aware of Rafe standing so close behind her that they were almost touching. It was foolish to be afraid, she lectured herself; Miss Hennessy and the Estacadas were within shouting distance. Judith entered the cabin and turned on the lights.

The living room and kitchenette were much as she had left them that afternoon. It appeared that Hodge had eaten a couple of pieces of fruit from the basket, but everything else remained untouched. Except, Judith remembered, the champagne bottle. Hodge had thrown it in the trash. The label was from a medium-priced vintner; it didn't seem right to waste it. While Rafe searched the bedroom, Judith looked for the garbage pail. It was under the kitchen sink, empty.

Judith was still rubbing her temple when Rafe emerged from the bedroom. "Nothing there, except his suitcase. The only thing with his name on it are a couple of pill bottles."

Distractedly, Judith nodded. "There was a business card in his wallet, I think. Lulu McLean will have to do her homework to track down Hodge's family and business associates." The full impact of Rafe's words suddenly struck Judith: "Just a suitcase? What about his briefcase?"

Rafe stared at Judith with an apparent lack of comprehension. "His briefcase? I didn't see one."

"It was on the bed this afternoon when I brought the

fruit basket. Now it's gone, and so is the garbage. There's not even a plastic liner. Where does Cilla put the trash?''

"There's a communal Dumpster by the Wicker Basket," Rafe said, looking puzzled. "Cilla cleans the cabins in the mornings. Maybe she forgot to line the can."

Judith shook her head. "I don't think so. Burrell said he threw out the champagne. And I left him a note about my not providing meals. That's gone, too."

Rafe uttered a short laugh. "Who'd throw a briefcase in the trash?"

"I don't know. The next question is *why*." Another thought occurred to her. "Rafe, did you take Mr. Hodge to his cabin this morning?"

"No," Rafe responded. "Remember, I had to go with Mrs. Barber to Laurel Harbor. I didn't have time to escort Mr. Hodge."

"Then how did he know where to find the cabins?" Judith's gaze was now steady as her nerves began to settle down.

Rafe lifted one dark eyebrow. "Good point. Are you saying he's been here before?"

"What else?" Judith gave a shrug.

"What did Doc say?" Rafe's chiseled features had taken on a dark cast as he moved out of the direct light. "Did he know Hodge?"

Judith considered Doc's reaction to both the name and the body. "I'm not sure." She also remembered how Esther Danfield had seemed to be trying to place Hodge. Cilla hadn't behaved in a completely natural manner, either.

"A real mystery man," Rafe said lightly. "Shall we head back?"

Although Judith had found no obvious threat in Rafe's demeanor, there was no reason to stay. At the door, she cast one last look at the cabin called Buck. It had brought tragedy to H. Burrell Hodge. Slowly, she closed the door. No, it wasn't the cabin that had cost Burrell his life. Someone had taken it, deliberately and cruelly. Judith was convinced that the obnoxious, overbearing man had been murdered. No one deserved that, not even H. Burrell Hodge.

By the time Rafe had walked Judith back to the house, she had put aside her earlier misgivings about being alone with him. He waited at the bottom of the stairs until she was safely inside. Rafe St. Jacques might exude a mysterious aura, but he behaved like a gentleman. Surely she could trust him.

Renie had scarcely moved. It was just after nine, and although she was tired, it was too early for bed. Judith realized she was famished. Sitting at the kitchen counter, she devoured crackers, cheese, and a pear. Then she stared at the phone and wondered if she should call Joe.

She didn't want to tell him about H. Burrell Hodge. But if his death was ruled a homicide, the story would make the daily newspapers. The metro police might even be called in since Hodge was a local resident. Judith ate another cracker, squared her shoulders, and dialed Hillside Manor's private number.

After the fourth ring, she heard her own voice on the answering machine. Annoyed, she was about to hang up without leaving a message when Joe's breathless voice came on the line.

"Jude-girl!" he exclaimed, using the nickname that had never sat well with Judith. "I just came in the door." The transmission between Chavez Island and the city snapped, crackled, and popped.

"Gee, did your training session last half the night?" Judith asked, wondering how to phrase her latest disaster report.

"No, we got done around five-thirty," Joe said, his breath coming more easily now. "I had to go over and fix Herself's toaster. She had a problem with her buns this morning."

Judith bit her lip. "Her *buns*?" Was Joe teasing her?

"You know," he said, sounding quite serious. "Those what-do-you-call-them? English muffins. Vivian always toasts them and adds about a stick of butter and an inch of marmalade. I've never understood why she doesn't get fat. I guess it's all the booze.''

The implied intimacy made Judith bristle. So did the reference to Herself's svelte, yet curvaceous figure. All her life, Judith had struggled to keep her weight down. "Maybe I should drink more," she said in a testy voice, then thought of Renie's recent debacle and started to take back the words.

But Joe was already speaking: "As a matter of fact," he said, apparently ignoring the hostility in Judith's tone, "Vivian and I talked about her drinking tonight. Incredible as it may seem, she's finally gotten to the point where she not only admits she has a problem, but she may be ready to do something about it. Wouldn't that be terrific?"

In all honesty, Judith didn't think so. As long as the great love of Herself's life was liquor, Judith felt relatively secure. The key word, Judith realized, was *relatively*. Feeling totally secure was elusive. Life had bombarded Judith too often, too hard, and in too many ways.

But Judith knew she had to lie. "That's wonderful. Is she thinking about going to AA?"

"She hasn't gotten that far yet," Joe replied, his voice fading in and out. Not only was the transmission from the islands poor, but apparently Joe was moving around the house with the cordless phone. "Somebody recommended a rehab outfit that's supposed to be highly effective. If I have any spare time tomorrow at work, I'll check into other available resources. It's best to present Vivian with options. That way, she doesn't feel so pressured. She's never liked to be steered or manipulated."

"That's good of you, Joe," Judith said somewhat stiffly. "What caused this sudden change?"

"It's not so sudden," Joe said, coming through more clearly now. "The first big change was the move from Florida. Consciously or otherwise, Vivian wanted to break her pattern of living. Then Caitlin's been around more the past few months," he went on, referring to the daughter he had had by Herself. "She has more influence on Vivian than

anybody. Last but not least, is . . .'' Judith could hear Joe
make what sounded like a gagging noise. ''. . . your mother.
The old bat—I mean, Gertrude—has talked turkey with
her. Vivian's mother died when she was twelve, and Ma
Flynn had been dead for several years when Vivian and I
got married. So there's been no maternal figure for most of
her life. As you know too well, your mother . . .'' The gagging sound was more restrained this time. ''. . . speaks her
mind. She seems to have had some influence on Vivian.''

Judith was shaking her head in amazement. For the time
being, her jealousy was put on hold. ''People never cease
to confound me,'' she murmured. ''Well, I hope it works
out for her.'' Judith almost meant what she said.

''We'll see.'' Joe now sounded as if his mouth was full.
Judith guessed that he hadn't had any dinner. ''How's it
going up on the island?''

Conflicting thoughts raced through Judith's mind. Joe
had put in a long day with the dreaded training session.
Then he had come home to face not only a minor appliance
repair, but a major life decision for Herself. Did he need
to know about H. Burrell Hodge?

Not yet, thought Judith. If the metro division was called
in, Joe might not find out for a while. The training classes
kept him out of the loop. There was no point in causing
him any further worry.

''One of the guests fell down the stairs,'' Judith said
airily, hedging her bets. ''Other than that, everything's
fine.'' She grimaced, thinking of Renie's bout with the
brandy. ''It's a gorgeous house and a beautiful setting. By
the way, I liked that Subaru rental a lot. Instead of trying
some other car, I think I'll get one just like it for the return
trip.'' As she spoke, Judith realized she hadn't told Joe
about the extension of her commitment at Chavez Cove.
That, too, could wait.

''I can check out prices,'' Joe said. ''What is it, a Legacy?''

''Right. The one I rented is loaded, which is nice. But I

think we should get a used model, maybe two years old. Don't you agree?''

"Makes sense to me." Joe yawned. "I guess I'll head up to my lonely bed."

Judith felt a pang. "I really shouldn't have come," she declared, thinking of various reasons why not, including at least one Joe couldn't guess.

"Hey, you're going to make a grand off this deal. That'll cover airfare and three nights in a decent hotel somewhere. Think January, not September."

"I'll try." Joe couldn't imagine how hard it was for Judith not to think of September. Most of the residents on Chavez Island couldn't seem to put it out of their minds. Judith wondered why. "We can certainly use some R and R after the holidays."

"We sure can," Joe agreed. "Compared with other things, a thousand-dollar getaway is cheap. If Vivian decides to go to that rehab place, it may not be covered under her medical insurance. It costs over eight grand for a stay at Adhab."

"Wow, that's a lot of . . ." Judith stopped short. "Did you say Adhab?"

"Right. I think it stands for Addiction and Rehabilitation, or something like that. They've got several places on the West Coast. Whoever told Vivian about them said they were very good. Pastoral surroundings, comfortable rooms, excellent food, and a crackerjack staff. Have you heard of them?"

"Maybe. But only in passing." Judith was digging around in her memory. Was Adhab really the name that Deputy McLean had mentioned in connection with H. Burrell Hodge? "Is their headquarters local?"

"I've no idea." Joe yawned again. "As I said, I'll try to check them and some of the other rehab groups out tomorrow. I'm sinking slowly into the west, Jude-girl. The class bell rings at seven-thirty. Love you."

"Me too," Judith said in a distracted manner. She hung up the phone very slowly. The world was full of acronyms.

Some of them were identical, though they stood for different words. On the other hand, there was no reason why H. Burrell Hodge shouldn't be connected with a rehab organization. He had certainly been vocal in his antiliquor sentiments. Perhaps his reasons were professional. Deputy McLean would find out soon enough. Judith decided that she, too, would enjoy the relaxing waters of the Jacuzzi.

The master bedroom's tub and shower were in an open area separated from the bed by only a chair and a writing desk. The sound of the rushing water awakened Renie. She struggled to sit up, blinking against the subdued lighting and obviously trying to figure out where she was.

"Bill?" Her voice was fuzzy. "What . . . ? Why . . . ? *Coz*?" Her eyes grew wide if slightly unfocused as she stared at Judith. "Oh God! I did something really stupid, didn't I?"

"Define stupid," Judith responded, testing the water with a finger. "How do you feel?"

"Ghastly. What time is it?"

"A little after ten. Everybody's gone."

"What's happening?" With a small groan, Renie swung her legs over the edge of the bed and faced the Jacuzzi.

Judith shot her cousin a reproachful look. "Can this discussion wait until morning? While you were cutting Z's, I was hustling. The deputy sheriff, Doc Wicker, the B&B guests, Rafe St. Jacques—and my husband, helping his ex-wife conquer alcoholism. Not to mention getting her buns out of the toaster, or some damned thing. I'm beat. Go back to sleep, and I'll tell you all about it tomorrow."

"I'm not tired anymore," Renie protested. "In fact, I'm starving. Did you eat all the prawns?"

"I didn't eat any of them." Judith turned off the tap. The huge ebony tub was a sea of churning bubbles. "Everything's in the fridge. Except the bread—it got dried out in the oven. Help yourself." Blissfully, Judith sank into the tub.

Renie left the master bedroom. Above the purr of the soothing waters, Judith heard her cousin opening the refrigerator door and the cupboards. Judith closed her eyes and sank deeper into the jasmine-scented bath. A Jacuzzi would make a wonderful addition to the third-floor family quarters at Hillside Manor. To heck with the guests. If she had it installed on the second floor, she'd feel obligated to raise her rates to pay for it. Nor would Judith be able to use it in the evenings when she needed it most. She wondered how much a Jacuzzi cost. Maybe that's how she should use the thousand-dollar fee, instead of taking a trip. Joe would like the Jacuzzi, too; she was sure of it. The pulsating jets gently eased her tired body; the total submersion calmed her jumbled mind. This was luxury, heaven, complete abandonment to the senses . . .

Judith sat up sharply. She had been drifting off to sleep. No wonder Renie had become so stupefied after a couple of brandies on an empty stomach. The Jacuzzi pampered all too well. Neither Judith nor Renie was used to such elite treatment. Turning the jets off, Judith opened the drain, got out of the tub, and toweled off.

"Don't you dare eat all those prawns!" she yelled out to Renie. "I haven't had a real dinner, either."

Her cousin was just dishing up when Judith entered the kitchen in her blue bathrobe. "I'm still hungry, too," she admitted with a sheepish look.

"Hey," said Renie, giving the salad an extra toss, "if we were in Europe, we'd just be sitting down to eat. It's only ten-thirty."

"You must feel better," Judith remarked, ruffling the damp hair at her neck.

Renie nodded. "I've got a headache, but the main thing is that I'm famished." To prove the point, she began wolfing down pasta and prawns.

"Okay," Judith sighed. "I'll recap what went on while you were out with the Sandman."

The cousins had both finished eating by the time Judith had gone over the evening's events. She'd tried to relate every detail and nuance. Renie had listened attentively, asking only occasional, pertinent questions. When Judith finally stopped to hear Renie's reaction, the goose wings on the kitchen clock pointed to eleven.

"What stands out," Renie said carefully, "is your idea that Burrell had been here before, and yet only Bates Danfield acknowledged him as someone he knew before his arrival today. At least Bates sounded as if he wasn't a complete stranger."

Judith agreed. "There are several peculiar things about this situation. The missing briefcase. The references to September. Doc's reasons for giving up his medical practice. Rafe's behavior."

"I thought you said Rafe was very gallant," Renie put in.

"He was," Judith allowed. "But there's still something about him that bothers me. He seems like a man with a past."

Renie rolled her eyes. "Everybody's got a past. You're hung up on that because he's got that mysterious, romantic look to him. So does our milkman. But his life's an open half gallon of one percent."

"No," Judith persisted. "It's not just that. It's what he said. I told you—about how people regret things and blame themselves, even when they're not entirely at fault."

Renie, however, wasn't buying Judith's argument. "Everybody has regrets. I regret hitting H. Burrell Hodge over the head with that dinner plate. I regret drinking that stupid brandy. I regret *coming up here with you.*" She gave Judith a wry smile. "It's not the pleasure of your company that upsets me. It's being on the short list of murder suspects. No matter how Burrell died, I didn't give him a very good send-off. And I'm sure you regret saying yes to Jeanne Barber."

"I'm afraid so," Judith admitted. "In fact, Herself has already managed to sink her hooks into Joe's hide."

"Oh, yes," Renie nodded. "Do tell me about her burned buns."

Judith did, remembering to include Joe's mention of Adhab. "So now Joe is going to be holding her hand while she dries out. If she decides to attend AA, what do you bet she'll drag Joe along to the meetings?''

"Coz," Renie said on a weary sigh, "Joe married Herself while he was in a drunken stupor. Not only wasn't he in love with her, he didn't really know the woman. Then, before he could figure out how to get out of the marriage, you hooked up with Dan. Joe was stuck, and it's to his credit that he and Herself stayed married for as long as they did. What was it—twenty-five years?''

"Not quite," Judith replied in a meek voice. "They'd been separated for a while when I met Joe again five years ago. Herself had moved to Florida a year or two before that. She wanted sunshine. But I guess she got tired of it. She does gripe about the rain, though. I never do. I like it.''

"Me too," Renie agreed. "The point is, whatever Joe felt for Herself must have grown out of simply being together. That can be love, I won't deny it. But it isn't the same kind of love that the two of you have for each other. And don't forget, Herself put Joe through a lot of misery.''

"Just like Dan did with me," Judith remarked, getting up to clear the table. "I suppose I loved Dan in much the same way that Joe loved Herself. You know," she went on as she looked up from the open dishwasher, "Joe and I've never really talked about that. Not specifically.''

"Maybe you should. It might make both of you feel better." Renie was checking the stove to make sure it was turned off. "More secure.''

"Secure." Judith breathed the word. "Yes, maybe it would. Then I wouldn't resent Joe trying to help Herself do something that's really admirable. H. Burrell Hodge was right about one thing—alcohol has ruined too many lives.''

"I'm not arguing the point," Renie declared. "But Burrell's attitude made me crazy. I wouldn't have agreed with him if he'd insisted the earth was round. That's the trouble with me—I let idiots like him drive me nuts. Look where it's got me.''

"Next to the stove?" Judith smiled at Renie.

Renie threw up her hands. "No, I mean it made me do something *I* regret. Deeply. Unless someone actually came along and whacked Burrell with a crowbar, I'll always feel responsible for his death."

Judith considered Renie's words, though not precisely in the context that her cousin had intended. "It *could* have been a crowbar," she finally said. "But I suspect it was something else."

Renie's eyes widened. "You really believe he was murdered, don't you?"

Slowly, Judith nodded. "Yes."

Renie shook her head. "Usually, I try to talk you out of your flights of fancy. But for once, I hope you're right."

SEVEN

IT HADN'T BEEN easy for Judith to get up at six o'clock to bake three kinds of muffins. She was still bleary-eyed when she removed them from the oven at a quarter to seven and slipped them into the two breakfast baskets. Renie, who hadn't been able to get to sleep right away after her long evening's nap, was still in bed when Judith headed out for the cabins.

The morning fog swallowed up the path and shrouded the view from the grassy area by Doe, Buck, and Fawn. It was a silent world where Judith trod, with the sound of the sea muffled in the distance. She tiptoed up to Fawn and placed the basket by the door, then did the same at Doe. Passing Buck, Judith shuddered. The little building looked eerie in the shifting mist. It was no wonder that she let out a small shriek when a figure suddenly emerged from the fog.

"Mrs. Flynn!" cried Cilla Carr, then immediately lowered her voice. "I didn't expect you out this early!"

Judith discovered she was breathing hard. "The feeling is mutual," she said with a hand at her breast. "Do you always start by seven o'clock?"

Cilla shook her head. "No, not unless people have checked out by then. But I guess Mr. Hodge checked out in more ways than one, huh?"

"I'm afraid so," Judith said. "How did you find out?"

"Doc called us last night. He got hold of the Danfields, too. I guess it's no wonder I didn't sleep very well. Though after I finally got that toilet fixed . . ." Cilla's voice trailed away as she set some of her cleaning equipment on the ground. "Have you notified Jeanne yet?"

"No," Judith replied, feeling another attack of guilt coming on. "I should have phoned you and the Danfields myself. But I feel like an interloper. Who needs a complete stranger to give them bad news?"

"It's not your fault," Cilla said, her elfin features sympathetic. "Besides, Doc is our local news source. He keeps tuned to the weather reports and whatever other news affects us on Chavez. Do you want me to call Jeanne for you?"

The offer was tempting, but Judith had an obligation. "No. I'll phone after eight. Whatever guests do at the spa should start happening by then."

"Probably." Cilla retrieved her mop, broom, and the pail with its load of cleaning products, rags, and plastic sacks. "I'll start in on Mr. Hodge's place. He probably didn't make much of a mess, though. He wasn't there very long."

The plastic sacks reminded Judith of the empty garbage can. "Did you come back to Buck yesterday after Mr. Hodge checked in?"

Cilla's green eyes grew puzzled. "No. Why?"

Judith made a wry face. "It's nothing, really. But . . . ah . . . I was wondering if you forgot to line the garbage pail."

The pixielike features quivered with the effort of concentration. "I don't think so. As a matter of fact, I know I didn't forget. You know how those garbage bags are sometimes almost impossible to open after you tear them off the roll? Well, the one for Buck was such a pain that I thought I was working with the wrong end. I finally pulled it apart, though, but I was kind of steamed. I don't like things that slow me down."

"So," Judith inquired casually, "when is the garbage picked up?"

Cilla's perplexity deepened. "It isn't—not the way you city people mean. Once a week, usually on Tuesdays, Rafe hauls it over to the Laurel Harbor dump. Did something important get thrown out?"

Again, Judith was faced with a dilemma concerning candor. Cilla Carr was such a friendly, open person—surely she could be trusted. "Mr. Hodge's briefcase is missing," Judith said. "I thought maybe somehow it got into the trash."

Cilla's blond brows lifted. "Like on purpose? Who'd do a thing like that?"

The young woman's apparent naïveté made Judith realize that she wasn't aware that H. Burrell Hodge's death might have involved foul play. Doc Wicker must have reported only a fatal accident.

"I don't know who'd toss his briefcase," Judith admitted, after making a decision not to further enlighten Cilla until the autopsy findings had been announced. "But it's definitely gone. Rafe and I went to the cabin last night to check things out."

"Oh?" Cilla's skin colored ever so slightly. "I don't know anything about it. I never saw a briefcase because I never saw Mr. Hodge. Do you want me to check the Dumpster when I empty the trash?"

"Would you?" Judith put on her most winning face. "He might have had valuable papers in there. His next of kin would want to get them back."

Cilla gave a noncommittal shrug. "Excuse me, I've got to get my rear in gear. But I'll look in the Dumpster. See you."

When Judith returned to the house, Renie was getting dressed. "I've got extra muffins," Judith announced. "I couldn't figure out a way to cut back on the recipe without screwing it up. We might as well eat Burrell's share."

It was the wrong thing to say. Renie poked her head through a University of Wisconsin T-shirt and glared at her cousin. "Thanks. Now the sheriff will figure my motive for murdering Burrell was to get not only the prawns, but the muffins, too.'' She yanked at the T-shirt. ''Why don't you get one of these that says 'I'm with Killer' and has an arrow pointing to me?''

Judith couldn't help but laugh. ''Stop it, coz. How about some scrambled eggs and bacon to go with the muffins?''

Still looking disgruntled, Renie turned to the lighted vanity mirror over the sink in the master bedroom. ''Okay. Some fruit wouldn't be amiss, either. Is it foggy out or am I still half-asleep—as usual?''

Renie was rarely fully functional before ten o'clock, but this morning she had apparently gotten enough sleep to render her semialert. Judith assured her cousin that it was indeed foggy. Renie made a grumping noise and proceeded to apply her makeup.

In the kitchen, Judith mixed eggs, split a grapefruit, and put bacon in a frying pan. Then she scanned Jeanne Barber's notes, looking for the phone number of the California spa.

It wasn't written down anywhere. Judith scratched around the counter by the telephone; she checked the calendar and the guest book; she even looked on the refrigerator door.

''Damn!'' she exclaimed as Renie entered the kitchen. ''That wretched Jeanne didn't leave her phone number in Palm Desert. I wonder if Doc has it.'' She dialed 4.

Doc, however, didn't have the number. Nor, he thought, would Jeanne have left it with Rafe or anyone else on the island. ''She must have forgotten,'' Doc said, stating the obvious. ''Her daughter probably knows what it is. You ought to be able to find Marcia's number in Jeanne's address book. Her married name is Andersen, with an 'e'.''

''Thanks, Doc,'' Judith said. ''How are you feeling?''

''What? Oh, better, thanks. I guess Hodge's death upset me more than I realized. How's your cousin?''

''Guilt-riddled,'' Judith answered with a glance at Renie who was tending the bacon.

''She shouldn't be,'' Doc asserted. ''The more I think about it, the more I'm certain that somebody intentionally bashed in Hodge's head. He couldn't have done that to himself unless he'd backpedaled into a solid oak beam at about fifty miles an hour. Tell Mrs. Jones to stop being so hard on herself.''

Judith passed the message along to Renie, who acknowledged it with a grateful, if unconvinced, little smile. After hanging up, Judith went into the master bedroom to look for the address book. She hadn't seen any sign of it in the kitchen.

Sure enough, it was in the drawer of the writing desk. Judith opened it to the A's. Marcia Barber Andersen and her husband lived on the other side of the state. Since it wasn't yet seven-thirty, Judith decided to wait to call until after she and Renie had eaten breakfast.

While the cousins downed their meal, Judith told Renie about meeting Cilla by the cabins. "I wish," Judith said in conclusion, "that someone would own up to knowing H. Burrell Hodge."

"Bates Danfield did," Renie pointed out.

"I think Doc knew who he was, and maybe Esther, too," Judith said thoughtfully. She rose from the table, taking away her empty plate. "I'm going to call Marcia Barber Andersen now."

Renie pitched the grapefruit rinds into the garbage. "What do we do then? Wait for the sheriff to haul me away?"

"Hardly." Judith had punched in Marcia's number. "Frankly, I feel at loose ends. The autopsy report won't be in until later today. There's no real work to do. And I don't feel right about going around asking a lot of ... Damn!" She put her hand over the mouthpiece. "It's an answering machine," she whispered, then removed her hand and spoke into the phone: "This is Judith Flynn at Chavez Cove. Would you please call me at your mother's number as soon as it's convenient? Thank you."

To Renie's surprise, Judith immediately dialed again. "Could you please give me the number for Adhab? No, I don't know the address." She waited. At last, the operator pulled up multiple listings. Judith opted for the corporate offices.

"If this is the right outfit," she said to Renie, "they've got a center halfway up the mountain pass, one across the sound, and another out on the peninsula. But the headquarters is in the 'burbs, across the lake. That's who I'm . . . Drat, they're not in yet."

"It's only eight o'clock," Renie noted. "Maybe whoever should be in is out. Permanently."

"You mean Burrell?" Judith blanched. "I never thought of that." She abandoned the phone with a futile feeling. "Let's call on the Danfields."

"Let's not," Renie said. "I don't feel like getting shot at this early in the day."

"Elrod Dobler knows us now," Judith reminded Renie. "He'll be okay. Besides, I'd kind of like to talk to Elrod."

"I'd rather talk to a Doberman than Dobler," Renie declared. But she went into the bedroom to get her jacket.

While Judith waited, there was a knock at the back door. It was Cilla, with her cleaning supplies.

"I checked the Dumpster," she said, bursting across the threshold. "Rafe must have gotten an early start. It was empty. He must have things to do in Laurel Harbor before the first ferry gets in."

Judith was puzzled as well as disappointed. "But there aren't any guests arriving today. The Estacadas and Miss Hennessy aren't due to check out until the weekend, and nobody knows that Mr. Hodge's cabin is . . . vacant."

"Rafe has to check for mail and other deliveries," Cilla explained, stepping down into the kitchen. "Say, you and your cousin cleaned up pretty well after yourselves." She began to delve in the trash can. "Oh, too bad! You broke one of Jeanne's favorite plates!"

Renie had approached and was standing on the step that led from the living room. "I'll replace it," she said in a woeful voice. "I was the one who did the damage."

Cilla examined the broken pottery. "I think it's out of stock. Oh, well," she said, giving Renie a cheering smile.

"Accidents happen. Look at poor Mr. Hodge."

Judith put a hand on Cilla's arm. "*You* look at him, Cilla. Tell me who you see. Mr. Hodge had been to Chavez before yesterday, right?"

Cilla flinched at Judith's touch. "I wouldn't know. I've never met the man. But maybe he came here, and I didn't see him."

Judith withdrew her hand. "What makes you think that?"

Placing the crockery pieces back in the garbage bag, Cilla made a frustrated gesture. "It was sort of odd—when I mentioned Mr. Hodge's name to my mother, she threw up."

"She *what*?" Judith was incredulous.

"You're kidding," Renie said.

Cilla shook her head. "No. Yesterday morning, I mentioned who all was coming to Chavez—like I usually do, because my mother keeps to herself and tends to live vicariously—" She darted both cousins an ironic look. "—and she turned all pale and clutched her stomach and said she was going to be sick. And she was. Then I had to leave to come over here and introduce myself."

Judith remained startled. "Did she recover?"

"Oh, sure. She always does." Cilla got a can of furniture polish and a dust rag out of her pail.

Renie was now looking as confounded as Judith. "Does she do this often?"

"Not exactly *often*," Cilla responded. "Just when something or somebody upsets her."

"Did she say why she was upset?" Judith queried.

"No." Cilla shook her head. "I don't ask. It's better that way. Otherwise, I get long, involved, nonsensical explanations. Like the Roto-Rooter man."

Judith felt as if she were getting a nonsensical, if not long and involved, explanation from Cilla. "Dare *I* ask?" she murmured.

"Sure," Cilla replied. "When we first moved here, the drain got stopped up. I worked and worked, but I couldn't free the line, so we had to call Roto-Rooter. They don't come right away, as you can imagine. It was a two-day wait. When the guy finally showed up, he looked like my mother's Uncle Rudy, who was killed on Iwo Jima. Mother was only two at the time, and I doubt that she remembered him, but she went into this big story about how he used to take her to the zoo and they'd watch the monkeys. She'd never been to the zoo since. Just seeing the Roto-Rooter man made her realize how much she missed the zoo—and Uncle Rudy.'' Cilla raised both hands in a helpless gesture.

''I see,'' Judith said, though she wasn't entirely sure she did. ''In other words, certain people—or situations—trigger sad memories.''

''You could put it like that, I guess.'' Cilla headed for the living room.

Still befuddled, Judith led Renie out through the front door. ''Poor Cilla. I thought *my* mother was daffy.''

''She is,'' Renie said. ''Actually, her mother's antics don't seem to bother Cilla too much. She takes them in stride.''

''Good for her,'' Judith muttered. Taking Gertrude in stride was easier said than done.

The fog was still thick as the cousins proceeded down the road. They were practically at the Wicker Basket before they could see the building's homely exterior. Doc was outside, fiddling with an outboard motor.

''Hi, Doc,'' Judith said in greeting. ''Have you got a boat?''

Doc smiled at Judith and Renie. ''You bet. It's just a little runabout. I keep it over at Salmon Gap.''

Judith gazed at the map that was displayed on her left. ''Isn't that on the other side of the island?''

''That's right.'' Doc used a tattered rag to wipe grease off his hands. ''But it's the only available moorage. I wouldn't feel right taking up space in Chavez Cove. Rafe doesn't have room, either. And the Danfields—well, they sort of reserve their dock space for themselves and their guests.''

Renie was studying the map, too. "What's at Salmon Gap?" she inquired.

"Not much," Doc replied, now wiping off his glasses with a clean handkerchief. "It's a nice little inlet with a decent stretch of beach. There's a makeshift boathouse, mostly for storing kayaks and canoes, and a floating dock. That's where I keep *Frannie*."

"*Frannie*?" Judith eyed Doc with curiosity. "I thought that was the name of Rafe's cruiser."

Doc resettled the glasses on his nose. "No, Rafe's is *Fannie*. It's a coincidence. I was here first." A faintly bitter note echoed in Doc's voice.

"Say," Judith said, deciding that it might be tactful to change the subject, "what did Rafe do before he came to Chavez Island?"

"He was a seaman, I believe," Doc answered, bending down to tinker with the outboard motor. "He's been all over the world."

"So how does he support himself?" Judith asked.

"We all sort of chip in," Doc said with a grimace as he apparently encountered a recalcitrant piece of machinery. "Jeanne reimburses him for bringing the bed-and-breakfast guests over from Laurel Harbor, I share my fee for manning the postal station, and everybody pitches in for deliveries. He doesn't make much, but he doesn't need much. Rafe prefers a simple life. His great love is nature."

"That cruiser must have cost a lot," Renie commented. "Where did he get the money to buy a boat like that?"

Doc grunted as he wrestled with something inside the motor. "That I couldn't tell you. I get the impression—just an impression, mind—that Rafe has some kind of nest egg. But he's not one to discuss personal matters. If you want to talk to him, stick to boats, the weather, and the environment."

"The strong, silent type," Judith murmured.

"Silent about himself, that's for sure," Doc agreed. "Strong, physically anyway."

Judith and Renie left Doc to his tinkering. The dampness

from the fog lent a chill to the air as they approached the picket fence that guarded the Carr house. Judith slowed her step, trying to peer through the heavy vapors.

"I can't even see the house in this fog," she remarked. "I wonder when this stuff lifts? It was gone by the time we got here yesterday around eleven."

Before Renie could speculate, a ghostly figure plunged through the wooden gate. Dressed all in white, with long, pale hair, the apparition made both Judith and Renie jump. Apparently, the figure was equally startled by the cousins: A little keening cry escaped its lips, before it cringed and began to slowly withdraw back through the gate.

Judith had recovered herself, and was trying to focus on the specterlike being. Through the swirling fog, she realized that it was a woman in a long nightgown and robe. "Mrs. Carr?" called Judith.

The figure stopped retreating. "Yes?" Mrs. Carr's voice quavered on the chilly air.

"It's me," Judith said. "Mrs. Flynn. Remember, from yesterday?"

Timorously, Mrs. Carr moved closer. She was a bit taller and thinner than her daughter, Cilla. As she neared the cousins, Judith could see very little resemblance between the two women except for their fair hair. Rowena Carr had sharp features, brown eyes, and no dimples. There was nothing elfin about her, though Judith might have described her appearance as fey. Indeed, her apprehensive demeanor was distinctly different from the rude creature of Monday afternoon.

"I thought you were *her*," Mrs. Carr whispered, then pointed to Renie. "Who is *this*?"

"My cousin, Mrs. Jones." Judith waited for Mrs. Carr's reaction. There was none, except that she cocked her head and eyed Renie in a birdlike manner. "You thought I was *who*?" Judith asked after a long pause.

"Never mind." Rowena Carr's voice was suddenly shrill. She placed her hands inside the sleeves of her robe, turned abruptly, and disappeared back into the fog.

"Woo-woo!" Renie exclaimed under her breath. "Definitely three eggs shy of an omelet!"

"She is a bit unpredictable," Judith said in her more charitable fashion. "Who do you suppose she was looking for?"

"Cilla?" Renie suggested. "Maybe she's coming back home from our place before she does the cabins."

In the distance, a foghorn uttered its mournful sound. "I wonder how Rafe navigates in this kind of weather," Judith remarked.

"Maybe he's got radar," Renie said. "He sounds a little weird, too. Does everybody who lives here have to be peculiar?"

"Cilla seems fine. Doc's okay, if a little close-mouthed about some things. And except for being forgetful—which I can't criticize, given my current mode of operation— Jeanne Barber is fairly normal. No one's mentioned anything odd about the late Duane," Judith pointed out.

"No one mentions the late Duane much at all," Renie noted. "He strikes me as a nonentity, except for carving three-eyed ducks."

"I never met him," Judith admitted. "I don't think he attended the class reunions with Jeanne."

"I don't like dragging Bill to mine. Nothing is more boring than watching a spouse try to remember who used to have hair and who didn't weigh three hundred pounds in high school."

The stone fence slowly appeared through the fog. Elrod Dobler showed up much faster. He all but sprinted down the road, shotgun at the ready.

"Good morning," Judith called out in an overfriendly manner. "How are you, Mr. Dobler?"

"You again," Dobler said wearily, lowering the weapon. "What now?"

Renie offered Dobler a big, phony smile. "Shot anybody lately, Mr. Dobler?"

"Naw." The gnarled little man shook his head. "I missed last night. Not by much, though."

Dobler had fallen in step with the cousins. "Last night?" Judith echoed. "Who was that?"

"How should I know?" Dobler demanded. "It was gettin' dark. I don't see as good as I used to. But that doesn't mean I can't aim."

"When was it?" Judith still tried to keep her voice on a conversational level.

"Hells' bells, I don't know. Six-thirty, maybe seven o'clock." Dobler eyed Judith suspiciously. "Why you askin'?"

"Just curious," Judith replied. "If you've sighted some strangers around here, I should know about it. Jeanne Barber would want me to do that, don't you think?"

"Nobody pays me to think," Dobler retorted. They had reached the entrance to Stoneyhenge. "I told you, I didn't see whoever it was up close-like. But the Danfields weren't expectin' nobody, so whoever it was, shouldn'ta been here." In a protective stance, the old man had turned his back to the wrought-iron gates. "Now what was it you two are wantin' this time?"

"We were just out for a stroll," Judith fibbed. "We could hardly pass by without saying hello. Are Mr. and Mrs. Danfield up?"

Dobler snorted. "Up half the night, after Doc called with the news about that Hodge fella. You'da thought he was their best friend or some damned thing. Maybe you can talk some sense into 'em." He went over to the little grill and pressed a button. "You got visitors. Missus Finn or whatever her name is, and the short one. Wanna see 'em?"

Esther Danfield's reply was distorted as it came through the grill, but her response was in the affirmative. A minute later, Judith and Renie were in Stoneyhenge's entry hall. Esther, wearing a quilted satin robe, greeted them warily. Her classic features seemed drained and there were dark circles under her eyes. She led Judith and Renie into the living room.

"Do sit," she said, indicating two blue sofas and a gold brocade loveseat. "I'll fetch coffee."

Settling onto one of the blue sofas, Judith put up a hand. "Please don't bother. We can't stay long. But I felt an obligation to call on you because of the . . . accident we had at Chavez Cove last night."

Esther Danfield couldn't conceal the stricken look on her face, though she made a noble attempt at equanimity. "Oh, yes," she said carefully. "That was a terrible thing. The poor man! How is his family taking it?"

"I don't know," Judith admitted, trying to assess Esther's responses while also taking in the living room's Belle Époque decor. "Deputy McLean was going to track them down. We haven't heard from her yet this morning. Of course it's still very early."

"Yes," Esther agreed, her long fingers plucking at the quilted satin. "Yes, it's quite early. These things take time, I suppose. Santa Lucia County is ill equipped for such emergencies. Well, now. I hope this hasn't completely ruined your stay?"

The comment struck Judith as fatuous. Obviously, the news of Hodge's death had deeply disturbed Esther. Perhaps she was rattled.

"It's been an awful blow," Judith said, with a quick glance at Renie, who was frowning into her lap. "Actually, I was hoping that since your husband knew Mr. Hodge, he might be able to help the sheriff's people contact the next of kin or at least the business associates."

Esther ran an agitated hand through her short silver hair. "I have no idea. I didn't see Mr. Hodge when he called on Bates yesterday. It's a shame he's not here right now. He went over to Laurel Harbor with Rafe St. Jacques."

Judith tried to hide her disappointment. She also couldn't help but wonder if Esther was telling the truth. "Oh—that's too bad. We shouldn't have bothered you, but Mr. Dobler acted as if Bates was at home."

A flicker of uncertainty crossed Esther's face. "He did? Oh, that's probably because he was out wandering in the woods when Bates left. Mr. Dobler's morning surveillance, you see." She made a wry, faintly apologetic face. "You must find our security system rather extreme. I do, too, but we humor Mr. Dobler, and trespassers are a very real problem, especially during the summer.''

Judith had assumed a sympathetic look. ''I thought Rafe was in charge of security.''

''He is, officially,'' Esther replied. ''But he can't be everywhere. Besides, Mr. Dobler takes a very proprietary view of the island.''

Renie, who had been studying the bold pattern of the nineteenth-century needlepoint rug, turned her gaze to Esther. ''According to Elrod, you had a trespasser last night, around the dinner hour. He took a shot at whoever it was. Do you think it was someone who didn't belong on the island?''

Esther made a helpless gesture with her hands. ''Honestly, I've no idea. Mr. Dobler is always shooting at something. He may not have seen a person at all. It could have been an unfamiliar sound, an animal, a bird. Firing his gun makes Mr. Dobler feel as if he's doing something useful.''

Renie made no effort to hide the fact that Elrod's cavalier discharge of firearms appalled her. ''But what if he hits somebody? Has that ever happened?''

Esther's laugh was musical. ''Heavens, no! His eyesight is very poor. I doubt that he could hit a target that's more than five feet away. I don't think he'd want to—Mr. Dobler is a very kind man under that gruff exterior. It's just that he's . . . well, he's never been a particularly gregarious person, and after he was widowed several years ago, he grew more and more cantankerous.''

Renie evinced surprise. ''Elrod had a wife?''

''You didn't know?'' Esther's forehead furrowed and she clutched at the lapels of her robe as she turned to Judith. ''Her name was Flora. Flora Barber, Duane's sister. Since you're a friend of Jeanne's, I assumed you knew that. But . . . Jeanne didn't . . . fill you in?'' Esther suddenly seemed short of breath.

''She left in such a rush that I was lucky to get some written instructions,'' Judith admitted. ''As for Duane Bar-

ber, I know next to nothing about him. In fact, I don't know
Jeanne very well. We haven't been close over the years.''

''Oh, of course,'' Esther remarked vaguely, relaxing her
hand and letting it drop into her lap. ''Flora was several
years older than Duane. She died of cancer about twelve
years ago. M . . . Mr. Dobler was bereft.'' There was another catch in Esther's voice, and a glint of tears shone in
her blue eyes.

Judith was touched by Esther's compassion. ''That's a
shame,'' she said as she got to her feet. ''We'll be on our
way. I just wanted to make sure that the regular residents
of Chavez Island don't think me irresponsible.''

''Hardly that,'' Esther assured Judith. ''Accidents happen.'' She paused at the door to the entry hall. ''It *was* an
accident, wasn't it?''

''That's what it looked like,'' Judith answered, not daring to meet Renie's gaze. ''Why would you think otherwise?''

Esther seemed to shrink inside her robe. ''Oh! I don't!
It's just that . . . Doc sounded rather strange on the phone
last night. Do stop by again. Shall I have Bates call you
when he gets back from Laurel Harbor?''

Judith said that would be fine. Outside, the fog was beginning to lift. There was no sign of Elrod Dobler on the
road.

''Let's go see Salmon Gap,'' Judith suggested.

''What's to see?'' Renie was digging her heels into the
dirt.

Judith shrugged. ''I don't know. Weren't we going to
explore the rest of the island? The fog's thinning out.''

They could see at least ten yards down the road now.
Above them, the mist swirled in the trees. The air had
warmed up already, promising another beautiful afternoon.
Somewhere, they could hear birds twittering. To all appearances, the cousins were on an island paradise. Not even
a dead body could completely ruin the appeal of their surroundings.

''Okay,'' Renie finally relented. ''I checked the map

back at Doc's. Salmon Gap is probably about a quarter of a mile from here.''

But there was an obstacle that Renie apparently hadn't noticed: At the next bend, just beyond the farthest reaches of Stoneyhenge's wall, the road came to an abrupt halt. There was no trail as such, only a barely perceptible path that was probably a deer run.

"How did you ever win any beads as a Camp Fire girl?" Judith asked her cousin. "You sure can't read a map."

"In my group, beads were earned by how many dough-nuts you could sell," Renie replied. "I sold a ton."

"Sold or ate?"

"It came to the same thing," Renie said, not looking at Judith. "Eventually, I got promoted to Faggot Finder."

"I don't think they call them that anymore," Judith said, stepping off the road and heading through the beaten-down ferns and berry bushes.

"Probably not. The language has changed. They don't sell doughnuts anymore, either. They've had mints for years. I liked the doughnuts better." Renie started to follow Judith, but stopped after they'd gone only about fifty feet. "Hey—do you know where we're going?"

Judith turned to look over her shoulder. "*You* don't."

"If this is a deer run, it doesn't necessarily lead to the beach. What we should do—according to the map—is take a right, then a left when we see the water. That's the way to Salmon Gap."

The suggestion had merit. "Okay," Judith agreed. "It shouldn't be too far. Stoneyhenge has a view of the water from its southern exposure. We just passed the end of the wall, so we must still be in line with the shore."

While the going was more difficult, the cousins were proved right: Within five minutes, they were at the edge of a bluff that overlooked the sea. The ground had become very rocky, and the footing was treacherous. Judith and Renie walked with great caution. As they moved along the bluff, the fog began to evaporate on the water. Soon they could see Perez Island in the distance, and at least two of the smaller islands. The cousins were about to shed their jackets when they reached a trail.

"This must be the hikers' route from Eagle Lake," Renie said. "We can go back that way. It should take us right up to the cabins."

"What about the north side of the island?" Judith asked as they began a zigzag descent down the face of the cliff.

"I don't think there's much to see," Renie responded, panting a bit. "It looked like a bunch of woods with no shoreline until you get to the inlet where Rafe lives. The helicopter pad is between his place and the Wicker Basket."

Except for the false lead about the road's continuation, Judith was mildly impressed by Renie's comprehension of the map. "So we'll go by Eagle Lake on our way back to the house?"

"Right." A shower of dirt and pebbles was dislodged as Renie misstepped. "Sorry, coz. This trail's kind of steep."

"We're almost down," Judith said, pausing to admire the lagoonlike inlet. The tide had just turned, exposing a horseshoe of pearl gray sand speckled with a few small rocks, sand dollars, and heart cockles. In the curve of the little bay, the floating dock bobbed while the runabout tied to it bounced on the waves. "There's Doc's boat," Judith noted, as the cousins hit the beach. "See? It says *Frannie*."

"It's cute," Renie commented as she studied the jaunty lines of the nineteen-foot craft. "There's the boathouse."

The boathouse was taller but not much wider than a phone booth. Finding the weathered little edifice unlocked, Judith couldn't resist peeking inside. "It looks more like an outhouse than a boathouse," she remarked, eyeing a kayak, a couple of canoes, and a half dozen paddles of various shapes and sizes. Judith closed the door, which was made of the same fir slats as the rest of the structure. "The kayak and canoes must belong to the residents."

Renie had again turned to stare at Doc's runabout. "It looks like Uncle Vince's boat," she said.

"It does," Judith agreed. "Except Uncle Vince is always

fiddling with his motor so that when we visit him and Auntie Vance on the island he can never take anybody out in the boat.''

"Uncle Vince is afraid of the water," Renie asserted, referring to their uncle and his wife who had retired to one of the larger islands inside the sound. "Uncle Vince is afraid of everything, including Auntie Vance."

"You can hardly blame him for *that*," Judith said, as they strolled along the water's edge. "Auntie Vance has such a sharp tongue. Even my mother is afraid of her. The last time Auntie Vance and Uncle Vince came down from the island, they . . . Hey, look at this!''

The cousins had almost reached the far side of the inlet. There, above the usual tidemark in the sand, were the faint impressions of footprints. They led on a diagonal from the last high-tide mark to the general direction of the trail which Judith and Renie had just descended. Either two people had made them, or someone had come and gone via the same route.

"These prints are fairly fresh," Judith said in a puzzled voice. "Has somebody been here this morning?"

Renie bent down to examine the impressions. "They may be fresh, but they're not very clear. Except for a couple of them, the sand is too dry to tell very much. It looks to me like a less-than-average-sized man or a slightly more-than-average-sized woman wearing some kind of sneakers or deck shoes."

Judith concurred. "Doc?"

Renie stood up. "Could be. What's your point?"

Judith gave Renie a sheepish grin. "I don't have one. But I think I should. Who did Elrod Dobler shoot at last night? Who did Rowena Carr see?"

"The answer, dear coz, is nobody. One is half-blind and the other is three-quarters nuts."

Judith didn't agree. She started back for the trail. "I'm guessing we had a visitor to Chavez Island in the last few hours. The question is," she continued, beginning the climb up the face of the bluff, "who was it? And when did he or she come and go? Most of all, why did whoever it was visit Chavez via Salmon Gap? It's the back door to the island. Could it be that our unknown caller had a date with H. Burrell Hodge?''

EIGHT

RENIE WASN'T ENTHUSIASTIC about Judith's theory. She all but scoffed as they reached the top of the bluff and headed along the trail to Eagle Lake. The route was well maintained, with solid, relatively even footing. Gradually, the cedar, fir, hemlock, sword ferns, and salal gave way to a verdant meadow dotted with bright buttercups and cowslips. A trio of deer grazed peacefully, looking up only when Judith and Renie drew within twenty feet.

"They like us," Renie whispered. "We've found friends."

But as the cousins moved quietly along the trail, all three animals leaped through the long grasses and raced off among the trees. Judith and Renie exchanged droll expressions. A moment later, they could see the lake, not much bigger than a city block. Two cedar snags rose out of the placid waters, and a beaver dam had been built at the far end. A kingfisher sat on one of the snags and a pair of canvasback ducks glided across the deep green water.

"Pretty," Judith murmured. Even though the deer had fled, the tranquil scene invited quiet.

It did not, however, invite humans to come much closer. As Judith and Renie moved toward the lake, the meadow turned marshy. Renie's sandals threatened to pull from her feet, and Judith's Keds grew damp.

"We'd better stick to the trail," Judith suggested.

Near the beaver dam, however, the trail branched into two forks. The path on the right seemed like the logical choice to Judith. Renie didn't agree.

"That's going to take us north instead of west," she protested. "In fact, I don't think it's going to take us anywhere. If I remember the map correctly, it peters out on the other side of the lake."

Judith appeared undaunted. "If that's so, let's see why it exists. Somebody—Rafe, maybe—is keeping the trails up very well. Why bother creating a spur that goes only about fifty yards to nothing of consequence?"

It seemed to Renie that Judith's logic was faltering. "I still say the other branch will take us back to the cabins," Renie averred.

Judith kept walking, but Renie was right. The trail ended at the edge of the woods. It led to something of consequence, however: In the shade of the giant evergreens, the cousins saw a small Grecian temple, with a half dozen Ionic columns supporting a dome. The building, which appeared to be made of limestone, stood on a slight rise and overlooked a carefully tended cemetery. The grounds were enclosed by a wall built from stones which Judith recognized as the same kind that had been used on the Danfield property.

"I'll be darned," Judith said under her breath. "Was this on Doc's map?"

"I don't remember seeing it," Renie answered.

There was no gate, only a discreet sign that read "Private Property—Please Keep Out."

"Does that mean us?" Renie inquired.

"Probably," Judith said, but she entered the little cemetery anyway.

The path that bisected the manicured lawn was covered with limestone pebbles. There were no more than a half dozen tombstones, but each was large and elaborately carved. The closest was also the most recent. The earth had still not settled completely over the new grave.

"It's Duane," Judith exclaimed. "Look, 'Duane Edward Barber, born April 11, 1937, died July 27 of this year.' He's got a duck on his headstone."

Renie gazed critically at the carving. "It's your run-of-the-mill mallard. Duane must have carved it himself. It's got lips. Ducks don't have lips." Gingerly, Renie touched the decoy. It wiggled. "This must be temporary," she said. "I'll bet Jeanne is having one made in limestone or granite to go with the rest of the cemetery."

Judith was less interested in the graveyard's aesthetics than in who was lying under the emerald green grass. "Look, next to Duane—Flora Barber Dobler, Elrod's wife. Esther was right—she was quite a bit older than her brother, Duane. There was about a twelve-year difference between them."

Renie admired the graceful angels which clasped the headstone with one hand and held out the other, apparently to Flora's departed spirit. "Do you suppose this is sacred ground?" Renie asked.

"I don't know," Judith said, making her way down the path. "Here are two more Doblers, Albert and Violet. They have a fawn sitting on them. I'll bet they're Elrod's parents. Born 1895 and 1900, respectively, died 1959 and 1964. 'Home at Last,' it says."

Farther down, at the foot of the temple, Judith found a large, simple monument with the name "DANFIELD" inscribed in bold, handsome letters. Underneath, in smaller, but matching letters, were the names "Arthur" and "Clarice." There were no dates.

"That's strange," Judith remarked.

Renie shrugged. "In a private cemetery, I suppose you can do whatever you like. That's a fairly old tombstone, though. I'd guess it was put there when the temple was erected. It's made of the same limestone."

"Could be." Judith glanced up at the temple. Seven steps led to the little rise, and she could see the name "DANFIELD" carved into the temple's base. "I wonder if somebody from the Danfield family is actually buried there, such as Bates's parents.''

Renie was squinting at the temple. "Maybe," she suggested, "the name puts their stamp on the cemetery itself.''

"That's possible.'' Judith moved off the main path to a plot that was nestled in the curve of a rock garden. The marker here was flat, and upon it lay a dozen dark red chrysanthemums. Judith bent down and carefully moved the flowers so that she could read the information on the plain granite stone. " 'Francesca.' That's all.''

Noting that the grass was still very wet from the fog, Renie knelt on the tombstone. "It's not a new one,'' she said, feeling the contours in the carved letters. "But that's about all I can tell. The flowers are fairly fresh, though.''

"We can ask Doc who Francesca is—was,'' Judith said, as Renie awkwardly stood up. "We could ask anybody on Chavez, for that matter. A cemetery is hardly a secret.''

"The Carrs wouldn't know, probably,'' Renie pointed out as the cousins walked back down the limestone path. "They just moved here in the spring.''

"True,'' Judith allowed. "But the rest of them would.'' At the entrance, Judith turned to admire the setting and the temple one last time. "It's a nice idea, having a graveyard just for those people who've lived—and died—on the island.''

"Right, really nice, really cute.'' Renie shot Judith an ironic look.

"Well, it is,'' Judith declared, now moving briskly down the trail. "It enhances the sense of community.''

Renie snorted. "I don't see these people being very chummy. The Danfields seem to keep to themselves, Rafe does his job, then takes off in his boat or tucks himself away in his hidey-hole, Mrs. Carr is goofy, and old Elrod would just as soon use his trigger finger to plug one of his neighbors as offer a helping hand. Only Doc and Cilla seem normal.''

Judith, however, wasn't inclined to take such a dim view of human nature. "Jeanne mentioned in her letter that everyone had been very kind after Duane died. It's just that we're strangers.''

"It's just that they're strange, if you ask me," Renie retorted.

The cousins had reached the fork where the main trail kept going straight ahead. Despite careful maintenance, the part of the track closest to the lake was quite marshy. Judith and Renie had to proceed gingerly to keep from getting stuck in the mud.

"It might be easier to walk in the grasses," Judith remarked, going off the trail. "My Keds are getting soaked."

"My sandals are about ruined," Renie admitted, following her cousin. "It's a good thing I brought five pair."

But after only a few steps, Judith suddenly sank up to her calves. "Damn!" she cried. "It must be a gopher hole!"

Grabbing Judith's arm, Renie tried to pull her cousin out of the depression, but Judith felt herself sinking farther into the mire. Struggling to get a firmer foothold, Renie braced her weight on her heels and tugged harder. Judith heard a sucking noise somewhere in the vicinity of her feet, then lunged upward. Renie pulled so hard that she fell over on her back. With another slurping sound, Judith bounded out of the hole and fell on top of Renie.

"Oooof!" cried Renie. "Move! You're smashing me!"

Judith tumbled over onto the grass. "My Keds are gone. They came off in the mud." She gazed wistfully in the direction of the hole from which she'd just been liberated.

"Forget the Keds. They're probably ruined anyway." Breathing hard, Renie sat up and surveyed her soiled clothing. "Damn! I'm a mess!"

Judith was eyeing her mud-covered feet. "I paid twenty bucks for those Keds," she grumbled.

"So what? I paid a hundred and twenty for these." She pointed to her sandals which had suffered mightily on the excursion.

Judith was now standing up, trying to wipe off her bare feet. "That was no gopher hole. It's too big and too deep."

Renie had twisted around in an attempt to check out the seat of her slacks. They were covered with mud and grass stains. "It's probably an otter burrow. Or maybe a muskrat house. Be thankful you didn't get your toes bitten off."

"I guess we found out why we should keep to the path," Judith said ruefully, as she shook clumps of wet earth from her green pants. "Unless you know the route, you stick to what you can see. Aha!" What Judith could see next to the deep hole were footprints in the muddy trail. There were at least a dozen of them, smudged and indistinct, but footprints nonetheless. "They're only on this part of the path for a couple of yards. As if," Judith said excitedly, "the person who walked this trail knew where to avoid stepping in a hole. What do you think?"

Renie yawned. "I think I want to get back to the house so I can change. Of course whoever walked here knew the route. *We're* the only pair of dunces on this island who don't know it. Except maybe the Estacadas. So what?"

Her enthusiasm dampened by Renie's remarks, Judith resumed walking more slowly. The trail dried out almost immediately as they moved away from Eagle Lake and found themselves once again in the forest.

"I'm just wondering if whoever made those footprints down at Salmon Gap also made the ones on this trail," Judith countered, though there was an apologetic note in her voice.

Renie sighed. "Give it up, coz. Stacie and Rob may have gone hiking yesterday. They probably combed the island, just like we're doing now. There isn't that much ground to cover. Or maybe it was whoever put those mums on Francesca Whoozit's grave. It might have been the person who tends the cemetery."

Judith wouldn't admit out loud that Renie was probably right. They walked for some time in silence, trying to ignore their damp and dirty state. The fog had completely dissipated, and the blue sky was studded with fluffy white clouds. It was only when they came out by the cabins that Judith spoke again:

"At least we didn't get lost. But how do you get to Rafe's place? Or to the helicopter pad?"

Renie put a firm hand on Judith's wrist. "Call AAA. I can already feel the damp seeping into my bones."

But before they could cross the flagstone walk, June Hennessy appeared from around the corner of her cabin. "Yoo-hoo!" she called. "Any news?"

Judith turned, shielding her eyes from the sun. "Not really. We've been out for a couple of hours. Maybe there's a message from the sheriff on our machine."

Drawing closer, Miss Hennessy stared at the cousins. "My! What happened? You've soiled yourselves."

With an abject glance at her wet, muddy clothes, Judith nodded. "I'm afraid so. I fell in a hole by the little cemetery at Eagle Lake."

Miss Hennessy shook her head. "That's a shame. You weren't injured, I trust?"

"Only some pulled muscles from trying to get out," Judith replied.

"I'm flatter than I used to be," Renie put in.

Judith ignored her cousin. "We'd better head back to the house. I really don't expect to hear anything until this afternoon."

Miss Hennessy nodded in her brisk manner. "Government employees move even more slowly in the Santa Lucias than in the city. Of course their idea of crime is litter. Thank heavens!" she added with a burst of appreciation. "Such a relief to live where you don't have to worry about sex fiends and other miscreants."

Fleetingly, Judith tried to recall the last time she'd worried about sex fiends. Living in the heart of the city, she probably should worry about them occasionally. Maybe being married to a policeman had made her careless.

"I don't suppose," Judith said in a casual manner, "that you ever met Mr. Hodge on any of your previous visits to Chavez Island?"

Miss Hennessy looked aghast. "Good heavens! No! Has he been here before?"

"I think so," Judith answered, unable to conceal the lack of certitude in her voice. "He didn't exactly say as much, but he seemed familiar with the locale."

"Perhaps," Miss Hennessy allowed, now wearing a prim expression that suited her plain white blouse, navy blue slacks, and matching cardigan. An antique cameo brooch at her throat was the only concession to adornment. The contrast between the disheveled cousins and their tidy guest made Judith squirm. "Mr. Hodge must have known Mr. St. Jacques," Miss Hennessy asserted, making Judith momentarily forget about appearances. "They wouldn't have spoken in such a way if they weren't acquainted with one another." Miss Hennessy sniffed with disapproval.

Judith was confused. "When was that? That Mr. Hodge and Mr. St. Jacques . . . spoke?"

"Oh, dear . . ." Miss Hennessy appeared to reflect. "I'm not certain. Late afternoon? On Chavez, I ignore the clock. It's my master the rest of the year."

Apparently, Renie was also bewildered. "Wait—are you saying that Rafe and Burrell had an argument yesterday?"

Miss Hennessy arched her gray eyebrows. "I abhor gossip. I'd call it a heated exchange. I happened to be sitting on the veranda reading a most fascinating biography of Mary Lyon, the founder of Mount Holyoke College. Such a marvelous woman and such a daring educator! I couldn't help but overhear. Mr. Hodge had a very loud voice, and the tenor of their conversation distracted me."

Judith's forehead furrowed. The previous evening, Rafe had implied that he'd had nothing to do with H. Burrell Hodge after bringing him to Chavez Island. Perhaps Judith hadn't understood Rafe correctly.

"You're sure it was Rafe St. Jacques?" Judith asked, a bit diffidently. "Did you actually see him?"

"I did not," Miss Hennessy replied. "I went inside. I'd reached a most exciting chapter in my book, about Mary Lyon attending Amherst. I was *agog*."

"Amherst," murmured Renie. "Wow."

Judith hoped that Miss Hennessy didn't realize Renie

was being facetious. "You didn't ... um ..." Judith sought for a tactful way to ask her next question. She didn't want Miss Hennessy to think she was prying. "They weren't arguing about the amenities or anything like that, were they?"

Miss Hennessy looked repelled. "I think not. I tried very hard to disregard their conversation. But it seemed to revolve around ferns."

"Ferns?" Judith blinked. "They were arguing about *ferns*?"

Miss Hennessy nodded gravely. "Mr. St. Jacques was all for them. Mr. Hodge was definitely against them. That's when I retired to my cabin."

"Well, certainly!" Renie said in a low voice.

"*Ferns*," Judith repeated in a baffled tone. She thought for a moment, then gave Miss Hennessy an off-center smile. "Sometimes people can be very odd. I'm glad Mr. Hodge wasn't complaining about his stay. Thank you, Miss Hennessy. We'll let you know when we have any news."

Miss Hennessy nodded abruptly, then marched off in the direction of her cabin. Judith and Renie resumed their route back to the house.

"Why," Judith asked after they were out of hearing distance, "would anybody quarrel over ferns?"

"The environment," Renie replied, looking just a bit smug. "Rafe is for it, Burrell was against it. Ferns are a hot topic only in that context."

Judith stared at her cousin. "You may be right," she said, vaguely surprised by Renie's acuity.

Renie gave a little shrug as the cousins came out into the open area by the rear of the Barber house. "Of course I'm right. What else, unless you're talking about floral arrangements?"

"It makes sense," Judith agreed. "What doesn't is that Rafe would have had to make a special trip to call on Burrell. Why would he do that if he didn't know anything about the man?"

" 'H. Burrell Hodge'," Renie intoned. " 'The Man Nobody Wants to Know.' Including me,'' she added ruefully. "I wish I'd never met him.''

Judith wished the same thing when she entered the back door, looked through the front windows, and saw Deputy Lulu McLean sitting in the lawn swing on the deck. "Oh, dear,'' breathed Judith, going to the front door, "there must be hot news, or Lulu wouldn't have come all the way to Chavez Cove.''

Lulu, however, wasn't alone. Seated on the step below the swing was Rafe St. Jacques. The pair appeared to be in deep conversation when Judith came out onto the deck.

"Well!'' said McLean, getting up with surprising grace for a woman of her size. In the full light of day, the deputy's color seemed heightened and the tendrils of red hair that peeked out from under her regulation hat shimmered in the sun. "You're back! We wondered what had happened to you.'' Her eyes raked the cousins' unkempt state. "Nothing good, it looks like to me.''

"We were playing Lewis and Clark,'' Renie said, as she joined Judith on the deck. "My cousin is Lewis, and I'm Clark. Sacajawea went out for cigarettes. What's up?''

Ignoring Renie's flippancy, McLean assumed a stern air. "We've got a homicide on our hands. H. Burrell Hodge was killed by a blow to the head with a blunt instrument.''

Renie swallowed hard. "How do you define 'blunt instrument'?'' Her voice came out in a squeak.

McLean literally looked down at Renie. "Something hard, heavy, substantial. A baseball bat, a hammer, a two-by-four. Why? Have you seen anything suspicious around here?''

None too deftly, Judith stepped in front of Renie. "We wouldn't know what to look for,'' Judith said. "Your definition has wide parameters.''

"Early days,'' McLean replied, "as they say in detective fiction. We didn't expect to have the autopsy results so soon, but things slow down this time of year. The coroner doesn't have to spend so much time patching up accident-prone tourists. But we've narrowed the field because of the way Hodge's skull was smashed. It was something about two inches wide, maybe circular or oval, and—as you can guess—very solid.''

Judith had seated herself on one of the benches. The description of the weapon didn't suggest anything specific. ''Are you in charge of the investigation?'' Judith inquired of McLean.

''I sure am,'' the deputy replied, with a toss of her head. ''I've got a couple of men going over Hodge's cabin. We'll give back his key when we're good and ready.'' She glanced at Rafe, who had stood up and was leaning against the rail of the deck. ''You know I mean business, don't you, big fella?''

Rafe's smile conveyed a touch of mockery. ''That's right. I'm confident you'll catch the culprit.''

McLean beamed at Rafe. ''You got that right, kiddo. Now let's get on with it.'' She swerved around, her hazel eyes fixed on Renie. ''You and I are going to have a little talk, Short Stuff. Tell me all about last night, starting with, say, six o'clock.''

''Six o'clock?'' Renie repeated in a faint voice. ''Was I there?''

''Don't get smart with me,'' McLean snapped, taking a menacing step toward Renie. ''You tell me what happened after H. Burrell Hodge arrived at this house around six.''

Judith could see from Renie's stormy expression that her cousin was at war with herself. But after a long moment, she appeared to give in. Indeed, Judith realized that her cousin was wearing her boardroom face, which was usually reserved for graphic-design presentations to CEOs and other corporate nabobs.

''Burrell barged in here just as we were about to eat,'' she began, her voice dropping a notch as she sat down on the bench next to Judith. ''He had a fixed idea that my cousin served dinner to guests. We'd tried to tell him otherwise, but he wouldn't listen.''

''I left a note at his cabin,'' Judith put in, and received a warning glance from McLean for her efforts.

Renie, however, darted a grateful look at Judith before resuming her narrative. "Burrell was overbearing, demanding, and rude. He had the nerve to upbraid us because we were having a cocktail."

McLean had moved next to Rafe at the rail. "You were *drinking*?" the deputy inquired in an insinuating tone.

Judith couldn't hold her tongue. "We'd had just one drink," she put in. "I made us each a refill, but Mrs. Jones said she'd rather eat."

"Butt out," McLean admonished Judith. "You've already been interrogated." She turned back to Renie. "Go on."

Renie's round face was puckered in concentration. "Burrell refused to leave. He became insulting. It was obvious that he didn't like women. He indicated that he considered them inferior." Judith caught the sly glimmer in her cousin's eyes. "Naturally, I was enraged."

"Naturally," McLean agreed, her broad face suddenly betraying a jot of sympathy. "So what happened next?" The deputy folded her arms across her jutting bosom and once again became the soul of officialdom.

"I blew my stack." Renie clasped and unclasped her hands. "I conked him with a plate. *On top of his head.*" She jutted her chin out and threw McLean a defiant look. "It didn't knock him out, it didn't kill him, and don't ever call me *Short Stuff* again!"

The merest flicker of respect showed in McLean's expression. "Okay, I won't. Keep talking. How did Hodge react after you delivered the blow?"

Renie winced at the terminology. "He was furious. He threatened to sue. Finally, he left."

"And?" McLean prodded.

As Renie hesitated, Judith again leaped into the fray: "At least a couple of minutes went by. Then we heard . . ."

"Belt up!" McLean roared, shaking a fist at Judith. "Do you want to get arrested for interfering with a police investigation?"

Judith shrank back onto the bench. She was just a little

ashamed of herself, imagining how Joe would react to interruptions from a witness.

Renie was fingering her upper lip. "You know, it's odd—I'm not exactly sure what happened next. We heard a thump and a cry—or maybe it was the other way around." Renie couldn't resist giving Judith a look that seemed to ask for help.

McLean said nothing. She now had one foot planted on an empty bench and was resting her elbows on her knee.

Apparently, it finally dawned on Renie that the deputy expected her to continue without prompting. "When we heard the noises—in whichever order they occurred—Mrs. Flynn and I raced out to the back porch. We saw Burrell lying at the bottom of the stairs. We thought he'd fallen. The steps are very long and very steep. Mrs. Flynn went down."

For a moment, the only sounds came from the chattering bluejays and the wind in the trees. Then McLean nodded once. "That's when Mrs. Flynn called 911, I assume?"

Judith started to open her mouth, thought better of it, and bit her lip. "Right," said Renie. "Then she called Doc Wicker."

"You discovered the body when?" McLean asked.

Again, Renie considered. "I'm not sure. Six-fifteen, maybe? We came in from the deck a little after six. Burrell arrived just a few minutes later. He bellowed and blustered for—what?" Again, she darted a glance at Judith. "Five minutes? Maybe not that long. I really don't know."

Without another word, McLean straightened up, squared her broad shoulders, and marched into the house. Judith rose from the bench and peered through the window to see what the deputy was doing. For the first time in a quarter of an hour, Rafe spoke.

"I suspect Lulu is checking the crime scene. This is her first chance to see it in full daylight. Just before the two of you got back here, she said she wanted to have a good look."

Judith was pacing back and forth in front of the windows.

"I can hardly believe Burrell was murdered. What will Jeanne Barber think?"

"She's bound to be upset," Rafe said with a frown. "This has been a bad summer for Jeanne."

"It's not so hot for me, either," Judith said grimly. "I feel responsible."

"It's not your fault," Rafe responded, then rested his dark-eyed gaze on Judith. "At least I assume it's not."

Renie had kept a lid on her temper long enough. "What's *that* supposed to mean?" she demanded.

Rafe gave a careless shrug. "Look, I'm unofficially in charge of security for the island. I feel some responsibility, too. But let's face facts—the number of suspects is limited." His cool gaze took in both cousins.

"Not necessarily," Judith countered. "Why couldn't someone we don't know about have come onto the island?" She waved a hand in the direction of the water where a dozen sailboats glided and dipped in the wind. "There are boats everywhere. If not here, they could dock at the Danfields, at Salmon Gap, at *your* place." Judith shot Rafe a meaningful look.

"Touché," he said lightly. "But no one did. I would have seen them."

"You wouldn't have seen anyone coming into Salmon Gap," Judith retorted. "And I believe someone did, probably about the time that Burrell was killed."

Rafe's eyes narrowed. "What makes you think that?"

"High tide was around six last night, which means the best time to safely navigate the waters into Salmon Gap would have been then," Judith explained, now sounding reasonable and calm. "I realize that an experienced sailor like you could probably manage under almost any conditions except maybe a minus tide. But as you told the Estacadas, it's very tricky when you don't know the local hazards."

"So?" Rafe appeared highly amused.

"We saw footprints this morning at Salmon Gap and on the trail by Eagle Lake," Judith went on doggedly. "They were fairly fresh. We think someone tied up at Salmon Gap, walked the length of the island, and—well, I leave the rest up to you.''

To Judith's disappointment, Rafe appeared neither impressed nor dismayed. ''It's possible, I suppose,'' he said in a casual voice, then broke into a grin. ''You've done some sleuthing, it seems.''

Judith felt the color rise in her cheeks. ''Under the circumstances, it's the least I can do. As I said, I feel responsible.''

Before Rafe could reply, Lulu McLean returned to the deck. She gestured at Rafe. ''Come on down and take a look. I want to see what you think.''

With his customary pantherlike grace, Rafe followed the deputy through the house. Judith grabbed Renie's arm.

''Let's see what they're looking at,'' she whispered.

The cousins hurriedly tiptoed to the back entrance. Renie remained behind the screen door, but Judith quietly slipped onto the porch and concealed herself on the love seat in the alcove. She saw McLean and Rafe at the bottom of the stairs, pawing at the tall, thick shrubbery which grew next to the house.

''Somebody *could* have hidden in there,'' McLean said. ''Check out the ground. Some of those flowers and plants look as if they've been trampled.''

Rafe rustled about in the rhododendrons. ''You're right. I wonder if you could get a footprint. Unfortunately, the Saint-John's-wort covers most of the ground.''

''I combed that area pretty well just now,'' McLean replied. ''Except for the trampling, I didn't see any other evidence.''

Rafe emerged from the bushes, brushing leaves from his dark hair. ''No cigarette butts, notepaper, lipstick-marked cocktail napkins?'' Though his back was turned and Judith couldn't see his face, his voice conveyed amusement. ''Come on, Lulu, you're slipping.'' To Judith's surprise, he reached out and playfully cuffed McLean's cheek.

''I don't expect to have this case handed to me on a silver

platter," she huffed. "It's my first time as primary on a homicide, after all." She poked Rafe in the chest. "You'd better not be mixed up in it, kiddo. I'd hate like hell to have to haul you in."

"Would you?" Rafe was now standing very close to McLean. With her regulation hat, she was almost as tall as he was. Judith's eyes widened as Rafe tipped up the brim of the hat and lightly brushed her lips with his. He said something low, which Judith couldn't hear. Fearing discovery, she skittered out of the alcove and dashed into the house, almost knocking Renie over in her haste.

"What's with them?" Renie inquired. "Collusion?"

Judith shook herself. "More like a collision—irresistible force meets immovable object. Or something like that. My, my." Judith now began to pace the living room.

"Hadn't you better try to track down Jeanne?" Renie had flopped onto the couch.

Judith glanced at her watch. "It's going on for noon. I'll try calling her daughter again." She started for the phone in the kitchen, then snapped her fingers. "Shoot! I forgot to check the answering machine for messages."

To Judith's relief, Marcia Barber Andersen had called at 10:08. In a girlish voice, she informed Judith of the number where her mother could be reached in Palm Desert, adding that Jeanne should only be disturbed in the event of a serious emergency.

"I think this qualifies," Judith said. But before she could punch in the spa's number, McLean and Rafe returned from outside.

"I'm heading out now," McLean announced, all but swaggering through the kitchen. "Rafe brought me over in his cruiser." The deputy smirked just a little. "By the way, I assume neither of you plan to leave Chavez soon."

"We can't," Judith blurted. "We're stuck for at least a week."

McLean nodded abruptly. "Good. Don't get any ideas about making an early exit. I'll be in touch. Come on, Rafe, let's head for Laurel Harbor."

When Rafe and McLean had disappeared down the stairs to the cove, Judith dialed the Palm Springs spa. She was transferred five times before Jeanne came on the line.

"Judith! Is something wrong? Do you have a question? What broke?"

Judith grimaced into the phone. "We've had a problem, Jeanne. Remember Mr. Hodge?"

"The late Mr. Hodge," Renie murmured, opening the refrigerator.

"H. Burrell Hodge?" Jeanne's voice had turned suspicious. "What about him?"

"He's sort of . . . dead," Judith said, avoiding Renie's bemused gaze. "Last night—early evening, actually—he . . . ah . . . um . . . got killed."

"What?" The word seemed ripped out of Jeanne's throat. "Judith, is this a joke? You always had such a wonderful sense of humor. I remember in Mr. Quimbly's botany class, you once brought in a plant that your mother found in the yard and it turned out to be poison ivy and we all ended up with . . ."

"No, Jeanne, this is no joke," Judith broke in, gaining momentum from Jeanne's aggravating digression. "Mr. Hodge was killed when someone hit him in the head. It wasn't an accident, according to the sheriff's department. It was a premeditated homicide."

The silence at the other end of the line indicated that Jeanne Barber was now taking Judith seriously. "Oh, good grief!" she finally exclaimed. "I can hardly believe it!"

"It's true," Judith averred. "Lulu McLean is in charge, and she seems capable. But I must ask you—as she may later on—if you have any idea who might have wanted Mr. Hodge dead."

This time the silence went on much longer. "No, of course not. How could I? I'd never met the man before in my life."

The insistent note in Jeanne's voice disturbed Judith, but she wasn't sure why. "Jeanne," Judith began somewhat wearily, "I've got a million things to ask you about what

I should do regarding insurance and the business aspects of what happened. But I have to say this—I'm convinced that H. Burrell Hodge had been to Chavez Island before yesterday. Please don't try to lead me down the garden path. I'm on the spot here, and I'm trying to do what's best for you—and for me. I'd appreciate your candor.''

"About what?'' Jeanne now sounded cross. ''Don't bother yourself. I can call my insurance company and my attorney and whomever else I need to contact from here. All I expect from you is to take care of the guests who are still alive. They *are* still alive, aren't they?'' The words dripped with acrimony.

"Certainly they are,'' Judith snapped. ''You might at least tell me why Mr. Hodge came to Chavez.''

"I've no idea.'' There was a pause, and then the frost melted slightly in Jeanne's voice: ''He didn't tell me, because I never spoke with him. Someone else made the reservation. A woman, as I recall. It was about a month ago, right after Duane died. I wasn't exactly at my best. Excuse me, Judith, I must make those phone calls. Don't call me— I'll call you.''

"Wait!'' Judith cried into the phone. ''Are you sure you know nothing about why Mr. Hodge would have called on Bates Danfield?''

An impatient noise erupted at the other end of the line. ''I do not.'' Again, there was a pause. ''I swear, Judith, on my late husband's soul, *I never heard of H. Burrell Hodge until last month*. Now do you believe me?''

Judith said she did. She had no choice.

Jeanne hung up.

NINE

JUDITH WAS ANGRY with herself. By the time the cousins had changed clothes, started the washer, and finished lunching on tuna-salad sandwiches, Renie was angry with Judith, too.

"Cut it out, coz," she ordered. "You're *not* losing your mind. You've had too many things to think about in the last twenty-four hours, that's all."

"But it was the perfect opening to ask Rafe about his argument with H. Burrell Hodge," Judith contended for the fifth time in the !ast hour. "Lulu McLean was outside, Rafe and I were talking about Burrell, and Rafe was insinuating that *we* might be involved in the crime. That's when I should have thrown his lie back in his face."

"You'll have another chance," Renie said in a reasonable voice as she closed the dishwasher and flipped the switch. "We aren't going anywhere for a while, remember?"

Judith made a face. "I can remember that part—but not much else. I wonder if I should call Mother?"

It was Renie's turn to make a face. "If you do, then I'll feel obligated to call *my* mother. I was hoping to put that off until tomorrow."

"How," Judith asked with a lift of her eyebrows,

"did you manage to forestall her so long?" Aunt Deb expected her only daughter to check in at regular intervals, approximately four hours apart, like a medical dosage.

Renie sighed as she climbed back onto one of the counter stools. "I told her the communications facilities were very primitive. It's not exactly a lie. In fact, it's sort of like one of your famous fibs. You know—skewed."

Judith did know. "I should have told a bigger one—like we were totally incommunicado." Reluctantly, she dialed her mother's number in the converted toolshed. Since Gertrude wasn't inclined to pick up the receiver immediately, the phone rang eleven times before Judith started to fret. "I hope she hasn't fallen . . . Maybe Carl and Arlene asked her over to lunch . . . She could be in the bathroom . . . It's not impossible that she's being ornery and not answering . . ." On the nineteenth ring, Judith hung up. "Damn— it always worries me when I can't get hold of her. I wonder if I should call Arlene."

"Try the old girl again in a few minutes," Renie suggested. "I'll call my mother now and get it over with."

Aunt Deb, who adored the telephone as much as her sister-in-law loathed it, answered before the first ring had been completed. Renie reached for her glass of Pepsi and settled in for the long haul:

"Yes, we're fine, Mom . . . No, it's too warm to wear a coat. Or mittens . . . Yes, it's a nice house . . . Yes, there's a roof. And doors. With locks. Windows, too . . . Well, when I said 'primitive,' I meant the telephone system, not the house itself . . . No, it's not at all like the family cabin . . . Yes, a real indoor toilet, two, in fact . . . Yes, running water and electricity and a dishwasher and a TV and a VCR and a CD player and a Jacuzzi . . . What? It's a bathtub, with jets that sort of massage you while you're . . . Yes, you could call it 'The Lap of Luxury,' I suppose . . . Yes, we're very lucky . . . Yes, you might say 'spoiled' . . ." Renie rolled her eyes at Judith. "No, I'm not going anywhere by myself . . . No, I won't talk to strangers . . . No, I don't have a cold—it's the transmission on this phone. I told you it wasn't . . . Yes, as a matter of fact, she just tried to call Aunt Gertrude . . .'' Renie mouthed something that Judith couldn't understand. ''Substituting for Sophie O'Dell? Yes, I know Aunt Gertrude would play cards even if she were completely paralyzed and on life support . . . Yes, I realize bridge is more important to her than God our Father . . . No, I don't know if God plays bridge . . . Yes, if He doesn't, she *will* be disappointed when she finally gets there . . . You know, they may not have *telephones* in heaven, either . . . Well, of course I don't know it for a *fact* . . . Of course I appreciate what a comfort the phone was to you when I was little and sickly and you were alone while Dad was off to sea and you couldn't drive and Aunt Ellen would have to spend the night to keep you company . . . Yes, I did puke a lot . . . Yes, I'd turn positively green . . . Yes, I remember Dr. Llewellyn's house calls . . . Yes, he couldn't have repeatedly saved my life unless you'd been able to call him on the phone . . .''

Renie had slumped onto the counter, her Pepsi drained along with her endurance. Judith, now assured that her mother was out somewhere happily engaged in a marathon of bridge, was studying the refrigerator for dinner possibilities. Steak appealed to her. She knew Renie wouldn't turn it down.

Judith was removing two thick New York cuts from the freezer when someone knocked at the front door. She could see an unfamiliar figure through the glass panes, a dark-complexioned young man with a shock of jet-black hair that stood almost straight up on top of his head.

''Yes?'' Judith said, opening the door just enough so that she could be heard.

''Hallo?'' The young man flashed a big, engaging smile. ''I am Mansur, Abu Hamid Mansur.'' He bowed.

''Ah . . .'' Judith glanced at Renie over her shoulder. But Renie was now facedown on the counter, still listening to Aunt Deb. ''How can I help you, Mr. . . . Mansur?''

''You may be calling me Abu,'' the young man replied, still beaming. Except for his hair standing on end, he wasn't quite as tall as Judith, and was on the lean side, with marked cheekbones accentuating limpid dark eyes. "You may be answering questions. And so forth."

"About what?" Judith wondered if the young foreigner could somehow be attached to the sheriff's office.

"About allegedly dead man." The grin disappeared and Abu inclined his head, apparently indicating respect for mortality. "He die here, precise?"

"I'm sorry," Judith said, still holding the door firmly in place. "I can't discuss the matter with strangers."

Abu shook his head. "Not strange. I of Laurel Harbor. I *Merchant*."

"I can't buy anything," Judith asserted. "Excuse me, I must get back to . . . work."

"I, too. Tell about dead man. You see him die?" Abu seemed energized by the concept.

Judith's patience was running out. "If you want to discuss this, contact Deputy McLean at Laurel Harbor. If you're a local merchant, you probably know her. Have a nice . . ."

Somehow, Abu had managed to get his foot inside the screen door. "No, no. I not selling today, I reporting. And so forth." He dug inside his well-cut corduroy slacks and brought out a business card. "I journalist. I press. I writer-man."

Judith gaped at the card. Sure enough, the printing read, "Abu Hamid Mansur, staff reporter, *Laurel Harbor Merchant*, a weekly newspaper serving the Santa Lucia Islands since 1910."

"So it's come to this," Judith murmured. "I knew the written word was going out of style."

"Style?" echoed Abu. "You know AP style? My editor say, 'Memorize, Abu, study, learn.' I try. I go to university. And so forth." The limpid eyes took on a pitiable cast.

"Come in," Judith relented, opening the door just as Renie finally hung up. "Meet Abu, coz. He's a reporter from Laurel Harbor."

"Hi, Abu," Renie said in a faint voice. She sat up, waving feebly. "Do you have a mother?"

Abu beamed at Renie. "Yes, she in Babol."

Looking dazed, Renie nodded. "My mother babbles, too."

"No, no." Abu wore an expression of dismay. "Babol, my home, it is near Caspian Sea."

"Really?" Renie was wiggling both index fingers in her ears, as if to clear them of her mother's lingering voice. "That's nice. You must not have to call her often. It's international long-distance. That's very expensive. Lucky you." Renie wandered out of the kitchen.

"Look," Judith said to Abu, "I really can't tell you much. I'm not the owner here."

Abu nodded. "Yes, I am knowing that. Mrs. Barber is trading house and cabins. And so forth. She gone to oasis?"

Despite Abu's fractured English, Judith gathered that he not only knew Jeanne, but was familiar with her whereabouts. "That's right," Judith said, suddenly struck by a brainstorm. "In fact, I talked with her only an hour or so ago. I can give you her number in California. It would be much better if you asked her all the questions."

Abu, however, looked dubious. "But she not here when dead man die. Already one story lost. Now need new story. *Merchant* print tomorrow. Must have story before go to other job."

"Doing what?" Judith asked as she wrote the spa's number on a piece of notepaper.

Abu flashed his big grin. "Drive boat between islands. Get tips sometime. No tips on *Merchant*. I water-taxi man."

"That figures," Judith said, again under her breath. She handed Abu the notepaper and put a hand on his slim shoulder. "I don't know anything about the murder. I'd never been to Chavez Island until yesterday. Honestly, Abu. I didn't see it happen. Call Mrs. Barber. Have you talked to Deputy McLean?"

Abu nodded. "Within the hour. She come from here to there. She say *murder*." The young man gave Judith a dark look. "Murder better story than hospital. But hospital good enough before murder."

Judith didn't try to follow Abu's logic—or language. Shepherding him to the front door, she smiled encouragement. "I'm sure you'll get a terrific story out of this. I understand there aren't very many murders in the Santa Lucias."

"That is truth," Abu replied, his expression uncertain as he was steered onto the deck. "Not many hospitals, too. Not for hashish. And so forth." At the top of the stairs that led down to the path, Abu turned. "You catch murderer, you tell *Merchant*?"

Judith couldn't help but smile, though she wasn't sure why. In the past, catching killers hadn't been a laughing matter for her. "Sure. You'll be the first to hear, Abu."

His face brightened. "Very fine. I write big story, be on talking TV shows, win Mr. Joseph Pulitzer's prize. And so forth. Bye-bye." Abu fairly bounced along the path that led to the cove.

Judith could see a small launch tied to the dock. No doubt Abu covered his beat by boat. It occurred to Judith that for all the tranquillity and beauty, life on the islands must be arduous. But, she reflected as she went back inside the house, it wasn't always tranquil. She and Renie had been on Chavez for only a little more than twenty-four hours. Almost all of them had been disruptive and disturbing.

Nor was there any respite in sight. When Judith went into the living room, she saw Renie letting in a middle-aged woman who looked oddly familiar. The visitor wore a crisp beige linen suit, three-inch sling-back pumps, and a soft black silk blouse. Her pale blond hair was done up in a neat French roll, and she carried a black shoulder bag that matched her shoes. Cosmetics had been liberally, if tastefully, applied to cover wrinkles and take the edge off of sharp features.

"This is Mrs. Carr," Renie said, giving Judith a puckish look.

"Rowena Carr," the woman said, holding out a gracious hand. "I don't believe we've met."

They had, of course, as Judith realized. She could hardly believe that this carefully groomed woman was the same person as the wild-eyed creature Judith and Renie had encountered on their morning walk. On the other hand, Rowena Carr apparently didn't recall meeting the cousins. Judith decided not to enlighten their guest.

"Do sit down," Judith urged, indicating the leather armchair that was positioned in front of the small grotto separating the living room from the stairs to the loft. "May I offer tea? Or a soda?"

"No, thank you," Mrs. Carr said with a small smile. "I can't stay. I came to offer my condolences. Doc Wicker told me about the tragedy you had here last night. My daughter and I feel very sorry for both of you. It's so difficult taking on someone else's responsibilities, and then having things go wrong."

"It's been tough," Judith admitted. "I talked to Jeanne this morning. Naturally, she's upset."

"Naturally." Rowena Carr's face was impassive. "By the way, I must presume upon you to ask a favor."

Judith tipped her head to one side, signaling encouragement. "Yes?"

Mrs. Carr opened her shoulder bag, took out a pair of black kidskin gloves, and slowly began to put them on her thin hands. She didn't speak again until each of her fingers had worked their way into the tight-fitting gloves.

"If you should learn that Cilla—my daughter—has gone down to see Mr. St. Jacques, would you please telephone me? She's not allowed to keep company with him." Mrs. Carr gave Judith a stern, direct look. "Jeanne Barber is always very reliable about passing on information to me."

"Oh." Judith exchanged a swift, puzzled glance with Renie. "Okay, we'll do our best. But frankly, I don't know how to get to Mr. St. Jacques's place."

Mrs. Carr's nostrils flared ever so slightly. "It's intentionally well concealed. The path goes off behind a large cedar stump next to the Eagle Lake trailhead.''

Judith tried to recall the stump. ''You mean by the guest cabins?''

''That's right.'' Mrs. Carr flexed her gloved fingers. ''The trail is Mr. St. Jacques's little secret. He has a great many of them, I'm afraid. Thank you both. I must be off now.'' She gave each of the cousins a gracious nod. ''Good day.''

Renie followed Mrs. Carr to the back door, waited to see that she reached the bottom of the stairs safely, and then turned to Judith. ''That woman's crazy even when she's sane. What gives?''

''I don't know.'' Judith shook her head in bewilderment. ''At least you were spared most of Abu and his butchered English.''

Renie snorted. ''*You* were spared listening to my mother.''

Judith shrugged. ''I still have to call mine later. How shall we spend the afternoon?''

Renie gazed up into the far reaches of the high ceiling. ''Why don't we just sit here and wait to see who shows up next? It's kind of like a variety show—there's a new act every fifteen minutes.''

''That,'' Judith declared, ''is why I want to get out of here. In fact, I was wondering if Rafe would take us over to Laurel Harbor. It might be fun to explore the town. We didn't get to see much of it when we got off the ferry from the mainland.''

Renie had her back to Judith and was looking out through the big picture window. ''Why not?'' she said after a pause. ''You can grill Rafe while we're out in open water. Maybe he'll throw us overboard. I can't swim, remember?''

Judith ignored Renie's remarks. ''Maybe we could have dinner in Laurel Harbor. The steaks will keep. I'll call Rafe.'' She went back into the kitchen.

But no one answered when Judith punched in Rafe's single-digit number. ''He should be back from transporting Lulu McLean to Laurel Harbor,'' Judith remarked. ''Unless he had to wait for deliveries on the mainland ferry.''

"Say," Renie said, adjusting the blinds as the sun began to hit the front windows, "speaking of deliveries, when do we get mail here?"

"Gee," Judith replied, frowning, "I'll bet we have to pick it up from Doc. Let's go over to the Wicker Basket. Maybe Doc will know where we can find Rafe."

Doc was inside the store, unloading vegetable cans. "Rafe brought these over this afternoon," he said, indicating the vegetables and three other cartons which looked to contain fruit, soup, and pet food.

"Who's got a pet around here?" Renie inquired. "All the animals we've seen have been wild."

"Nobody." Doc was putting the last two soup cans on the shelf. "But Cilla wants a dog. I promised her I'd stock up before she picked one out. I didn't expect a whole case of Meaty Beef. There hasn't been a dog around here since Harry's drowned."

"Harry?" Judith looked puzzled.

Doc's hand seemed a trifle unsteady as he straightened the cans. "That was a long time ago," he said abruptly, keeping his eyes on the vegetables.

Something clicked in Judith's memory. "One of the Danfields mentioned somebody named Harry. He worked here, right? Like . . . what was his name? Tom Lowman?"

"That's right," Renie chimed in. "Tom, Dick, and Harry. You're Dick, aren't you Doc? Hickory-dickory-Doc." She laughed in a self-conscious manner. "Sorry, I couldn't resist. And I haven't been near the brandy jug today. Honest."

Doc finally seemed satisfied with his efforts at facing out the vegetables. He turned slowly and smiled at Renie. "I know that. I'm just trying to figure out what to do with all that dog food, especially if Cilla changes her mind about getting a pet. How can I help you ladies?"

"Two things, actually," Judith said. "We were wondering if Rafe could take us over to Perez Island so we could stroll around Laurel Harbor. I tried to call him, but he was out.''

Doc was using a Swiss Army knife to open the canned fruit carton. ''Rafe's kind of a will-o'-the-wisp. When he's not going between here and Perez, he spends a lot of time just cruising around on that boat of his. It's a fine day—I imagine he's off exploring some of the outer islands. Now that the tourists are mostly gone, he'll have them to himself.''

''Oh.'' Judith sounded disappointed. ''Say, Doc, do you know why Mrs. Carr is opposed to Cilla seeing Rafe?''

Doc made an attempt to smooth his fluffy white hair. ''I told you, Rowena Carr is a bit eccentric. She gets notions about people. In Rafe's case, she probably thinks he's too old and too worldly for Cilla. As the only eligible man under sixty on the island, it would be natural for Cilla to develop a crush on Rafe. He's quite good-looking.''

The explanation seemed plausible to Judith. Yet it struck her as almost too smooth, too pat. Doc began unloading more fruit. Judith had one more question for him.

''We walked over to Salmon Gap and back this morning,'' she began. ''We found the little cemetery. It's lovely. Who's Francesca?''

The can of peaches that Doc had been transferring to an upper shelf fell out of his hand. He kept his back to the cousins as he fumbled around on the floor. ''Damn! It's rolling all over the place . . . Now where did it go . . . ?''

At last, he looked up. ''The Danfields—Bates's parents—established the cemetery around the time of the First World War. Chester Danfield settled on Chavez just before the turn of the century.'' Doc had recovered the peaches and was placing them on the shelf next to the pears. ''Chester's wife refused to move from the city, so he left her. He built a cabin more or less where Stoneyhenge is now and became a bit of a hermit. When he died along about 1917, his wife wouldn't bury him in the family plot. She said that if he wanted to live alone on Chavez, he could be dead alone there, too. Arthur—that would be Bates's father—wanted to bury the old man at sea, but he couldn't get permission. Maybe it had something to do with the war, I don't know. So he established the cemetery and built the temple over his father's grave. I guess he thought his mother would give in and be buried there, too. But Mrs. Danfield made her wishes known that she wanted to be laid to rest in town. She passed away shortly before Arthur married, around 1921, I think.'' Doc finished unloading the fruit cans, then began folding the cardboard box, presumably for recycling. ''Arthur and his wife, Clarice, liked the place so much they decided to build a real house. Stoneyhenge was the result.''

''It's a beautiful place,'' Judith said. ''I gather from talking to Bates that the family has always had money. Investments, of some sort.''

''So I hear,'' Doc responded in a noncommittal manner. ''Whatever it is that Bates does to earn his keep doesn't make very many demands on him. In the twenty-two years I've been here, I've never seen that man put in a day of real work.''

Renie was inspecting a can of smoked oysters. ''You'd think,'' she remarked, hastily putting the can back when she saw the exorbitant price on the bottom, ''Bates would get bored.''

Doc nodded in agreement. ''I would. Esther, too. Oh, once in a while they go away for a few days, but not often and not far. It makes you wonder, doesn't it?''

Judith wasn't sure what Doc meant. ''You mean . . . about their lack of drive? Or involvement? Or . . . ?'' She made a helpless gesture with her hands.

''Those things, yes,'' Doc replied, now opening the dog food box. ''Heck, I'm not sure what I mean. But when I see that handsome house and those wonderful furnishings and how Bates and Esther always look as if they've just stepped out of some magazine ad for a country squire and his lady—well, I have to speculate a little.'' He laughed, sounding vaguely embarrassed. ''I'm probably foolish, imagining things that aren't there. That's easy to do up here on the island, especially in the winter when you can't get out as often and nobody comes around. Too much time alone. Yes, it bothers me once in a while. But,'' he added, with a musing glance at the cousins, ''it never seems to bother Bates and Esther. I have to wonder why.''

Speculating on human nature was one of Judith's favorite pastimes. She took Doc's words seriously and tried to come up with some sort of explanation. Her mind drew a blank.

''I guess,'' she said in apology, ''I don't know them well enough to understand their behavior. They have children. Surely they keep involved with them. Esther mentioned that they might be coming up to the island soon for a visit.''

Doc chuckled, though there was an edge to his voice. ''Esther is always saying they're coming for a visit, but they never do. I haven't seen Eugenia or Elliott in five years. Maybe they sail into the Danfields' dock, and I don't know they're here. That could be. But neither Bates nor Esther ever mention the visits when they come to get—''

Judith snapped her fingers. ''The mail! I almost forgot! That's the real reason we stopped by.''

''Oh, of course.'' Doc went behind the counter and pulled out a Nike shoe box marked ''Barber.'' Apparently, his postal system consisted of keeping the mail in shoe boxes with the individuals' names lettered in black-felt pen. Judith could see a Rockport box bearing Rafe's name, a Timberlands box for Elrod Dobler, and an Adidas box on which the name ''Lowman'' had been crossed out and ''Carr'' had been inked in underneath.

''Two days' worth,'' Doc said, handing Judith two thick rolls of mail which were held together with wide rubber bands. ''Most of it's probably junk. But don't throw any of it away—Jeanne gets a lot of catalogues, and she enjoys going through them. Do you want me to have Rafe call you if I see him in the next hour or two?''

Judith gave Renie a questioning look; Renie shrugged. ''I guess so,'' Judith said to Doc. ''It's not yet two. We'd still have time to spend at Laurel Harbor.''

''Okay,'' Doc said, returning to his dog food. ''By the

way,'' he called to Judith and Renie as they headed for the door, "I hear it's official. We have a murder on our hands.''

Judith turned in the doorway. "You thought so all along, didn't you, Doc?''

Doc nodded solemnly. "My opinion was formed strictly from the physical evidence. Somebody hit Hodge hard enough on the back of the head to fracture the skull and cause internal bleeding. That's not an accident.'' He winked at Renie. "It's not a dinner plate, either.''

"So what's your guess, Doc?'' Judith asked.

"You mean whodunit?'' Doc chuckled again. "I haven't any idea. If I had to take a wild stab, I'd say that somebody with a boat followed Hodge to Chavez, waited around the grounds of the B&B, and clobbered him a good one. How does that sound?''

Judith gave a little nod. "Not bad—for a wild stab.''

"It had to be something like that,'' Doc said in a voice that was intended to be casual but which conveyed a note of desperation. "Nobody on Chavez had any reason to kill him.''

Judith thought it best not to dispute the point. "Let's hope Lulu McLean knows how to do her job. I understand she's never led a homicide investigation before.''

"She'll do just fine,'' Doc said. "Say, I don't suppose you want any dog food?''

Renie leaned across the threshold. "Is it cheaper than your hot dogs?''

Doc smiled at Renie. "Not much. But it *is* Meaty Beef.''

"I'll try it tomorrow,'' Renie said with a little wave.

Judith hoped her cousin was kidding. But maybe not.

"Rats!'' Judith exclaimed as they headed back up the road to the Barber house. "I tell you, I'm slipping! Did you notice how Doc led us down the garden path about the cemetery?''

"I thought it was interesting,'' Renie replied. "A veritable Danfield saga.''

"A veritable diversion, you mean.'' Judith sounded

cross. "Doc never did tell us who Francesca is—*was*. Every time I try to pin one of these islanders down, they go off on some tangent and I don't get any answers. It's aggravating! And what gripes me most is that I get so engrossed that I forget to pursue my original query."

"They're elusive, all right," Renie admitted. "But I'm not sure Doc deliberately misled you. He seemed quite caught up in the Danfield story. It sounds as if he's got some questions of his own. About them, at any rate."

"It's like a conspiracy," Judith grumbled as they trudged along the uneven dirt road. "Evasion, ambiguity, half-truths, maybe untruths—and just plain silence. We're missing something, something big. But what is it?"

Renie was gazing up through the network of vine maples which grew over the road. Some of the leaves had already turned a bright red-orange. "What about that weapon? Circular or oval, about two inches wide. What does that bring to mind?" Renie wondered out loud.

"It's too big to be a hammer," Judith replied. "I was thinking about those tools that Cilla misplaced. Did she mention a crowbar?"

"I don't think so," Renie said. "A hammer, a wrench, a . . . I forget. Was there anything else?"

Judith frowned. "I'm not sure. She's such a whirlwind that it's hard to follow her."

They had come out into the clearing by the house. Rob and Stacie Estacada were sitting on the back steps. Rob looked upset, and Stacie had been crying.

"We want to leave," Rob announced. "We heard that Mr. Hodge was murdered. Can we get the rest of our money back?"

Judith had no idea what Jeanne Barber's policy was when it came to cancellations. Hillside Manor was more than fair, Judith had always thought, allowing refunds if guests canceled before four o'clock in the afternoon. It was now five minutes to two. Given the circumstances, Judith didn't blame the honeymooners for wanting to get as far away as possible from Chavez Island.

"You've already paid through the rest of your scheduled stay?" Judith asked.

Rob nodded. "I put the whole thing on my Visa when we made the reservation. Twelve hundred dollars, plus tax. We should get everything back but last night's stay. That was two hundred. Plus tax," he added after receiving a nudge from his bride.

"I'll run it through," Judith said. She didn't see how Jeanne could refuse to offer a refund. "May I see your card? I'll take it inside and run it through for a credit."

Rob reached into the back pocket of his jeans and pulled out a wallet. Stacie clung to him, her head on his shoulder. "Where will we go now, lovey-buns?" she asked in a small voice.

"Canada, maybe." Rob kissed the top of her head. "We'll call from Laurel Harbor." He kept rummaging through the wallet. "Darn—I don't see my Visa card. Or my MasterCard or my ATM card." He pulled away just enough to look into Stacie's face. "Did you take them, honey-lips?"

"No," she said, somewhat indignant. "I haven't charged a thing. I'm waiting until I get my own cards with my married name. What would I use them for here anyway?"

"I had them on the ferry," Rob insisted, now removing everything from the wallet, including his cash. "Damn! Where could they have gone?" He gave Stacie a helpless look.

"They're probably back in the cabin," she said.

"I never took them out of my wallet. I know I didn't." Rob's forehead wrinkled with concern.

Judith offered the pair a sympathetic smile. "Don't fuss. I can check your credit card number on the original bill. I'll mail you a copy of the refund."

"That's not the point," Rob protested. "Where are my cards?" Now he gave his wife an accusing look. "Stacie, you'd better not be one of those women who swipes her husband's credit cards and buys a lot of stuff and then acts like she didn't do anything wrong! I've had buddies with wives and girlfriends who pull that stunt, and it's not cute!''

Stacie backed away from Rob, her eyes flashing. "You creep! How dare you talk to me like that! Go ahead, go to Canada! I hope you have a great time—by yourself!'' She stormed off down the trail that led to the cabins.

"Jeez!'' Rob's anger was mingled with embarrassment as he turned to Judith and Renie. "I guess I made her mad. Do you think she'll get over it?''

"Probably,'' Judith said, a bit distractedly. The hostile interlude had given her time to think. "Rob, were you and Stacie gone from the cabin late yesterday afternoon?''

Still looking sheepish, Rob considered. "We went for a walk earlier. Then we played some badminton. After that, we had a swim down in the cove by the dock. I guess it was around five when we got back. I fired up the barbecue then, and we . . . ah . . . went inside for a while to wait for the coals to get hot.''

Recalling the state of *dishabille* in which she and Rafe had found the Estacadas, it was obvious to Judith that more than the coals had gotten hot. "Did you see anybody— anybody at all—around the cabins in the afternoon? Besides my cousin and me, I mean.''

Rob's forehead furrowed again. "I don't think so. Why?''

Judith didn't know whether or not she should be candid. Finally, she decided that honesty was the best policy. The Estacadas were leaving, in any event. "Something may have been taken from Mr. Hodge's cabin yesterday. I'm wondering if it's possible that whoever took it also went into your cabin and got hold of your ocredit cards. Did you lock up when you went swimming?''

Rob's face fell. "No. I mean, it seemed so safe here. So isolated—*you* know. And sure, I left my wallet. I wouldn't take it to the beach.''

"That's what I figured,'' Judith said. "If I were you, I'd report those cards as stolen right away. And then I'd apologize to Stacie and promise her a wonderful Canadian honeymoon.''

The suggestions seemed to buoy Rob. "Good idea," he said. "Can I use your phone?"

Judith assured him that he could. She led the way up the stairs with Rob and Renie trailing behind her. Knowing it would take Rob a few minutes to get hold of the credit card companies, Judith and Renie retired to the living room.

"I wonder," Judith mused as she sat down on the sofa next to Renie, "if I should check the mail. There might be some reservation requests that I should tend to." Slipping the rubber band off the first packet, she sorted through four catalogues, three travel brochures, and a letter from the Santa Lucia Chamber of Commerce. The second batch revealed more catalogues, the PUD bill, a real estate flyer, and another letter. It was not, however, addressed to Jeanne Barber, but to H. Burrell Hodge.

Judith's jaw dropped.

TEN

"I DON'T THINK," Renie remarked dryly, "that Burrell will be opening that letter. Go ahead, what difference can it make?"

"It's from Laurel Harbor," Judith said in a curious tone as she noted the postmark. "It was mailed yesterday, in care of Jeanne Barber. The return address is Perez Properties."

Renie flicked her finger at the real-estate flyer that Judith had placed on the coffee table. "That's the same outfit who sent this. But it's only an ad."

With a deep intake of breath, Judith tore the envelope open and extracted the one-page letter. " 'Dear Mr. Hodge,' " she read aloud. " 'We look forward to your arrival in Laurel Harbor on Thursday of this week. In the meantime, we hope you enjoy your stay at Chavez Cove. Ella Stovall, our top agent, is anxious to show you the property in which you've expressed an interest. The smaller parcel is already listed with us, but we are optimistic about your expansion plans. Our office is located two blocks from the ferry terminal, next door to Ferguson's Hardware. If you intend to stay over, we would like to take you to dinner. Also, please let us know if you would like us to find you accommodations. It wasn't clear from your previous correspondence whether or not you already had a reservation in Laurel Harbor or the surrounding area. You may reach me at . . .'' Two telephone numbers followed, one at work, the other at home. The letter was signed Simon Dobler.

''Hunh!'' Judith exclaimed, handing the letter to Renie. ''*Simon* Dobler? He's got to be related to Elrod. It can't be a coincidence. That's not exactly a common name.''

''Call Simon Dobler. Or . . . what's her name?'' Renie scanned the single typed sheet. ''Ella Stovall.''

''I have to wait until Rob gets off the phone,'' Judith said, craning her neck to see if the young man was still at the kitchen counter. ''It looks like he's on hold.''

''So are we,'' Renie said, putting her feet up on the coffee table. ''What do you think? Burrell was involved in real estate?''

Judith chewed on her forefinger. ''I should try to call Adhab again. What if it is a recovery center, the same one Herself is considering? Directory Assistance listed several of them, and now that I think about it, they were all in remote areas—the mountains, the peninsula, I forget where else. Maybe Burrell or his bosses were planning to expand. Maybe,'' Judith went on, her voice climbing with excitement, ''that's why he wanted to see Bates Danfield.''

Renie made a clucking noise with her tongue. ''Then Bates lied. He said Burrell was one of his advisors. At least that's what he implied.''

''Right,'' Judith agreed. ''But I understand why Bates would do that. If he owns most of the island, would he want anybody to know he was thinking of selling off property to a rehab center?'' Suddenly, her eyes grew wide. ''Ah! Now I know what Abu was talking about! Sort of. He said something about a hospital. It was so garbled that I thought he meant he would have had a smaller story if Burrell had been hurt and had had to go to the hospital, but now it was a much bigger article because he'd been killed. But that's not it, I'll bet. I'm guessing he meant there were *two* stories—one about building a recovery center— which he might call a hospital because of his limited En-

glish—and the other, the murder itself. I should have listened more closely.''

Rob Estacada was listening in the doorway between the
kitchen and the living room. "Excuse me," he said as Judith paused to catch her breath. "I'm done. Those were
one-eight-hundred numbers, so there's no charge. It was a
toll-free number to the hotel in Port Royal, too. I made a
reservation at a place a friend recommended. It's supposed
to be really quiet and out-of-the-way. It's called the Clovia.
Do you know it?''

Judith and Renie exchanged horrified looks. Five years
earlier, they had spent a few days at the Clovia, also in
search of peace and relaxation. Instead, they had found a
body in the elevator. But surely, Judith thought, history
couldn't repeat itself. Not for the Estacadas, at any rate.

"The *Clovia*," Judith said, with a lame little laugh. "I
thought you said the . . . *Monrovia*. Yes, it's charming, right
on the bay, near the park. Very nice. You'll love it.''

"I hope so," Rob said uncertainly. "I'd better go have
it out with Stacie. Do you think you could ask the guy with
the cruiser to take us over to Laurel Harbor in about an
hour?''

Judith promised to try. When Rob was gone, the cousins
went into the kitchen. Her first call was to Rafe. He still
didn't answer. She dialed Perez Properties next. A woman
answered, identifying herself as Ella Stovall.

Judith went through a rather elaborate—but truthful—
explanation of who she was and why she was calling. "You
have heard about Mr. Hodge's death, I assume?" she con-
cluded.

Ella, who sounded relentlessly good-natured, said she
had. "A real shock. We don't have murders in the Santa
Lucias. Drownings, yes. Murders, almost never. Poor
Jeanne Barber! What a rotten summer she's had!''

Briefly, Judith commiserated over Jeanne's unhappy fate.
Then she changed the subject: "What I didn't understand
is why H. Burrell Hodge was here in the first place. But
I'm sure you've informed Deputy McLean why Mr. Hodge

came to the Santa Lucias.'' Judith paused, but there was no response. "Haven't you?''

"No," Ella replied. "I haven't seen Lulu. Not today." The real-estate agent sounded puzzled. "Oh! You mean the sheriff would want to know Mr. Hodge's intentions as part of the murder investigation, right? I didn't think of that. Is it important?''

"It could be," Judith said. "Naturally, everybody on Chavez wants to know." Now Judith veered from the truth: "They've been driving me crazy with questions.''

Ella burst out laughing. "All seven of them? Hey, Mrs. . . . Flynn, is it? Don't let them rib you. The Santa Lucias are a hotbed of gossip. They know why Hodge came to Chavez. I'll bet they know why he was coming to Perez, too. He owns a big addiction recovery business, with several centers around the western part of the state. He was looking to open at least one more, maybe two. Perez and Chavez would make ideal sites, depending on the specialty. Perez has a regular hospital—the only one in the Santa Lucias—for consultation with medical people. Chavez is sufficiently isolated to provide all the privacy that recovering addicts would want. I had a great site for him over here, real possibilities beyond his initial requirements. Naturally, I hoped to broker the Chavez sale, if it went through. But now," she said with a heavy sigh, "I suppose everything's down the drain. It's a good thing I never count my commission until I close the deal.''

"Then I take it that Mr. Hodge was trying to buy property from the Danfields?'' Judith queried.

Ella Stovall laughed in a throaty manner. "Now, Mrs. Flynn, don't put words in my mouth. I've probably already said too much. You wouldn't want to get me in trouble with Mr. Dobler, would you?''

"Would he be any relation to Elrod?'' Judith asked, with a glance at Renie.

"Sure," Ella answered cheerfully. "Simon is old Elrod's son.''

"Really." Judith noted Renie's quizzical expression and

sought to enlighten her cousin. "Elrod's son, huh? Why am I surprised that Elrod has a son?"

"I've no idea," Ella said in a voice that indicated she really didn't. "A daughter, too. Hey, got to run. A couple of would-be vacation-home buyers are just coming in the door."

Judith relayed the details to Renie over glasses of soda. "So I don't need to call Adhab again," she said. "At least not for now. We know why Burrell came to the islands. The problem is, we still don't know why he was killed. Or who did it."

Renie had gotten up from the counter and gone to the refrigerator to get more ice for her soda. A glance in the direction of the back porch caused her to mouth the single word "Esther." Judith was still trying to figure out what Renie was saying when a timid knock sounded at the door.

"Hi, Esther," Renie said in greeting. "Come in. Want some pop?"

"Oh—no, thank you," Esther replied, entering the kitchen. On this late-summer afternoon, she wore a fawn-colored silk blouse, cocoa brown slacks, and a single strand of pearls. Her short hair was impeccably coiffed and her cosmetics were as discreet as they were perfectly applied. "I felt like getting out for a bit and thought I'd stop by to see how you were managing. We heard the coroner's verdict. Isn't it shocking?"

It hardly seemed proper to expect that Esther Danfield would want to sling a leg over one of the tall kitchen stools, so Judith invited their caller to come down into the sunroom. All three women descended the single step and arranged themselves in white wicker chairs.

"We weren't shocked so much as alarmed," Judith said, getting up almost immediately to adjust the blinds. "Doc thought all along that it wasn't an accident."

Esther, however, found no comfort in Doc's opinion. "What's this world coming to? I can't believe that Chavez is no longer safe. What shall we do?" She sounded almost frantic.

Judith tried to reassure Esther. "Elrod's got a gun. You have a security system. Of all the people on this island, you and Bates are best protected from danger."

Esther shuddered. "I don't know. Isn't it true that if someone wants to kill you, *really* wants to, they can? What if the killer is . . . ?" She clamped her lips shut and frowned into the philodendron that grew out of a lamp stand at her side.

"Is what?" Renie asked.

"Oh—I'm not sure what I mean!" Esther uttered a high-pitched laugh. "Really, this is all so unbelievable! My nerves are absolutely shattered. I haven't been this upset since . . . in years."

"Since what?" Renie seemed to have the bit in her slightly buckteeth and was running with it. Judith sat back and watched.

"Since years ago. Never mind." With a trembling hand, Esther fingered her pearls.

"Say," Renie said brightly, "how about a drink? Not pop—a serious drink. Maybe it will help your nerves, Esther."

Esther looked mildly horrified. "Oh, not this early in the day!" She glanced at the diamond-studded watch on her left wrist. "Well . . . it *is* going on three o'clock. A gin martini, if you have it. Thank you."

Renie got up to tend bar. Judith considered mentioning the real-estate issue, but decided to wait until after their guest had consumed a bit of gin. "Jeanne Barber is going to be upset," Judith finally said. "More upset, I mean. The Estacadas are checking out this afternoon."

It was the wrong thing to say. Esther stiffened in her chair and stared at Judith. "No! They're that frightened? You see—that's what I was talking about! No one is safe!"

"But they're honeymooners," Judith pointed out in a reasonable tone. "Besides, I think Mrs. Estacada tends to overreact."

"Can you blame her?" Esther demanded. "I'd leave,

too. In fact, I told Bates this afternoon that we should go
away. If we could . . .''

Renie presented Esther with her martini. ''If you could
what?'' Renie inquired, sitting back down.

Esther gave a shake of her head. ''I just meant that . . .
Well, you can't just pack up and go . . . That is . . .'' She
gave another shake, spilled a bit of the martini on her
sleeve, frowned, and took a deep drink. ''This is very
good,'' she announced, with just the hint of a smile.

''Thank you.'' Renie preened a bit, though Judith sensed
it was more for her benefit than Esther's. The martini glass
was big enough to be a pudding dish. Upon closer inspection, Judith realized it *was* a pudding dish. Esther, however,
didn't seem to mind. She sipped slowly, but deeply, and
briefly closed her eyes. ''This is rather restorative,'' she
remarked.

''Good,'' said Renie in an unusually amiable tone. ''By
the way, Doc Wicker told us about the Danfield history
today. They certainly go way back. We saw the cemetery
this morning, too. It's a lovely spot.''

Mentioning the cemetery did not have a salubrious effect
on Esther Danfield. ''Please . . . that's so morbid. I've never
liked it.'' She took another deep drink. ''Let's talk about
something else.'' Esther nodded at the bookshelves that ran
under the counter separating the sunroom from the kitchen,
beneath two of the windows, and down one narrow strip of
wall. ''Jeanne has a very nice library. I've borrowed several
of her books over the years. My hobbies are reading and
classical music, especially opera.''

''I love to read, too,'' Judith put in, as Renie got up and
went out through the kitchen into the living room. ''I used
to be a librarian. It was enjoyable work. Being surrounded
by books was a wonderful feeling.''

Esther agreed wholeheartedly. ''There's nothing like putting on a favorite recording and curling up with a good
book,'' she said with a pleasurable sigh. ''Music in particular takes you to another world.''

Judith nodded. ''I'm not very knowledgeable about classical music, though. I love the ballet. My cousin's the opera buff.''

''If you're a trained librarian, you must have gone to college,'' Esther said wistfully as the strains of Puccini's *La Boheme* floated through the speakers that were placed at strategic points around the house. ''I wanted to teach, but my parents didn't think training for a career was necessary for girls. Maybe they were right, but I always felt I could have made a contribution. Educating young people is a noble calling. I once felt very strongly about it. Not that my feelings mattered.'' Esther's fine features sagged. ''Of course, that was the late fifties. Women attended college only to find a husband, according to my parents.''

Judith started to point out that she and Renie had both completed degrees. But before she could get the words out of her mouth, Renie returned to the sunroom and Esther began swaying to the music.

''The last act,'' she murmured into her martini. ''Poor Mimi! She's finally reunited with Rodolfo, but it's too late—she's dying.'' A glint of tears shown in Esther's blue eyes.

''It's the most moving of operas for me,'' Renie said on a tremulous sigh. ''So personal, intimate, timeless. If only they could have gotten Mimi to a *doctor*.'' She shot Judith a goading look.

''A doctor?'' echoed Judith, as Mimi entered the garret, weak and nigh onto death. ''Oh! Yes, that reminds me . . . Esther, do you know why Doc Wicker gave up his practice? He strikes me as the type who would have made a wonderful family physician.''

While tears still welled up in her eyes, Esther's face became impassive. ''It was a long time ago. Doc doesn't like to talk about it.''

Renie was on her feet again, one hand moving in tune to the music. Musetta offered her earrings to pay for Mimi's cordial; Colline sang a farewell to his overcoat before pawning it to buy medicine. ''Say, Esther,'' Renie said brightly, ''how about another martini from Renie?''

Esther's blue eyes widened. "Oh, no, I couldn't!" Her gaze dropped to the almost-empty glass. "Well . . . perhaps just a tiny bit to freshen it."

As Renie headed back to the kitchen, Judith shook her head. "I still say it's a shame. I can't understand why a man like Doc—who seems so conscientious—would throw away a medical career. Such a waste! In fact, it's selfish."

"But . . ." Esther began, then stopped as Mimi told Rodolfo she wasn't really sleeping, she'd only been pretending until the others had left them alone. "Dear me," she gulped, removing a lace-edged handkerchief from the pocket of her slacks. "This is so touching!"

Renie returned with a second martini. True to her word, this time the glass was only half-full. Esther, however, lapped up the drink like a cat. "You mustn't blame Doc," she sniffled. "It was so sad . . ." Rodolfo compared Mimi's beauty to the sunrise; Mimi said he was wrong, it was more like the sunset . . . "Pitiful, really," Esther went on. "I was reminded of it yesterday. It was this time of year—actually a week or so later, the first day of autumn . . ." Her voice grew faint, as she leaned toward the nearest speaker.

"Yes?" Judith said encouragingly, as Rodolfo and Mimi reminisced about their first meeting.

Esther seemed to have fallen under a spell. "A . . . young couple had come to stay at the cabins. The woman was about to give birth. She'd been warned by her doctor not to venture far from a hospital. But . . . she scoffed. She was adventuresome. They were down at Hidden Cove. The woman went into labor . . ." Esther paused to dab again at her eyes. Musetta returned with a muff for Mimi's chilled hands. "The birth was very difficult. Doc did everything he could. I believe it was the first time he'd faced a complicated delivery, and he had nothing with him but his regular medical kit." Pausing, Esther bit her lower lip as the tears trickled down her cheeks. While Mimi slept, Rodolfo kept watch, and Musetta prayed to the Virgin. "Miraculously, the baby survived." Swallowing hard, Esther clutched the pudding dish with both hands. "But despite Doc's every effort, the mother . . . died."

So did Mimi. Rodolfo's anguished cries rang throughout the house. The orchestra played its final heartrending notes. Esther was sobbing aloud. Judith winced, and Renie looked a trifle sheepish.

"Say, Esther, maybe I should make some coffee," Renie offered.

The opera's climax seemed to snap Esther out of her trance. She shuddered, blew her nose, and cast a repugnant glance at the empty pudding dish. Then, from over the crumpled handkerchief, she stared at Renie with red, reproachful eyes. "You're really quite shameless, you know."

Renie nodded. "It was a dirty job, but someone had to do it. Nobody on this island will tell us anything. That's not fair. Not when we get stuck with a dead body."

Indignant and unsteady, Esther got to her feet. "You tricked me. That's cruel."

Judith was at Esther's side. "Not as cruel as whoever murdered H. Burrell Hodge. If the residents of this island keep everything to themselves, the killer may never be caught."

Esther glared at Judith. "What's that got to do with poor Doc? What happened to him is in the past. Doc has atoned for his lack of skill and experience many times over. Oh, he tried to continue practicing medicine, I believe he even considered joining the Peace Corps, but his heart wasn't in it. Nor was it all his fault. There were . . ." Esther flinched as if she'd been struck. "There were extenuating circumstances." Giving a final wipe at her eyes, Esther squared her shoulders. The gesture seemed to help her gain control of her limbs and her emotions. "Now you've pried and prodded until you know what happened to Doc. I hope you're satisfied. Good-bye." With her head held high, Esther went through the kitchen and out of the house.

Judith eyed Renie. "That *was* pretty outrageous, coz," she said in a chiding tone.

"Oh, phooey!" Renie retorted. "It was no more outrageous than one of your long, drawn-out, circumlocuitous attempts to get information out of unwitting suspects. Face it, Esther wouldn't have told us a damned thing if I hadn't loosened her tongue with a little gin and lowered her emotional defenses with some tear-jerking music."

Judith wasn't convinced that Renie had done the right thing. What was worse, she didn't think that Esther's revelations were very helpful. "I don't see what Doc's loss of a patient has to do with H. Burrell Hodge. To top it off, now we've alienated Esther Danfield. I was more interested in asking her who's the Francesca buried in the private cemetery."

"Esther didn't want to talk about the cemetery," Renie pointed out, still sounding defensive. "It gave her the creeps."

"True." Judith spoke absently, as she paced the length of the sunroom. "There's something odd about Esther's story, though. It wasn't . . . cohesive."

"Of course it wasn't cohesive," Renie snapped. "She was guzzling gin and listening to Puccini. You'd prefer Abu's inverted pyramid version?"

Judith started to make a testy reply, then brightened. "*The Merchant*! If we can get Rafe to take us to Laurel Harbor tomorrow, we could go through the newspaper's files. Maybe that will tell us something, not just about the twenty-year-old tragedy, but H. Burrell Hodge's development plans."

Recognizing that it wouldn't be prudent to balk while Judith was out of sorts, Renie shrugged. "Okay. But shouldn't you try to get Rafe so that the Estacadas can get out of here this afternoon?"

Judith looked at her watch. "It's after three-thirty. That's too late for us to go today. But the Estacadas have until six-thirty to catch the last ferry. Or does it actually leave at seven-thirty? I forget."

Renie apparently had also forgotten. She said nothing, but followed Judith into the kitchen. This time, Rafe answered. He would be glad to take the Estacadas to Laurel Harbor. He would also be glad to take the cousins there the following day. What time? Judith suggested eleven o'clock. After assuring Judith that he would go up to the cabins to alert the Estacadas, Rafe hung up.

"Well, that's that," Judith said, still seated on the stool at the kitchen counter. "Now we've got two empty cabins. I wonder if Burrell's heirs will want the money back for the rest of his stay. They're entitled to it." She flipped open the guest registry which Jeanne kept by the phone. "According to this notation, he paid with a credit card. I think I'll call Lulu McLean and see if she's tracked down his next of kin."

Judith was on hold for over five minutes, waiting for the deputy to come to the phone. "There are no next of kin," McLean declared after Judith had phrased her request. "Hodge was married years ago, but it didn't last. No kids. No siblings that we can find, no other relatives. He was a loner, in terms of his personal life. If you want to reimburse somebody, try Adhab."

"Adhab," Judith repeated innocently. "Is that the recovery center?"

"You got it," McLean replied. "They don't have much of a central-office staff, just an office manager, a receptionist, and an accountant. Everything is pretty much handled through the individual centers."

"Thanks," Judith said, hoping she sounded appropriately grateful. "How's the investigation going?"

"Slow," McLean answered. "Is there anything else I can do for you, Mrs. Flynn? I'm pretty busy here."

"I was just wondering how long you've been in the islands," Judith said. "That is, it occurred to me that if you've only recently arrived, it must be hard to get to know your territory. It's so spread out."

"I've been here six years," McLean responded. "Don't worry about me. I know what I'm doing."

"I hope so," Judith remarked after ringing off. She saw

Renie's puzzled expression and related the other half of the conversation.

"So relax," Renie said. "Maybe McLean's made more progress than she let on."

"No," Judith countered. "I believe her when she says it's slow going." Slipping off the stool, Judith started for the front door. "Come on, let's sit outside and let the fresh air stir our brain cells."

Renie, however, needed sustenance. After getting a soda refill and a box of pretzels, she joined Judith on the deck. "Well?" Renie inquired, making herself comfortable on one of the benches by the rail. "Have you any ideas?"

"I do, as a matter of fact," Judith replied. "I've been thinking about motive. If you lived on Chavez Island, how would you like to have a rehab center in your midst?"

"I wouldn't," Renie answered swiftly. "The island is too small for that kind of thing. It would change the whole tenor of the place."

Judith nodded. "Exactly. So let's assume that Doc wouldn't be pleased; neither would Cilla and Mrs. Carr, or, for that matter, Jeanne Barber."

Renie popped two small pretzels in her mouth. "Except Jeanne wasn't here."

Judith continued as if she hadn't heard her cousin. "And Rafe would really hate the idea, because not only does he seem to treasure his privacy, but he's an ardent environmentalist. No wonder he and Burrell were arguing over ferns."

"What did I tell you?" Renie proffered the pretzel box to Judith.

"The only ones who might be for the project are the Danfields, and by association, Elrod Dobler," Judith went on, taking a handful of pretzels and putting them in her lap. "Burrell went to see Bates Danfield, which suggests he is the seller. His evasiveness about Burrell indicates that he hadn't told Esther what was going on. I have a feeling she still doesn't know, but I could be wrong about that. I wonder what she meant about not being able to leave the island.''

Renie took the pretzel box back from Judith. ''Esther seemed scared. *Really* scared, almost as if she thought somebody was out to get her. What would that have to do with Burrell and Adhab?''

''I've no idea,'' Judith admitted. ''She's the nervous type, though. Too thin.'' Over Renie's shoulder, Judith could see a cruiser skimming across the water away from the island. ''I think that's Rafe's boat,'' Judith said. ''He must have loaded up the Estacadas.''

Renie turned to look, and in the process, knocked the pretzels off the bench. The box fell into the bushes. ''Drat,'' Renie grumbled, getting down on her knees and stretching an arm to retrieve the fallen snack. ''I'll bet the birds around here would enjoy some of these . . .'' Clutching the pretzels, Renie turned a stricken face to Judith. ''My God! I completely forgot! It must have been the booze!''

Judith regarded her cousin with curiosity. ''Forgot what?''

Scrambling to her feet, Renie hovered over Judith. ''Last night, while you and Doc were examining Burrell's body, and I was feeling like a guilt-ridden criminal, I was moping around in the shrubbery across from the back stairs. I saw something odd. Come on, coz, let's go see if it's still there.''

Judith hurriedly followed Renie through the house, though they both slowed down when they reached the treacherous back staircase. ''What was it?'' Judith asked, hanging on to the banister.

''I'm not sure,'' Renie answered. ''I was so upset thinking I'd killed Burrell that it didn't register. It was wood, like a handle. I suppose I thought it had come out of that storage shed between the house and the garage.''

Judith remembered that Renie had been staring at the wild rhododendrons. Racing across the turnaround area, she began searching the ground. Renie joined her, rubbing her temple in confusion.

"I don't recall the blackberry vines . . . Looking at them, I mean . . . Do you see anything?"

Judith did. Renie was right: The object that lay half-concealed by some brown fallen leaves from the rhododendrons had a wooden handle. Gingerly, Judith brushed the leaves aside.

"It's a mallet," she said in wonder. "With an iron head."

Next to Judith, Renie peered down through the shrubs. "So it is. What do you think?"

"I think the head isn't two inches wide. Almost, though. The coroner may have been quoted in general terms." Straightening up, Judith looked skyward, as if for inspiration. "Lulu may have concentrated on looking in the shrubbery on each side of the staircase, not over here across the turnaround. But if she did search this section, she must have missed seeing the mallet in the dark. My guess is that it was deliberately hidden, not dropped."

"How do you know?" Renie asked in a skeptical voice.

"Because those rhododendron leaves are old, from last year. The ones that dropped late this summer wouldn't be so desiccated. And the iron head shows no sign of rust. If it had been there as long as the leaves on top of it, there would be rust." Judith contemplated her next move. "I wonder if we should call the sheriff."

"Why," Renie asked, "would the killer dump that mallet—assuming it's the alleged blunt instrument—so close to the scene of the crime? Why not take it into the woods or throw it in Eagle Lake?"

Judith admitted she couldn't guess. "If it hadn't been placed so carefully under those leaves, I'd say somebody dropped it. Somebody innocent, maybe. But it's almost as if it were meant to be found."

"Maybe the killer didn't expect us to come running out last night," Renie suggested. "Maybe he—or she—figured Burrell would drop dead without a sound."

"That's possible," Judith said. "Come on, we'd better call McLean. We might catch her before Rafe heads back to Chavez. He can give her a ride over here.''

The deputy was out, but Judith left a message. Throwing caution to the wind, she decided to risk making a fool of herself and tell the person at the other end that the murder weapon might have been found.

The cousins had just returned to the deck when they heard someone at the back door. This time it was June Hennessy. She looked worried.

"The Estacadas have left," she said. "The young woman was a flighty sort, but her husband seemed reasonable. Yet they've fled. I must confess, it gives me pause. I shall return to Perez Island as soon as it's convenient. I probably should have gone with the Estacadas, but I didn't realize they were leaving so quickly."

Judith's shoulders slumped. "You must do as you like," she said a bit stiffly. "You'll want a refund, I suppose?"

But Miss Hennessy surprised Judith. "No. Jeanne Barber can apply it to our faculty retreat in the spring. We take all three cabins, and get in before the rates go up. It's still expensive, especially on a teacher's salary. That's why I always come in the off-season."

"Okay," Judith agreed, somewhat appeased. "I'll try to get hold of Rafe St. Jacques as soon as he gets back from Laurel Harbor. If you don't mind staying overnight, my cousin and I plan on going to Perez around eleven o'clock tomorrow morning."

Miss Hennessy frowned. "Well . . . I *could* stay. I'm not highly strung, like *some*. No spunk—that's what's wrong with the young women around here. Tears, hysteria, complete lack of self-control. At Laurel Glen, we instill self-discipline. It's the cornerstone of a successful life." With pursed lips, Miss Hennessy paused in apparent reflection on the soundness of her personal philosophy. "However, now that I've made up my mind to go, I have plans for class preparation. A jump start, as it were. If it's not too great an inconvenience for Mr. St. Jacques, I'd prefer to leave today."

Judith said she'd do her best to arrange transportation.

After Miss Hennessy left, Judith dialed the Carrs' number. Luckily, Cilla answered instead of her mother.

"Cilla, do you own a mallet?" Judith asked.

"I sure do," Cilla answered, sounding a bit cross. "Did you find it?"

Making a thumbs-up sign, Judith glanced at Renie. "I think so. Does it have a wooden handle and an iron head?"

"Yes." An exasperated sigh floated over the scratchy phone line. "Honestly, I'm sick of having my tools disappear! Usually, I'm not so careless. I guess my mind's more messed up than I thought."

"When did you last see your mallet?" Judith asked, still keeping eye contact with Renie.

"Yesterday afternoon," Cilla replied promptly. "I put up the badminton net for the Estacadas. I used the mallet to drive the metal poles into the ground. Where did you find it?"

Judith hesitated. "Out by the garage," she finally said, deciding that it might not be wise to state the specific spot.

"I'll get it in the morning when I clean house," Cilla said. "Thanks." Her voice dropped. "Thanks for being so kind to my mother. She told me about calling on you."

"Uh . . ." Judith wondered if she should mention the fact that Rowena Carr didn't recall seeing the cousins until introducing herself at the Barber house. "Does your mother have memory problems?"

"She has a lot of problems," Cilla replied. "Don't blame yourselves for any of them. Bye now."

The phone rang while Judith still had her hand on the receiver. It was Lulu McLean. "What's this about finding a possible murder weapon?" she demanded.

Judith explained. McLean's attitude became less belligerent. "A mallet, huh? Could be. You didn't touch it, did you?"

"Of course not." Judith considered telling the deputy that Mr. Flynn was a policeman. But before she could say anything further, McLean was speaking again.

"Okay, I just saw Rafe at the county extension office.

I'll try to grab him before he takes off. Meanwhile, go keep an eye on that mallet. I wouldn't want it to wander away.''

Judith replaced the phone. "She's coming over. That's fine. Then Rafe can take June Hennessy *and* Deputy McLean back to Laurel Harbor."

Renie was opening the liquor cabinet. "Last night I didn't think I'd ever feel like drinking again. But I could manage a small screwdriver. How about you?"

The goose wings showed that it was a quarter after four. "Why not? We can take our drinks down to the turnaround."

Renie was uncapping a bottle of Russian vodka. "What for? Why can't we sit on the deck, like normal people?"

"Because McLean wants us to keep an eye on the mallet," Judith replied with a droll expression. "I know, it sounds silly. But at least she's taking us seriously, so we should humor her."

"That's dumb," Renie declared, getting a pitcher of orange juice out of the refrigerator. "McLean won't be here for at least half an hour. We can run down just before five and make it look as if we'd been guarding the goods the whole time."

Judith started to quibble, thought about sitting on the hard stairs or the uneven ground, and shrugged. "Okay. The mallet's been there since yesterday, if it really does belong to Cilla. She said she used it to put up the badminton net for the Estacadas."

Renie mixed their drinks. "If all the guests are going away, why are we staying?"

The idea hadn't yet occurred to Judith. "Good point. Why would Jeanne want to pay me for what amounts to house-sitting? Nobody else has reservations until Monday. Maybe Cilla could take over until Jeanne gets back Wednesday. I'll call later and see what she thinks."

Glasses in hand, Judith and Renie retreated to the deck. A few more clouds had gathered in the sky, and the air felt much cooler. Overhead, the noisy bluejays were arguing again. Judith put her feet up and tried to relax.

"Where were we with our hypotheses when you suddenly remembered you'd seen a blunt instrument?" Judith asked.

"What difference does it make if we're going to be out of here tomorrow?" Renie was sitting in the lawn swing, moving lazily back and forth.

"Well . . ." Judith plucked at her lower lip. "I guess it doesn't. Still, I sort of hate to let go."

Renie turned slightly, giving Judith an amused look. "Why do I think you won't really leave?"

"I can use the money," Judith said in a self-righteous tone, "especially if we're going to buy another car." She wagged a finger at Renie. "Just to prove my good intentions, I'm going to call the car-rental company on the mainland. If we go back tomorrow, maybe I can rent that Subaru Legacy for the return trip. There can't be that many people renting cars this time of year."

Renie waited on the deck while Judith called the rental office on the mainland. The woman who answered said that the Legacy Judith had dropped off Monday morning had gone out that night. Perhaps Mrs. Flynn would like to try a different model?

Judith said that would be fine, but it would have to be a four-door sedan. That was no problem, the woman replied. They had a nice maroon Impreza that had just come in. The detail man would have it ready in an hour or so. The agency insisted on doing a thorough job of cleaning and maintenance before releasing its cars. The Impreza would be gassed up and ready to go by morning. To expedite matters, Judith gave the necessary information, including her temporary address.

"I'm staying at Chavez Cove," she explained.

The woman laughed in surprise. "Really? What a coincidence. That Legacy you dropped off yesterday was rented by a woman from the same address."

Judith also laughed. "That is a coincidence. Was it a Mrs. Barber?"

The woman thought so. Whoever it was planned to drop

it off at the airport before taking a flight to California. Judith finished relaying the information and hung up.

"You see?" Judith said to Renie. "I plan on going. Assuming that it's okay with Jeanne."

Renie looked at Judith. Her round face merely hinted at her disbelief. After depositing their unfinished drinks in the refrigerator, the cousins went out the back door to wait for Deputy McLean.

"One of us should have stayed on the deck," Renie said. "McLean will come up from the dock. She'll have to use the front door. Shall I go back inside?"

Judith made a face. "I suppose." She glanced up at the steep planes and angles of the Barber house. There was no way that the cousins could see anyone arriving from their position in the turnaround. While the water side was almost entirely made of glass, the opposite facade was solid wall, except for the back door. All that was visible was the covered staircase and the overhang from the roof.

Renie trudged back up the stairs. Glancing at her watch, Judith noted that it was almost five. She wandered over to the wild rhododendrons, noting how much rangier they were than the dense, compact hybrid variety by the stairs. Poking her head into the shrubbery, she gazed down at the spot where she'd seen the mallet.

It was gone.

ELEVEN

JUDITH FELT HER spine tingle. Someone had crept into the turnaround while the cousins sat on the deck, enjoying their drinks and talking. It was very likely that that someone had been a killer. The thought of having a murderer move stealthily within thirty yards of their comfortable circumstances was very unsettling, but Judith couldn't allow fear to distract her. She saw no signs of footprints, but neither the grassy strip next to the shrubbery nor the dry dirt and gravel in the turnaround would take much of an impression. She was still muttering to herself in dismay and disbelief when Bates Danfield came up the road.

"Mrs. Flynn," he said in a serious voice. "May I have a word with you?"

"What?" Judith was so absorbed in the loss of the mallet that she hardly heard Bates. "Okay, what is it?" The irritation in her voice was impossible to conceal, though it wasn't intended for Bates Danfield.

He, however, seemed to feel otherwise. "I'm the one who should be annoyed," Bates began, his patrician features showing displeasure. "It seems that you've upset my wife. Indeed, your actions were disgraceful. What, pray tell, was the point of such an ignominious charade?"

Judith tried to put the missing mallet out of her mind. She failed, for she could hear voices emanating from the vicinity of the back porch. They came from Renie, Deputy McLean, and Rafe St. Jacques.

"Where is it?" McLean demanded, pounding down the stairs with reckless abandon. "Oh, hullo, Bates. What are you doing here?"

Judith swallowed hard. "It's gone. Someone must have taken it."

McLean reddened with anger. "What? I told you to keep an eye on it! Or is this some kind of joke?"

"It seems," Bates said in a supercilious tone, "that Mrs. Flynn and Mrs. Jones are fond of jokes. It's a pity that no one else finds them amusing."

Renie's eyes had grown wide as she gazed at Judith, McLean, Bates, and, finally, Rafe, who also seemed puzzled. "What now?" Renie inquired, sounding almost as vexed as the deputy.

Judith sighed heavily. "As I said, the mallet's gone. Do I need to fill out an affidavit?"

"I think you do," McLean declared. "Or at least make a formal statement. Where was this alleged mallet found?"

"What mallet?" Bates inquired, now looking confused as well as outraged.

"Good question," McLean muttered, as Judith led her to the place in the shrubbery where the mallet had been lying only an hour ago.

"It was under some of those old rhododendron leaves," Judith said, then quickly offered her logic to support why she believed the object had been purposely hidden. "It belongs to Cilla Carr," Judith said in conclusion. "At least Cilla thinks it does."

Rafe was also studying the ground beneath the bushes. "Cilla has a mallet. I've seen it in her toolbox."

With arms folded across her breast, McLean paced the width of the turnaround area. "This is a real screwup." She paused just long enough to flash censorious glances at Judith and Renie. "As a matter of fact, you two are the biggest screwups I've met in a long time. How the hell did Jeanne Barber get mixed up with the likes of you?''

''That's not all,'' Bates put in. ''I feel obliged to report what they did to my wife.''

McLean whirled on Bates. ''To Esther? What did they do?''

Bates shot a malevolent look at the cousins before he replied. ''They forced hard liquor on her and played disturbing music. She's lying down right now, trying to recover from the trauma of it all.''

''Oh, good grief!'' Renie stamped her foot, and twirled around in an angry circle. ''That's ridiculous! Nobody made Esther drink martinis! She came here complaining of frayed nerves. We were just trying to be hospitable.''

''What about the insidious music?'' Bates demanded.

''*La Bohème*?'' Renie's expression was incredulous. ''Come on, Danfield—that's not exactly a Nazi interrogation tune.''

''Esther was undone,'' Bates said stiffly.

''I'm done,'' McLean announced. But instead of heading back through the house, she started down the road. ''C'mon, Rafe,'' she called over her shoulder. ''We're going to see Cilla. Maybe she can tell us something about this so-called mallet.''

Having remained silent during the last few minutes, Judith had given herself the opportunity to regain her composure. ''Look,'' she said to Bates, ''I'm sorry your wife is upset. She really didn't have that much to drink. And how could we know that Puccini would affect her so deeply?'' Judith carefully avoided looking at Renie.

In a truculent gesture, Bates shoved his hands into the pockets of his Norfolk jacket. ''You should have been able to tell how sensitive she is just from talking to her,'' he responded, though the edge of his anger seemed dulled. ''I suppose she talked and talked about . . . everything.''

''Not exactly everything,'' Judith said, sensing that Bates was on a fishing expedition. ''Just . . . certain things.''

''About what ?'' Bates's voice was anxious.

"Oh . . ." Judith appeared to be thinking. "About borrowing books from Jeanne Barber. Doc Wicker. Her parents."

Bates gaped at Judith. "Her parents? What did she say?"

"Um . . . Mostly it was their attitude toward girls and going to college and such. They sounded rather old-fashioned."

"Oh." Bates's shoulders slumped in the Norfolk jacket. "I see. And Doc?"

"Esther told a very sad story, about the mother Doc couldn't save." Judith offered Bates a piteous smile. "It explained why Doc gave up medical practice. We were curious about that."

The muscles along Bates's jaw tightened. "Esther told you about Doc? What did she say? Precisely, that is."

"Precisely?" Judith wrinkled her nose, then glanced at Renie for help. "That Doc hadn't been in practice long and he had never dealt with a difficult delivery and it all went wrong. The baby lived, but the mother didn't." Judith looked again at Renie.

"That's right," Renie chimed in. "Oh, and that the mother had been warned not to go too far from a hospital because it sounded as if her own doctor knew she was going to have problems. But she and her husband came up to Chavez anyway."

"That's it?" Bates's glance darted from cousin to cousin.

"I think so," Judith replied.

"I see." Squaring his shoulders, Bates gave a single nod. "Well, I don't want my wife taken advantage of like that again. You do understand, I trust?"

"We do," Judith promised. "If anyone should be mad, it's Doc. I guess he doesn't like having that story told."

"Probably not." Bates's anger had finally dissipated, along with his concern. "You're sure Esther didn't mention anything else that might have caused her distress?"

Judith shook her head. "Not that I recall. She wasn't here very long."

"Very well." Bates managed a thin smile. "I think the world of my wife. It unsettles me greatly when she's distraught. I'll be going now. Good day."

"Okay," Renie said, after Bates had disappeared down the road, "what was he afraid that Esther told us?"

Judith was already trying to figure that out. "Didn't I say the story lacked cohesion? First of all, why didn't they try to get the pregnant woman off the island and over to the hospital in Laurel Harbor? Had the helicopter pad been put in twenty-some years ago? Rafe wasn't here then, but somebody must have had a boat. The Danfields, probably. Why didn't they send for emergency assistance? We're not talking about the Dark Ages."

"Maybe," Renie suggested, "it was the weather. Remember, I told you how my dad always said it could be dangerous to travel by sea when summer turns into fall? Didn't Esther say that the tragedy took place on the first day of autumn?"

"You're right," Judith said. "Yes, the weather might have been bad. But you'd think the emergency people could get around, wouldn't you?"

"I don't know," Renie replied. "There's always the coast guard."

"We don't know the whole story," Judith declared. "Bates Danfield doesn't want us to know the whole story. That's why he was so worried about what Esther told us. But even after drinking a martini out of a soup tureen, she held back. I noticed that at the time. She'd falter, and then sort of cover her tracks."

Renie nodded. "She was cautious, even in a semialcoholic haze. But it wasn't a soup tureen, it was a pudding dish."

"And her parents," Judith went on, ignoring the correction. "I don't think Bates wanted Esther to tell us anything about her parents."

"And she didn't," Renie noted, "except to say that they had some arcane ideas."

The cousins suddenly stared at each other. "What," Judith asked, "are we talking about? None of this has anything to do with H. Burrell Hodge or Adhab or the present."

"You're right," Renie admitted. "We're beating ourselves up for nothing."

"Then why is everybody around here so close-mouthed?" Judith demanded.

"Because that's the kind of people they are," Renie replied. "That's why they're isolated. They don't really want to have anything to do with other people. They have their secrets, and whether or not they're worth keeping doesn't really matter. They don't want to share any part of themselves with the rest of the world."

Judith knew that Renie was right. "I didn't mean it when I told Esther that Doc was selfish," said Judith, more to herself than to Renie. "But in a way, it's true. They're all selfish. The Danfields are rich, and people with money are always afraid that other people are trying to get it away from them. Rowena Carr has mental problems, and Cilla is trying to keep the world from getting to her mother. Rafe has something buried in his past, I'm sure of it. He's hiding out in Hidden Cove, which is certainly fitting. And Elrod Dobler definitely has a proprietary attitude toward the Danfields, and by extension, toward the whole island. These people live here, they die here, they get buried here. It's a world unto itself."

"You left out Jeanne Barber," Renie put in.

"So I did." Judith smiled wryly. "I wonder why Jeanne and Duane came up here twelve years ago. Their daughter probably wouldn't have been out of high school. It must have been kind of hard on them."

The answer to that question seemed to be at hand as June Hennessy strode down the path from the cabins. "I came to see if Mr. St. Jacques could take me over to Laurel Harbor," Miss Hennessy said. "Have you seen him? He's not at Hidden Cove, and his cruiser's gone."

"He's tied up in Chavez Cove," Judith said with a smile. "I'm sure he'll take you over to the big island when he gets back from the Carrs. Deputy McLean is with him.''

Miss Hennessy gazed at Judith with open curiosity. ''Well! Has the deputy discovered who killed Mr. Hodge? I certainly hope so!''

''She's still working on it,'' Judith admitted. ''Say, Miss Hennessy, how did Marcia Barber go to school from here? My cousin and I were figuring that Jeanne and Duane must have moved up here while she was still a teenager?''

''I've never met Marcia,'' Miss Hennessy replied without much interest. ''I'm not even certain how old she is. She may have graduated by the time the Barbers bought the Chavez Cove property.''

Renie, who had been idly searching for four-leafed clovers along the edge of the turnaround, looked up. ''Who'd they buy this land from? I can see that the cabins are old, but I know they built the house. What was here before that?''

''Nothing,'' Miss Hennessy answered. ''Or so I understand. Remember, I didn't start coming to Chavez until five years ago. Though I recall Jeanne mentioning that she and Duane purchased the property from Elrod Dobler.''

Judith gaped at Miss Hennessy. ''*Elrod Dobler?* I thought the Danfields owned most of the island.''

Miss Hennessy uttered a short little laugh. ''So they'd like you to think. But it's not true.'' She gave the cousins a knowing smile. ''Until the Barbers came, Elrod Dobler owned everything, lock, stock, and sand pebble. I'll fetch my luggage and drop off the key. Mind if I wait on your deck for Mr. St. Jacques?''

Judith and Renie had been chewing on Miss Hennessy's tidbit for at least five minutes when McLean and Rafe returned from the Carr house. Perhaps the schoolteacher was misinformed. Surely the crusty old lout with the sawed-off shotgun couldn't be a wealthy property holder? Perhaps Miss Hennessy had Elrod confused with Simon Dobler. Elrod lived in a guest cottage; the Danfields lived at Stoneyhenge. They dressed like rich people, they talked like rich people, they acted like rich people, they had the patina of rich people.

"*Patina*," Judith was muttering as Rafe and McLean appeared on the road. "Maybe that's the key, as in surface, as in superficial."

Renie had no opportunity to respond. McLean was looking disgruntled, and Rafe wore an unusually harried air.

"Cilla can't be exact about how big the head of the mallet is," McLean groused. "An inch, two inches—somewhere in between. I don't suppose you two could tell me."

Judith cleared her throat. "I'd say under two inches. But it's just a guess. I told you, I didn't touch it."

"I think it could be the weapon," Rafe said, with a deferential glance at McLean. "How many other items on this island fit that description?"

McLean didn't respond. With her lips clamped together, she signaled for Rafe to follow her. They went up the stairs. Judith and Renie brought up the rear.

"Look," McLean said before heading out the front door, "I don't know what to make of you two." She glowered at Renie. "You actually saw this mallet thing last night, right after Hodge was killed, but you didn't say anything until this afternoon." Turning to Judith, she wagged a reproachful finger. "Then, after you've both seen the mallet, you don't stand guard over it until I can get here. Meanwhile, somebody pinches it. Did you see anyone near the house after you called me to say you'd found the mallet?"

Given the parade of visitors to Chavez Cove in the last few hours, Judith had to stop and think about who had arrived when. "Only June Hennessy and Bates Danfield. But of course anyone could come into the turnaround without us seeing them. As you can tell, you have to be actually on the stairs before you have any kind of view between the house and the shrubbery."

McLean gave a slight nod, indicating that she was unaware of the layout. "Okay," she said to Rafe in a dejected tone, "let's go."

"Wait!" Judith exclaimed. "I forgot! Miss Hennessy

wants to go back with you. She's checking out, too.''

Judith had barely uttered the words when June Hennessy's voice trumpeted through the house. ''Yoo-hoo! Anyone home?''

Hurrying to admit Miss Hennessy, Judith silently berated herself for her faulty memory. McLean pounced as soon as the schoolteacher entered the kitchen. Had Ms. Hennessy seen anyone in the turnaround on her previous visit to the house? Had Ms. Hennessy happened to notice anything unusual? Had Ms. Hennessy sensed anything untoward?

''I'm not *Ms.* Hennessy,'' the schoolteacher replied in a haughty voice. ''I'm *Miss* Hennessy. The designation of Ms. is a pariah. It means *nothing*. Are women such as you ashamed of your single state? *I'm* not. Indeed, I'm proud of it.''

Lulu McLean seemed taken aback. ''Look, you don't understand. Ms. is like Mr.—you can't tell from a man's title if he's married or not, right? Why should it be any different for women?''

''Because women *are* different,'' Miss Hennessy retorted. ''They're superior in every way. All this nonsense about equality! I wouldn't lower myself to become equal!''

''Okay,'' McLean said wearily. ''I see your point. I think. Now how about seeing anything in the turnaround?''

''You mean at the bottom of the back stairs?'' Miss Hennessy's ire cooled. ''No, certainly not. Although . . .'' She frowned. ''When I left this house roughly an hour ago, I did *hear* something. A rustling sound is the best way I can describe it. Naturally, I thought it was an animal of some sort. That's not unusual around here.'' She gave McLean a defiant look.

The deputy was undaunted. ''Where was it coming from?''

Miss Hennessy's frown deepened. ''Why, I'm not sure. I really wasn't paying attention. My mind was focused on my departure.''

McLean nodded. ''Okay, I guess that's the best you can do. Let's haul ass for Laurel Harbor.''

Miss Hennessy made a disapproving face, but Rafe was already heading for the dock. "A moment," Miss Hennessy said, beckoning to Judith. "Should you find my cameo brooch, please send it on to Laurel Glen Academy. I must have mislaid it. Very vexing—I'm not usually careless." With a nod, she followed Rafe to the steps that led into the cove.

Five minutes later, the cousins had rescued their screwdrivers and were sitting on the deck. "I'll call Jeanne before we start dinner," Judith said. "I should call Mother, too."

Renie's eyes danced. "Why, if we're leaving tomorrow?"

"I mean," Judith explained a bit defensively, "if Jeanne insists that we stay, I'll call Mother. Otherwise, you're right. We'll just show up and surprise her."

"Uh-huh." Renie was definitely skeptical.

"Okay, okay," Judith said crossly. "I'll call Jeanne right now. It's going on six. She ought to be done for the day with her mud wrap and her kelp balm and her goat hormones."

This time, Judith reached Jeanne on the second transfer. In a voice throbbing with apology, Judith relayed the coroner's verdict. "It's had a dampening effect on the other guests. That's understandable, of course. People often overreact. In all honesty, I doubt that the others were in any real danger . . ."

Jeanne jumped on only one word: " '*Were*'? What do you mean, Judith?"

"Ah . . . as in they were here, but now are gone? The Estacadas checked out earlier this afternoon. Miss Hennessy just left about ten minutes ago."

"Oh, good heavens!" Jeanne sounded annoyed.

"I know, it's a big pain," Judith said hastily. "So I was wondering if you wanted me to stay on. According to your reservation list, no one else is coming until Monday."

"This is a disaster," Jeanne declared. "I'm losing hundreds of dollars! Call the state association's central booking

office. Let them know that the cabins are vacant. Maybe
something can be salvaged from this mess. No, I don't want
you to leave! Not counting tonight, there are five more days
that we might be able to fill. Unless,'' she added in an
ominous voice, ''no one will come to Chavez because of
the murder.''

''I wouldn't worry about that,'' Judith said quickly. Too
quickly, she realized when she heard Jeanne's sharp intake
of breath. ''I mean, people often are intrigued by misfortune. You know, like tours of famous crime scenes.''

''That's repellent,'' Jeanne said. ''Please call the state
association. I'm surprised you didn't think of doing that
already.''

''I wouldn't have done it without consulting you first.''
Judith managed to sound vaguely indignant. ''By the way,
Jeanne, who did you buy this property from?''

''What? Why on earth do you want to know that? Look,
I've checked with the insurance company and my lawyer.
Now that we know it was murder, I have no liability. You
don't need to worry about anything except putting people
in those empty cabins. Really, Judith, I had no idea you
were so nosy! Why don't you ask me what kind of a sex
life Duane and I had? Or if we ever met Marcia's real
parents? Just tend to business—that's what I'm paying you
for. I must go, it's time for my alfalfa dinner graze.''

''Jeanne!'' Judith hadn't heard much of the other
woman's last few words. ''What about Marcia's real . . . ?''

But Jeanne had hung up.

Judith gave Renie a sheepish look. ''Heh-heh. We're not
leaving.''

Renie, who was leaning in the doorway between the
kitchen and the deck, inclined her head. ''I never thought
we were. Shall I make french fries to go with the steak?''

''Fine,'' Judith said, dialing the state B&B association's
number. ''I'll do the salad after I shanghai some paying
guests.''

Getting a recorded message, Judith remembered that Ingrid Heffleman closed down the state association's office

at five. Judith had Ingrid's home phone number. The director answered almost immediately.

"Judith," Ingrid finally said after listening to the woeful tale at the other end of the phone, "how do you keep getting mixed up in these debacles? I hate to tell you this, but there are some members of the association who don't feel you should continue serving on the board."

"Really?" Judith couldn't keep the eagerness out of her voice. She'd only agreed to join the board after a great deal of coercion, mainly from Ingrid. Meetings were always tedious affairs, accompanied by weak coffee and limp cookies. "If you insist, I'll step down."

"*I* don't insist," Ingrid responded. "I'm pleased to have you serve. But there are others in the hostelry business who don't approve of the notoriety that you've brought to us upon occasion. They certainly won't like this latest catastrophe!"

"Pretend it's really Jeanne's," Judith said. "Which it is. She just doesn't happen to be here. Do you think we can place any guests between now and Monday?"

"I don't know," Ingrid replied dubiously. "It's short notice, and the season's basically over. I'll see what I can do."

"I appreciate it," Judith said warmly. "So does Jeanne."

Ingrid emitted a little snort. "If Jeanne appreciates it so much, why doesn't she stick around?"

"It's because of Duane," Judith said. "She needed a break after the trauma of his sudden death."

"I don't mean *that*," Ingrid countered. "I mean, why is Jeanne selling the Chavez Cove B&B? The deal's been in the works since before Duane died."

Judith put a hand to her head. "I didn't know that," she said dully. "Has she found a buyer?"

"Not yet. It won't be easy. Not everybody wants to get stuck out on a little island like Chavez. But don't tell anybody I said so," Ingrid added, dropping her voice. "Okay, Judith, my husband just got home from work. I'd better see what kind of pizza he wants me to order. I'll let you know if I come up with any reservation possibilities. Take care and try to keep the body count down. See you.''

Furious, Judith flung the guest registration across the kitchen. Renie, who wasn't used to such a display of temper from her cousin, jumped. ''What's wrong now?'' she asked in a mild tone.

''Everything! I hate everybody on this island! It's nothing but a big rock full of stupid secrets! I wish—I *really* do—that Jeanne had told us we could leave. Now it turns out that Jeanne is trying to sell this place. I don't blame her in a way—maybe she's sick of these people, too.'' Judith began to simmer down. ''Now I'll have to call Mother. She may not remember anything, but at least she'll tell me about it.''

''Huh?'' Mystified, Renie looked up from the potatoes she'd been peeling.

Judith paid no heed. The phone rang in the toolshed seven times before Gertrude picked up the receiver. ''How was bridge?'' Judith asked, forcing herself to sound cheerful.

''Whose bridge?'' growled Gertrude. ''My partial plate's loose. Can you take me to the dentist tomorrow?''

''What?'' Judith's false cheer faded. ''No, of course not. I'm not coming back until next Wednesday.''

''Coming back? Where've you been?''

''I'm up here at . . . Oh, Lord,'' Judith said, briefly turning away from the mouthpiece. ''Where do you think I am?''

''In your kitchen, where else? It's almost suppertime. In fact, it's past *my* suppertime.'' Judith and Joe's six o'clock dinner hour was a long-standing bone of contention between mother and daughter. ''What are we having?''

''Mother,'' Judith said carefully, ''I'm not at home. I'm at Chavez Cove in the Santa Lucias. Renie and I left yesterday morning. Do you remember that?''

''You're crazy,'' Gertrude declared. ''Why are you calling me on the phone when you could move your fat tail about twenty yards from the house to my suitcase-sized apartment? You get lazier by the day, Judith Anne. How about beans and wienies for supper?''

''Why not?'' Judith answered in a weak voice. ''I'm hanging up now, Mother. I'll see you soon.''

''You'd better,'' Gertrude said in a warning tone. ''I'm half-starved. Sophie O'Dell served us slop-on-a-mop for lunch. At least that's what it tasted like. No substance. No flavor. No pro-*tein*.''

''That's a shame, Mother. Bye, now.'' Judith winced as Gertrude banged the phone down in her ear. ''I think I'll have another drink,'' Judith said, sounding dazed. ''Maybe I'll take up smoking again. Do you have any heroin with you, coz?''

''That bad, huh?'' Renie poured cold water over the potato slices. ''Did she mention your fragile health as a child?''

''She doesn't remember that I ever was a child.'' Judith corrected herself: ''No, she doesn't remember that I grew up.'' Forlornly, Judith gazed at Renie. ''Which is it, coz?''

Renie shook her head. ''As somebody wise once said, 'When did the child become the mother? And when did the mother become the child?' It's tough. What's worse, is that it's not just our present. It's our future, too.''

With a sad little smile, Judith faced the liquor cabinet.

To the cousins' surprise, the rest of the evening was peaceful. No one dropped in, no one telephoned, no bodies were found at the bottom of the stairs. After dinner, Judith and Renie made hot chocolate and watched a video. Then they each selected a book from Jeanne's library and read for an hour. Around eleven-thirty, Renie decided she would adjourn to the loft. Judith could have the master bedroom to herself.

''You're not nervous?'' Judith inquired.

Renie shook her head. ''Not really. I think whoever killed Burrell has no reason to do ditto to us. Don't you agree?''

"Yes, I do," Judith replied. "Snipers are random killers. So are serial murderers, in a way. But not the kind of person who does in H. Burrell Hodge. Burrell strikes me as the type who invites murder."

The thought stayed with Judith as she prepared for bed a few minutes later. She had read somewhere that the victim almost always held the key to the killer's identity. The trick was to study every facet of the dead person's life history, attitudes, and habits. Judith knew some of the facts about Burrell, but not enough. Despite his overbearing manner, he ran a small empire that was devoted to doing good. He had failed at marriage and lived alone. He was apparently well-off, bent on expansion. He despised drink, and, presumably, drugs. And, what struck Judith as most important, *he had been to Chavez Island before the day he died.*

Sitting on the edge of the bed facing Jeanne Barber's tidy desk, Judith was certain that somehow Burrell was connected to at least one person who lived on the island. Which one? Or was it all of them? When had he come to Chavez before Monday? Why had he come?

Judith's gaze fell on Marcia Barber Andersen's wedding picture. She was pretty, in an insipid sort of way. She didn't look at all like Jeanne. Maybe she resembled Duane. There was a picture of him on the desk, too, with his arm around Jeanne. They were both wearing resort clothes and had leis around their necks. Hawaii, Judith was sure; perhaps a silver anniversary trip. Duane was fair-haired, with a pleasant face and just a slight bulge around the midsection of his flowered shirt.

But Marcia didn't look like him, either. She was dark and petite. Judith recalled Jeanne's angry remark: "Why don't you ask if we ever met Marcia's real parents?" Or something very like that. Marcia must have been adopted. Judith stared at the picture for a long time before she turned off the light.

An idea took root. Judith thought it might blossom into a motive for murder.

TWELVE

THERE WERE NO muffins to bake or baskets to deliver the next morning. Judith and Renie both slept in. When Judith awoke shortly before eight-thirty, Renie was still asleep. Letting her cousin slumber on, Judith finished breakfast and was having a third cup of coffee when Cilla Carr arrived with her cleaning equipment.

"I hate Lulu McLean!" Cilla declared as she hurtled into the living room. "Do you know what? She thinks I killed that Mr. Hodge! Isn't that stupid?" Grasping a can of furniture polish, Cilla started spraying every wood surface in sight.

Judith eyed Cilla with curiosity. "Because of the mallet?"

"That's right. I hardly know her, but for some reason she's never liked me. According to her, I'm the only person in the whole world who owns a mallet. And if I don't know where it is, then it must be the murder weapon. So I did it." Cilla waved her hands above her head. "I never even met that guy! Why would I kill him?"

"Maybe your mother knew him," Judith said, trying to make it sound like a joke.

Cilla, however, wasn't laughing. "That's dumb! Why would my mother know Hodge?"

Judith lifted one shoulder. "I don't know much about you or your mother. Did she work? Are you from around here? What's your background? Those are the kind of questions that Lulu McLean is bound to ask." Judith had been wanting to ask them, too.

"My mother and I lived in Ketchikan, Alaska, for over twenty years. She was the bookkeeper at a fish cannery. When she decided to take early retirement five years ago, we moved to the Lower Forty-Eight. Oregon at first, then Idaho. Finally here. Alaskans don't like cities." Cilla lowered her voice as well as her eyes. "Mother's had her emotional problems. People make her nervous. She likes Chavez. It's remote, quiet. It suits her."

Judith gave Cilla a probing look. "And you?"

Somewhere in the reaches of the high ceiling, a voice barked a command: "Pipe down!" Gazing up, they could see Renie's face peering through the loft's railing. "Somebody's trying to sleep up here!"

"It's nine-thirty," Judith called. "Most people are up."

"Most people are stupid," Renie retorted, then disappeared.

Judith smiled at Cilla. "My cousin's not a morning person. Why don't we go out into the kitchen and have a cup of coffee? You don't have to clean the cabins today."

"But I do," Cilla protested. "Miss Hennessy and the Estacadas didn't check out until yesterday afternoon."

"There's still no rush," Judith pointed out. "I don't have anyone coming today. That I know of. Let's sit for a while. Then I'll come along and give you a hand with the cleaning."

Sitting at the trestle table, Judith steered the conversation back to the Carrs' choice of Chavez Island. "How did you hear that there was a place for sale? It seems kind of chancy that you found an available house here."

Cilla shook her blond curls. "Not really. Earlier this year, my mother got a letter from somebody who knew we were looking for a setting like Chavez Island. It turned out to be perfect."

"You bought from a couple named Lowman, I understand," Judith said in what she hoped was a conversational tone.

Cilla shook her head. "Not the Lowmans. They were renters."

"It must have cost a lot," Judith said rather vaguely.

"Not really," Cilla replied, her attention diverted by a full-grown raccoon which was standing on its hind legs at the screen door. "My mother says we got the place for next to nothing. I suppose most people don't want to be so isolated." Rising from the bench, Cilla went to over to look at the raccoon. "Isn't he adorable? It's too bad we're not supposed to feed them. I don't see how anything so cute can be so mean."

"Appearances are deceiving," Judith murmured. "With people as well as animals. Cilla," she went on in a more normal voice, "are you acquainted with Jeanne's daughter, Marcia? She must be about your age."

"I've never met her," Cilla said, bending down to make cooing noises at the raccoon. "Mother and I didn't move here until last spring, remember?"

Given her recent track record of forgetfulness, Judith was pleased that she had, in fact, remembered. "But," she added, rising from the trestle table, "I thought you might have met her when she came to visit her folks. Or when her father died."

The raccoon gave up its fruitless begging and lumbered away. "I did see her at Duane Barber's funeral in Laurel Harbor," Cilla said, straightening up after retying one of her tennis shoes. "Marcia was there with her husband. But I didn't actually meet her. Mother handled all the condolences for both of us."

"Duane Barber was too young to die," Judith remarked, taking the coffee mugs over to the sink. "I know the loss was hard for Jeanne. It must have been tough on Marcia, too. My own dad died when I was twenty. He had a rheumatic heart. Sometimes I feel as if I never really knew him."

"Same here," Cilla agreed. "I never knew my father when I was growing up. I was a love-child." Cilla showed her dimples. "No one used to talk about things like that. But now it's common. And I don't mind, not really. Especially now." For a moment, the young woman's face clouded over. Then she lifted her chin and her elfin features again became animated. "It's stupid to be ashamed of falling in love. Sometimes things just don't work out. There must be good reasons why not. I think my mother was very brave."

Judith tried to picture Rowena Carr in the throes of reckless passion. The image was more than a little blurry. But, as she'd just told Cilla, appearances could be deceiving. "So she raised you on her own?"

Cilla nodded, her busy hands wiping up crumbs from the counter. "It was okay, most of the time. It's only been in the last few years that Mother has been . . . unstable. She hit fifty, and it was like somebody pushed a button. Bzzzt! She refused to admit she was middle-aged. That's when she started dyeing her hair and wearing too much makeup. Her emotional state became fragile almost overnight. I used to have these fantasies," she went on, neatly arranging the phone book, the napkin holder, and a mug full of pencils and pens, "that my father had his own fishing fleet or that he was a trapper or one of those recluses who lives a thousand miles from civilization. He couldn't be with us because he had to follow his calling. In a way, I guess that's true. Isn't it weird how things you imagine often turn out to be right?" Cilla had grown wistful.

The remark mystified Judith. "Are you saying you finally met your father?"

A sly look crept into Cilla's eyes. "Let's say I've seen the light. Or had it shown to me. Whoa!" Cilla cried, bursting out of the kitchen and into the living room. "I've got work to do! The day's moving right along. Shall I start with the cabins first and come back later when your cousin is awake?"

"That's fine," Judith replied. "But I'm going to help

with the cabins.'' It occurred to her that she could do a little investigating of the premises so recently occupied by her departed guests. Judith winced a bit as she considered that one of them had departed permanently.

The fog was lying in again as Judith and Cilla walked along the path to the cabins. ''You know,'' Cilla was saying as they reached the three flagstone walks, ''I wish I knew how I misplaced that mallet.'' She pointed to the woodpile where the badminton and croquet sets were kept along with a stack of horseshoes. ''I must have left it here after I set up the net. Anyone could have taken it, I suppose.''

Judith said nothing. Cilla was right—up to a point. The sports-equipment area was literally off the beaten track. Only the game participants would notice an object left lying on the ground.

''Where was the net set up?'' Judith inquired. ''It's not there now, it's next to the woodpile.''

Cilla indicated a grassy section between the nearest flagstone walk and the woods. ''You can see the holes.'' She moved forward a few steps and bounced up and down. ''Here's one. The other is over there.'' She pointed toward Judith.

''It's a hole, all right,'' Judith said, noting the one-inch circle amid the grass, clover, buttercups, and a few wild strawberry runners. ''Do you think you left it by one of the holes or over by the rest of the sporting equipment?''

''I wouldn't leave it on the ground,'' Cilla responded with feeling. ''Somebody might trip over it while they were playing. I'm sure I put it back in my tool kit.''

Judith decided to let the matter drop. The two women went inside the cabin that had been occupied by the Estacadas. Rob and Stacie had left the place in considerable disarray. The bed was not only unmade, it was virtually undone. Empty mineral water bottles had been abandoned in every room, including the shower stall. The remnants of Judith's breakfast basket littered the living room and kitchenette. There were dirty dishes, glasses, and silverware on most of the surfaces, and something had been spilled on the braided rug. The circular area was still damp, as well as discolored.

Cilla shook her head in dismay. ''Sometimes people are pigs.'' She bent down to sniff at the rug. ''Champagne. It ought to come out with a bit of scrubbing.''

It took Judith and Cilla over half an hour to put the cabin straight. They were relieved to find that June Hennessy had left her lodging neat as a pin. Cilla took on the perfunctory cleaning task while Judith searched for the schoolteacher's missing cameo brooch. Finding no trace of it, Judith went next door to check on Burrell's cabin. It had been tidied since she and Rafe had searched the premises Monday night. Judith knew that Deputy McLean's underlings had gone over the cabin with a fine-tooth comb, though they apparently had found nothing of significance. Still, Judith felt obligated to make one last pass.

The effort proved unproductive. McLean's subordinates had removed all of Hodge's personal effects, presumably to ship them back to Adhab. For a few moments, she stood quietly in the living room, wishing the walls could speak. Of course she heard nothing, except the wind in the trees. Judith went back outside just as Cilla came out of June Hennessy's cabin.

''All done,'' Cilla announced. ''I'll do your place next. Unless your cousin's still asleep.''

''She'd better not be,'' Judith averred. ''We're due to leave for Laurel Harbor in about twenty minutes.''

''You're going with Rafe?'' Cilla's face softened at the mention of his name.

Judith nodded. ''I wonder—does he pull into Chavez Cove, or should we go down to his place?''

''He'll pull in at your dock—Jeanne's dock, I mean.'' Cilla averted her gaze. ''Rafe likes to keep his private world private. It's a darling little house on stilts. He's got all these stuffed birds and old bones and tusks and even an umiak that hangs from the ceiling. Sometimes he takes care of sick animals or birds. He knows so much about nature.

I enjoy talking to him about Alaska. He spent quite a bit of time there.''

"Doing what?" Judith asked.

Cilla's brow clouded. "Something with ships. He was a sailor. Not like in the navy, but oceangoing vessels. I think. Rafe doesn't talk about that much. But he likes to show off his souvenirs, especially the stuffed seabirds.''

"It seems you're welcome at his hideaway,'' Judith noted, as they came out of the woods by the Barber house.

"I love to visit the animals,'' Cilla replied a bit stiffly.

Judith recalled Rowena Carr's disapproval of her daughter keeping company with Rafe St. Jacques. But it was none of Judith's business. Cilla was a grown woman, though her insular life prompted Judith to think that, emotionally, she was still quite young. It was still none of Judith's business.

Renie was not only up but dressed. She was just clearing away her breakfast dishes when Judith and Cilla arrived.

"I couldn't get back to sleep,'' Renie said in a miffed tone. "Some people have no respect for others. All that loud talk put me on edge.''

"You slept for over nine hours, you lazy twerp,'' Judith chided. "Let's head for the dock. Rafe should be along in a couple of minutes.''

Leaving Cilla to her chores, the cousins descended the stairway to the cove. The fog was lifting, allowing Judith and Renie a partial view of the water. The sailboats were gone, but a large cabin cruiser was moving at a stately pace, while several noisy gulls flew in its wake. At the far end of the dock, a heron stood majestic and motionless. He took wing only when the bow of Rafe's boat nosed into the cove a few minutes later.

Rafe assumed the role of tour guide during the first half of the trip. He spoke with affection of the orca whales, the sea otters, the cormorants, the kingfishers, the seals, the dolphins, the murres, even the ubiquitous gulls.

Feeling the sea spray caress her face, Judith listened attentively. "You mentioned that Eagle Lake was a bird sanctuary,'' she said as the cruiser bobbed on the open water.

"But we didn't see many birds. Just some ducks, as I recall."

Rafe's profile turned grim. "It used to be a bird sanctuary. It will again, I hope. God knows, I'm doing my best to keep it hospitable for all kinds of birds."

"What happened?" Renie asked as the brisk breeze whipped at her chestnut curls.

Rafe was slow to respond. "It was one of those terrible misfortunes. Seven years ago, almost to the day." He paused, and when he spoke again, his tone was much lighter. "Where do you plan to have lunch in Laurel Harbor? I'd recommend The Green Grill. They have a wonderful vegetarian menu. Be sure to try their zucchini omelet. Of course they don't use real eggs. That wouldn't be healthy."

Renie's horrified expression indicated The Green Grill might as well serve live germs. "We'll think about it," Judith hedged. "Say, Rafe, speaking of greenery, I understand you and Burrell had a bit of a dustup about ferns. Why would he be against them? Ferns are lovely."

From his place at the helm, Rafe glanced over his shoulder. "Ferns? You must have misunderstood. I never discussed ferns with H. Burrell Hodge. Or anything else, for that matter. The only time I saw him was when he came over from Laurel Harbor with the two of you Monday morning."

Judith exchanged puzzled looks with Renie. "Oh," Judith said in a small voice. "I guess I didn't hear right. Someone told me you'd called on him at his cabin Monday afternoon."

Rafe had turned back to face the bow of the boat, but Judith thought he tensed ever so slightly. "No, it wasn't me. I never saw Mr. Hodge after he arrived." The statement seemed final.

The fog had lifted by the time they arrived in Laurel Harbor at eleven-forty-five. Rafe had errands in town which would take at least a couple of hours. When did the cousins want to return to Chavez Cove?

Judith had hoped to spend the entire afternoon on Perez Island. She hemmed and hawed until Renie spoke up.

"With no guests, we're bored to tears. Could you come back for us around eight? Or do you have running lights?"

Rafe seemed unruffled by the request. "Of course. I often make trips in the dark. Eight o'clock right here then?"

Agreeing on the appointed time and place, the cousins allowed Rafe to point them in the direction of The Green Grill. As soon as he had disappeared, Renie grabbed Judith by the arm. "Anything but vegetarian food! I'd rather eat a brick!"

Judith laughed. "How about House of Grease across the street? It's not called that, but I'll bet it lives up to the name."

The Beef Reef provided the cousins with all the deep-fried selections that a clogged artery could desire. Judith chose the Reuben; Renie went for the beef dip, rare. Salads slathered in Roquefort dressing and baskets of french fries completed their entrees.

"Rafe told a foolish lie," Judith said, her eyes roaming around the restaurant's rough-hewn interior. Horse collars, cowbells, shovels, and pitchforks hung from the unvarnished cedar walls. Despite the potential view, there were no windows. Illumination was provided by red, green, and amber lanterns that looked as if they'd been stolen from a railroad line. The dozen or so customers sat on low-backed chairs at bare wooden tables. But the place was clean, and the food was hearty. "Everybody who lives on Chavez Island lies," Judith continued after sinking her teeth into the Reuben sandwich. "Either that or they don't say anything."

"I suppose," Renie mused, "that Rafe didn't want anyone to know he'd quarreled with Burrell. Still, it doesn't mean Rafe killed him. Ferns aren't usually a strong motive for murder."

"Hey," Judith reminded Renie, "you're the one who figured that the ferns were part of a bigger picture—Adhab versus The Environment. Think about it. You also said that these people on Chavez don't like other people. To a nature lover like Rafe, what's a human life compared to saving the ecology of the Santa Lucias?''

Renie grew thoughtful. ''Put like that . . . Maybe. I can kind of see Rafe bashing in Burrell's skull with that mallet. *If* the mallet was the weapon. But I can't envision Cilla or Mrs. Carr or Esther doing the dirty deed.''

Judith arched an eyebrow. ''Cross all the women off the suspect list? Come on, coz—*you* bashed him first.''

Renie winced. ''Okay, okay—but I used a domestic item. A woman's weapon, as it were.'' She gobbled up three big french fries before continuing. ''That 'misfortune' Rafe mentioned—but didn't elucidate—that was another September disaster. I wonder what it was? Something about the Santa Lucias back then rings a bell with me. What do you remember from seven years ago?''

''I remember trying to salvage the rest of my life after Dan died,'' Judith responded dryly. ''I'm afraid I was kind of self-absorbed back then.''

Ten minutes later, the cousins were absorbing the sights and sounds and smells of Laurel Harbor. Set on a hill above a curving bay that was large enough to encompass a much smaller island known as Little Perez, the town sloped upward and receded into the forest. Judith guessed that there were probably no more than two thousand full-time residents. There were commuters who worked on the mainland, and, Judith had heard, some Hollywood types who retreated to the Santa Lucias when they weren't actively involved in moviemaking. On this golden September afternoon, the main street which ran parallel to the harbor was fairly busy. Apparently, quite a few visitors lingered on Perez Island. The salt air was tinged with gas fumes and food smells. Sporting goods, hobbies, bicycle and boat rentals, souvenirs, clothing, food, drugs, and sundries were featured in the stores housed in an architectural range that ran the gamut from Victorian gingerbread to California contemporary. There was a movie theater, a hotel, two coin laundries, and at least five restaurants and four taverns. Signs pointed to various churches, schools, and the hospital. Laurel Harbor seemed to have something for everyone.

"Aha!" Judith exclaimed, pointing to a window that was filled with small colored photos of every size, style, and price range of houses. "It's Perez Properties. Shall we?"

Renie shrugged. The real-estate offices included one large room with three desks and an inner office. A plump middle-aged woman with a sleek blond pageboy looked up when the cousins entered. The nameplate on her desk read "Ella Stovall."

Judith made the introductions. Ella's big smile faded only a jot when she realized that Judith and Renie weren't prospective buyers, but the temporary inhabitants of Chavez Cove. "Coffee?" she inquired, indicating a small table with a big urn and several paper cups.

"No, thanks," Judith replied, after she and Renie had sat down in the modular vinyl chairs next to Ella's desk. "We're doing some snooping," Judith went on, having decided to be candid. "As you may have guessed, we're kind of on the spot. You deal with newcomers all the time. You know how suspicion runs in small communities. The local folks probably think we killed Mr. Hodge."

"I don't." Ella Stovall had grown serious. "But then I'm not from here originally. It's natural for people to think the worst of strangers. They always make better villains than the neighbors. By the way, I spoke to Lulu McLean about an hour ago. She'd already found out from Adhab's headquarters what Mr. Hodge wanted in the Santa Lucias. Basically," Ella continued with a faint show of reluctance, "he was on a scouting expedition. Chavez, Perez, Sanchez, and Salvador Islands all have properties that would have been of potential interest to him. Unfortunately, I never had the chance to meet with him. He was supposed to be here today or tomorrow. Of course, that isn't going to happen. Lulu also said they were releasing the body today." Ella now looked downright grim.

Judith nodded faintly. "So an actual deal wasn't in the works?"

"Not officially. But," Ella added, "Mr. Hodge might have been in private negotiations. You'd be surprised how people try to circumvent real-estate agents. They think they can save the cost of a commission. What they don't realize is that they can buy themselves a lot of grief."

"I'm curious about something else," Judith said, sensing that she'd reached a dead end as far as the real-estate angle was concerned. "Who actually owns the bulk of Chavez Island? I've heard two different versions."

Ella's hazel eyes turned wary as she darted a glance at the closed door of the inner office. "I'm not trying to be difficult, but that's a question I'm not free to answer. Sorry."

Renie leaned an elbow on the desk. "We can check it through the county rolls."

Ella gave Renie a faint smile. "That's what you'll have to do, I guess."

The door to the inner office opened. A stocky man wearing a shirt, tie, sport coat, and slacks saw the cousins and offered a wide smile that stopped just short of his eyes. He was in his late forties, with receding brown hair, an aquiline nose, and a small, almost dainty mouth. Judith was sure that he was Simon Dobler, though except for the size and stature, she saw little resemblance to the crusty Elrod.

Ella was quick to make introductions. Simon shook hands with Judith and Renie. He kept smiling, but there was still no warmth in his eyes.

"We met your father," Judith said. "He's quite a guy."

Simon's flinch was almost imperceptible. "Pappy can be a curmudgeon sometimes. He lives in the past, when trespassers and poachers could be stopped by pointing a gun. I try to tell him he'll get sued one of these days."

The phone had rung on Ella's desk. She picked it up, while the cousins rose and moved a few feet away so that their conversation wouldn't disturb Ella.

"You have a sister, I hear," Judith remarked, as a fair-haired young man came into the office, nodded at Simon, and sat down at one of the other vacant desks.

"Yes," Simon answered. "Excuse me," he gestured at the young man who was sorting phone messages. "I must check in with Allan. Nice to meet you."

Judith and Renie looked at each other. It appeared they had outworn their welcome. With a wave to Ella, Judith started for the door. They had gone only a few steps when Ella called after them.

"Sorry about that," she said, joining them on the sidewalk. "Look," she went on, lowering her voice, though except for a couple of older women who were chattering away as they headed into the bakery next door, no one could have heard, "I feel silly being so tight-lipped about who owns what on Chavez. The truth is, I'm not sure myself. But the one thing I do know is that Mr. Dobler doesn't like his employees talking about it. It seems silly, but there it is." She gave the cousins a helpless look.

"That's okay," Judith assured the real-estate agent. "What bothered me most was how abrupt Mr. Dobler was just now. Is his sister in a mental home or something?"

Ella burst out laughing. "Hardly! You just caught him on a bad day. Business always goes downhill this time of year, and he pouts all the way through March. As a matter of fact, his sister is in one of the finest homes in the islands. You know the place—Stoneyhenge. Haven't you met Esther Danfield?"

"Oh, well," Judith said in a lost voice as she and Renie headed for the offices of the *Laurel Harbor Merchant,* "I guess I shouldn't be surprised. If small towns are inbred, why not tiny islands?"

"Maybe this explains the confusion about who owns what," Renie suggested. "Both families had property on Chavez, and then they merged."

"That's possible," Judith allowed, pausing to peer through the newspaper office's front window. She saw two desks, some file cabinets, and a couple of computer terminals. She didn't see Abu until Renie opened the door.

"Chavez ladies!" Abu cried in pleasure. "You be coming in! You be telling Abu much news. And so forth." He bowed several times.

"We don't have much news," Judith said in an apologetic voice. "What we'd like is a favor."

It took five minutes to make Abu understand the request to go through back issues of the paper. There was no index, and previous editions of the *Merchant* were kept in binders by year.

"You read stories by Abu?" the young man asked excitedly. "I come to here in August only. Mr. Fernandez, twenty-six, formerly Laurel Harbor, quit and go to big city. Abu make many American dollars here, six each hour."

"That's . . . grand," Judith said, keeping her smile fixed in place. "Where's the editor?"

"Editor man?" Abu looked at the nearer of the two desks as if he expected someone to pop up from under the empty chair. "Mr. Grainger, fifty-three, of Orca Point, eat middle meal. Return at two. Paper come then, too. And so forth."

Judith understood the part about Mr. Grainger being at lunch and assumed that Abu was trying to tell the cousins that the weekly edition of the *Merchant* would be delivered about the same time that the editor got back. With a friendly nod, she pulled out the volume that was dated from seven years earlier. Renie got stuck with Abu's guided tour of the previous week's issue.

It didn't take long for Judith to find what she wanted in the September back issues. Mr. Grainger, or whoever had been the editor seven years ago, had used huge black type to proclaim the news that the Santa Lucias had suffered an environmental catastrophe: OIL SPILL MENACES ISLANDS. The subhead read "Sea Life Destroyed in Wake of Tanker Disaster; Loss Could Be in Millions." There was also a somewhat grainy three-column photograph of a large ship in open waters.

Renie, unfortunately, was still making tactful comments

about Abu's most recent journalistic efforts. Judith gave up trying to catch her cousin's eye, and began reading the article itself. The story was depressingly familiar: A supertanker, bound for one of the big refineries on the mainland, had started to leak oil just off Chavez Island. The spillage, ultimately totaling over one hundred thousand barrels of crude, had spread as far as Perez and Sanchez Islands. The damage to marine life, shore-nesting birds, and sea mammals wasn't yet known, but was estimated to be enormous.

The story jumped to an inside page with a better-quality photo that was infinitely more heartrending. A fair-haired child stood on a stretch of sand, peering down at three dead terns. Judith continued reading.

"The *Petroleum Monarch*'s captain, Lawrence M. Larrabee, has refused to answer questions about what caused the spill. However, his first mate, Rafael St. Jacques, issued a personal, public apology. St. Jacques did not blame anyone in his statement, though he indicated that the facts behind the disaster would come out in a hearing which will be held . . ."

Renie had finally finished admiring Abu's reporting. While Abu answered the telephone, she sidled over to Judith and immediately spotted Rafe's name. "Wow! So he was involved in that mess! I remember it now—I think it turned out that the captain got fired because he drank or something. It was sheer carelessness. And Rafe was there. I'll be darned."

"Apparently," Judith said, keeping her voice down, "that's his deep, dark secret. Maybe he felt he shared the blame. Maybe that's why he settled in the Santa Lucias— to make amends."

"And?" Renie prompted.

Judith stared at her cousin. "And what?"

"And what's it all got to do with H. Burrell Hodge?"

Judith shook her head. "I don't know. Nothing, maybe. Except in a broad sense—Hodge was coming to the islands to screw up the environment. Rafe wanted to stop him."

Abu had gotten off the phone and picked up a camera.

He turned, bowing to the cousins. "Abu go. Cars crash, Jack Rabbit Road, no hurts, some dents, picture to take. And so forth." He bowed again before scurrying out the door.

Amused, Judith and Renie looked at each other. "Serena Jones, Judith Flynn, Heraldsgate Hill," Judith said, unable to resist mimicking Abu, "temporarily put in charge of local newspaper. And so forth. What do we look for next?"

Renie perched on the edge of the desk Abu had just vacated. "What do you want to know?"

Judith thought. "A history of the island might come in handy. The paper's been around since 1910." She scanned the shelves, but discovered that the bound volumes only went back to 1960. "They must store the rest of them someplace else. Let's see . . ." In a flutter of dust, she removed the volume from twenty-five years ago. "Doc's debacle—we'll see if the story's here. Esther said it happened on the first day of fall, so it should be in the last or next to last issue of September."

But there was nothing about a woman dying in childbirth or a baby surviving. "The editor might have considered it an invasion of privacy," Renie noted. "Smaller communities often invoke their own forms of censorship. Did you check the births?"

"There weren't any in these editions," Judith said, pointing to the issues dated September twenty-third and September thirtieth. "I don't imagine they had a big population explosion around here in those days."

On a whim, Renie flipped to the first issue in October. Under a line drawing of a stork was a headline that read "Welcome Baby Islanders." "There are two births," Renie said. " 'Mr. and Mrs. Edmund Bolger, Deer Creek Road, Sanchez Island, a girl, Cathleen Lynn, six pounds, ten ounces, September twenty-ninth.' Little Miss Bolger must have just missed the deadline. Hey!" Renie suddenly grew animated. "Listen to this! 'Mr. and Mrs. Bates Danfield, Stoneyhenge, Chavez Island, a boy, Elliott Arnold, seven pounds, nine ounces, October second.' " She wiggled her eyebrows at Judith. "Well?"

Judith rubbed her chin. "Well what? Are you giving me a quiz this afternoon?"

Renie's enthusiasm dwindled. "I had an off-the-wall idea. But thinking it through makes it sound stupid. You know—there aren't all that many babies born around here, at least not back in the sixties. Doc delivers one to an ill-fated mother, and about ten days later, Esther has a boy. It seems strange, that's all."

Except for the hum of the computers, the newspaper office grew silent. Judith was sorting through Renie's somewhat garbled idea. "Coz," Judith finally said, "did you look at Marcia Barber Andersen's wedding picture? How old do you think she is?"

Renie considered. "Early, mid-twenties. But when was it taken?"

"I don't know," Judith replied slowly. "As I recall, Jeanne mentioned something about her daughter getting married fairly recently, say within the past year. Marcia's adopted." Judith gazed expectantly at Renie.

"So? You think she's the kid whose mother died?"

"It's possible. Except that the Barbers didn't live here twenty-five years ago."

"Then it's not likely. Would you move to a place because the doctor who delivered your adopted baby happened to run a general store there?"

Judith sighed. "You're right. It's lame. And it's too much to be a coincidence. I imagine they moved here because Duane's sister, Flora, was a resident." Her eyes wandered to the rest of the bound *Merchant*s. "I wish I knew what we were looking for."

A man about the same age as the cousins came through the door. He was of medium height with thinning gray hair and a long, melancholy face. "Are you waiting for me?" he asked in a mournful voice.

"Maybe," Judith answered brightly. "Are you Mr. Grainger?"

"I am," the man responded with something that sounded like regret. "Ned Grainger, editor, publisher, and bearer of burdens. What can I do for you? Not much, probably."

"That depends on how long you've been in Laurel Harbor," Judith said, smiling encouragement.

"Too long," Grainger replied, sitting down at the other vacant desk. "Newspapering isn't what it used to be." He waved a weary hand at the computer screen that was staring back at him. "Who reads? Except off of one of these damned things. It's depressing."

"You've been in the business . . . ah . . . how long?" Judith prodded.

"I cut my teeth on a weekly in Utah," Grainger lamented. "I went on to Idaho, Wyoming, finally here. Everywhere I got work, circulation dropped off. Display ads started to shrink. Even the classifieds dried up. There were cow-pies in Wyoming bigger than our annual advertising income. It was pathetic."

"I don't suppose you were here in the mid-sixties," Judith said wistfully.

"There were a few bright moments back in July and August," Grainger continued, not looking at either of the cousins. "Somebody said we were getting a new coffee-house, maybe one of those discount chains, too. But it never happened. Betsy's Bridal Boutique and Cold Storage closed down. So did Herbie's In-And-Out-In-An-Hour-Or-Else Auto Upholstery. It's just one damned thing after . . ."

Judith and Renie tiptoed out of the *Merchant*. "I don't even want to ask him about Abu," Judith said as they reached the sidewalk. "How were his stories, by the way?"

"Amazingly coherent," Renie replied. "Skillful editing, I'd guess. What now?"

"Another quiz question?" Judith grinned at Renie. "How about the county offices? Believe it or not, I'd say they're located in that dark red building that looks like a big barn up the street. There's a flag on top."

The big red barn was indeed the seat of Santa Lucia County. Despite the style and age of the exterior, the interior was remarkably up-to-date. A tall, thin woman with masses of white hair piled on top of her head led the cousins to the record section, which was on a brand-new computer system. No one was at either of the two terminals, so Judith and Renie commandeered them both.

"I'll do deaths," Judith said. "You take births."

Renie wrinkled her pug nose at Judith. "You always get the stiffs. What do I do with the births?"

"Key in Danfields, Doblers, et al. See what happens."

What happened to Judith wasn't very enlightening. She came up with the death dates for Bates Danfield's grandfather and parents. She also found Elrod Dobler's parents and his wife, Flora Barber Dobler. Then she pulled up Duane Barber. Again, there was nothing startling except the mildly interesting information that Duane and his sister, Flora, had been born over on the mainland not far from the gateway to the Santa Lucias.

"Zip," she murmured, turning to see how Renie was doing. "Anything hot?"

"I found the two Danfield kids, Elliott, and the girl, Eugenia, who was born a little over two years after her brother. I also pulled up Simon and Esther Dobler. Esther's your age, coz."

"She looks younger," Judith grumbled.

"She does not. And she acts about eighty, especially when she's drinking gin out of a pudding dish." Renie typed in another name. "Oh, my God!"

Judith swiveled in her chair. "What is it?" she demanded, trying to keep her voice down.

Renie was staring transfixed at the computer. "It's a birth. For Francesca Emily Wicker, born September 21, 1960 . . ." Grabbing Judith's arm, Renie shoved her cousin in front of the screen. "Daughter of Francesca Ernestine and Richard Emery Wicker. Coz, Doc delivered his own daughter! And then his wife died! Check the deaths, quick!"

Judith did. Francesca Ernestine Wicker had died the same day that her daughter was born.

THIRTEEN

EMERALD GREEN GRASS covered the sloping knoll that led down from the county courthouse to the street. A sprinkler system was making lazy loops between the driveway that led to the parking lot and a not-quite-life-size statue of an early Spanish explorer. Judith and Renie sat down on a wooden bench that was just out of range of the sprinkler. They were both still shaken by their discoveries in the records office.

"No wonder," Judith said in a faint voice, "Doc doesn't want to talk about why he gave up practicing medicine. Imagine! His own wife died while he was delivering their child!"

Renie was shaking her head and trying to ignore a fox terrier that was sniffing at her latest pair of designer sandals. "I suppose they had an ob-gyn where they lived, but that Doc and his wife—like so many young people—figured they knew it all. So off they went on their camping trip. I've heard other stories like that, where women have gone into premature labor on top of a mountain or down in a canyon or stranded on a desert island. Luckily, they usually don't die."

"But Francesca did, and is buried in the private cemetery. I wonder why," Judith said in a thoughtful voice. "I mean, why not in a cemetery where they lived? Doc didn't come here—as far as I can piece together—until two or three years after the tragedy.''

"Sentiment, maybe," Renie suggested, as the fox terrier attempted an experimental nibble on a bare toe. "Beat it, you little creep! I hate dogs!"

"The baby was named Francesca, too," Judith mused. "Now why would Doc give her up?"

Renie pulled her feet away and tucked them under the bench. "Who said he did?" Panting, the dog crawled under the bench, too. "Go away! Take your stupid fleas with you!"

"You're right," Judith responded in a thoughtful voice. "The girl would be mid-twenties—as we already calculated—and could be on her own by now. But no one has mentioned her. If Doc raised her, surely someone would have alluded to the fact."

The dog had gotten hold of the sandal's left T-strap. Renie pulled on the animal's ear; the fox terrier tugged at the strap. Renie pulled harder; the strap snapped. Renie swore, swooped down on the dog, and started booting it away from her. The dog began to bark. The left sandal fell off. Renie swore again, louder and more colorfully. An elderly couple who had had just gotten out of an aging sedan, a shirtless young man on rollerblades, and a mother pulling two children in a wagon all stopped to stare. The dog reared back, baring its teeth. Renie, with one sandal on and one sandal off, bared hers. Alarmed, Judith stood up and wondered what she could do to break the stalemate.

It was June Hennessy who stepped in. Just as Renie got down on all fours and looked as if she were about to bite the dog, Miss Hennessy put two fingers in her mouth and emitted a shrill whistle. "Edelweiss!" she shouted. The dog took one last look at Renie and ran joyfully to Miss Hennessy.

"My word!" Miss Hennessy exclaimed, looking startled. "It's you! Both of you! From Chavez Cove! Of course!" Her voice finally lowered a jot. "You mentioned coming to Laurel Harbor. Whatever did you do to aggravate Edelweiss?''

Having retrieved her sandal and gotten to her feet, Renie had a full head of irate steam. Judith gritted her teeth and stepped between her cousin and Miss Hennessy. ''Edelweiss got a little frisky with Mrs. Jones's footgear. It's okay—neither of them bit the other one.''

'' '*Okay*'?'' roared Renie. ''What's '*okay*' about having another pair of hundred-dollar sandals ruined?'' She turned an infuriated countenance on Miss Hennessy. ''If it's so '*okay*,' how about ponying up the money to replace the damage done by your ugly mutt?''

Having picked up Edelweiss in her arms, Miss Hennessy grew almost as outraged as Renie. ''People who pay extravagant sums for apparel deserve to have their possessions destroyed! It's decadent! That money could be used to help educate a disadvantaged child! When was the last time you expended some of your obvious surplus to provide schooling for the needy?''

''Last week,'' Renie retorted, ''when I wrote three tuition checks for my idiot children! Don't talk to me about education! My husband's a teacher, too!''

The original gawkers had now been joined by another half dozen people, who had begun to murmur among themselves. To Judith's horror, Abu pulled up in a very old, very battered compact car. It was painted red, white, and blue, with a scattering of stars and large hand-drawn letters that read ''*Lanrel Harbor Merchaut*.'' The car kept backfiring even after Abu turned off the ignition.

''Chavez ladies!'' Abu beamed. ''Is this fights? Are dangers nigh? And so forth?'' He brandished his camera, then began clicking away.

The arrival of Abu somehow served to calm Renie. Or perhaps it was the telephoto lens pointed in her direction. In any event, Renie gave one last swing of the broken sandal and began to wander off toward the courthouse parking lot. Judith was left to face June Hennessy and Abu's clicking camera.

"My cousin isn't a dog lover," Judith said with an apologetic smile. "I am, though. My first husband and our son and I always had a dog." It was true: Judith had only given up keeping dogs when she moved back to the family home on Heraldsgate Hill and Sweetums had tried to turn Mike's little mutt into Hirsute Helper.

Miss Hennessy had begun to simmer down. "Edelweiss sometimes gets excited around strangers," she admitted, stroking the animal's neck. "He never likes it when I leave him. He's still very agitated since I returned yesterday. But of course Jeanne Barber doesn't allow pets at Chavez Cove."

"I can understand that," Judith murmured, keeping one eye on Renie, who was now on the other side of the street reading what looked like an historical marker. Abu, meanwhile, had finished clicking off his roll of film and had taken out a notebook.

"As long as you're on Perez," Miss Hennessy was saying, "you ought to visit Laurel Glen Academy. It's only two miles out of Laurel Harbor."

It took a moment for Judith to remember that Laurel Glen was the name of Miss Hennessy's private boarding school. "I'd like to," she fibbed, "but we don't have much time. I should get back to see if there are any guests coming in tonight or tomorrow. Jeanne wants me to try to fill the unexpected vacancies."

An expression of chagrin crept over Miss Hennessy's face. "Yes, that young couple and I left you in the lurch. As did Mr. Hodge, though I suppose he can't be blamed."

"No," Judith agreed with a grimace, "he can't."

The onlookers had started drifting away, but Abu was now at Judith's side. "Here is Miss June Hennessy, Laurel Glen Academy headmistress, and Mrs. Flynn—first name no given, Chavez Cove"—Abu checked his watch which looked to Judith as if it were very expensive—"3:06 P.M., Wednesday, September fourteenth, why is anger? Is political upheaval? Social unrest? Economic chaos? And so forth?"

"Abu," Judith said patiently, "this is not news. News is when Man Bites Dog. In this case, woman did not bite dog, though she tried. Therefore, nothing needs to be reported. But thank you, Abu, for asking." With a purposeful stride, Judith began walking away. It was immaterial to her whether or not June Hennessy followed.

Miss Hennessy did, however, with Edelweiss trotting at her side. "I understand," she said in a low voice, "that Deputy McLean hasn't yet found the killer. I stopped in at the sheriff's office just now to speak with her." Miss Hennessy nodded at the barnlike building behind her. "I presume you were also calling upon Miss McLean."

"Ah . . . not exactly," Judith replied, dismayed by the realization that she hadn't thought of seeing the deputy while they were in the county offices. "But you say there are no new developments?"

With her mouth set in a grim line, Miss Hennessy shook her head. "At least none that Miss McLean would reveal to me. Now I feel very foolish indeed for having attempted to help her. She's far too aggressive and overbearing. Isn't she aware that it's as important to be a *lady* as well as a *woman*?"

Judith and Miss Hennessy had reached the street, which had no curb but began where the grass ended. Across the way, Renie wandered about in a large circle, gazing at the sky. "You tried to help Deputy McLean?" Judith asked, seizing upon the one fragment of Miss Hennessy's discourse which seemed pertinent to the murder investigation. "How?"

"Perhaps 'help' is too strong a word," Miss Hennessy cautioned. "I merely pointed out that while I was taking a brisk walk Monday evening around six-thirty, I saw someone on the road that goes by what's now the Carr house. It was growing quite dark, so all I could make out was a form up ahead of me. By the time I reached Stoneyhenge— such a lovely home!—whoever it was had disappeared. Perhaps they turned in at the gate. But I realized later that the person might have been in the vicinity of Chavez Cove about the time of . . . the unfortunate incident with Mr. Hodge.''

"You're certain you couldn't tell if it was a man or a woman on the road?'' Judith asked.

Miss Hennessy made a rueful face. "Unfortunately, I'm nearsighted. And as I mentioned, it was almost dark. Indeed, on that part of the road with all the trees growing so close together, it's even darker. Miss McLean asked the same question.''

For a moment, Judith was silent. "You didn't happen to go by the Barber house while you were on your walk, did you?''

"No. I'm sufficiently familiar with the island to know where to cut through from the cabins to the main road," Miss Hennessy explained. "There's a footpath—a deer run, really—that goes off through the woods. It was still light enough when I started out to see clearly.''

Again, Judith lapsed into thought. Three people had now claimed to have seen someone walking on the road, possibly within the time frame of Burrell's death. Elrod Dobler wasn't certain about the time, and Rowena Carr wasn't certain about much of anything. Still, their accounts, along with that of Miss Hennessy's, indicated that someone had been out on the road, perhaps shortly after the murder.

"Did you hear a shot while you were walking?'' Judith inquired, trying not to become distracted by Edelweiss, who was now running in circles around Miss Hennessy and barking in an imperious manner.

Miss Hennessy looked startled. "A shot? My, no! Was that odious little man at Stoneyhenge firing his loathsome gun?''

Judith nodded. "He says he did, but he's not sure when.'' Noting that Renie had walked back toward the central business district, Judith politely took her leave.

She caught up with Renie at the only stoplight in Laurel Harbor. "Where are we going?'' Judith asked.

"To a cobbler,'' Renie answered. "I can't explore Perez Island with one sandal.''

Sam the Shoemaker was located between the drugstore and the bank. It took less than five minutes to reattach the sandal strap. Unfortunately, the repair cost about three times as much as Renie would have paid on Heraldsgate Hill. She was still griping when Judith saw copies of the *Laurel Harbor Merchant* being delivered to a newspaper box at the nearest corner.

"Let's grab a cup of coffee and read all about it," Judith suggested.

After purchasing a latte for Judith and a mocha for Renie at an espresso stand by the ferry terminal, the cousins found another bench, this one perched at the edge of the bluff overlooking the bay. A long line of vehicles was gathering in the loading area, presumably for the three-fifty ferry.

"This isn't half-bad," Judith said as she skimmed the first of two front-page articles about H. Burrell Hodge's murder. "You're right—I suspect Ned Grainger does a heavy rewrite job on Abu's copy."

The straight news account was not only grammatical, but accurate. Judith, however, wasn't pleased to see her name in print. " 'The body was discovered by Judith Flynn, who has temporarily taken over the running of Chavez Cove for owner Jeanne Barber.' " Judith made a face. "I hope this story hasn't gotten into the city papers."

Renie was reading over Judith's shoulder. "Good. They don't mention me at all. Or is that because I'm one of the suspects?"

"Abu or Ned Grainger probably got my name off the forms Lulu McLean filled out," Judith said, hoping to console her cousin. "Look, this other story gives some background on Burrell. Somebody did their homework."

According to the sidebar article, Harold Burrell Hodge was fifty-one years old, and the owner and manager of The Addiction and Rehabilitation Institute, otherwise known as Adhab. He had founded the organization some fourteen years earlier, starting with the mountain facility. Since then, he had established nine other centers throughout the Pacific Northwest as well as in Alaska and Hawaii. Some were devoted exclusively to patients who were addicted to alcohol, others focused on drugs, one was nicotine-oriented, two treated all aspects of substance abuse, and another specialized in sexual dysfunction.

"I wonder what *that* means," Judith murmured.

Renie raised her eyebrows. "Functioning all of the time? Functioning some of the time? Functioning none of the time? All of the above?"

Judith returned to the article. " 'The late Mr. Hodge felt he had a mission in life,' " she read aloud. " 'As a young man, he had suffered from alcoholism. After his recovery at the age of twenty-six, he realized that not only did he not need to retreat from the world, but that he should step up and contribute to helping others who had sunk into a morass of addiction.' "

"Hmm," Renie murmured. "That sounds like a press release. The *Merchant* probably got it from Burrell's headquarters."

"Could be," Judith agreed, then continued reading out loud: " 'Mr. Hodge, who had had a brief failed marriage while he was still drinking, left no survivors. In his own words, he felt he belonged to anyone and everyone who suffered from the disease of addiction. At his request, there will be no services, but memorials may be sent in his name to The Addiction and Rehabilitation Institute at . . . ' " Judith emitted an odd little laugh. "He sounds so altruistic. I suppose he was. But face-to-face, he was kind of awful."

"A dry drunk," Renie declared. "They're the very worst kind. They spend their whole lives *not* drinking and making everybody else pay for their deprivation."

Judith gave Renie a slightly reproachful look. "That's not really fair, coz. I'm not even sure it's the right definition. Anyway, Burrell spent much of his life helping other people."

Renie didn't say anything, but she didn't appear convinced. Judith let the subject drop. "The main story only alludes briefly to Burrell's presence on Chavez Island.

' . . . Exploring the possibilities of opening another center in the Santa Lucias.' Not much help there.''

"It'd be interesting to find out what Burrell did to the environment at those other sites," Renie remarked. "We're not talking about toxic waste here. But building anything can screw up an ecological system if you're heedless. I envision Burrell as barreling ahead, paying no attention to the concerns of others. That's what he did with us when he wanted our prawns.''

Judith suppressed a smile. Only Renie could compare sharing her shellfish with clear-cutting a stand of two-hundred-year-old Douglas firs. "It seems we have two people involved in environmental disasters," Judith noted. "Burrell, with his plans for expansion, and Rafe St. Jacques, who was first mate on the *Petroleum Monarch*.''

"One has regrets, the other didn't give a hoot," Renie said. "Or so we're led to believe.''

Out beyond the jutting arm of land that wrapped around the far end of the bay, a superferry could be seen heading for Laurel Harbor. Judith was always amazed that the huge, bulky four-deck vessels could maneuver so agilely through the narrow passages indicated by the buoy markers. Of course there was the occasional mishap, when a ferry rammed the dock or went aground. Rarely was anyone hurt, since the big boats were always inching their way so close to shore.

The cousins watched for a few moments in silence. Gulls swarmed and circled above the ferry, which had slowed to a crawl upon entering the narrow channel. September's golden haze cast a filter across the horizon, a sign that summer was fading into fall. More cars and RVs and trucks and even a bus had now pulled into line. Foot passengers, many with bicycles, were preparing to board at the slip. At the sound of the ferry's first blast on the whistle, a dozen or more people emerged from various storefronts on the main street and began hurrying back to their vehicles. Judith, who was always an ardent people-watcher, sat back to enjoy the minor spectacle.

"What about Doc?" asked Renie, who was never as in-trigued as Judith by observing the foibles and fancies of her fellow human beings. "Have you figured out if he has a motive to kill Burrell?"

Judith didn't answer right away; she was too busy watch-ing a pudgy young man who had locked himself out of his car. "What? Oh, you mean with regard to Doc's tragedy? No," she added as a ferry official came to the young man's assistance, "I don't see how that ties into Burrell."

The ferry let out another blast on the whistle, a low, moaning sound that reverberated off the bluff. Like a huge white beetle negotiating a pile of pebbles, the superferry crept closer to the slip, angling between the pilings until the bow gently bumped against the dock.

"Motive is hard to come by," Judith murmured, now watching as the ferry crew tied up the vessel with thick braided ropes. "What is there, except for the environ-ment?"

"Not much," Renie replied, finishing her mocha and ris-ing to throw the paper cup into a trash can behind the bench.

"Though I wonder . . ." Judith went on, as if she hadn't heard Renie. "That part in the newspaper article about Bur-rell retreating from the world—where would you retreat, coz?"

"Huh?" Renie sat down again on the bench. "A five-star hotel, probably in Paris. I'd have to check a Michelin guidebook. The George V comes to mind. Hotel kitchens and restaurants shouldn't be rated by stars—they should use pork chop symbols. Yes, a five-pork-chop hotel. That would be nice."

Judith grinned at her cousin. "I'm talking about real peo-ple, not my relatives. Well?"

"My turn to take a quiz?" Renie gave a shake of her head. "I don't know—a cabin deep in the woods? A desert island? Your mother's toolshed?"

"The desert island comes closest." Judith's grin had subsided into a quizzical little smile. "Did you notice what the H. in Burrell's name stood for? It's in the sidebar story.'' Judith tapped the *Merchant*'s front page.

Renie snatched the paper out of Judith's hand. ''Harold Burrell Hodge. So?''

Judith's little smile remained in place. ''Harold—as in Harry. There was someone by that name who worked on Chavez Island. What if Burrell returned to settle here? It makes sense, don't you think?''

Renie appeared to be thinking. Judith waited for the results, meanwhile watching the foot passengers stream off the superferry. ''I think,'' Renie said slowly, ''that you're stretching it.''

Judith, however, wasn't easily swayed. ''We know that Burrell had been to Chavez before his arrival Monday. The question is, when? It needn't be six months ago or even six years ago. Nothing much has changed on the island for at least fifty years. What if Burrell was the Harry who lived down at Hidden Cove?''

The vehicles had started to drive off the ferry, heading up the winding road that led to the heart of town. The ferry official was still trying to unlock the pudgy young man's car, using something that looked like a long wire. A big beer truck rumbled off the ferry, followed by a bread truck, a produce truck, and a dairy truck. Laurel Harbor was about to be restocked.

''You could ask Doc, I suppose,'' Renie said in a doubtful voice.

''I intend to,'' Judith retorted, sipping at the last of her latte. ''Let's invite Doc to breakfast tomorrow morning.''

Renie looked alarmed. ''Breakfast? Morning? Like before ten? Do I have to be there?''

''Suit yourself,'' Judith replied, now fixed on the steady stream of vehicles which were coming off the ferry. ''Do you suppose any of these people need a place to stay tonight? Maybe I should be down on the dock holding a sign.''

''Check in with the Chamber of Commerce,'' Renie suggested. ''It's on the other side of the bank.''

"That's a good idea," Judith said, getting up from the bench. "I should have thought of it myself."

Three minutes later, the cousins were at the Chamber of Commerce office, but it was closed. A hand-printed sign indicated that whoever staffed the premises would "Be back soon."

"Drat," Judith exclaimed. "It sounded like a good idea."

"It was," Renie noted. "Don't lose heart. Here comes Ella Stovall. Maybe she's got some hot news."

The real-estate agent from Perez Properties was hurrying across what had turned into a busy street with the super-ferry's arrival. "Mrs. Flynn!" she called. "Good, you're still here!" Huffing a bit, Ella reached the sidewalk. "Doc Wicker just called me. He thought I might be able to run you down." Ella caught her breath and chuckled. "He knows I keep my eye out for anything that moves along the main drag. Some woman named Heffelump or something has been trying to reach you. She finally phoned Doc."

"Oh!" Judith beamed at Ella. "That would be Ingrid Heffleman, from the state B&B association. May I use a phone in your office to call her?"

Ella said that would be fine. The three women couldn't cross the street until six cars, a swaying RV, two pickup trucks, and a motorcycle had passed. Perez Properties appeared empty when they arrived. Using her calling card, Judith dialed the long-distance number in the city. Ingrid had two reservations, both married couples from out of state, who were looking for accommodations in the Santa Lucias.

"I could have sent them to Perez or Sanchez," Ingrid said in a dry tone, "but I felt obligated to help you out. They're arriving tomorrow, probably in the afternoon."

"That's wonderful," Judith enthused. "Jeanne Barber will be pleased. Can you give me their names and method of payment?"

Ingrid complied. "That'll be two nights for each of them.

If anybody else comes along, I'll keep Chavez Cove at the top of the list. By the way,'' she added slyly, ''we're starting to make plans for the annual state association meeting in February. We need someone to cater the luncheon on the sixteenth. Do you think you can manage that, Judith?''

Judith slumped over Ella's desk. ''Um . . . er . . . well, probably. Is it a buffet?''

''That's right,'' Ingrid replied crisply. ''A hundred to a hundred and fifty people. Three hot dishes, four kinds of cold sandwiches, five salads, two desserts, and assorted condiments. Rolls, of course, and beverages. I'll put you down.''

Judith thanked Ingrid, though for what she wasn't sure, and hung up. ''I'm dead,'' she gasped, getting out of Ella's chair. ''I should have known there'd be a trade-off. There always is with Ingrid.''

''It sounds,'' Ella said in an amused voice, ''like you're a busy woman.''

''Too busy,'' Judith murmured, then forced a smile for Ella. ''Say, we're going to have dinner here in Laurel Harbor tonight. Would you care to join us?''

Ella looked very pleased. ''I sure would. It'll make up for not eating out with H. Burrell Hodge. I love to eat, but I hate to cook. Want to try Charlie G.'s? It's the best place in town. Except that it isn't—in town, I mean. It's about a mile from here, at Orca Point.''

''It sounds fine,'' Judith said. ''Shall we meet you here a little before six?''

The time was perfect for Ella, who insisted upon making reservations. ''You never know this time of year. Perez is still pretty busy,'' the real-estate agent informed the cousins.

Back on the sidewalk, Judith and Renie wondered how they could kill the next hour and a half. It was almost four-thirty, and the superferry had loaded. Another blast of the whistle signaled its departure. Judith couldn't help but think what it must be like to be dependent on the comings and goings of a ferryboat to keep in touch with the rest of the world.

"It's like the pioneers," Renie said. "Of which I'm glad I was never one. Give me taxis and freeways and a straight shot into downtown. All this isolation would drive me crazy. Of course the people who live here *are* crazy, or they wouldn't have come in the first place."

Judith didn't argue. "So what should we do during the next ninety minutes? Talk to Lulu McLean? Browse the shops? Visit Laurel Glen?"

"I'll take Number Two," said Renie. "Lulu won't tell us anything, and I don't want to see that damned dog again. I'd be forced to bite him. Shops are good. Maybe I can find some new sandals. I don't think this strap is going to hold very long."

What began as a desultory stroll among the shops of Laurel Harbor gained momentum when Judith and Renie discovered McBetsy's, an upscale boutique in a beautifully restored Victorian house two blocks from the main thoroughfare. The fashions were in keeping with the architecture, romantic confections in gauzy chiffon and delicate silk. Judith succumbed to a peach-and-plum floral that fit snug around the bodice and flowed to mid-calf. Renie was torn between ivory pleats and a deep blue drape. She solved the dilemma by getting both. The price tags had made the cousins gulp, but they rationalized their extravagance by contending that such filmy, flirty designs could not be found anywhere in the city, and perhaps nowhere else on earth.

It was ten to six when they left McBetsy's. Renie had failed in her quest for sandals, but decided she could make do with the remaining three pairs she'd brought along for the trip. Feeling sufficiently exhilarated to keep guilt at bay for at least a couple of hours, Judith and Renie hurried off to meet Ella Stovall.

During the drive in Ella's comfortable van, the cousins got to see some of Laurel Harbor's outskirts. Splendid new homes sat cheek by jowl with modest older bungalows, all sharing a water view. There were brick homes, mobile homes, wood-frame homes, and stucco homes. Hand-lettered signs posted along the route to Orca Point offered free kittens, dahlias for sale, and horseback rides.

Charlie G.'s sat at the tip of a promontory high above the water. The weathered cedar exterior, big picture windows, and sharply slanting roof evoked a style popular in the nineteen-seventies. Ella, who not only seemed to know all of the restaurant's staff, also appeared to be on first-name terms with most of the diners. It took her and the cousins almost five minutes to wend their way to a window table.

Over cocktails, Ella offered a brief account of her life and times: She had been born and raised in a medium-sized city on the mainland, but had moved to Perez Island as a bride almost thirty years earlier. The marriage hadn't lasted, though it had produced two children. Her ex had left the island, but she had remained with her son and daughter.

"My son, Allan, works with me. You saw him this afternoon," Ella explained. "I doubt if he's going to make real estate his career, but dealing with people is always good training. Now tell me all about yourselves and how you ended up at Chavez Cove just in time for a murder."

Judith and Renie complied, each giving an abbreviated version of their backgrounds. Ella was a good listener. Judith could see how she managed to win the confidence of her clients.

"So," Judith said, after explaining that she'd known Jeanne Clayton Barber in high school, "Chavez Cove is on the market?"

"It's not officially listed," Ella admitted, "but Jeanne and Duane let it be known early last summer that they were shopping the place. I gather that Jeanne told the state B&B board or whatever you call it that she and Duane would consider a reasonable offer."

"Why would they sell after all these years?" Judith inquired with a little frown. The issue raised questions in her own mind: Down the road, would she think about getting rid of Hillside Manor? Would running a B&B become too much of a burden as she grew older? What would happen when Joe retired from the police force? Could they manage three flights of stairs after they hit sixty-five?

". . . Rather than Jeanne," Ella was saying, and Judith realized that her musings had made her miss some of the answer. "Duane never really pitched in, as far as I can tell. He had all those damned duck decoys—excuse my French—and he just sort of moldered at Chavez Cove. Then, when he died, Jeanne must have decided it was time for her to move on—literally."

"So who owned the cabins before the Barbers came along?" Renie asked as their waitress brought them each a second drink.

Ella handed over her empty Manhattan glass and picked up the fresh cocktail. "Now you're getting into that property ownership thing," she said with a wry little smile. "My boss, Simon Dobler, has this little conceit. He likes to give the impression that he's a hardworking real estate guy who's just plain folks. It's good for his professional image. But the truth is," Ella went on with an ironic look for Judith and Renie, "he's fabulously wealthy. It's not the Danfields who own everything in sight—it's the Doblers. Simon and old Elrod are probably the richest men in the Santa Lucias."

Despite the rumors, Judith was surprised. Was it June Hennessy who had told her that Elrod Dobler was a land czar? Judith should have believed Miss Hennessy. Unlike the Chavez Island residents, the schoolteacher didn't feel a need to lie or evade.

After the cousins had expressed both awe and amazement, Ella continued with her tale. "It's a typical example of one man's folly being another man's fortune. At one time, the Danfields owned the whole island. By the Danfields, I mean Bates's grandfather. Then along came his parents, who weren't very lucky in the financial department. They poured money into Stoneyhenge, which was actually built—physically, I mean—by Elrod Dobler's father, Brigham Dobler. He was a builder from the mainland. That was in the early twenties.''

Ella paused to take another sip from her drink. "I can't believe I'm telling you this." She gave an incredulous shake of her head. "Oh, well. Anyway, along came The Crash in twenty-nine. Arthur and Clarice Danfield suffered big losses. They couldn't afford to pay off Brigham Dobler and had to default. Brigham got Stoneyhenge, but he didn't want to live there—he had a virtual castle on the mainland. His only son, Elrod, was just a kid, so Brigham put the property in trust and allowed the Danfields to live there until Elrod was twenty-one. But Elrod was never your normal kind of guy—he didn't want a big fancy house. I'm told Elrod despised his father's ostentation, and, after Brigham died, his son sold off the castle. About that same time, Elrod came of age. He allowed the Danfields to stay at Stoneyhenge since he preferred something more modest, specifically, what's now the Carr house, which he bought from Arthur and Clarice. And there he stayed, even after he married and had his family.''

"Fascinating," Judith remarked. "But that doesn't answer who had the cabins."

Ella gestured at Judith with her glass. "I'm getting there. Arthur and Clarice Danfield drowned one night about thirty years ago, just after I moved to Perez Island. Believe me, it was almost enough to make me think twice about living in the Santa Lucias. They'd started out on what seemed to be a beautiful, calm night, and then suddenly a storm came up when they were halfway between Chavez and Perez. The launch was overturned and their bodies were never recovered." Ella shuddered at the memory. "It was awful. In fact, it happened just about this time of year."

Judith glanced at Renie. " 'Remember September,' " she murmured. Renie gave a faint nod.

"The cabins were built by Arthur and Clarice back in the late thirties," Ella continued. "It was their attempt to bail themselves out of their money troubles. It was the tail end of the Depression, and, unfortunately, nobody had much money. Tourism in the Santa Lucias wasn't exactly a booming business. Just after World War II broke out, Arthur and Clarice were forced to sell the cabins—as well as the property on which they stood—to Elrod Dobler. He'd just turned twenty-one, and of course they were grateful that he hadn't thrown them out of Stoneyhenge. After the war, the cabins did fairly well, but Elrod wasn't much of an innkeeper. Neither was his wife, Flora. They didn't need the money, so they just sort of bumped along, and if lodgers showed up, fine, and if not, that was even better.''

Judith couldn't help but consider the luxury of indifference in the hostelry business. In her own case, it wasn't an option. With or without a husband, Judith had always earned her way in the world. ''Why didn't they just tear them down?'' she asked.

''Elrod doesn't like change,'' Ella responded. ''After Flora died, he solved the problem by talking his brother-in-law, Duane, and his wife, Jeanne, into buying the property. They got it for a song, and I'm assuming that's how they managed to build such a gorgeous house. Although I was in the real-estate business twelve years ago when all this happened, I didn't handle the sale. Elrod's son, Simon, had founded Perez Properties in the early seventies, so he was the agent.'' Ella lifted both hands in a gesture of conclusion. ''Now you know everything that I shouldn't have told you.''

Judith shrugged. ''It's a matter of record, isn't it?''

Ella nodded. ''But it's still not a subject of casual conversation around these parts.'' From across the table, she leaned closer to the cousins. ''As I mentioned, Simon Dobler prefers keeping his empire a secret. Never mind that most of the old-timers know the truth. They're not the ones who're buying property in the Santa Lucias. Besides, you have to understand how it is in a small, isolated community like this. Secrets are gold. They're power. They're what make us important and alive.''

Renie was twirling a swizzle stick in her fingers. ''I understand. As I mentioned in my brief biographical sketch, my husband and I lived in a small town when we were first married. Bill—my husband—makes a comparison between small-town dwellers and people who live in huge cities like New York. Even though they're at the extreme ends of the population scales, Bill says that in each case, the inhabitants have to fight for their own identities. In New York, for example, they do it by being overly contentious and aggressive. They assert themselves in ways that aren't always appropriate or necessary. As for the small towns, individuals have . . .''

''. . . All the answers,'' Judith interrupted with a kick for Renie under the table. Getting sidetracked wasn't going to help ferret out information about the residents of Chavez Island. ''I mean, I still don't know who sold to Doc Wicker or the Carrs. Was it the Danfields or Elrod Dobler? And why does Elrod now live in Stoneyhenge's guesthouse?''

Their waitress had reappeared, inquiring if the women would care for another cocktail or prefer to order. The three women unanimously agreed that they were ready for food, though they hadn't made their choices. Could they have another two minutes? With a smile, the waitress said she'd be back.

Mulling ensued. At last, Judith and Renie succumbed to Ella's suggestion that they try the house special, which was sockeye salmon cooked over an alder fire in the Native American manner.

''You'll love it,'' Ella declared. ''They do it outside, in an enclosed area. It has a smoky flavor that's irresistible.''

Renie was already salivating, but Judith was keeping to the conversational matter at hand. ''Doc Wicker? The Carr house?'' Her eyebrows lifted in an inquisitive manner.

Ella waved a hand. ''The Carr house is an easy one to answer. After Mrs. Dobler died, Elrod couldn't bear to live there without her. He's a crusty, cantankerous old coot, but he was devoted to Flora. Elrod rented out his place to a series of people, the last couple being Tom and Peggy Lowman. Then, for reasons that elude me, when Rowena Carr and her daughter arrived last spring, he sold the place out-right. I didn't handle the sale—Simon did—but I gather they got it below market value. Of course by then Elrod had been living in the guesthouse at Stoneyhenge for several years. After all, Esther is his daughter. Not that she's proud of it—in fact, Esther isn't proud of anything except the facade of genteel wealth.''

"But,'' Judith pointed out, "it's not a facade. Esther Dobler is a rich woman. It's her husband, Bates, whose family lost almost everything.''

Three Caesar salads appeared, accompanied by the flourish of a peppermill. Ella didn't continue speaking until the waitress had left their table. "Esther doesn't have a dime. Elrod turned everything over to Simon. He and Flora had some very archaic ideas about girl children. A husband and a family, that was every young girl's goal, as far as they were concerned. Esther got both, so that was enough.''

"She also got the house,'' Renie noted between large forkfuls of romaine. "Who pays for the upkeep?''

"Simon,'' Ella replied. "Or Elrod, whichever you prefer. Simon manages the money. Elrod doesn't want to be bothered.''

"And Doc?'' Judith prodded.

"Doc.'' Ella put her fork down and sighed. "What's now the store and his apartment was once a stable and later a storage shed. The Danfields still owned it, about all they had left on the island except for Hidden Cove, the cemetery and some acreage in the woods. Doc showed up one day—this is hearsay, though I was living in Laurel Harbor at the time—and insisted on buying the land from Bates and Esther. They needed the money, I guess. Doc bought it and renovated it and set up his store. At least that's what I've heard. I wasn't in real estate then.''

"That sounds simple enough,'' Judith said, wondering why it also didn't sound quite right. "The same for Hidden Cove?''

"Yes. I got in on that deal with Rafe St. Jacques because Simon and his wife were off on a three-month tour of Eu-

rope,'' Ella explained. ''It was a cash sale, twenty grand.''
She paused to allow the cousins a moment to absorb the
amount. ''Even four years ago, that was cheap for water-
front property. Of course that old boathouse was almost
falling down. The place was abandoned after that drunken
idiot who holed up there was run off the island twenty years
ago.''

Judith sat up at full attention. ''What drunken idiot?''

Ella shrugged. ''Some young guy who was supposed to
do a lot of the stuff Rafe St. Jacques does now. He was
there about a year, a year and a half. It didn't work out.
He drank. There was an incident—I'm not sure what, I was
in the middle of my divorce. Anyway, he had to leave.''

Judith fixed her dark eyes on Ella's placid face. ''Do you
remember his name?''

Ella lifted one plump shoulder. ''I'm not sure . . . As I
said, my own life was a mess at the time . . . It was . . .
Harry. But I don't remember his last name. Breaking up is
hard to do, even when your husband is a louse. I guess I
wasn't paying attention.''

Judith guessed that Harry's last name was Hodge.

FOURTEEN

THE ALDER-SMOKED SALMON had been delicious. Renie
raved about it all the way back to the Laurel Harbor
marina. Ella Stovall didn't mind taking credit for her
recommendation. She and the cousins parted company
with effusive compliments all around.

But as soon as Ella had dropped off her companions,
Judith's mood turned ruminative. "It was Burrell," she
declared, shivering a little as the evening breeze came
off the water. "Didn't I tell you that Chavez Island
would make an ideal retreat from the world?"

"I could retreat there if Charlie G.'s delivered,"
Renie replied in a dreamy voice. "Or I could dig a pit
and cook the sockeye myself. I could have it every day,
with toast for breakfast, on bagels for lunch, then spread
all over crackers for hors d'oeuvres, and at dinner, in
oh, so many ways . . ."

"Stick it," Judith muttered, keeping an eye on the
dozen or more lights which twinkled out beyond the bay.
It was almost eight o'clock, and Rafe should be arriving
any moment. Despite the imminent change of seasons,
the marina was busy, with every conceivable type of
boat, from luxury yacht to little runabout.

"If only," Judith was now saying, more to herself
than to Renie, who still seemed to dwell in a haze of

alder smoke, "Ella hadn't been dumping her husband twenty-some years ago. Otherwise, she'd have known the details we're missing. She has a knack for noticing what goes on around her. So many people don't."

"New potatoes," Renie murmured. "That's the thing. Why do some people serve rice with salmon? It doesn't work. Those new potatoes at Charlie G.'s had just enough parsley, a touch of garlic, and something else . . . What was it? I couldn't quite place the flavor."

"Tom, Dick, and Harry," Judith said, pacing the width of the dock which swayed just a bit on the tide. "Tom was Mr. Lowman, Dick was Doc Wicker, and I'm absolutely convinced that Harry was Harold Burrell Hodge. It explains so much, including why he knew the island."

"Now buttered baby carrots are always nice, but these had a trace of rosemary," Renie rhapsodized. "Talk about tender! They actually did melt in my mouth. I think I swallowed them whole."

"Most of all," Judith went on, stepping aside for two young couples who had just come off a sleek sailboat, "it could explain why he was killed. What awful thing did the young, drunken Burrell do that might have caused someone to wait over twenty years to get revenge?"

"Getting back to the salad," Renie began, "I'm good with anchovies. Not that I'd like to make a meal of them, but one or two in a Caesar, and I . . ."

Judith heard an engine cut less than a hundred yards from shore. She watched the lights approach as the boat veered toward the dock. "It's Rafe," she announced. "Let's go."

Rafe St. Jacques asked several polite questions about the cousins' visit to Laurel Harbor. But when he reached the point of inquiring about dinner, Judith cut him off, lest Renie again start lauding the local cuisine.

"I didn't realize," Judith said in her most sympathetic voice, "what you went through with the *Petroleum Monarch*. No wonder you gave up the sea. As a commercial venture, I mean."

Since Rafe's back was turned as he stood at the helm,

Judith couldn't see his face. But she noted how his shoulders tensed and that there was a long, awkward pause before he responded.

"It sounds as if you've been investigating me," he finally responded in a tight, even voice. "I have to ask why."

"Curiosity," Judith replied lightly. "My cousin remembered something about an environmental disaster in the Santa Lucias about seven years ago. We had some time to kill, so we stopped in at the local newspaper office."

The broad shoulders seemed to relax just a bit. "It was the worst thing that ever happened to me," Rafe said in a low voice. "I'd warned the captain. He wouldn't listen."

"He drank, I understand," said Judith.

Rafe didn't answer. The cruiser cut smoothly through the inky water as the lights from other vessels shimmered like so many stars in the late-summer night.

"What happened to him?" Judith persevered.

"Larrabee?" Rafe hunched over the wheel as the cruiser picked up speed. "I don't know. He was dismissed."

"And you quit?"

"Yes." Again, Rafe paused. "I had fifteen years in with the shipping line. I was due for a captaincy in the next few months." Slowly, he turned to look at Judith. In the darkness, his chiseled features grew even sharper and a shade more intimidating. "The sea was my life. But it wasn't just the adventure of ships. It was the marine life, the plants the animals, the birds, the fish . . ."

"Smoked over an alder fire," sighed Renie.

Judith shot her cousin a warning glance; Rafe apparently didn't hear Renie. "The sea," he went on, "is the cradle of the world. Everything comes from the sea. Many people worship the earth, but they're wrong. They should worship the sea. I did. I do. And when that drunken moron of a Larrabee failed to exercise even the most elementary precautions . . . well, I went quite mad. I would have killed him if some of the other crew members hadn't stopped me. The least I could do was try to make amends. I quit, took my severance pay, retirement, the whole shot—and worked for almost three years, helping to clean up the spill. When I finished—not that it's ever finished—I decided to live on Chavez permanently. I felt I belonged there, where the tragedy had been felt most deeply. So that's where I stay, at Hidden Cove, nursing the birds and the otters and whatever other form of marine life I can find.''

Judith couldn't help but express her admiration for Rafe. ''That's very commendable. It must mean a great deal of self-sacrifice.''

Rafe had turned back to observe their course. The night was quiet, except for the constant churning of the sea and the throb of the engine. ''We all owe the world something,'' Rafe said simply. ''Giving back to the environment is the least I can do. I still think there must have been some way I could have prevented Larrabee from acting so recklessly. But I don't know what.''

Noting the hopelessness in Rafe's voice, Judith sought words of comfort. ''Maybe you couldn't have taken any action short of mutiny,'' she said.

''Maybe.'' Rafe now sounded weary.

''I can see why you were so strongly opposed to H. Burrell Hodge's plan to build a rehab facility on Chavez,'' Judith said, in what she hoped was still her most sympathetic tone.

Rafe said nothing. The cruiser moved smoothly over the water as Chavez Island loomed up in the darkness.

''It wasn't a bust,'' Judith averred, kicking off her Keds in the living room of the Barber house. ''We found out a lot of very interesting things.''

Renie, who was finally through dwelling on her sumptuous meal, flipped open a can of Pepsi and yawned. ''So where does it leave us?''

''With more motive,'' Judith declared, putting her feet up on the coffee table. ''The only problem is, I don't know what the motives are. We've got money, which is always sound. Esther and Bates without any—money, I mean—

Elrod—or Simon—with all of it. But I don't see how it ties into Burrell, unless it has something to do with him buying up what's left of the Danfield property.''

"Like the cemetery?" Renie wrinkled her pug nose. "Okay, there's some woodland, too, I gather. But if the Danfields wanted money, it would be in their interest to keep Burrell alive."

"True," Judith admitted. "I really don't think that's it. I have a feeling that the answer lies with Doc Wicker."

Renie gave Judith a quizzical look. "As in what happened when his wife died?"

"Maybe." Judith frowned in concentration. "Burrell—or Harry Hodge, as he was known in those days—must have been at Hidden Cove about the time that Doc's tragedy occurred. Now who would know what really happened?"

Renie wore a dubious expression. "What else *could* have happened? Mrs. Wicker went into labor, there were complications, Doc didn't have enough experience—and the mother died but the baby lived. It seems pretty straightforward to me."

Judith shook her head in an impatient manner. "No. Remember what we talked about earlier? Where were the emergency personnel? Where was the coast guard? Where," Judith went on, her eyes suddenly bright with excitement, "was the boat that should have taken the Wickers to the hospital at Laurel Harbor?"

Renie didn't respond immediately. When she did, she spoke in an uncharacteristically studious voice: "Harry—Burrell—was in charge of transporting people to and from the islands, just like Rafe is now. At least we think Burrell was on Chavez at that time. But something happened. What? A fifth of Old Sluggo?"

"Maybe," Judith allowed. She was now sitting with both feet on the floor, her chin on her fists. "Doc would know. Let's go see him."

Renie's mild protests were overcome. It wasn't yet nine o'clock. Doc would still be up. Of course he'd be reluctant to talk about the tragedy. But a murder had occurred, and the residents of Chavez Island had to start opening up.

"Doc strikes me as a basically decent man," Judith said, putting on her jacket. "He'd want to see justice done."

Renie's face showed an emotion that for once Judith didn't readily recognize. As soon as her cousin spoke, Judith realized it was apprehension. "Maybe," Renie said quietly, "Doc already did. Sometimes people think of murder as justice. I think they call it justifiable homicide."

The ground floor of the Wicker Basket was dark when Judith and Renie arrived. Judith knocked several times but got no answer. A single light shone in a dormer window on the second floor. Judith wondered if Doc might have fallen asleep over a book or while watching TV.

"Rats!" Judith grumbled. "I guess it'll have to wait until morning." She gave one last look at the amber glow behind the curtains.

The cousins had just started back down the road when a familiar voice called out to them. It was Doc. He doffed his Greek fisherman's cap and hurried in their direction.

"I never get late visitors," he said with a smile that struck Judith as strained. "I just came back from calling on the Carrs. What can I do for you?"

Now that she was face-to-face with Doc, Judith felt disconcerted. "Have you got a minute, Doc? We'd like to talk to you about something . . . important."

Somewhat to Judith's surprise, Doc didn't invite the cousins upstairs. Instead, he ushered them into the store and all the way back to a small room which he apparently used as an office. The old oak desk was piled high with invoices, shipping forms, newspapers, magazines, catalogues, and—which Judith found poignant—medical journals. There was only one chair, but Doc offered it readily.

"I'll clear off a place on the desk," he said, "for whichever of you doesn't need the chair. I can stand."

Renie was already edging onto the desk, so Judith took the chair. She felt faintly foolish, with Doc standing rather stiffly by the door and Renie trying not to knock various items off the desk.

"It's about Harry," Judith began, knowing her eyes were filling with sympathy for Doc. "You remember him as Harry Hodge."

All the color drained from Doc's face. He removed the fisherman's cap and wiped his brow with an unsteady hand. "Harry Hodge," he said in a hollow voice. "Harry . . . Hodge! My God!"

Doc passed out.

"You can't call a doctor when the doctor's passed out," Renie said reasonably after Judith urged her cousin to get help. "You get smelling salts or throw a bucket of water on him or something."

"Yeah, right, sure," Judith muttered, kneeling beside Doc and feeling for a pulse. "He's alive. That's an improvement over some of the people we've met on Chavez Island."

Indeed, Doc was already beginning to stir. He groaned, put his hands to his eyes, and grimaced. Then he was staring up at the cousins with tired, unfocused eyes. "Oh, my!" he said in a weak voice. "How stupid of me! I must have forgotten to take my blood pressure medicine." Clumsily, he tried to get up. Judith gave him a hand.

"You take the chair," she said. "Or would you rather let us help you get upstairs?"

"I'll be all right," Doc assured Judith. "Maybe it was just shock. It's been a long time since I've heard that name spoken."

"But not so long since you saw him last," Judith said, suddenly aware that Renie was no longer in the little office.

"What?" Doc was sitting back in the chair, adjusting his glasses, which had fallen off when he fainted. "I'm sorry, I don't understand."

"Harry Hodge," Judith repeated. "Harold Burrell Hodge."

To Judith's mystification, Doc frowned, then nodded

slowly. "So it was Harry. I couldn't help but wonder."

Renie returned, bearing bottled water and a paper cup. "I thought you might want some of this," she said. "I took it off the shelf. Do you give yourself a discount?"

Doc allowed himself a small smile. "I pilfer now and then," he replied. "Thank you. That's very kind."

Judith, who was now half-leaning, half-sitting on the desk, waited patiently for Doc to finish his drink. At last, he resumed speaking. "When I heard that someone named Hodge was coming to Chavez, naturally I wondered. But Hodge isn't an uncommon name. Maybe I didn't really want to know. I'd spent twenty-five years trying to forget. Even after he'd been killed, and I saw his body, I still wasn't sure it was him. Twenty-five years is a long time."

Judith recalled Doc's reaction upon seeing Burrell at the bottom of the steps. She also remembered that afterward, he'd supposedly felt ill. "You were 99 percent convinced, though, weren't you?"

Doc tipped his head to one side. The glasses were still crooked. "Well . . . I wouldn't say that. Expired people always look different. So much of what we recognize is mannerisms, attitude, gestures. You see," he added with an almost chilly stare, "I never saw him alive while he was here this time."

Judith tried not to flinch under Doc's gaze. "No, I guess you didn't. But it must be him. Harry, I mean. He knew his way around the island. He was a reformed alcoholic. His first name was Harold."

"Oh, I don't doubt that it was him," Doc said, now speaking in his usual, kindly manner. "You don't want to wish anybody ill, and yet there's some part of you that can't help but feel smug when a person gets what you think he deserved." Doc put his head in his hands. "Isn't that terrible? Look at all the good Harry did—and I'm gloating! That makes me far worse than he ever was. Alcoholism is a terrible disease."

Renie, who had propped herself up against a filing cabinet, made a clucking noise with her tongue. "True, except that people do one of two things when they have a disease—they get over it, or they die from it. Burrell—Harry—seemingly recovered. And yet . . .'' Her words trailed off.

Judith glanced at her cousin. As was so often the case, she knew what Renie was thinking. ''Maybe he did die of it—only twenty-some years later.''

Abruptly, Doc removed his hands from his face. ''What do you mean?''

''I mean, that maybe something he did while he was still drinking caused his death.'' Judith felt nervous as she uttered the statement. ''We heard he was thrown off the island. Do you know why, Doc?''

Behind the crooked glasses, Doc's gaze was steady. ''No. I wasn't here when that happened.''

It wasn't the answer that Judith had expected. Suddenly, she felt at a loss. There was something about Doc—his innate dignity, his obvious need to guard his privacy, his natural reserve—that kept Judith from pressing him for answers. He seemed the soul of integrity. But, like so many of the other island dwellers, had he lied? Early on, Doc had stated that he didn't know H. Burrell Hodge. But even then, he must have suspected that Burrell and Harry Hodge were the same person. Judith fervently wished that there was someone on Chavez who would stick to the truth.

Maybe there was. A surreptitious glance at her watch showed Judith that it was just after nine-thirty. Perhaps it wasn't too late to pay another call.

''Are you going to be okay?'' Judith asked Doc.

He nodded and smiled. ''I'm fine now. The last few days have kind of gotten to me. Old age must be setting in.''

''Not quite,'' Judith said encouragingly. ''Strain can knock any of us for a loop. See you tomorrow, Doc. We'll be getting some new guests.''

Outside, Renie started for the road that led to the Barber house. But Judith was going in the other direction. ''What now?'' Renie demanded.

''I thought we'd pay a visit to Elrod Dobler,'' Judith

replied, keeping her voice down. "Can you imagine him
hemming and hawing and telling tall tales?"

"I can imagine him loading and aiming and firing his
gun," Renie retorted. "I don't think that going to see Elrod
after dark is a very good idea."

Judith started to argue, then decided that maybe Renie
was right. "Okay, we'll do it in the morning. Maybe I
should call Joe."

Five minutes later, Judith was on the phone. Just before
the call was about to switch over to the answering machine,
she heard a masculine voice at the other end. To her astonishment, it wasn't Joe.

"Ah . . . er . . . excuse me," she said, sounding rattled.
"I must have the wrong—"

"Judith?" the voice broke in. "It's me—Bill."

"Bill?" Judith goggled at Renie who was putting a bag
of popcorn in the microwave. "What are you doing at Hillside Manor? Or did I dial your number by mistake?"

"No," Bill answered. "Those cleaning fluid smells at
our house are overpowering. Joe asked me if I'd like to
stay in Mike's old room. How are you two doing?"

"Uh . . . fine, swell, great." Judith kept her gaze fixed
on Renie who was now looking confused as well as anxious. "Do you want to talk to your wife?"

Bill did, though Judith knew that Renie's husband had
an aversion to the telephone that was almost as great as
Gertrude's. "By the way," Judith said before she handed
the phone to Renie, "where *is* Joe?"

"He went to a meeting with Vivian. Is Renie there?" It
was obvious that Bill wanted to keep the call to a minimum.

Renie took the receiver. "Don't tell me you inhaled,"
she said.

A popping sound emanated from the microwave. Judith
stood by, watching the timer. As expected, Renie's conversation with Bill was short and to the point: "Progress?
. . . Paint? . . . Mail? . . . Kids? . . . Work? . . . Love you."
Renie hung up. "I didn't realize it at the time," she said
in a wondering tone, "but I think one of the reasons

I married Bill was so that I wouldn't have to engage in long phone conversations. It makes up for talking to—or being talked at—by my mother.''

"Nothing makes up for talking to our mothers," Judith said, somewhat distractedly. "I wonder what kind of meeting."

"Huh?" Renie gave Judith a puzzled look.

"Joe went with Herself to a meeting," Judith said. "Maybe it's AA. Maybe it's Adhab. Maybe it's a tryst at a seedy motel."

"Right." Renie yawned, then pushed Judith out of the way as the microwave went off. "Quit imagining things. Concentrate on the lighter side of life. Like murder."

Judith tried to do just that. As Renie melted an alarming amount of butter and poured it over the popcorn, Judith got a can of diet soda out of the refrigerator and tried to put the day's jumble of information into some kind of logical order. She was about to follow Renie into the living room when a noise at the front door startled her. Under the floodlight, she saw two raccoons clambering around on the deck.

"They must have smelled the popcorn," she remarked. "Don't they ever give up?"

"Nope," Renie said, collapsing onto the sofa and stuffing her face. "They're greedy."

Judith couldn't suppress a grin. "And you're not?"

"I'm merely hungry," Renie replied. "Here, have some. It's pretty good."

For a few minutes, the cousins munched and sipped in companionable silence. There was more thumping and bumping on the deck, but they chose to ignore the intruders.

"It's too late to watch a video," Judith finally said, noting that it was now ten o'clock straight up. "Shall we turn on the news?"

"I never watch the news on TV," Renie declared. "All those cardboard anchorpersons smiling their way through grim death and disaster makes me gag."

Judith, however, often switched on the late newscast. "Let's catch the headlines," she suggested, reaching for the remote control on the coffee table. "I gather that Burrell's murder still hasn't made the media in the city."

"Bill wouldn't know," Renie said. "He doesn't watch the TV news, either. Sometimes all he reads in the paper is the sports. With the kind of teams we've got, that's usually depressing enough. Then he has to give himself therapy."

The set came on, predictably showing a beaming blond anchorwoman recounting a light plane crash which had killed a family of four in the southern part of the state. She smiled her way through the bloodied victims of a war halfway around the world, an African famine, and the fatal overdose of a rock musician. With a cynical expression, Renie kept devouring popcorn; Judith was moved by the tragedies, sitting motionless with her diet soda poised halfway between her lap and her lips. Despite the anchorwoman's fixed smile, Judith could swear she heard someone crying in the background.

"It's the producer," Renie said, taking a big swig of Pepsi. "Even some television people have a heart."

Judith suddenly pressed the Mute button. "No, it's not. Somebody *is* crying. Listen."

Renie did. "It's the raccoons," she said. "They've got a new tactic. Real tears, to go with their banditlike eyes."

But Judith wasn't about to be swayed. "It's not coming from the deck, it's in the other direction." She rose from the sofa and went to the back door. The fairy lights that glittered in the ivy didn't reveal anything unusual. Judith cautiously opened the door. There was no one on the porch or in either of the alcoves.

But the sound of weeping grew louder. Going to the top step, Judith looked down. She remembered all too clearly the sprawled form of H. Burrell Hodge lying at the bottom of the stairs. To her astonishment, a figure sat huddled on the last step. Judith darted back inside, but left the door ajar.

"Coz!" she hissed. "Somebody's outside!"

Renie put aside the magazine she'd been perusing,

grabbed another handful of popcorn, and hurried to join Judith. Gripping the handrail, the cousins descended warily. The sobs were deep and heartrending. Within the last six steps, Judith recognized the disheveled pale blond hair of Rowena Carr.

Judith and Renie kept their distance. "Mrs. Carr," Judith called softly. "Is something wrong?"

The distraught woman's head jerked up but she didn't turn around. "Oh! Oh! Ohhh!" She buried her face in her hands and began to sob again.

Now Judith moved closer, placing a gentle hand on Mrs. Carr's shaking shoulder. "Why don't you come inside? It's chilly out here tonight."

Rowena Carr kept sobbing; Judith's hand remained on the other woman's shoulder. At last, Mrs. Carr seemed to gather strength. She grasped the rail and raised herself to a standing position. The tear-streaked face she turned to Judith was terrified.

"Am I going mad?" she asked in a trembling voice.

Judith didn't feel qualified to answer the question. "Let's have some hot cocoa," she suggested. "Then we'll talk about what's bothering you."

The words seemed to soothe Mrs. Carr. Docilely, she let Judith and Renie lead her up the stairs and into the living room. A nod from Judith sent Renie to the kitchen to make cocoa. Judith insisted that Mrs. Carr sit on the sofa.

"Does Cilla know you're here?" Judith asked, remembering to turn off the muted television set.

Mrs. Carr shook her head. She was very pale, and the limp blond hair hung in tangles around her shoulders. In the full light of the living room, Judith could see that their unexpected guest was wearing a waltz-length nightgown and slippers under a tan raincoat. The slippers didn't match.

"I keep forgetting," Mrs. Carr murmured, more to herself than to Judith. "Jeanne isn't here. She's been such a help to me since we moved to Chavez Island."

"In what way?" Judith inquired, pulling the rocking chair closer to the sofa.

Mrs. Carr wasn't looking at Judith. Her gaze seemed to be fixed on a basket of African violets that sat on the coffee table. "Jeanne insisted I was normal," Mrs. Carr finally said. "There was nothing wrong with me. Not really. I just needed . . . medicine. But I don't like medicine. I don't like hospitals. I don't like doctors."

"I see," Judith said vaguely. "Are you . . . Christian Scientist?"

Now Mrs. Carr did meet Judith's gaze. "Oh, no! Not that there's anything wrong with being a Christian Scientist—but my feelings aren't based on religious principles. It's experience that's taught me to avoid the medical profession. They can only bring you grief."

"Goodness," Judith remarked, "I don't think that's always true. Doctors save lives all the time. They prevent tragedies. They give us all a better quality of life. Oh, I'll admit that sometimes they make mistakes, just like anyone else—they're human, after all—but by and large, there are a lot of dedicated health-care providers out there."

Mrs. Carr sat up very straight. There was no sign of tears now, and her voice had grown firm. "I only know from what I personally experienced."

"Which was?" Judith phrased the question casually.

"We should never have come here." The brief calm deserted Mrs. Carr as she swiveled and twitched on the sofa. "Cilla thought it would be good for me. But it isn't. It was a terrible idea. Of course she couldn't know."

"Know what?" Again, Judith kept her voice conversational.

A sudden, frightened expression flooded Mrs. Carr's pale face. "It's not something I can discuss," she declared, rising from the sofa. "Not with strangers. Not with anybody. I should go home. Cilla will worry."

Before Judith could protest, Renie entered the living room bearing a tray with three steaming mugs. "Hot chocolate! Get your rich hot chocolate here! Hurry, hurry!"

The diversion seemed to fluster Mrs. Carr. She plopped back down on the sofa and eyed Renie with something akin to alarm. "Oh! Cocoa! My! Well, perhaps just a taste . . ."

If Renie's entrance had detained Mrs. Carr, it also silenced her. She blew on the cocoa, tested it with her tongue, blew again, and finally took a sip. But she said nothing. Judith, meanwhile, cudgeled her brain, trying to come up with words that would unlock their guest's flow of speech.

It was Renie who finally spoke: "You know," she said from her place in the deep armchair, "all this isolation isn't good for people. Have you and Cilla thought about moving to the city?"

The cocoa mug shook in Mrs. Carr's hand. "My, no!" she exclaimed in a horrified voice. "Cities are dreadful places! I'd be afraid to leave the house! Why, Ketchikan was almost too big! That's one of the reasons we left." Her voice grew calmer as she set the mug down on the coffee table. "That, and . . . other things. Now I must be going." Though she seemed unsteady, Mrs. Carr stood up and headed for the back door.

Judith hurried after her. "Let me see you down the stairs," she insisted.

"I can manage," Mrs. Carr said stiffly.

Judith wouldn't be deterred. She held on to Mrs. Carr's arm with one hand and the rail with the other. When they reached the bottom of the stairs, Judith asked if her guest felt capable of walking home alone.

"Oh, yes," Mrs. Carr replied. "It's not really a physically debilitating condition. But I do feel tired and depressed and nervous and anxious and . . . yes, irritable most of the time. And I forget things and just suddenly feel that the whole world is against me." She uttered a weary sigh.

"If you have all those complaints, you should see a doctor," Judith said in her most compassionate manner. "I'm sure someone can recommend an excellent physician right here in the Santa Lucias."

Mrs. Carr's eyes were very bright in the glow of the fairy lights. "I know the best doctor in the Santa Lucias. I wouldn't ask him to help me if I were dying." Her mouth set in a grim line. "How could I? He already killed my sister."

With a flap of her mismatched slippers, Mrs. Carr scurried across the turnaround and down the dirt road.

FIFTEEN

JUDITH'S HOT CHOCOLATE had grown cold by the time she returned to the living room. Renie was back on the sofa, complacently eating the last of the popcorn.

"We've got to talk to Cilla first thing tomorrow," Judith said, collapsing next to Renie. "Why didn't I figure this out sooner? Why did I think it was Marcia Barber?"

"Huh?" Renie turned to look at her cousin. "Why did you think Marcia Barber was *what*?"

Judith faced Renie. "Somehow I kept thinking that because Marcia was adopted, she might be Doc and Francesca's daughter. But I'm not even sure how old Marcia is. Cilla's about twenty-five, which is the right age for her to be the Wicker girl. If Rowena Carr meant what I think she did, then she's Cilla's aunt, not her mother."

"Oh, brother!" Renie let out a big sigh and leaned back against the sofa pillows. "Where did this wild idea come from?"

Judith told Renie what Mrs. Carr had said at the bottom of the stairs. Renie listened at first with skepticism, but became more credulous as Judith spoke.

"So," Renie finally said, "you think Mrs. Carr was referring to Doc Wicker when she mentioned the best physician in the islands? And the sister who died was Mrs. Wicker? Are you sure you're not building something out of nothing?''

"Well, no," Judith admitted. "I can't be positive. But it makes sense. Remember how Cilla said her mother fell apart and got sick whenever somebody stirred up old memories? That's what she did when she heard about H. Burrell Hodge. Why did Rowena Carr react that way unless she knew him?''

"That doesn't mean Rowena knew him on this island," Renie objected. "What about Ketchikan? Doesn't Adhab own a facility in Alaska?''

"That's true," Judith agreed. "But if there's one thing we've learned in the last few days, it's that everybody on Chavez Island seems connected. Why else would Rowena and Cilla Carr move here? Cilla said her mother got a letter telling them about the Lowman property. Who sent that letter to the Carrs? They tried several other out-of-the-way places after they left Ketchikan, but they didn't stay. Now they're here, and they bought a house." Judith suddenly snapped her fingers. "How do they support themselves?''

Renie made a wry face. "If cleaning three cabins and a house can pay the freight, I'm giving up the graphic-design business and buying a new mop. Investments, I suppose. Mrs. Carr's retirement. An inheritance?''

"Mrs. Carr isn't any older than we are," Judith said in a thoughtful voice. "According to Cilla, she's early, maybe mid-fifties. How much retirement would she get as a book-keeper with a fish cannery? How could she sock away any big investments with a daughter to raise? An inheritance is possible. But there are other ways people can make money." Judith shot Renie a sly look.

"Blackmail?" Renie gasped.

"I don't think Mrs. Carr would call it that," Judith said. "But let's face it, these people have secrets. Maybe they'd pay to keep them quiet.''

Renie was definitely dubious. "Who?''

Judith turned equivocal. "I don't know. The Danfields

don't have any money. Rafe's secret—as far as we know—
isn't exactly criminal, and if Elrod Dobler has anything to
hide, he'd shoot whoever threatened to spill the beans."

"That leaves Doc," Renie noted.

"Not blackmail then," Judith mused. "Payment for
services rendered."

"You mean because Rowena raised Francesca? Or Cilla,
as she's known?"

"Support money. That's straight up."

"Where does Doc get it? Even at those inflated prices,
he can't make much off the store."

"Maybe I'm wrong," Judith sighed. "Maybe Cilla isn't
the Wicker baby."

"You make her sound like a toy," Renie said with a
little laugh.

Judith, however, wasn't smiling. "I suspect Cilla doesn't
know the truth. If it *is* the truth."

"Why keep her birth mother a secret?" Renie wondered
aloud.

"I don't know." Judith frowned. "Why was Doc calling
on the Carrs tonight?"

Renie shrugged. "Why not?"

"If only Doc would talk. He knows everything. Including the truth about Harry Hodge."

"He's not the only one," Renie noted.

"What do you mean?"

"You already said it—Elrod Dobler. Shall we put on
bulletproof vests tomorrow and pay him a call?"

Judith's first duty in the morning was to go with Cilla
and make sure that the cabins were presentable for the incoming guests. Cilla was her usual bouncy self, humming
a merry tune as she led the way along the trail. Judith
started to ask if she knew her mother had been at Chavez
Cove the previous night, but thought better of it. There was
no point in spoiling the young woman's buoyant mood.

"I thought we'd put the guests in Fawn and Doe," Judith
said as they came out on the flagstone path. "If these peo-

ple have heard anything about Mr. Hodge's death, I wouldn't want to have them in Buck where he stayed.''

"Good idea," Cilla said. "Time heals all wounds. I don't suppose you've heard anything about what happened to my mallet?''

Judith shook her head. "Not a word. Lulu McLean is keeping her own counsel.''

Cilla emitted a little snort. "She's probably waiting to catch me off guard so that she can arrest me. I'll bet whoever killed Mr. Hodge just happened to wander onto the island. A drug addict, maybe. You know, someone that his rehab center couldn't cure and who wanted to get back at him. That's probably who Mother saw the night he was murdered.''

They had reached the cabin called Doe. Judith regarded Cilla with curiosity. "Your mother really did see somebody Monday evening?''

Cilla's eyes grew wide. "Sure. She doesn't really imagine things, she just magnifies them. But she said it was a woman. That doesn't seem likely, does it?''

In Judith's experience, anything—and anybody—was likely when it came to murder. The fierce human emotions that drove young people, old people, gay people, straight people, middle-aged people, rich people, poor people, and just plain ordinary people to destroy the lives of other people were universal. But Cilla was young, and maybe a little naive.

"It's hard to say," Judith replied ambiguously. "Did your mother recognize whoever it was?''

"No." Cilla let out an exasperated sigh. "She won't admit it, but my mother needs glasses. She won't see an eye doctor. I think I'll buy her a pair of those magnifiers at the drugstore in Laurel Harbor and glue them on her. Anything would help. She can hardly see the TV, let alone read.''

Judith gave Cilla an understanding smile. "My mother drives me nuts sometimes, too. She's getting very forgetful. But," she added, "so am I.''

Cilla smiled back, displaying her dimples. "You're probably just too busy. I get that way when I have a lot of things on my mind. Which reminds me, I want to check out the toilet in Doe. The plumbing in these cabins is really old."

Judith nodded. "I'll take the welcome basket to Fawn. Do you need my key for Doe?"

Cilla shook her head. "One key fits all. I can take that basket in for you."

Judith handed over the collection of goodies. "By the way, Cilla, you haven't found any of the things our recent guests were missing, have you?"

Cilla looked puzzled. "Like what?"

Judith ticked the items off on her fingers. "Mr. Hodge's briefcase. Rob Estacada's credit cards. And Miss Hennessy's brooch."

"No." Cilla shook her head. "I remember the briefcase disappeared, but I didn't know about the credit cards or the brooch. Gee, that's weird. We've never had anybody steal anything since I've been on Chavez. Are you sure those things weren't misplaced?"

"It seems like too much of a coincidence that all three sets of guests would lose something," Judith said. "Though I can see Stacie Estacada mislaying the credit cards, and while Miss Hennessy insists she's not careless, she was in a big hurry to get out of here the other day. The briefcase, however, is another matter."

"Maybe," Cilla said, her eyes widening, "whoever killed Mr. Hodge took it. The briefcase might have contained that person's history as a drug addict."

Judith tried to conceal her doubts. "Anything's possible," she said vaguely. "I'll go check on Fawn."

As expected, everything in the cabin formerly occupied by the Estacadas was now in order. Cilla, however, had insisted upon dusting and airing out the cabins. Judith left the door open, then went outside to wait.

The morning haze was thicker than usual, and the air had grown quite chilly. Judith reminded herself that the first day of fall was now less than a week away. Aimlessly, she wandered around the grassy area between the flagstone walks. Seeing the barbecue pit, she checked to make sure that the bags of charcoal briquettes were covered. She also took a quick inventory of the sports equipment: badminton racquets, a tin of birdies, the net and poles, a set of horseshoes, the rack of croquet mallets with the colored balls, pegs, and wickets lying in a box on the ground. Judith started to walk away.

She stopped. With an eager step, she ran back to the croquet set. The red, green, blue, yellow, black, and orange mallets weren't lined up exactly with the balls. The red mallet was sitting behind the orange ball. Judith knew that the equipment was always stored by color. Jeanne Barber— or someone—had seen to that. *What if . . . ?* she thought.

"Cilla?" Judith had rushed to the front porch of Doe. "*Cilla?*"

There was still no answer. Feeling a rush of panic, Judith went inside. Relief swept over her as Cilla came out of the bathroom.

"That stupid toilet's backed up again," she complained. "Now I'll have to get my tools. I'd better check the lines in Buck and Fawn, too. You're lucky that the Barbers put in first-rate pipes. At least they help with the crummy water pressure we have here on Chavez."

Judith wasn't particularly interested in the island's plumbing problems. "Cilla, do you know if anybody's played croquet since Monday?"

Cilla dimpled at the question. "Not that I know of. The Estacadas played badminton. But I don't think they tried croquet or horseshoes. Don't honeymooners prefer other games? Purple passion and all that?"

Judith, however, wasn't thinking romantic thoughts. "I'd better head back to the house," she said. "Thanks for everything."

"Sure," Cilla replied cheerfully. "I'll be there in a while to do your cleaning. You don't have to stick around—I've got my key."

"Fine," Judith replied vaguely. Her mind was racing as she hurried down the trail. Why hadn't she noticed those croquet mallets earlier? But of course she had—she simply hadn't considered the possibilities. Were there other things she also hadn't noticed or taken in or understood? Judith had the disturbing sense of missing quite a bit. Indeed, just now Cilla had said something that she felt was important. Badminton? Dusting? Keys? Plumbing? Passion?

Shaking her head, Judith started up the stairs to the back door. Before she'd gotten to the fourth step, she stopped and turned around. Where had Burrell been standing when he was struck from behind? The thick shrubbery reached just beyond the bottom stair. If he'd paused for any reason—such as hearing an unexpected sound—his assailant could have leaped from a hiding place in the bushes, slammed him in the back of the head, and rushed off. It would have been quite simple, really. It was all in the timing. But who knew that Burrell would be at the Barber house around six o'clock? Everybody, Judith figured. Burrell had been vocal in his insistence on being fed by the cousins.

Or perhaps he'd been followed. By the dinner hour, dusk was already settling in. Burrell was completely self-absorbed. He might not realize that someone was behind him on the trail. Yet, none of these mental gyrations explained how Cilla's mallet had ended up under the leaves on the other side of the turnaround. Still feeling frustrated, Judith wandered across the open space. She glanced at the closed doors to the garage and storage shed. Had Deputy McLean or her subordinates checked what was inside? The heavy padlocks indicated that they had not. According to Jeanne, Judith had the only set of keys.

"Hey," Renie called from the top of the stairs, "did you eat all the bacon? I can't find it."

Startled from her reverie, Judith turned and looked up. Renie was still in her bathrobe, with a towel wrapped around her head. "It's under the link sausages. I'll be right up."

The goose clock indicated that it was just after nine. Judith poured herself a cup of coffee and sat at the counter. "Let's play a game," she said.

Renie, who was breaking eggs in a pan, glanced over her shoulder. "Sure. Let's call it Breakfast. I'm It. Watch me eat. But don't ask me to think. It's too early."

"All the better," Judith said. "I'll say a word , and you say the first thing that comes into your head. Word association. We'll start with . . . dust."

"Bacon," Renie replied promptly.

Judith winced. "Key."

"Eggs."

"Plumbing."

"Toast."

Judith sighed. "This isn't working. Forget it." Swiveling on the stool, she watched the fog rising out of the trees. Judith felt as if she were in a fog, a thick cloud that covered her brain and made her feel completely ineffectual. "There's too much stuff going on—or that has gone on—on this island." She sighed. "And too little that we know." Watching Renie settle in with her food, Judith noted that her cousin's eyes had taken on a glimmer of intelligence. "Lulu McLean may be chasing the wrong mallet. I'm going to call her."

The deputy was in. For once, she evinced some interest in Judith's information. "It could have been a croquet mallet," McLean allowed. "They're a little bigger than one of those hammer things, aren't they?"

"Maybe." Judith really wasn't sure. "But I think you should check the croquet mallets for hair and fibers and prints."

"Well!" McLean now sounded huffy. "Aren't you the forensics expert! Would you like to set up a lab in your kitchen?"

"Um . . . I read a lot of detective novels," Judith said in an apologetic voice. "Besides, we wouldn't want any of those mallets disappearing, would we?"

"No, we wouldn't," McLean said grimly. "Okay, I'll be over in an hour. Stay put, will you?"

Judith hung up the phone. "Drat. Now we can't go see Elrod Dobler. McLean's coming to Chavez Cove to check on the mallets."

Renie was removing a second slice of toast from the toaster. "We'll catch Elrod later. There's no guarantee that he's going to be any help."

"Maybe not." Judith leaned her elbows on the counter and sank into deep thought. She didn't say a word during the course of Renie's meal. At last, when Renie was loading the dishwasher, Judith finally spoke: "I'm remembering September. From twenty-five years ago. How's this for a scenario?"

"What?" Renie unwound the towel from her head and fluffed up her damp hair.

"Francesca Wicker goes into labor while she and Doc are staying on the island. The predicted difficulties arise, complicating the delivery. Doc realizes he can't handle the situation by himself. Naturally, he's terrified. He asks Harry Hodge to take him and Francesca to Laurel Harbor. But Harry is drunk. Doc can't manage the boat alone because he has to cope with his wife. It's the equinox, and a storm comes up. A helicopter can't land—assuming there was a landing pad back then. The coast guard may already have had more than it could handle. What happens next?"

Renie gave Judith an exasperated look. "I told you—it's too early for games."

Judith ignored her cousin's pique. "Doc asks the Danfields—or Elrod—for help. They have a boat—they've always had a boat, as far as I can tell. But Doc is refused. Why? Because Esther Danfield was also expecting a baby about the same time. Remember, the newspaper said her child was born about ten days later. Despite their lack of real money, Esther and Bates have this lord and lady of the manor complex. I can see them turning Doc down. It would be a terribly selfish act, but somehow it fits."

Renie sat back down on the stool next to Judith. "Your

logic makes some sense. It's certain that something awful happened, or Francesca wouldn't have died. That something might have been preventable. Maybe it was simply the weather, though, and nobody could get off the island. Look what happened to Bates's parents during another September storm.''

''That's true,'' Judith admitted. ''But I still think Burrell—Harry Hodge—played some part in the tragedy. Doc acknowledges that Harry was here. It had to be when Francesca died, because Doc also said he wasn't around when Harry left the island. We know Doc went off to join the Peace Corps or whatever, and then returned to live on Chavez a couple of years later. Harry was gone by then. He must have been sent packing by the Danfields or Elrod.''

Renie sat in thoughtful silence for a full minute. ''Doc named his daughter Francesca, after her mother. But that's not Cilla's name—it's Priscilla. If Doc went off to do penance in the Third World, he couldn't have taken a baby with him. Maybe you're right—he gave her up to his sister-in-law, and she changed the kid's name. Another Francesca might have been too painful a memory.''

Judith nodded with vigor. ''I think we're finally onto something. The only problem is,'' she went on, growing somber, ''I don't like where it's leading.''

''To Doc?''

''Right.'' Judith sighed. ''You mentioned justifiable homicide last night. I can't help but wonder if that's what Doc thought, too.''

''Maybe it's not Doc,'' Renie said. ''There's one other person who had a good reason to seek revenge.''

Judith locked gazes with Renie. ''Rowena Carr?''

Renie lifted one shoulder. ''She could claim she was nuts. Maybe she is.''

''Hunh.'' Judith rested her chin on her hands. ''I wonder.''

Judith didn't get the opportunity to speculate further. A chipper voice sounded at the back door.

"Hey-hey-hey and what do you know!" Cilla cried, bursting into the kitchen. "I found my mallet! Sure enough, the toilet in Buck was plugged up, too. When I went to fix it, I found the mallet in the bathroom! Now how do you suppose it got there?"

Judith and Renie stared at Cilla. "That's a good question," Judith said slowly. "Why would anybody move it from the shrubbery off the turnaround and take it to one of the cabins?"

"Frankly," Cilla declared as she emptied the kitchen trash can, "I don't care how it got there. Now if I could just find my wrench and hammer . . . Oh!" Her mouth dropped open as she gaped at the cousins. "I see what you mean! Or do I?"

Judith gave a faint shake of her head. "Probably not. Because I don't see it myself." She glanced at the metal box which sat by the back door. The handle of the mallet protruded from the screwdrivers, pliers, and other tools. "Lulu McLean's on her way over here. You'd better let her have a look."

"Lulu!" Cilla was scornful. "She'll probably arrest me on the spot. In fact," she went on with a guileful expression, "I'll leave the tools here, if you don't mind, and come back to clean house later. There's something I should do before Lulu gets here."

"Like what?" Judith asked in a sharper tone than she'd intended.

Cilla looked startled, then blushed becomingly. "I . . . Sometimes . . . About once a week, I clean Rafe's place. He's a tidy person, but . . . it needs a woman's touch."

"Decorating," said Renie. "That's the thing. We're redoing our kitchen because we had a small inferno recently. I imagine you can give Rafe some decor tips. Your mother strikes me as someone who might have artistic talent. Does she pitch in?"

The blush deepened. "No. Mother's not the least bit artistic," Cilla replied. "Numbers are her thing."

Renie smiled ingenuously. "Still, it must be nice for a

bachelor like Rafe to have you women fawn over him. I'll bet your mother bakes him pies.''

"Mother doesn't bake." Cilla had become nervous, almost agitated. "Look, I'd better get going . . ."

"Quilts," Renie said, gazing up at the beamed ceiling as if she were reading off a list of potential female accomplishments. "Sweaters. Mittens. Argyle socks. Surely your mother must do something with her time?"

"She doesn't do it for Rafe," Cilla retorted. "Mother doesn't like him. She thinks he's . . . bad."

Renie was now playing her middle-aged ingenue role to the hilt. "Is he?" she asked in a shocked voice.

"Of course not!" Cilla said with fervor. "He's a wonderful man! He's . . . he's haunted, that's all. But Mother blames him for . . . our misfortune." Cilla hung her head.

Judith and Renie exchanged swift, puzzled glances. "You mean . . . ?" Judith began, but for once, words failed her.

In one of her exaggerated gestures, Cilla threw her hands up in the air. "Oh, pooh and double pooh! This is the end of the twentieth century! Who cares about love affairs and children born out of wedlock? I'm not ashamed of it! Why should Mother care if anybody finds out that Rafe St. Jacques is really my father?''

Judith was gulping down aspirin tablets as if they were chocolate-covered peanuts. "I can't stand any more of this," she declared, turning a stricken face on Renie. "Is it true? Is it possible? Am I the one who's going crazy?"

"It's all a dream," Renie said in a dazed voice. "Pretty soon we'll wake up in our own little beds and discover that we never went to Chavez Island, that my kitchen never caught fire, that your car didn't crash into the wall at Falstaff's, and that our mothers have never caused us an ounce of trouble." With that pronouncement, Renie slid right off the stool and onto the kitchen floor in an extreme gesture of despair.

"Get up," Judith urged in a cross voice. "Somehow

we've got to sort all this out. Let's start with Rafe. I'll admit, his age is a little hard to guess. I figured around forty, but he could be older—or younger. Let's say he's forty-five—that would certainly make it possible for him to be Cilla's father. But if so, my theory about Doc Wicker's baby is shot to smithereens."

Renie struggled to her feet. "It would explain why Rowena Carr doesn't want Cilla hanging out with Rafe. She hasn't yet forgiven him for leaving her with a baby to raise."

"Maybe." Judith rubbed at her temples. "So what happened to the real Francesca Junior? Maybe she's Marcia Barber after all."

"Maybe she was adopted by somebody in North Dakota and has never heard of Chavez Island," Renie said. "If so, lucky her."

"Rats!" Judith pounded at the kitchen counter and hurt her knuckles. She was massaging them when Lulu McLean arrived with Rafe St. Jacques.

"Rafe got into Laurel Harbor just as I was about to leave," McLean announced with a kittenish glance at her companion. "Okay, take me to your mallets."

Wearily, Judith pointed at the back door. "There's one of them. Cilla's showed up in her toolbox."

"I'll be damned," McLean breathed, gazing at the object. "Where's Cilla?"

The query startled Judith, who turned to stare at Rafe. "She was going to Hidden Cove to clean your place. I take it you missed her?"

Rafe shrugged. "I left early this morning. I had a breakfast meeting with a biologist from the university lab on Sanchez Island."

Lulu McLean was slipping on a pair of nylon gloves. She picked up the mallet and placed it in an evidence bag. "Okay," she said, looking stern. "Let's see that croquet set."

"I can show you," Rafe volunteered. "It's behind the cabins by the woodpile." He put a familiar hand on Mc-

Lean's arm and steered her through the back door.

"I guess that puts us in our place," Judith said. "Now what?"

"Frankly," Renie said, "facing Elrod Dobler's shotgun sounds like a snap after all this. Shall we?"

"Why not?" sighed Judith. "We'd better go now so we'll be back when Rafe brings the guests from Perez Island. He'll probably get Lulu to Laurel Harbor about the time the ferry comes in."

The fog was still drifting across the road as the cousins walked past the Wicker Basket. Doc was nowhere to be seen, nor was there any sign of Rowena Carr when they passed the neat little Victorian house farther down the road. Indeed, except for the wind, the island seemed strangely silent. Not even the gulls were making their presence known on this September morning.

The stone fence appeared first, then the iron gates, and, finally, the outline of Stoneyhenge. But there was no sign of Elrod Dobler or the Danfields. Judith approached the metal grill and fumbled with the buttons.

"Esther?" she called, hearing her own voice echo back. "Bates?"

"Elrod!" barked a voice from somewhere in the fog. "Hands up!"

"Screw it, Elrod," Renie said in a tired voice. "It's us, Jeanne Barber's stand-ins."

Elrod materialized out of the mist. "What now?" he demanded, sounding as weary as Renie.

Judith forced herself to put on her most engaging face. "Mr. Dobler, we need to talk to you. We're in a pickle."

"Who isn't?" Elrod retorted. "Life's a pickle, and a sour one at that. Start talkin'."

Judith shook her head. "Not here. Can't we sit down like civilized people, in the guesthouse?"

The astonishment that crossed Elrod's wrinkled face indicated that such an idea was as foreign to him as flying to the moon. "I don't have no guests," he said in a truculent tone. "Who do you think I am, some ritzy society snob?"

"I think," Judith said plaintively, "that you're a very wealthy landowner who prefers his own company. Which I understand. But what we want to discuss is very important, not just to you, but to everybody who lives on Chavez Island. Chavez means a lot to you, doesn't it, Mr. Dobler?"

The old man leaned on the shotgun. "It's my home," he said simply.

"Then let us try to help you save it," Judith persisted. "Right now, it's sinking into a sea of lies and evasions and murder."

"Tcaah!" Elrod spit into the dirt. "People! They ruin everything!"

"Exactly," Judith nodded. She waited for Elrod to make up his mind.

"Okay," he finally agreed. "Come on. But don't expect anything fancy. I got needs, but no wants. Life oughtta be simple."

It was, up to a point. Everything in the little stone cottage was even older than its occupant. Dark, heavy oak furniture, a well-worn Oriental rug, sagging damask draperies, and lamps that looked as if they'd been converted from gaslights suggested that Elrod had equipped his home with leftovers from his father's mainland castle. The atmosphere was gloomy, almost sepulchral, especially when Judith noticed that the room's focal point was a small shrine: Above the mantelpiece of the small stone fireplace hung an oil portrait of a handsome woman dressed and coifed in a style from fifty years ago. A half dozen tapers burned at each side of the painting, and a fresh bouquet of dahlias and mums stood in a tall crystal vase.

"Flora?" Judith asked in a whisper.

Elrod couldn't seem to bring himself to look at the portrait. "Yep." He remained standing and didn't offer the cousins a seat.

"I'll try to be brief," Judith began.

"You're damned right you will," Elrod broke in.

"My cousin and I know quite a bit about various events that have taken place on this island," Judith went on as if

Elrod hadn't interrupted. "We know about Arthur and Clarice Danfield's financial reversals. We know how Doc lost his wife when their child was born. We know that Rafe is doing penance for being involved in a big oil spill off Chavez. We know that Rowena Carr is deeply troubled, but that somehow she and her daughter are managing to live on next to nothing. We even know," Judith continued after taking a deep breath, "that H. Burrell Hodge is the same Harry Hodge who used to work on the island before he got fired for being drunk. And, of course, we know that Esther Danfield is your daughter and Simon Dobler is your son."

If Elrod was surprised by Judith's recital, it didn't show. "Ain't you the smarty-pantses?" he said in a sarcastic voice. "If you know so much, why are you askin' me questions?"

"Because," Judith said simply, "you know most of the answers. For instance, why didn't Doc Wicker take his wife to Laurel Harbor when she went into labor?"

The old face sagged. "Oh, my!" Elrod sat down on the arm of a faded mohair sofa. "That takes me back, it does!" Feverishly, he rubbed at what was left of his thinning gray hair. "Don't you go blamin' Esther! It was that damned Bates who caused the trouble. Him 'n that drunken Harry. I shoulda knowed when Hodge showed up the other day it was him. I shoulda knowed he'd cause more trouble. That was his real first name, far as I'm concerned. T. for Trouble."

"You didn't recognize him when he came to see Bates?" Judith inquired.

"Hell, no." Elrod put a shaking hand in front of his face. "See that? More'n I can do half the time. My eyes ain't so good. Anyways, he was a lot different—older, fatter, balder. 'Course he was sober. Never saw him sober when he was a young'un. I can't think why Bates ever let him live down at Hidden Cove. Maybe it was because nobody else wanted to. That boathouse wasn't more than a shack in those days, leaky roof, busted windows, no heat or running water. Rafe's got it fixed up real nice now."

Elrod had gotten off the track. Judith tried to steer him back in the right direction. "So what did Harry and Bates do that was so awful?"

" 'Course Harry didn't want much money," Elrod went on as if he hadn't heard Judith. "And Bates didn't have none to speak of, so he paid the kid in booze. Stupid. But that's Bates all over. Sometimes I wonder. Maybe Esther woulda been better off getting herself educated and being a schoolmarm. Marriage isn't the answer for everybody. But you coulda fooled me—my Flora was tops. Esther wasn't so lucky, but then she never went out in the world to find anybody. Bates was right here, under her nose."

Judith had never considered the courtship of Esther Dobler and Bates Danfield. But Elrod was right: The two young people had been raised together on the island. Even if they had gone to school in Laurel Harbor, propinquity was an overpowering aphrodisiac. Then there was the money issue. The Danfields must have been desperate to marry their son to the Dobler daughter.

Despite the detour the conversation was taking, Judith couldn't resist a question. "Has it been an unhappy marriage?"

Elrod stared at his scuffed work boots. "Esther and Bates don't know what happy is. You know something?" He looked up at the cousins. "Oh, that's right—you know everything. But maybe not this—if you're a monkey in a zoo, how do you know what it's like for the monkeys in the jungle? Those two never got out much in the real world. They know Chavez Island, and that's about it. Me 'n Flora thought we was protectin' our girl. Simon was another matter—he's a boy. But maybe we made a mistake. I reckon it's too late now."

"It's never too late," Renie put in, her voice unusually soft.

"Ehhh?" Elrod shook his head. "Maybe. Maybe not."

"The trouble?" Judith said, also very quietly.

Elrod frowned at the cousins. "Hey—why don't you two

sit down? You're makin' me nervous, standin' around like that. Try a couple of them easy chairs.''

Judith removed a birdwatcher's guide and sat down; Renie picked up three boxes of shotgun shells before seating herself. Elrod hunched his shoulders and rested his chin on his fists.

''So there we were, back in September of . . . I forget the exact date, about twenty-odd years ago. Along comes this young couple to the cabins, paddling from Perez in a canoe. The damned thing had sprung a leak. Harry said he'd fix it, but 'course he didn't. Too damned drunk. The next day, the little woman—Missus Wicker—started havin' her baby. Now don't go askin' me what went wrong, 'cause I'm no medico. But Doc—only we called him *Mister* Wicker then, 'cause we didn't know he was a doctor—told Harry he had to take them in the launch to Laurel Harbor. Harry said okay, just bring the missus down to Hidden Cove. Well, that weren't so easy. But Doc finally got her there only to find Harry passed out and no gas in the engine. Somehow, Doc brought Harry around and sent him tearin' off to my place. I didn't have no boat—never saw the need of it. What did I want with goin' to the big islands? Chavez was good enough for me. Anyways, I went with Harry to Stoneyhenge to get Bates to take his nice big cruiser. But a storm was brewin', sudden-like.''

Elrod stopped, stood up, and walked in his bowlegged fashion to the window. He opened the damask drapes slowly, revealing a view of the water through the trees. The fog had dissipated, but gray clouds hung over the island. As the wind picked up, Judith could see whitecaps on the incoming tide. She felt as if Elrod had somehow managed to re-create that autumn day from a quarter of a century ago.

''Bates wouldn't risk the cruiser, damn his hide.'' Elrod shook a fist in the direction of the main house. ''I didn't know nothin' about runnin' the thing. Harry said he'd give it a try, but Bates wouldn't let him. They got into it then, nearly comin' to blows. Esther came cryin' and yellin' into the room, sayin' if they didn't stop, she'd have *her* baby. I grabbed Harry and got him out of there. By the time we got back to Hidden Cove, it was too late. Missus Wicker was dead, and the newborn baby was bawlin' its head off. Doc was bawlin', too. It was a terrible thing.'' Elrod closed the drapes.

On the mantel, the tapers flickered and danced, apparently caught in a draft. The wind could be heard in the chimney, and the trees that surrounded the guesthouse seemed to moan. Elrod sat back down on the sofa, his weathered face now drained.

Judith cleared her throat. ''What became of the child?'' she asked in a gentle voice.

''Damned if I know,'' Elrod responded. ''Doc finally got hold of the coast guard, and they came to take him and the baby to Laurel Harbor. He came back the next day, askin' if his missus could be buried on the island. Seems he couldn't stand the idea of takin' her back wherever he come from. Bates was feelin' pretty bad by then—as well he might—so he said okay. That's the last we seen of Doc until about three years later, when he showed up and settled in. I guess he couldn't stand bein' far from his missus. That made sense to me. I'd never leave my Flora. That's why I don't go off Chavez, not for no reason. Funny, ain't it? Those two women who never knew one another in this life are lyin' up there together at Eagle Lake. And here Doc and I stay, a couple of old duffers just spinnin' out our days till we see 'em again in the next world.''

To her chagrin, Judith realized that there were tears in her eyes. Reaching into the pocket of her slacks, she pulled out a crumpled tissue. ''That's a very moving story,'' she said, trying to smile in sympathy. ''I take it Harry left soon after the tragedy?''

Elrod nodded. ''Bates got rid of him. I reckon it was his way of makin' up for bein' a horse's behind. But at least Bates was sober. Then again, maybe that makes it worse. Bates knew what he was doin' when he turned Doc down. Harry didn't. It was Doc who had that helicopter thing put in after he moved here. He never said nothin' about why he done it, but we all knew. Nobody'd ever get stuck on Chavez again.''

Judith discreetly blew her nose. ''This is a sad place in many ways,'' she remarked. ''Is anyone happy here, except Cilla?''

''Cilla?'' Elrod's mouth turned down. ''Cilla Carr oughtta get out while she still can. If she waits much longer,'' he added in an ominous tone, ''it'll be too late.''

The wind blew out the tapers on the mantel. Flora Dobler's portrait faded into the shadows. Her husband put his head in his hands. Judith was sure that he wept, too.

SIXTEEN

RENIE URGED JUDITH to get a grip on her emotions. "It's very sad, it's very moving, but you and I know it's not healthy to dwell on past tragedies. Grovers don't wallow in what-might-have-been."

Judith dabbed at her eyes as they walked back down the road. "At least we know what happened with Harry and the Wickers. It's just about what we figured. Part of the puzzle that's missing is Cilla and her mother. I wish," she went on in a wistful voice, as the Victorian gingerbread facade of the Carr house appeared before them, "that we could really talk to Rowena. But I don't think it'd do much good."

"Probably not," Renie agreed, though she slowed her step to match Judith's as they approached the picket fence.

Judith sighed. "We're still guessing that Rowena is Francesca Wicker's sister. I got the impression that El-rod didn't know of any connection, but I should have asked anyway. Maybe he'd know if Rafe is really Cilla's father."

The Carr house looked quiet, though the wind stirred the tall dahlias and the mountain ash trees. "You know," Judith said, her voice suddenly eager, "we've never seen Hidden Cove. It's not yet eleven. Rafe won't be back from Laurel Harbor for a while. Let's go have a look.''

Renie didn't argue. Five minutes later, the cousins were trying to find the way to Rafe's hideaway. Rowena Carr had told them that the path started near an old cedar stump somewhere between the cabins and the Eagle Lake trailhead. Close inspection showed several cedar stumps, no doubt left from a stand that had been cut when the land was cleared to build the cabins.

Renie, however, noticed that one of the larger stumps had an old gouge covered with oyster fungi. ''This could have been the original blaze for the path,'' she said.

Sure enough, on the other side of the exposed roots, a narrow trail dropped sharply downhill. Here, in the heavy shade of the evergreens, the ground had little chance to dry out. Judith and Renie trod carefully as they made their way among the ferns, salmonberries, and what looked suspiciously like nettles.

After about fifty yards, small springs emerged on both sides of the trail, trickling ever downward. As the ground grew even wetter, the cousins were glad to see that a series of wooden steps had been wedged into the earth. They hadn't gone much farther when a sloping roof appeared before them, and then a glimpse of quiet, dark green bay.

Rafe's house was three stories high, but very narrow, with the front portion supported by stilts. Like the Barber residence, the waterside was made almost entirely of glass. As Judith and Renie reached the beach, they could see much of the interior. The bedroom was a loft on the top floor, the living room and kitchen were in the middle, and a workshop and den were at ground level.

''It's a *real* den,'' Renie said in wonder. ''Look at all those animals!''

Several varieties of birds roosted not only on perches, but on the furnishings. A ferret wandered between a bookcase and a TV set. Two beavers poked their heads out of a large metal tub. An aquarium hosted various kinds of fish.

"It must be Rafe's wildlife hospital," said Judith. "It's a nice idea, but I'll bet it smells bad."

The cousins ambled along the beach, which was narrow and crescent-shaped. The dock was predictably empty. Rafe's kayak stood on end next to the house. There was also a bucket half-filled with butter clams.

"Mm-mmm," Renie murmured in appreciation. "I could go for some chowder about now. It's getting to be lunchtime."

"Don't even think about it," Judith said, tugging at Renie's arm.

"Do you suppose we could dig clams at Chavez Cove?" Renie inquired in a hopeful voice.

"Jeanne didn't mention it." Judith was standing by what appeared to be the only door, located at the side of the house. There was no porch or steps. "I wonder," she mused, then grasped the doorknob.

It turned easily. Judith stepped inside.

Now it was Renie who protested. "You're trespassing, coz," she said in an anxious voice. "Let's get out of here. Rafe could be back at any time."

"No, he couldn't. The ferry didn't get in until ten-forty-five. He's got to drop the guests off—assuming they were on that run—and then get over here. It's eleven-ten. We've got a few minutes to spare."

"But you should be there to greet your guests," Renie persisted.

"Cilla can help them. Rafe knows the drill. I'm covered. Besides, I really don't expect them until this afternoon." Judith was wandering around the workshop, which was filled with tools, books, and what looked like a complete veterinarian pharmacy.

But it was the pictures on the walls that caught her eye. Some were clipped from newspapers and magazines; others were actual photographs, both in color and in black-and-white. Each was hand-labeled with the single word, "VICTIM." The images of a sea lion, an otter, a whale, a muskrat, salmon, steelhead, sea-run cutthroat trout, and at least a dozen different kinds of birds lined the workshop. But one of the glossy eight-by-tens drew Judith like a magnet: It was a woman. Judith moved in for a closer look.

Above the "VICTIM" tag line, she recognized the morose face of Rowena Carr. "That's eerie," Judith murmured.

Renie scrutinized the photo. Rowena's hair was carefully combed in a French roll and she wore a high-necked dress with a double strand of pearls. "I don't get it. 'Victim' of what?"

"I don't know," Judith said in a vague voice. "It looks like a blowup of a smaller picture. Doesn't it seem kind of grainy?"

Renie, who was farsighted, moved farther away. "I don't have my glasses. From what I can tell, it looks recent, though."

"Let's go," Judith said, suddenly anxious to get out of Rafe's house. "Does any man ever keep pictures of the women he's wronged and label them?"

"If any man ever did, it'd be Rafe," Renie said, as Judith closed the door behind them. "That guy has a guilt complex about a lot of things."

Judith frowned. "So Rowena Carr is the only woman he seduced and abandoned?"

"Why don't you ask him?" Renie said, poking Judith in the arm. "Here comes the cruiser."

"Damn!" Judith breathed. She and Renie were standing in plain sight at the foot of the steps which led to the trail. The cruiser had nosed alongside the dock, with Rafe on the deck, making ready to tie up. He seemed startled to see the cousins, but lifted a hand in greeting.

There was nothing to do but wait for Rafe. "What's our story?" Renie asked out of the side of her mouth.

Judith sighed. "How about the truth?"

"Which is?" asked Renie.

But Rafe had secured the cruiser and was now heading for shore. He jumped lightly to the ground and offered his most engaging smile. "You must have known your guests weren't on the ten-forty-five," he said. "Were you looking for me?"

Judith met his gaze straight on. "We wanted to see how you'd redone the old boathouse. It's very nice. Did you do the work yourself?"

Rafe nodded. "It took over a year. My main concern was to provide an animal shelter. I'm not a vet, of course, but I've studied wildlife problems, especially those related to environmental hazards. Did you see my little family through the window?"

"Yes," Judith replied, now gazing back at the house's bottom floor. "Yes, we saw them through the window."

Rafe stared at Judith for a long moment before his expression became sardonic. "As well as from inside, I'd guess."

Judith felt her cheeks grow warm. "Well . . . yes. We were intrigued."

"I usually lock up during tourist season," Rafe commented in a placid tone, "but there's not much boat traffic around Hidden Cove this time of year. "What did you think?" The azure eyes seemed to pinion Judith.

"I think," she replied carefully, "that you're a dedicated person. I also think you have a rather peculiar collection of pictures. They struck me like one of those kids' puzzles— 'Which one doesn't belong?' "

"You mean Rowena Carr." Rafe nodded again, though more faintly. "We forget how much people are affected by environmental disasters. Everybody gets excited about the wildlife, the plants, the nonhuman elements. But there are other victims. In Rowena's case, the *Petroleum Monarch* ruined her future. Twenty years ago, she put her life savings into the company's stock. After the disaster, the stock plummeted. I gather she had some kind of mental breakdown. Finally, she had to quit her job. That's when she and Cilla moved from Ketchikan."

"I see," Judith said thoughtfully. "Was it irony that prompted you to write to them about the Lowman property?"

Judith's guess drew a blank from Rafe St. Jacques. "I didn't write to them." His chiseled features were puzzled. "I'd never heard of the Carrs until they moved to Chavez this spring."

The cousins had to make do with canned clam chowder. It wasn't bad, but Renie complained that Jeanne Barber's commercial supply fell far short of Auntie Vance's legendary recipe.

"No bacon, for one thing," Renie griped. "It's not thick enough. And I doubt that these are butter clams. They're too rubbery."

"I tell an occasional fib," Judith said, gazing out through the kitchen window at the overcast afternoon, "but it's always in a good cause. These people lie for no apparent reason. Cilla's right—there's no stigma these days about illegitimate children. Why doesn't Rafe own up to having fathered her?"

"Horse clams," Renie declared. "I'll bet that's what they are. Or geoducks. I'd write a letter of complaint if they used geoducks. You might as well eat a garden hose."

"It could be money," Judith went on, absently crumbling crackers in her chowder. "But Cilla's too old to qualify for child support."

Renie waved the soup spoon at her bowl. "Auntie Vance uses real cream. I'll bet this is some kind of concentrate made from powdered milk."

"Who else would write to Mrs. Carr? Who else would know them or where they'd gone?" Judith kept staring out the window. "The only other explanation is if Rowena really is Francesca Wicker's sister. We could find Francesca's maiden name on the death certificate at the county courthouse."

"Butter," Renie said in a firm voice. "Not margarine, not shortening—real butter. You don't need much because you fry the bacon first in the kettle, and then . . ."

"Coz!" Judith had finally tuned into Renie's culinary reflections and found them irritating. "Stop dwelling on food and help me think this through. Would somebody at the courthouse read Francesca's death certificate over the phone?''

"If you want to be read to, call the library," Renie huffed. "Sometimes you don't take me seriously. Auntie Vance's clam chowder is just as important as Francesca Wicker's maiden name. It's Auntie Vance's heritage, her claim to immortality. When she's gone—God forbid—we'll remember how tough she was and how she insulted people and the way she'd criticize everybody up one side and down the other. But that negative part will fade, and what we'll have left of Auntie Vance is the good stuff—her generosity, her energy, her good heart under that prickly exterior. In other words, we'll have her clam-chowder recipe, her chicken and noodles, her apple pies, her whole damned legacy of making and baking for other people. Now why is that not important?''

Judith was taken aback. "I never looked at it that way," she said, wondering as much at her own lack of perception as at Renie's eloquent appreciation. "And here I was, just figuring you were fixated on filling your stomach.''

Renie shot Judith a disdainful look. "Everybody has some kind of immortality. Auntie Vance's is cooking for other people. Mine is eating what people cook.''

Judith laughed. "You're shortchanging yourself, coz. Some of your design work will live on. A hundred years from now, people will say, 'See that concept? Serena Jones was the first to come up with it.' ''

Renie looked askance. "A hundred years from now everything will be electronic, and substance will replace style. I'm part of a dying breed, like Ned Grainger and his weekly newspaper. It's Bill who will leave a legacy. It won't be tangible, but his teaching and his counseling and his very presence among students will affect generations yet unborn. He scoffs, but it's true.''

Judith reflected on Renie's words. "You're right. The same goes for Joe. On a day-to-day basis, all he can see is putting together evidence and making a case stick and getting criminals off the street. But in the long run, a police-man's job is at the very heart of what makes society work. Otherwise, we'd have anarchy, and . . ." She stopped, her mouth falling open in astonishment. "Coz! I've been a dun-derhead!"

Despite Renie's complaints about the clam chowder, her bowl was empty. She had just picked it up when Judith made her pronouncement. "What are you talking about?" Renie asked.

Judith ran an agitated hand through her silver-streaked hair. "Let me sort this out. In fact, I'm going to call the courthouse first, and then Cilla, and after that, Doc, and we should go see Bates and Esther . . ."

Judith had dialed Laurel Harbor and gotten a response even before she finished speaking. Since events moved at a leisurely pace in the Santa Lucias, it took three minutes to get connected with someone in the county auditor's of-fice. By that time, Judith had composed herself, and Renie had loaded the dishwasher.

But except for deaths involving property disputes, Judith was informed that certificates were generally filed with the health department. She waited again to be transferred. At last, a friendly voice who identified herself as Monica read-ily agreed to pull Francesca Wicker's death certificate.

"You know," Monica said after she returned to the phone five minutes later, "I remember this tragedy. It hap-pened when I was just a kid, but it made a big impression. In fact," she laughed in a rueful manner, "I vowed never to have any kids. Now I've got three of them. I guess I changed my mind."

"All I really need," Judith said patiently, "is the de-ceased's maiden name."

There was a pause. "It's Carr," Monica finally said. "That's C-A-double-R."

"Ah!" Judith felt vindicated. "Thanks so much. That's all I needed to . . ."

"I'm sorry I took so long to find the certificate," Monica broke in. "But it wasn't in the file. Somebody came in this morning to ask for it, and it hadn't been refiled.''

Judith's triumphant expression faded. ''Who was it?'' she asked, trying to ignore Renie who was mouthing questions.

Monica giggled. ''Mr. Tall, Dark, and Handsome. My coworker, Katie, is still swooning. I think his name is Rafe. Romantic, huh?''

To Judith's relief, Cilla answered the phone at the Carr residence. This time, Judith felt compelled to exercise discretion. ''Please don't think me a big snoop,'' she began in an apologetic manner, ''but I have an odd query for you. Unless I'm mistaken, you just found out who your father was in the last couple of days. Is that right?''

Cilla hesitated. ''Yes, it is,'' she said in an uncharacteristically strained voice.

''Who told you?'' Judith asked.

''I'll have to take care of that later,'' Cilla said in a guarded tone. ''Maybe at your house?''

Judith glanced at the goose wings. It was almost one-thirty. ''Yes, that's fine. Half an hour?''

''Around two then,'' Cilla said, still in that circumspect tone. ''See you.''

Judith dialed Doc's single-digit number, but before the phone could ring, Renie severed the connection. ''Stop it!'' she ordered. ''What's going on?''

''I'm tying up loose ends,'' Judith said in an impatient voice. ''Don't you see? We've been accusing everybody on this island of telling lies. But we were wrong. Oh, there was some misinformation—unintentional, really—and a few misleading inferences, especially with the Danfields pretending to be rich. But only one person has been lying. The irony is that . . .'' Judith stopped as a strange whirring noise filled her ears. ''What's that?'' she asked in an unusually loud voice.

Renie was grimacing. ''It sounds like thunder,'' she shouted. ''But it isn't.''

The cousins rushed out to the deck. Above the trees, they

caught sight of a helicopter. In another moment, it was out of their viewing range. The sound of the rotors faded, and then stopped altogether.

Renie stared at Judith. "The copter pad?" Renie asked.

"I guess." Judith rubbed her temples. "Drat, we don't know where it is. Who could be flying in?"

"The pad's somewhere between Eagle Lake and Hidden Cove," Renie said. "I remember that from Doc's map."

"Let's go," Judith said, starting for the back door.

"What about Cilla?" Renie inquired, hurrying after her cousin. "I got the impression she was coming over here."

"Not right away," Judith replied, "but I'll leave her a note."

Renie's memory of Doc's map proved faulty. By the time the cousins had tried several false leads from the area by the cabins, they decided to check the map again. But before they could turn around, a figure emerged from the trail to Eagle Lake.

"Jeanne!" Judith cried in astonishment. "What are you doing here?"

Jeanne Barber was carrying her two suitcases, the garment bag, and a large shopping bag. She set all four items on the ground as soon as she reached the flagstone walk. "I couldn't stay away another minute," she declared in a fretful voice.

The whirring noise again filled the afternoon air. Judith and Renie looked up as the helicopter rose over the trees and headed away from the island. The women didn't speak until the sound of the rotors had faded.

"But everything's fine," Judith asserted, picking up one of the suitcases while Renie grabbed the garment bag. "Two of the cabins are booked for tonight, and there are probably more reservations coming in. I called Ingrid at the state association."

Jeanne nodded abruptly, then reclaimed the other suitcase and the shopping bag. "I know. I talked to Ingrid, too. That's why I'm here. I simply couldn't stay away any longer, knowing what a mess things were in."

"But they're not," Judith protested. "We've got everything under control."

Jeanne was moving briskly toward the path to Chavez Cove. "Nonsense. From what Lulu McLean told me on the phone this morning, the killer is still at large. Everybody on this island is a suspect. I feel responsible for putting you in charge. I realize now that it was a big mistake."

"Now just a minute," Judith said angrily, as she and Renie hurried to keep up with Jeanne. "It's not our fault that Mr. Hodge got killed. In fact, we've been doing some investigating on our own, and it turns out that he used to live . . ."

"Spare me," Jeanne snapped. "All I want to do is get home, unpack, and collect myself. Then I'll deal with this debacle the best I can."

The cousins trudged along in silence, though they couldn't help but exchange dark looks. When they reached the house, they found a note from Cilla.

"What's that?" Jeanne demanded. "A threatening letter?"

Judith tried to hold her temper. "Of course not. Cilla was supposed to stop by, but she's going over to Laurel Harbor with Rafe to meet the three-fifty ferry. I guess she had some errands to run."

Jeanne was standing just inside the back door. Her gaze raked the living room, the kitchen, and the stairs that led to the loft. "It *looks* all right," she said, more to herself than to the cousins.

"Why wouldn't it?" Judith asked in a testy tone. "Say, Jeanne, how come you arrived by copter instead of ferry?"

Jeanne was already taking her bags into the master bedroom. "I just missed the twelve-thirty. I didn't want to wait around for the three-fifty. I assumed the guests would be on that run, and I wanted to get here first. Luckily, the Santa Lucia Helicopter Service was standing by on the mainland after bringing over some Hollywood type from Sanchez." She frowned at Judith and Renie, who hadn't ventured all the way into the bedroom. There was no sign in Jeanne's cold manner of the gushing, faintly scatterbrained old high-school chum who had greeted the cousins on their arrival Monday morning. "It's too bad if Rafe's left for Perez," Jeanne said, opening one of the suitcases and removing what looked like a laundry bag. "You could have gone with him to catch the three-fifty. Why don't you call and see if he's still at Hidden Cove?"

"Now just a minute," Judith said, taking a bold step into the bedroom. "We're not ready to leave. We have to pack. We have some loose ends to tie up. Frankly, I'd prefer not leaving until morning."

Jeanne paused in the act of hanging up a blue silk dress. "Suit yourselves. You can stay tonight in the cabin that's not occupied." She swept a hand over Judith's toiletries, which sat next to the sink. "Get this stuff out of the way. I've got to finish unpacking before my guests arrive."

Feeling not unlike a common garden pest, Judith began gathering up her belongings. Renie, however, wasn't about to be bullied.

"Listen up," Renie barked, marching to the top of the four steps that led to the lower part of the bedroom. "My cousin and I've gone through hell and back while you sat on your scrawny butt down there in Palm Springs wallowing around in eel wax or whatever it was. The least you can do is be courteous. If I hear one more peep out of you, your husband's duck decoys won't be the only thing around here with irregular features."

Stunned by Renie's outburst, Jeanne turned away. Renie gave one sharp nod at Judith and stomped out of the bedroom. Judith continued collecting her toiletries. Though she and Jeanne worked in close proximity, they didn't speak. When Judith had closed the locks on her suitcase, she turned to Jeanne and spoke in a composed, serious voice.

"Renie is inclined to speak her mind. But I'm not blaming her. I don't think you should either."

Jeanne uttered a weary sigh. "These past few months have been very difficult. To make matters worse, my doctor in Laurel Harbor took me off my estrogen. Sometimes I don't seem to know myself.''

''I have an inkling of what else is bothering you,'' Judith said, her gaze level with Jeanne's. ''I think it would be better if you talked your way through it. Believe me, I've been there. I know more about these things than you could guess.''

Jeanne shook her head. ''There's no point.''

Judith refused to be put off. ''I honestly don't think you knew H. Burrell Hodge before he came to Chavez Island.''

''Of course I didn't! I already told you that!'' Jeanne's skin darkened under her newly acquired tan.

''But I do think,'' Judith continued doggedly, ''that you knew why he came. What puzzles me is why you left.''

Jeanne's shoulders drooped a bit. ''Look, Judith,'' she said, lowering her voice, ''keep out of it. Maybe I sounded harsh just now. My nerves are shot. Staying at the spa didn't help me relax—all I did was worry about what was happening here. I should never have let Marcia talk me into going. And now that I'm back, I have to deal with things in my own way, on my own. I'm sorry it has to be like this, but I really think it'd be best if you and your cousin got out of the house right now. You can spend the night in one of the cabins or you can catch the next ferry to the mainland. It doesn't matter to me. Just . . . go.''

Judith went. It took a few more minutes for Renie to finish packing and for both cousins to make sure they hadn't left any personal items in other parts of the house. At the last minute, Judith remembered to leave the keys on the kitchen counter. But she kept one for the cabins.

''Why,'' Renie demanded as they made their way down the long staircase, ''are we spending the night? Even if we miss the three-fifty, we could still get on the six-thirty.''

''I didn't say we were staying,'' Judith answered. ''I need time to think. Obviously, Jeanne doesn't want me to do that inside her house.''

By the time Judith and Renie reached the cabins, the clouds had lifted to reveal patches of blue sky. Since Judith had already assigned Doe and Fawn to the arriving guests, only Buck remained open.

"Burrell wasn't here long enough to leave an aura," Judith remarked, placing her suitcase near the hearth.

Renie, however, was looking uneasy. Judith asked if she felt spooked.

"No," Renie replied, sinking into a corduroy-covered armchair. "But I wonder if McLean will let us leave. Specifically, me. Don't you figure I have to be a suspect?"

"No," Judith said with conviction. "The coroner's report showed that Burrell wasn't killed with a dinner plate."

"I could have hit him twice," Renie pointed out.

"Lulu McLean may not be a lovable sort," Judith said, sitting down on the plaid sofa, "but she's smart. She can see that an angry person might blow up and bop somebody over the head. But that's a safety valve. You wouldn't get mad all over again, chase Burrell down the stairs, and hit him with a mallet."

"You're right," Renie conceded. "I'd have to be a real nut to pull a stunt like that."

Judith gave her cousin a twisted little smile. "That's true, you're not *that* nutty." The smile disappeared. "I'd sure like to hear what the lab found on that croquet mallet."

"I'd sure like to hear what you've figured out so far," Renie said, now sounding a bit cross. "I thought we were going to talk to Doc and the Danfields."

"I don't know that we need to—now," Judith added cryptically. "But we could use Doc's phone to call the sheriff's office and ask about the mallet. Let's wander over to the Wicker Basket."

Renie didn't look pleased, but she knew from experience that Judith needed time to let her logical mind sort through her theories, hypotheses, and guesswork. "I'm going to the bathroom," Renie announced. "Then we'll go to the Wicker Basket."

Judith sat quietly, waiting for Renie. She was almost certain that she knew who had killed H. Burrell Hodge. She was less certain why he'd had to die, but if her guess was right, then the motive was clear. But Judith also realized that there was virtually no proof. Perhaps the croquet mallet would offer some evidence. Judith was still mulling when Renie came out of the bathroom, cursing under her breath.

"The blasted toilet's backed up," she complained. "Cilla's right—there's no water pressure in these old cabins. Shall we call her from Doc's?"

"She's probably over at Laurel Harbor with Rafe," Judith said. "We could leave a message with Mrs. Carr."

When the cousins arrived at the Wicker Basket, Doc was standing outside, talking to Bates and Esther Danfield. Doc's greeting was warm, but the Danfields both regarded the cousins with a marked reserve.

"I tried phoning you," Doc said to Judith, "but Jeanne answered. I wanted to find out why that copter flew in. Now I know. She's back."

Bates was looking very grave. "We thought there'd been another disaster. Naturally, we're relieved. You'll be leaving, I take it?" His expression became hopeful.

Judith started to reply, but Renie beat her to the punch. "We're not sure," she said. "Judith's thinking about buying Chavez Cove from Jeanne. It's up for sale, you know."

Esther blanched. "No! That is ... We heard rumors ... But not ... *you!*" She gazed at the cousins with something akin to horror.

Judith decided to go along with Renie's ruse. "I've considered expanding my horizons before," she said with a little smile. "It all depends on whether we can strike a fair bargain."

"Chavez Cove should stay in the family," Bates declared, then hastily amended his statement. "By that I mean someone connected to the island."

"You might be right," Judith said lightly, then turned to Doc and asked to use the phone. The cousins went inside while Doc remained with the Danfields.

Lulu McLean refused to reveal the lab findings to Judith. Despite pleading, coaxing, and cajoling, McLean wouldn't talk. "Tell me this much," Judith finally said. "Do you have enough proof to make a case?"

"No," McLean said flatly. "Are you hinting that you know something we don't, or are you just trying to impede justice?"

"I'm not impeding it, I'm seeking it," Judith asserted. "What do I have to do to make you believe I'm serious?"

McLean's laugh sounded more like a snort. "Hand the perp over. Then I'll believe you."

"Okay," said Judith. "I will." This time, Judith hung up first.

"Damn!" Judith exclaimed as the cousins set foot on the porch of their cabin. "I forgot to call Cilla about the toilet! And now I have to use it before we leave."

"There's a plunger," Renie said in a dubious voice.

Between the seedy rentals and the ninety-year-old house on Heraldsgate Hill, Judith had coped with plenty of plumbing problems. She had no luck with the plunger, however.

"I need a snake," she said, coming out of the bathroom and casting about the kitchen for anything that might make do.

Renie was in the living room. "How about this?" she called.

Judith saw her cousin unwinding a piece of wire from some logs in the woodbasket by the fireplace. "I'll try it," Judith said. "Maybe I can shape it into kind of a fishhook thing."

"I can do that." Renie twisted, turned, and tucked the wire until it resembled a U-shape. "Good luck."

Judith tried to find the least uncomfortable position next to the toilet. The bathroom, with its shower stall and sink, was very cramped. "I should have gloves," she muttered. "Coz!" Judith yelled. "You got any gloves in your suitcase?"

"I don't do gloves," Renie replied, coming to stand in the doorway. "You know that."

"I thought you might have a pair of Bill's stashed some place," Judith said, angling the wire into the toilet bowl. "I found a pair of Joe's socks in my suitcase."

"Wear them instead of gloves," Renie suggested with a grin.

"Like mittens," Judith grumbled. "Some help." She felt the wire go deep inside the toilet and strike something soft. "Maybe it's a wad of toilet paper or tissue or . . ." Grunting with exertion, Judith finessed the wire until she got a tenuous hold on whatever was plugging the line. "Look out!" she cried, pulling up fast and hard. An off-white object fluttered and flipped onto the floor, like a dying fish.

"Well!" Renie exclaimed. "Now you've got one glove. Are you going to try for two?"

Judith gazed in wonder at the off-white nylon glove. "You bet I am."

"You have to have a pair," Renie remarked in an amused tone.

Waving the glove's mate victoriously, Judith stood up. "I sure do. But I don't intend to make a fashion statement, coz. I have the feeling that the last person who wore these suckers was a killer."

SEVENTEEN

"SEVENTY-FIVE DOLLARS?" Renie screamed into the phone at Doc Wicker's. "*One-way? Apiece?* Forget it! I'll swim!"

"You can't swim," Judith countered as Renie banged down the Wicker Basket's phone. "You don't know how."

"We're not paying a hundred and fifty bucks to take a helicopter to Laurel Harbor," Renie asserted in a defiant voice. "We'll wait until Rafe can ferry us over there."

Doc, who was standing behind the counter, cleared his throat. "I don't think Rafe is coming back tonight. He made his last run to Chavez when he brought the guests over to Jeanne's cabins around four-thirty."

Judith stared at Doc. "You mean he's gone again?"

Doc nodded. "He . . . ah . . . had a date. He left word that he wouldn't be back until tomorrow."

"A *date*?" Renie was incredulous. "With what—a walrus?"

Doc chuckled. "I know, Rafe seems all caught up in his wildlife and environmental causes, but he likes women, too. In fact," he went on, lowering his voice though there was no one else in the store, "I understand that he's engaged."

Judith smiled in delighted surprise. "I think that's wonderful! Who is she?"

Doc shut one eye in a confidential wink. "It's a secret. There should be an announcement soon."

The cousins were bemused. But Rafe's romantic life wasn't uppermost in Judith's mind. "We still have to get off this island," she said. "It's not quite five-thirty. We have plenty of time to catch the last ferry if we leave right away. Do you think Bates Danfield would take us in his yacht?"

Doc's face hardened. "Ask him, if you like."

Judith realized her gaffe. "Oh, Doc . . . I'm sorry!" She put out a hand and touched him lightly on the arm. "We know . . . about Bates and Harry and the storm and . . . everything."

Doc hung his head. "I thought you might," he said quietly.

The wind had come up and was sighing in the trees above the Wicker Basket. "What happened to the child?" Judith asked softly.

Doc licked lips which suddenly looked stiff and dry. "You don't know?"

"I think I do," Judith replied. "She's alive and well and cleaning cabins."

Though Renie gasped in amazement, Doc merely nodded. "Someday we should tell her. But until she and Rowena moved here last spring, it didn't seem necessary. I not only couldn't save her mother, but I rejected Cilla. I've been too ashamed to admit that."

"She's turned out well," Judith said. "I think she could handle it."

Doc shrugged. "Maybe. Of course, I rationalized everything at the time. I was going to sacrifice myself to the Third World, save the needy, play the saint. I couldn't take an infant with me. But what I was really doing was running away. So I came back here, where Frannie is buried." A faint smile touched his mouth. "My little boat, you see."

"Yes," Judith said. "I finally figured that out, too."

"But I couldn't bring myself to practice medicine," Doc continued. "That was very foolish. I wasted my life."

"It's not too late." Judith was aware that she had said the same thing about Esther Danfield. It could be said of almost everyone on the island. Missed opportunities, refusal to change, fear of the unknown—the Chavez residents were held hostage by more than the sea.

"I don't know," Doc said, though there was a lack of resolution in his manner. "It's Cilla I worry about. While they were in Alaska, things seemed to go well with them. My sister-in-law changed little Francesca's name to Priscilla—she couldn't bear calling her after Frannie. But Rowena did a wonderful job of raising the girl. And then things changed. I thought if they moved here, I could help them. That's why I wrote that letter, telling them the Lowman property was available. But Chavez is no place for a lively young woman like Cilla. She should be on the mainland, or at least one of the bigger islands."

"But she won't leave her mother. Her *stepmother*," Judith corrected herself.

"She could," Doc said, anger flaring in his face. "My sister-in-law is a very stubborn woman. All that talk about not seeing a doctor! She's just being silly. Why won't women face middle age? You'd think menopause was a criminal activity! If Rowena would start taking her estrogen, she'd be just fine."

Judith and Renie couldn't help but look at each other and grin. "So that's it," Judith said. "Hormonal imbalance. I should have guessed. She's about my age, and I've been on estrogen for almost ten years. So's Renie."

"It's a common malady," Doc sighed. "Maybe that's what I should do—set up a clinic for Women of a Certain Age."

"That's not a bad idea," Judith said.

"Listen, ladies." Doc leaned his elbows on the counter. "Are you willing to take a chance and let me cart you over to Perez? It's not too dark yet, and we can all squeeze into *Frannie*."

Judith's eyes grew wide. "Would you?"

Doc would. The cousins grabbed their suitcases. Twenty
minutes later, they had crossed the island and reached Salmon Gap. There were whitecaps on the water and the evening sky had clouded over. As Judith and Doc climbed into
the boat, Renie drew back.

"I don't know if this is such a good idea," she said. "I
can't swim."

"You won't have to," Doc said. "She may not be big,
but she's sturdy." Gently, he patted the side of the little
craft. "I may have let her down years ago, but *Frannie*
always sees me through."

Judith didn't know if Doc was talking about the boat—
or his wife. Maybe they were the same.

The crossing was bumpy, but Doc pulled into the marina
at Laurel Harbor right before seven. The superferry was in
its slip, loading for the final departure of the day.

"We made it!" Renie cried in jubilation. Impulsively,
she leaned over and kissed Doc on the cheek. "Thanks!
You're a good sailor."

Doc smiled broadly as the cousins stepped onto the dock.
"You're good sports. I'm heading back now before it gets
any rougher." His face grew serious under the Greek fisherman's cap. "Thanks for everything. You've given me a
different slant on things."

Judith was touched by Doc's gratitude. But before she
could respond, Doc revved the motor and began pulling out
into the bay. As the little boat headed for open water, the
Frannie's running lights seemed to wink at the cousins.

"Let's go," Renie urged. "I'm starved. We can eat on
the ferry."

Judith looked at Renie with what might have been regret.
"We're not catching that ferry," she said. "I thought you
knew."

Renie's jaw dropped, then anger sparked in her eyes.
"You thought I knew *what*? You never tell me anything!
What the hell are you doing now?"

Judith tapped her shoulder bag. "The gloves. We've got to turn them in to Lulu McLean. But before we do that, I want to go for a little spin."

Renie made a menacing move toward Judith. "I'll spin you! Like a damned dervish! This is crazy! If we don't get on that ferry, we'll be stuck here for the night!"

Judith shrugged. "So be it. But I'm not quitting when I'm so close to the truth." She started up the dock. "Come on, let's see if we can find Ella Stovall."

With ill grace, Renie gave in. All the way up the hill to the main part of town, she kept glancing over her shoulder, casting longing looks at the superferry's bright lights. "This sure is fun," she groused. "Carrying a heavy suitcase and probably sleeping on the courthouse lawn and not getting any dinner! What next, scrubbing our faces with Brillo pads?"

Judith didn't answer. Nor would she admit that the uphill climb with the burden of luggage and shoulder bag had winded her. When they reached the main street, she was more than a little dismayed to find the Perez Property office locked and dark.

"Damn!" she breathed. "Now where's a pay phone?" She scanned the street, then noticed that there was a light on in the *Merchant*. Abu's red, white, and blue beater was parked outside. "Never mind," she said, huffing as she crossed to the newspaper office. "All we need is wheels."

"I'll bet Abu's only got three on that old wreck," Renie muttered. "You aren't going to ask him to drive us, are you?"

"We don't have much choice," Judith said.

Abu was at his computer terminal, deep in concentration. He jumped when the cousins came through the door. "Yiii! Chavez ladies, Mrs. Flynn, Mrs. And So Forth! You bring news to Abu?"

"We may at that," Judith replied. "Is it possible that you could drive us somewhere?"

Abu's dark face grew animated. "To where you go?"

"I'm not exactly sure," Judith admitted. As precisely as possible, she described her destination.

"Abu find," the young man nodded. "Come, we get into official newspaper automobile."

Judith and Renie left their luggage in the office. Renie was muttering under her breath as they walked out to the street. The interior of Abu's car was also decorated, mostly with remnants of soda pop cans and fast-food meals. Renie reluctantly climbed into the backseat, while Judith gingerly sat down next to Abu. As he turned on the ignition, the entire vehicle shuddered. So did Judith. After two blocks, it occurred to her that he was heading for the ferry terminal instead of going inland.

"Say, Abu," Judith said mildly, "shouldn't we have turned around?"

Solemnly, Abu shook his head. "Abu always point official newspaper automobile toward Mecca first. Then go wherever going."

"Oh." Judith sat back and tried to relax. She was thankful that she couldn't see Renie. No doubt her cousin was looking as if she'd like to kill somebody. Judith had a good idea who Renie would choose as her victim.

Just before reaching the now-empty loading area, Abu made such a sharp U-turn that it threatened to topple the car. Then he gunned the engine. The vehicle convulsed some more. As they left Laurel Harbor behind them, ominous noises sounded from under the hood, in the chassis, and even the glove compartment.

It was now completely dark. The road on which they were traveling led through the heart of the island. They could see lights from the houses that were scattered along the way, but not much else. Only an occasional car passed them from the opposite direction, and no motorists in their right minds would be driving fast enough to catch up with Abu's beater.

The strange noises grew louder. Judith couldn't help but express alarm. "Is that . . . normal?" she inquired in an anxious voice.

"Normal?" Abu echoed. "What is normal?"

"That's what I was wondering," Judith said, just as Abu let out a howl and applied the brakes. The vehicle bucked, emitted a deafening belch, and skidded off the road, knocking over a "For Sale" sign. Abu had just missed a mailbox and the barking dog that he'd apparently been trying to avoid. The animal now stood on his hind legs with his front paws leaning on the right-hand rear door. Only his ears showed through the window.

Judith had braced herself on the dashboard. She felt shaken, but otherwise unhurt. Nervously, she turned around to look at Renie. Her cousin was lying with her head against the backseat.

"Are you okay, coz?" Judith asked in a frightened voice.

"I'm dead," Renie replied. "I died and went to Mecca." She sat up and glared at Judith. Then, as the dog kept barking, she turned and pounded on the window. "Beat it! You stupid mutt, you almost got us killed!"

Opening the passenger door a scant inch, Judith peered at the dog. "It's Edelweiss," she said in a bemused voice.

Abu was hunched over the steering wheel. At last he spoke, in a detached, dreamy voice: "Abu Hamid Mansur, twenty-three, of Babol and Laurel Harbor, maybe injured in official newspaper automobile mishap on Pheasant Run Road, Thursday, September fifteenth. Chavez ladies want to buy very used car? And so forth?"

Judith did her best to see if Abu was seriously hurt. It appeared that he was not, though she advised him that he'd better remain in the car until help arrived.

Renie was now leaning over the front seat. "What help?" she demanded, as the dog continued to bark. "We're out in the middle of nowhere."

"Hardly," Judith replied. She pointed to the fox terrier who was now sitting on the ground and howling. "I'm sure that's Edelweiss. Unless I've misjudged, the turnoff to Laurel Glen Academy is straight ahead. Let's ask June Hennessy to call for help."

Renie, however, refused to get out of the car. She waved

a hand in Edelweiss's direction. "That dog will eat me! Or at least my shoes!"

Annoyed, Judith stepped out onto the shoulder of the road. Edelweiss leaped up, raced over to Judith, and tried to lick her hand. "Come on, coz!" she yelled at Renie. "He likes us. Maybe we've finally made a friend in the Animal Kingdom."

Through the window, Renie was looking dubious. But she finally got out of the car. Edelweiss sat again, now panting at Renie.

"Look," she said to the dog, "I doubt we can be real buddies, but let's call a truce. Okay?"

Edelweiss seemed willing. Indeed, he ran ahead of the cousins, as if leading the way. Twenty yards ahead, just off the main road, twin brick pillars indicated the entrance to Laurel Glen Academy. The white iron gates stood open, no doubt because school was not yet in session. From what Judith could see of the layout, there were at least two large buildings, and several smaller ones. A playing field was on their right. To the left, lights shone in a brick cottage that was surrounded by a tidy garden.

The doorbell chimed a few notes from what Judith recognized as one of Beethoven's symphonies. A moment later, June Hennessy appeared, wearing a quilted ivory bathrobe. She looked startled though not displeased to see the cousins. Edelweiss plunged inside. "I was wondering where he went," Miss Hennessy said, her fond glance following the dog out of the tiny foyer. She turned back to Judith and Renie. "I hoped you'd visit Laurel Glen." The schoolteacher's tone conveyed eagerness. "Better to see the academy in daylight, though. But do come in."

"Actually," Judith said with an apologetic air, "we have a problem. Could you call the sheriff for us? We got involved in a car accident."

"My word!" Miss Hennessy's thick eyebrows quivered. "Was anyone hurt?"

"We're okay," Judith said, "but we're not sure about

the driver.'' She thought it best not to mention Edelweiss's unwitting role in forcing Abu off the road.

With a brisk step, Miss Hennessy led them into her sitting room and immediately went to the telephone. ''Where did the accident occur?''

Judith started to explain, then threw up her hands. ''Just tell them to come here. We can lead the way in person.''

Both June and Renie looked puzzled, but the schoolteacher gave a nod. ''Of course.'' Quickly, she dialed the sheriff's number. The exchange was brief and to the point. ''They'll be here right away,'' she said to the cousins after hanging up the phone. ''Shall I make tea while we wait?''

''No, thanks,'' said Judith. She and Renie had seated themselves on a chintz-covered sofa. The small room was furnished in a far more feminine style than Judith would have expected. June Hennessy's plain taste in wardrobe didn't carry over to her decor.

''Well.'' June had sat down on a lyre-back chair next to the telephone table. Ramrod-straight, she folded her hands in her lap. ''You must have seen the two larger buildings. One for classrooms, the other's a dormitory. We've a full-time staff of ten, though only eight are teachers. There's a counselor and a groundskeeper. Naturally, I handle all the administrative work, though I teach one class each semester. I couldn't bear not to be in the classroom.''

Judith nodded in understanding. ''You're very dedicated, Miss Hennessy. I admire that.''

Miss Hennessy gave what was intended as a modest shrug. ''Young people are our future. There's no higher calling than the teaching profession. I've put every cent I have into this school. Much of my time is devoted to fundraising. I've been fortunate. Some generous people have stepped forward. They realize education is the answer to society's ills.'' Miss Hennessy's eyes shown with zeal. ''We can never do enough to help disadvantaged children. Never.''

''That's true,'' Judith said sadly. ''But sometimes, even for the worthiest causes, a person can go too far.''

Miss Hennessy's chin shot up. "Nonsense! I've given Laurel Glen everything I have, all that I am. My contribution will not only affect this present generation of students, but the next, and the next." Her voice had risen, and she was speaking more rapidly. "How many others have struck out on their own to salvage the disadvantaged? How many care? How many even notice? Someday the world will recognize what I've done and be grateful!"

"H. Burrell Hodge isn't grateful," Judith said, still in that same sad tone. "That's because he's dead. You struck out, Miss Hennessy—literally. I meant it when I said I admired your dedication, but I despise the fact that you went too far. No matter how Mr. Hodge intended to ruin your school, you shouldn't have killed him with that croquet mallet. If Laurel Glen goes on, it'll have to do it without you."

June Hennessy scoffed at Judith. Her laugh was derisive. "I knew nothing about H. Burrell Hodge or his intentions! This is preposterous!"

"I saw the 'For Sale' sign next to your property just now," Judith asserted. "In fact, we knocked it over. It was a well-known fact that Burrell was looking at various properties, both on Chavez and here on Perez. You were the one who told us how quickly news passes in the Santa Lucias. The land adjacent to your school would have been ideal—secluded, remote, rural. But I suspect Burrell wanted more than that—he wanted the school itself. The letter that Perez Properties sent him indicated he had expressed interest in more than the parcel next door. Laurel Glen is a perfect setup for a rehab center. And you can say all you want about fund-raising and using your own money, but nobody short of a billionaire could keep this place going when the students pay virtually no tuition. You were going to be forced to sell and give up your dream. You couldn't bear that, so you killed Burrell. But another buyer would have come along, or eventually you would go bankrupt. I can only guess how many other lives you'd sweep away in your struggle to keep Laurel Glen. Unfortunately, it's a losing battle. You might as well give up now.''

"Ridiculous!" June Hennessy shouted. But she was shaking so hard that she could barely open the front door. "Edelweiss!" she called in a piercing voice.

The fox terrier came running down the hall and leaped on Renie. Judith tried to grab the dog's collar, but couldn't get a firm hold. Renie and Edelweiss grappled on the sofa. But Edelweiss was now licking Renie's cheek in an obvious show of affection.

The dog's apparent defection seemed to unhinge June Hennessy. She rushed to the front door. With her ivory robe flapping at her ankles, she ran out into the night—and straight into the arms of Abu Hamid Mansur.

"Don't let her get away!" Judith shouted. "She's a . . . scoop!"

The young reporter seemed to understand. Miss Hennessy was a big woman and Abu was a small man. At first, it appeared that she would overpower him by sheer size. With a growing sense of alarm, Judith and Renie watched them wrestle.

"Where are the sheriff's people?" Judith muttered frantically. Then, seeing that Miss Hennessy had Abu in a headlock and was about to thrust him into a small hedge, Judith started to run to the rescue. At that moment, Edelweiss streaked out of the cottage, causing Judith to stumble and almost fall.

But Abu was not without resources. As the dog prowled around the combatants in an apparent show of canine indecision, Abu broke free and let loose with a series of rapid movements that resulted in sending June Hennessy flying into space and landing under a rosebush. Triumphant, Abu directed an epithet at his vanquished foe.

"You, Miss June Hennessy, Laurel Glen Academy headmistress and teacher of history, very bad woman. Lucky for Abu he room in college with Japanese student knowing karate. And so forth!"

As Abu turned to beam at the cousins, a sheriff's car pulled into the drive.

*   *   *

Renie was only mildly disappointed that Charlie G.'s didn't have the sockeye salmon on the menu that Thursday night. "I'm in the mood for oysters anyway," she said after the waitress had brought the cousins' drinks and taken their orders.

Almost two hours had passed since June Hennessy and Abu had dueled in front of the small brick cottage. When the two sheriff's deputies had shown up, Judith had shouted at them to arrest Miss Hennessy for murder. She had recognized them as the same two men who had accompanied Lulu McLean on the night of Burrell's murder. One of them regarded Judith's accusation as if it had come from the lips of a lunatic; the other had reacted in a more cautious manner. The two had argued for several minutes. Surely, the first officer insisted, a local person of Miss Hennessy's fine reputation couldn't be a criminal? *You never knew about people*, the other deputy asserted. If nothing else, maybe they should collar both Miss Hennessy and Abu for disturbing the peace. Despite his victory, Abu showed more battle scars than did the headmistress. The lawmen finally agreed to take in Miss Hennessy and to let Abu go to the Laurel Harbor Hospital's emergency room to be treated for cuts, lacerations, bruises, and a possible broken toe.

A second patrol car would be summoned, to take Abu and the cousins into Laurel Harbor. They would also take the dog. Abu had bonded with the fox terrier, vowing to watch over the animal ". . . as if he were faithful camel." Judith had said she thought that was nice.

"I wish," Judith said after taking a sip from her Scotch, "that Lulu McLean had been on duty tonight. I'm not giving those nylon gloves to anybody but her."

Renie sighed into her bourbon. "I suppose now—after letting me wonder if you'd lost your mind—you'll tell me how you figured it out."

Judith offered Renie a lame little smile. "It was *you*, coz. When you talked about Auntie Vance's legacy, and then especially about Bill and his teaching. I realized that a mo-

tive for murder wasn't always money or jealousy or revenge. It could be a dream of immortality. That's what June
Hennessy had. It's ironic—both she and Burrell were basically well intentioned. I honestly think June wanted to
help disadvantaged youngsters and that Burrell wanted to
cure addicts. But they were both very flawed human beings,
more so than most. Ego, I guess, in both cases. I'd considered June as a suspect along the way because I thought that
if Burrell was considering buying property adjacent to the
academy, she would resent the intrusion.'' Judith made a
rueful face at her own choice of words. '' 'Resent' is putting it mildly. She'd hate having drug addicts or alcoholics
or maybe sex perverts next door to her school. That was
the very kind of sordid environment from which she was
rescuing her students. But the more I thought about it, the
more I realized that nobody could support a school like that
without a secure tuition base. All her bragging about seeking money from the private sector was sort of like Bates
and Esther pretending to be rich.''

Through the window, the soft amber lights of a distant
freighter plied the waters. Renie admired the view, then
turned back to Judith. ''There was a lot of pretending and
self-deception going on. Is that what you meant when you
said only one person was actually lying?''

''Right,'' Judith replied. ''June Hennessy told all the lies.
That was ironic, because I tended to believe her since she
wasn't a Chavez resident. Doc and Rafe and all the rest
hedged and evaded, but they didn't actually lie. Oh, Bates
wasn't straight with Esther about who Burrell really was or
why he'd come to Chavez. But Bates's intentions were understandable. He knew that Esther would be upset if she
realized that the man she'd known as Harry was back. I
think the Danfields suffered guilt pangs of their own for
not taking the Wickers to the hospital in Laurel Harbor
twenty-five years ago. I also think that's why Rowena and
Cilla got the Lowman house so cheap. Elrod felt bad, too.
Either Doc told him who the Carrs really were or somehow
Elrod figured it out—he's no dummy. I'll bet he pays Cilla

for her housekeeping duties, too. Elrod Dobler is ornery, but he's fair.''

Renie didn't agree wholeheartedly. ''Elrod and his wife weren't fair to Esther. She's always lived in a cocoon. Her world is very fragile. I suppose that's another reason Bates dodged the Hodge issue—he didn't want his wife to find out that Burrell was trying to buy property on Chavez for a rehab center. That kind of intrusion might shatter Esther.''

Judith concurred. ''The best thing that could happen is for Jeanne Barber to sell the house and cabins back to the Danfields. It would give them something to do.''

Renie sipped at her bourbon, then waggled a finger at Judith. ''You digress. What were the lies?''

''So I do,'' Judith said with a faint grimace. ''For one thing, Rafe and Burrell never quarreled—June invented that little scene. In fact, she tried to set up Rafe. Consciously or otherwise, his motive was most like hers—to stop Burrell from building another rehab center. She lied about seeing someone on the road to Stoneyhenge Monday night— she was there, giving herself an alibi in case anyone noticed that she'd left her cabin. She said she didn't hear Elrod fire his gun—that couldn't have been true. But if he or the Danfields had remembered exactly when Elrod shot at the supposedly unknown figure, then it would have literally put holes in her story. Of course she lied about hearing a noise in the shrubbery. She must have retrieved Cilla's mallet on her way out after coming to tell us she was leaving the island.''

''I still don't get the part about the mallets,'' Renie put in, buttering a roll to tide her over until their food arrived. ''Why was Cilla's planted by the turnaround?''

''A diversion,'' Judith said. ''In a couple of ways. When Cilla went to Doe to unplug the toilet, June took the mallet and the nylon gloves. The way I figure it is this—June followed Burrell to Chavez Cove, waiting for her chance. She brought both mallets, and while he was in the house making you crazy, she ditched Cilla's in the bushes. That mallet was a tool, and more suggestive of a weapon than the innocent croquet mallet. Of course it would reveal no sign of having been used in the crime, so it had to temporarily disappear after it had been found to make it look as if the killer had wiped it clean.''

Renie's smile was wry. "The croquet mallet might have gone unnoticed if you hadn't realized it was the wrong color in the wrong place. How could June have made such a mistake?"

"In the simplest possible way—it was dark and she was in a hurry. If," Judith continued, "she saw her error later, she probably was afraid to move the mallet for fear of leaving prints.''

"Which brings us to the gloves," Renie remarked.

"Yes. And the murder itself." Judith paused, her expression very serious. "While Burrell was driving us crazy in the kitchen, June hid next to the steps, wearing the nylon gloves and wielding the croquet mallet. As soon as Burrell got to the bottom of the stairs, she leaped out and slugged him. All she had to do was go back to the cabins, replace the croquet mallet, and flush the gloves down Burrell's toilet. She'd already found out that the old plumbing couldn't handle much in the way of refuse.''

"You mean," Renie said with a small grin, "the original toilet problem was—excuse the expression—a dry run?"

"Exactly. This was a meticulously planned crime. The nylon gloves had to go. June didn't dare put them down her own toilet, and had to take a chance that the plumbing in Buck worked okay. Remember, the keys to the cabins were interchangeable.''

Enlightenment was dawning on Renie. "The Estacadas' credit cards—Burrell's briefcase—June's cameo brooch! But the brooch was never really lost. June . . .''

". . . Merely hid it, but reported it missing to make it look as if all the guests were victimized. The credit cards were another ruse because it was the briefcase theft that was important. Burrell's plans were in there . . .''

". . . Along with a copy of the original letter he wrote to

Perez Properties about buying Laurel Glen. June was the one who . . .''

''. . . Forced the locks to see if Burrell was in fact on a real-estate mission. But she couldn't take the briefcase then because . . .''

''. . . Burrell would have reported it missing and raised the alarm. So June had to wait until he was dead, and even then, it wasn't easy to dispose of the briefcase, so she simply . . .''

''. . . Put it in her own luggage!'' The cousins were on a roll, their affinity so great that their brains whirled in sync. They burst out laughing.

''We should have known,'' Renie said, finally serious. ''June said she only came to Chavez during the off-season. But we found out from Jeanne that the summer rate was in effect until next week. June must have heard through the grapevine that Burrell was coming, and made her plans accordingly. She mentioned that news traveled fast between the islands.''

''Right,'' Judith agreed. ''I hate to admit it, but that part went right by me. School doesn't open until the first week in October, so I suspect that June usually comes at the end of September. But maybe the biggest lie she told was the one to Cilla. That could have caused some serious problems.''

''Cilla?'' Over her highball glass, Renie regarded Judith quizzically.

''I never got the chance to ask Cilla who told her that Rafe was her father. But she had to hear about it sometime Monday. When Cilla came back from fixing June's toilet late Monday afternoon, she was upset, and it wasn't just because of her missing tools. Cilla started to explain why she might have mislaid her things, but she stopped herself. Obviously, something traumatic had happened.''

''But why would June say such a thing?'' asked Renie. ''Was she just trying to make trouble?''

''That's possible,'' Judith allowed. ''Though there may have been another reason. June knew that Cilla was infatuated with Rafe. I think she hoped to make Cilla turn against him, so that if he were accused of killing Burrell, he'd have one less defender on Chavez. But Cilla's outlook on life and love was very different from June Hennessy's. As with so many other things, Cilla saw the revelation in a romantic light. I trust she'll accept the truth in the same way.''

''Doc has a lot to offer as a father,'' Renie noted. ''Let's hope he can start by putting Rowena on estrogen. That'll make life easier for everybody, including Cilla. Maybe he can be a real father to her now, and see that her life isn't wasted cleaning cabins on Chavez Island. Cilla has so much going for her. You know,'' Renie went on, buttering a second roll, ''she had a crush on Rafe. Maybe they can work something out.''

Judith shook her head. ''Doc said Rafe is getting engaged, remember?''

''Oh!'' Renie clapped a hand to her forehead. ''In all the other excitement, I forgot. You don't think . . . ?'' She let the question trail off.

''No. Judging from what Doc said, Cilla still thinks Rafe is her father. If he's about to acquire a fiancée, it's not anybody from Chavez.''

The waitress brought two spinach salads. Renie glowed when she tasted the honey-mustard dressing. Judith, however, was still wrapped up in the murder investigation.

''Real evidence is still sketchy,'' she said with a little frown. ''The correspondence between Burrell and Perez Properties will help. So will the books at Laurel Glen, which I'm sure will reveal that the academy is in a deep financial hole. But all that's merely motive. It's the nylon gloves I'm counting on.''

A dab of honey-mustard dressing remained on Renie's upper lip. ''How so? I assume criminals wear nylon gloves to keep from leaving fingerprints.''

''They do,'' Judith said with a droll expression. ''Which is their mistake. The perp doesn't leave fingerprints on whatever he or she has been handling—but they do leave them on the inside of the gloves. I learned that from Joe.''

Renie regarded her cousin with frank admiration. ''You're an apt pupil, coz. Bill should be so lucky with his students. By the way, what about those footprints at Salmon Gap and Eagle Lake?''

Judith was looking rueful. ''Innocent, I think. Maybe the Estacadas or Doc or just about anybody. But for a while, I had a nutty idea that Jeanne Barber might have sneaked back to the island and killed Burrell. I just couldn't figure out why. Jeanne still thinks that his murder was the worst thing that could happen to her bed-and-breakfast. I tried to get her to talk about it, but she wouldn't. I wanted to tell her that the tragedy wouldn't decrease the value of the property. I was afraid of the same thing after the fortune-teller got killed at Hillside Manor, and it turned out to be a plus.''

Renie had finally managed to get rid of the salad dressing on her lip. ''I told you so at the time. People are ghouls.'' Suddenly her gaze veered away from Judith toward the entrance to the bar. ''People are . . . unpredictable,'' said Renie in amazement. ''Don't look now, but I'm guessing that here comes the bride-to-be—with Rafe.''

Judith did her best to cast a discreet glance in the direction Renie had indicated. She failed. Her eyes widened, her mouth fell open, and she just plain gawked. Rafe, in a dark suit, white shirt, and tie, was sufficiently dashing to make any woman stare. But what really knocked Judith for a loop was the woman at his side. Attired in a short blue silk organza dress that revealed creamy white shoulders, long, shapely legs, and just enough cleavage to ignite a man's imagination, Lulu McLean was a stunning vision. Her red curls had been cleverly arranged to soften her features, and the subtle use of cosmetics displayed her fine complexion to excellent advantage.

Having been caught gaping, Judith could think of only one thing to say: ''Hey—how about those nylon gloves?''

Justifiably bewildered, McLean and Rafe approached the cousins. Up close, Judith spotted the ring on McLean's left hand. It wasn't a diamond, but some sort of sparkling azure stone that matched the sea—and Rafe's eyes.

"Excuse me—would you please explain what you're talking about?" Even McLean's voice seemed more feminine.

As she removed the gloves from her shoulder bag, Judith explained. The deputy's eyes lighted up. McLean turned to Rafe. "Hey, these two aren't as dumb as they look!"

Rafe gave McLean one of his engaging, enigmatic smiles. "I've always said appearances can be deceiving."

Judith gave McLean a slightly sheepish look. "Amen."

"What do you mean," Joe asked in a voice that was half-angry, half-baffled, "that we can't go to Mazatlán in January?"

It was the question that Judith had dreaded. It was six-fifteen, Friday evening, and she had been home less than two hours. Following dinner at Charlie G.'s, the cousins had been required to go to the sheriff's office and discuss their findings in detail with Lulu McLean. It turned out that the deputy had not known about June Hennessy's detainment. Not wanting their romantic evening spoiled, Rafe had surreptitiously turned off his intended's beeper.

Consequently, McLean had sat behind her desk in the blue silk organza dress and listened to Judith's theories. In spite of herself, McLean was impressed, especially with the presentation of the nylon gloves. While they weren't conclusive in and of themselves, the deputy believed they might not only reveal June Hennessy's fingerprints inside, but that there was a chance the outside might contain minuscule fibers from the croquet mallet. And yes, McLean admitted, the mallet had shown traces of hair which matched the victim's. Meanwhile, a full-scale investigation was being launched into the financial status of Laurel Glen Academy.

Judith and Renie hadn't checked into their motel in Laurel Harbor until after midnight. In the morning, they had called on Ella Stovall and Abu Hamid Mansur to thank them for their help. Ella was agog about the arrest of the headmistress. Abu was expecting a job offer from the *New York Times.* The cousins made the twelve-thirty ferry which actually departed at one-fifteen. Judith was able to rent another Subaru Legacy on the mainland. She'd dropped Renie off around four-thirty after her cousin had called from the car-rental agency on the mainland and learned that the work on the Jones's kitchen had been completed that afternoon. Bill was back home. Renie couldn't wait to see what makeover the workmen had wrought.

Fortunately, Arlene Rankers had everything well in hand for the current guests at Hillside Manor. Gertrude hadn't missed Judith because she insisted her daughter hadn't gone anywhere except maybe to the grocery store to get some almond clusters. There was a letter from Mike saying that he and Kristin had definitely set a June date for their wedding.

But it was Joe that Judith was reluctant to face. Lulu McLean thought the trial of June Hennessy would be held sometime right after the New Year. The cousins would be expected to testify. Still, that was only one of the reasons why the trip to Mazatlán wasn't feasible.

"It's like this," Judith said, sitting down at the kitchen table. Dinner was in the oven, the guests were enjoying their sherry and hors d'oeuvres in the living room, and Gertrude was fuming in the toolshed because her supper was late. "Renie and I had a little problem up at Chavez. That's why we came home early. Jeanne Barber flew back from California yesterday."

Joe scowled at Judith. "What kind of a problem?"

"Well . . . It wasn't our fault, even though Renie kind of flew off the handle when one of the . . ."

The telephone cut Judith short. Joe was sitting closer to the receiver, so he picked it up. "What? . . . No, that's okay . . . Don't panic . . . Fine, I'll be right there." Joe rang off, then turned to Judith. "That was Vivian. She hasn't had a drink since Monday, but she has an awful urge right now. We've been to two AA meetings, and she's getting a sponsor.'' He pushed his chair back from the table and stood up. ''Until that happens, I've offered to go with her. It's the least I can do.''

Judith didn't know whether or not she imagined the hint of apology in Joe's voice. ''Sure,'' she said. ''Go ahead. I'll save your dinner for when you get back. It's crab casserole. What time does the meeting end?''

Joe was in the hallway, putting on his jacket. ''Meeting? It's not a meeting. I said Vivian wants a drink. If I'm with her, she won't get so drunk. Hey, Jude-girl, Rome wasn't built in a day!''

After Joe had gone, Judith sat at the table for several minutes, her chin on her fists. She should have known that Herself's drinking problems wouldn't be solved so easily. None of life's problems were easy. Being married, even to the love of your life, wasn't easy. Having an elderly mother whose memory was slipping wasn't easy. Thinking about your only child's upcoming wedding wasn't easy. Explaining to Joe that she'd gotten mixed up in another murder wasn't . . . necessary.

Judith got up and went to the stove, where she ladled out Gertrude's casserole portion, then added fruit salad and a buttered roll. Maybe when it came down to the actual trial, only depositions would be required. Maybe Jeanne Barber would reimburse Judith for helping out at Chavez Cove. Maybe there was a really good deal somewhere out there on a secondhand Subaru Legacy. Maybe somehow she and Joe could put enough money aside in the next three months to go to Mazatlán after all.

Maybe was a wonderful word, Judith thought as she trooped through the twilight to the toolshed. It was tentative, but it held hope. Judith, after all, was basically an optimist. If she hadn't been, she would never have survived the years with Dan McMonigle.

''Hello, dopey,'' said Gertrude. ''You're an hour and a half late with my supper. What it is? Cat stew?''

At that moment, Sweetums crept out from behind Gertrude's chair. He smelled the crab in the casserole and went for Judith's ankles. Judith shook him off, arranged her mother's meal on the card table, then went into the tiny kitchen in search of cat food.

"You should have fed Sweetums earlier," Judith called. "You're not the only one who gets cranky when dinner is late."

"What?" Gertrude shot back. "I can't hear you. I'm deaf, you know."

"When you want to be," Judith said under her breath. She filled Sweetums's bowl with his favorite food. The cat gave Judith a perfunctory rub with his furry body, then plunged into his dish.

"I can call the dentist for you Monday, Mother," Judith said when she returned to the sitting room.

"I already went," Gertrude replied. "My partial's fine now."

Judith sat down on the sofa which originally had been in the main house's living room while Grandma and Grandpa Grover were alive. "Who took you?"

"Auntie Vance and Uncle Vince. They came down from the island and brought apple cobbler. For Deb, too." Gertrude lapped up fruit salad. "Vance is always griping about the ferry schedule. I don't see why they want to live up on that rock anyway. They had a real nice little place right here in town. Close."

Too close, Judith had always thought. As good-hearted as Auntie Vance was, she needed distance from the rest of her relatives. While the island on which she and Uncle Vince lived was only an hour away from the city, it provided just enough geographical and emotional space.

"Island life has its charms," Judith remarked in a non-committal tone.

Gertrude looked up from her plate. "How would *you* know? When was the last time *you* were on an island?"

"Mother," Judith said, trying not show her exasperation, "I told you—Renie and I spent the week in the Santa Lucias."

"Santa Lucias, O Sole Mios, and a big pizza pie!" Ger-

trude was scornful. "Never heard of 'em! The next thing I
know, you'll be telling me that you and my dingbat niece
flew to the moon! The two of you come up with some
pretty harebrained excuses to keep from helping Deb and
me. Say, what's in this casserole—garters? You can't tell
me it's real crab!"

"It is," Judith said, still exerting patience. "The first
ones of the season are in. I picked up two at Falstaff's on
my way home."

"On your way home from where?" Gertrude rasped.

"From . . ." Judith clamped her mouth shut. It was
pointless to argue with her mother.

But Gertrude was humming, albeit off-key. "La—la—
daaa—da-tata, la—la—daaa—da-tata . . ."

Judith recognized "Santa Lucia." "Mother," she
interrupted in a serious voice, "are you sure you don't remember things or are you just trying to get my goat?"

Despite her criticism of the casserole, Gertrude smacked
her lips as she devoured the last morsel. "I forget a lot of
stuff," she said, also serious. "It bugs me. The other day,
I forgot your father's first name." Gertrude shot Judith a
swift, remorseful look. "But I haven't forgotten your father. Names and places and all that—they're not so important, are they?" Again, her small eyes swerved in Judith's
direction. "It's people that count."

"That's right," Judith agreed. "People—and how we
feel about them."

"You're not gone now," Gertrude said, her voice just a
little quavery. "That's what matters."

Judith rose and went to stand by her mother's chair. She
put a hand on the older woman's shoulder. "It's okay to
be forgetful. Sometimes I'm that way, too. But I think you
were teasing about not knowing that Renie and I went to
the Santa Lucias."

Gertrude looked up at her daughter. The wrinkled old
face was expressionless, but her eyes were sly. With an
effort, she reached around to pat Judith's hand. "Maybe."

Judith started to remonstrate with her mother, then

thought better of it. Being forgetful wasn't the end of the world. In many ways, Gertrude was still sharp. Warped as it sometimes was, she kept her sense of humor. And under all the carping and criticism, Gertrude loved her daughter.

Maybe was good enough for Judith.

Despite the chatter of the guests in the living room, the house seemed empty when Judith returned. She debated about whether or not to wait to eat dinner. Joe might be gone less than an hour, or most of the evening. Finally, she decided to eat. But appetite eluded her.

If she had to be honest, she still wasn't happy with Joe's offer of help for Herself. Judith knew she was being selfish, but the feelings wouldn't go away. And Judith certainly wasn't happy about Joe keeping his ex-wife company over drinks.

Scraping most of the crab casserole and all of the fruit salad off her plate, Judith sighed. Her eyes trailed to the bulletin board on the wall next to the phone. The corkboard was completely covered with messages, reminders, and notations. It needed to be cleaned out. A swift perusal showed that some of the memos were two years old. Judith started sorting through them.

A slip of paper which Judith recognized as coming from Joe's notebook fell to the floor. On it were some cryptic markings. "SF," "Fri 10-7, D. 9:15 a. m., A. 10:50 a. m.," "Sun 10-9, D. 7:45 p. m., A. 9:05 p. m.," "St. Fran bridal suite."

Judith clasped the small piece of paper to her breast and giggled with delight. It wasn't hard to decipher Joe's code. October seventh was her birthday; he had planned a surprise getaway weekend in San Francisco at the bridal suite in the St. Francis Hotel. Judith didn't need to worry about going to Mazatlán in January. She had something truly exciting in her immediate future. Maybe she could even stop fretting about Joe's attention to Herself's unfortunate needs.

Maybe. But a sense of peace and—yes, Judith realized—

security seemed to settle over her. Maybe it wouldn't last. But for now, it was enough.

She was suddenly hungry. As she removed the crab casserole from the oven, the phone rang.

"Abu Hamid Mansur, twenty-three, soon formerly of Laurel Harbor," said the elated voice at the other end of the line. "Telling Mrs. Flynn, Heraldsgate Hill, of Abu's great journalism success. Thanking Mrs. Flynn for story which wins Abu much praise and many job offers. Abu going to Mecca."

Puzzled, Judith hesitated before responding. "To . . . ah . . . give thanks?"

"No," Abu asserted. "To new job. In Mecca, Indiana. Many dollars, seven-fifty each hour, better car without big shakes, not so much water, lower rent for Abu and Edelweiss. And so forth."

Judith congratulated Abu. Then she finished dishing up her meal, sat down at the table, propped the evening newspaper in front of her, attacked the food with gusto—and so forth.